Praise for the Gereon Rath series

'Kutscher successfully conjures up the dangerous decadence of the Weimar years, with blood on the Berlin streets and the Nazis lurking menacingly in the wings.' *Sunday Times*

'Gripping evocative thriller set in Berlin's seedy underworld during the roaring Twenties.' *Mail on Sunday*

'*Babylon Berlin* brings a fresh perspective to images and material that might otherwise seem shopworn, and its frenetic rhythms are particularly apt for a moment when we appear to be dancing our own convulsive tango on the edge of a fiery volcano.' *New York Review of Books*

'If you like crime, historical or translated fiction, this gives you all three.' **Nicola Sturgeon**

'James Ellroy fans will welcome Kutscher's series, a fast-paced blend of murder and corruption set in 1929 Berlin. Kutscher keeps the surprises coming and doesn't flinch at making his lead morally compromised.' *Publishers Weekly*

'The novels on which the dramas are based are even more rewarding than television's slick production...' *The New European*

Volker Kutscher was born in 1962. He studied German, Philosophy and History, and worked as a newspaper editor prior to writing his first detective novel, *Babylon Berlin*, the start of the award-winning series of novels to feature Gereon Rath and Charlotte (Charly) Ritter and their exploits in late Weimar Republic Berlin. The Gereon Rath series was awarded the Berlin Krimi-Fuchs Crime Writers Prize in 2011 and has sold over one million copies worldwide. A lavish television production of *Babylon Berlin* was first aired in 2017 in the UK on Sky Atlantic. Volker Kutscher works as a full-time author and lives in Cologne.

Niall Sellar was born in Edinburgh in 1984. He studied German and Translation Studies in Dublin, Konstanz and Edinburgh, and has worked variously as a translator, teacher and reader. He lives in Glasgow.

THE FATHERLAND FILES

VOLKER KUTSCHER

Translated
by
Niall Sellar

SANDSTONE PRESS

First published in Great Britain by
Sandstone Press Ltd
Dochcarty Road
Dingwall
Ross-shire
IV15 9UG
Scotland

www.sandstonepress.com

First published in the German language as "Die Akte Vaterland"
by Volker Kutscher
© 2012 Verlag Kiepenheuer & Witsch GmbH & Co.
KG, Cologne/ Germany
© 2010, Volker Kutscher

Translation © Niall Sellar 2019

The publisher acknowledges support from Creative Scotland
towards publication of this volume.

The translation of this work was supported
by a grant from the Goethe-Institut which is funded by the
German Ministry of Foreign Affairs.

ISBN: 978-1-912240-56-2
ISBNe: 978-1-912240-57-9

Cover design by Mark Swan
Typeset by Iolaire Typesetting, Newtonmore
Printed and bound by CPI Group (UK), Croydon CR0 4YY

'The year 1932 will be our year, the year the Republic emerges victorious over its opponents. Not one more day, not one more hour, will we remain on the defensive – we attack! Across the board! We must be part of the general offensive. Today we cry – tomorrow we strike!'

Karl Höltermann, SPD, December 1931

Prologue

Sunday, 11th July 1920

On the move again, stealing through the forest, he leaves his shelter and advances through the trees. No one will hear him, no one will see him. There is a heaviness in the air, deep in the thicket he feels the warmth; summer has arrived with a vengeance. Tokala pauses and takes a deep breath. The scent of lime-tree blossom and winter barley fills the air in the fields over by Markowsken, and already he can smell the lake.

As he draws nearer his pace slows. If he shows himself then it is only to strike fear into those around. He doesn't like it when they enter his forest, doesn't care for their loud cries, their reckless tramping through the undergrowth. He doesn't like their contempt for everything he holds dear.

A mirror hangs in his hut and, sometimes, before he ventures out, he rubs black earth into his face until his eyes glow wildly and, when he bares his teeth, he resembles a beast of prey. In the twilight it renders him as good as invisible but, with the sun high, he has chosen to dispense with his disguise. To be all the stealthier, he wears moccasins made of elk leather and in them he prowls quiet as a cat.

Tokala must be careful. The lake belongs to their realm. People don't dare enter his forest. They are afraid – afraid of the moors, and the Kaubuk.

1

Yes, the Kaubuk, they call him. They have long since forgotten his old name, which he can barely remember himself, and still less are they aware of his new one, which he adopted when he bade farewell to their world, many winters ago. His true name, his warrior name: Tokala, the fox.

Like a fox he moves through the forest, taking cover in his den. They let him go about his business in peace, and he reciprocates in kind. Neither meddles in the other's world, their unspoken agreement for years. It is dangerous in their world, but now and again he must risk it, must venture into their cities and villages by night when he needs new books or paraffin oil – or crops that refuse to grow on his patch of moorland.

His caution is justified. He has almost reached the lake when he hears humming and singing, and pauses mid-motion to listen. A woman's voice, an indeterminate melody. Slowly he steals towards his hiding place on the shore. Tokala has recognised her, has identified her voice, even before he sees her summer dress shimmering red and white through the trees.

Niyaha Luta, he calls her.

He has seen her once before, by the same spot a few weeks ago, and on that occasion, too, he crouched in hiding not daring to move. Though invisible in the dim of the thick undergrowth, she seemed to be looking straight at him when she gazed up from her book. The clatter and tinkle of metal told him she hadn't stolen away alone, and, indeed, shortly afterwards, a man with a bicycle emerged from the forest. It was clear that she had been expecting him when she kissed him. It was *she* who kissed him, not the other way round, and thus Tokala knew this was neither their first meeting nor some chance encounter.

That was the moment he withdrew from his hiding place into the darkness of the forest.

Now she has returned, and Tokala is crouching in his hiding place once more. He sees her dress, a red, feather-like pattern on radiant white; sees her bare legs dangling in the water. She is sitting on that same sunlit branch jutting out over the lake and, just as before, she is reading from her book.

There is a crackle of branches, and a man emerges from the forest. Not the man with the bicycle, but another, and Tokala sees in her eyes that his presence is unexpected. She snaps her book shut as if she has been caught doing something illegal.

'So this is where you've been idling,' the man says.

'I'm not idling, I'm reading.'

'Here, in the wilds? When the whole region has come to perform its patriotic duty, even the peasants from Jewarken and Urbanken?'

These days there is much talk of patriotic duty and the Fatherland. Tokala doesn't understand such talk, or why men in uniform chase him when he brings back bottles of paraffin oil from Suwalki or salt in exchange for his pelts. It makes no difference to him, Tokala, whether he is in the Markowsken forest or Karassewo, yet *they* behave as though it were the difference between heaven and hell. He has never understood the meaning of the border. The forest is the same, on both sides, and Tokala will never understand why one tree should be Prussian and the next should be Polish.

There is a splash as the man wades into the shallow shore water, and makes for Niyaha Luta.

'What are you doing so far out in the forest? Aren't you afraid you might wander onto the moors? Or into the Kaubuk's hands?'

'I'm not a child any more. Stories like that don't scare me.'

'Indeed you are not.' Tokala doesn't like the way he

3

looks at her. 'You're a grown woman. You can even *vote*.'

'I already did, straight after church. If that's what you're worried about?'

She means to sound brave, but Tokala can sense the tremble in her voice.

'What I'm worried about ...' He gives a contemptuous snort. 'And afterwards you had nothing better to do than ride out here ...'

Fearfully, she looks around. As if the man with the bicycle could appear at any moment. Tokala crouches in his hiding place, sharing her concern.

'Is it because of that red handkerchief hanging from the rail of the town mill bridge?' She says nothing, but the man moves closer, reaching the branch on which she is sitting and gesturing towards the bark. 'Someone's carved a heart here,' he says.

'Oh, have they now?' She sounds more spirited, but it is her desperation talking.

'A.M.,' he says, picking at the wood with his fingers. 'And next to it J.P. Freshly carved.' She says nothing, but Tokala can see the fear in her eyes. 'A.M.? Sounds a lot like you, my dear.' His index finger traces the letters in the bark. 'But who is J.P.?'

Tokala sees her fear gradually morph into rage. 'What are you trying to say?'

'That you've bagged yourself a suitor. Well, here's what I think about that!'

The man is screaming now. Tokala covers his ears with his hands, but the noise pierces the air.

'I never promised you anything!' She has jumped down from the branch and is standing with her bare feet in the shallow water, glaring at him furiously.

'Is that right?' he said, 'but you *have* promised the Polack something, is that what you're saying?'

'That's none of your goddamn business!'

4

'People are already talking about you! You're not even eighteen and here you are carrying on with this Pole, making doe-eyes at him!'

'I never promised you anything, and never, do you hear me, never, would I let a man like you anywhere near me!'

The man lurches backwards, as if physically pained by her words. As if she has dealt him a blow with a stick. Then he steadies himself, speaking softly now. 'But you let *him* do whatever he likes. The Polack!'

'He isn't Polish, he's Prussian. Just like you.'

'You admit it then!'

'So what I if I do? Maybe someday I'll marry him.'

'A Catholic? A Polish sympathiser?'

'I don't think that's any of your concern.'

'You don't?'

'That's right. I don't know what you want. Now get lost and leave me in peace.'

'The hell I will. Someone here's got to teach you some manners. Seeing as your father clearly hasn't.'

'Don't you dare touch me!'

The man takes a step towards her and her eyes glare at him but, still, he is undeterred.

'Just one kiss,' he says, and it sounds anything but affectionate. 'If you're going to kiss the Polack, then I have every right to kiss you too!'

He seizes her thin arms with both hands. She tries to repel him, but, crouching in his hiding place, Tokala sees the man tighten his grip and press his mouth on her face. She tries to swerve, but he is too strong.

'Let me go,' she cries, finally wrenching her mouth free.

'What's the matter? I thought a whore like you couldn't get enough.'

The man forces her to the ground, into the shallow water, as, still, she defends herself. He is wicked. Tokala knew it all along. 'Leave me alone!' she screams, but the wicked

5

man ignores her and her screaming subsides to a gurgle. Her head must be underwater.

Tokala averts his gaze, and sees another woman and another man, not in the lake this time but in a hut, in the glow of a paraffin lamp. The woman is bleeding from the eye, the face of the man inflamed; he is drunk and furious, and he strikes her and tears open her nightgown . . .

Tokala pushes the image to one side and looks back towards the shore. A voice inside urges him to intervene, but a second holds him back. It is not for him to meddle in their world! How many city dwellers visit harm upon their wives? That is their world, and Tokala knows it is rotten. That is why he left it behind. The city folk don't interfere with his business, and he doesn't interfere with theirs. That's the way his life has been for years, and it is the only life he can imagine for himself.

He can't bear it any longer, he must return to his forest, he can't stay another second. Crawling slowly backwards, the way he has read in books, he catches sight of the wicked man pulling at her summer dress, hears the fabric rip, sees him position himself on top of the defenceless woman and unzip his fly, while his other arm presses her to the ground, knees splaying her thighs. Tokala hears her scream, and once more it chokes to a gurgle as her head is briefly submerged. Again he sees the woman with her torn nightgown, her lifeless eyes.

Still picturing that final image, he bursts forth into the forest, runs as fast as his legs can carry him, as far away as possible from the violence of their world. The evil he once fled has returned and, even here, he is no longer safe. Racing on, the lake now far behind, he reaches the middle of the forest where he stops and lets out a cry so loud that the birds around him take flight. He stands there impotent and helpless, and screams.

It is hopeless! You cannot partake of their world without

6

experiencing its pain, without summoning its evil, not even as a spectator. That is the lesson you have learned. Now you realise, beyond any doubt, why you must keep away from their world; why living far away in the woods is the only right course of action.

PART I

Berlin

2nd to 6th July 1932

The sun beating down on dead bodies doesn't know about the future, doesn't see the big picture, it just knows where to send the flies.

ED BRUBAKER, SLEEPER, SEASON TWO, #7

1

Reinhold Gräf had never seen Potsdamer Platz so dark and deserted. It was a quarter past five in the morning, the neon signs had long been extinguished, and the buildings that lined the square loomed like dirty cliffs against the sky. The black Maybach, out of whose side window the detective gazed, was the only vehicle on the otherwise busy junction. Even the traffic tower was unmanned, its lights glowing dimly behind the glass. Gräf pressed his forehead against the car window and watched the raindrops form little pools on the windscreen, buffeted by the airstream.

'That's *Haus Vaterland* there, isn't it?' Lange piped up from the rear seat. 'The one with the dome.'

Gräf signalled for the driver to stop and folded down the window.

The cop standing in the rain on Stresemannstrasse had already seen the murder wagon. 'Goods entrance, Inspector!' The man gestured towards Köthener Strasse and saluted.

'Inspector's on his way,' Gräf said. He folded the window back up and instructed the driver to take a right.

He wasn't in the best of moods. The sole accompanying officer was Assistant Detective Lange, who, like Gräf, had been on night shift in Homicide. They had roused the stenographer, Christel Temme, from her bed, before collecting her in Schöneberg, otherwise there was only the driver. Gräf hadn't been able to reach anyone else in the

11

twilight hour between midnight and morning, not even an inspector. Despite being on standby, Gereon Rath wasn't answering his phone. After four failed attempts Gräf had lost heart and climbed into the Maybach with Lange, picking up the stenographer en route and heading for the crime scene. The journey had passed in silence, broken only by Lange's superfluous remark.

Of course it was *Haus Vaterland*. Köthener Strasse took them along the dim rear side of the building, past an endless row of high round arches, meagrely lit by the gas of the street lamps. Once upon a time Ufa, the film production company, had resided here, but since then the Kempinski group had spared no expense in redeveloping the enormous complex from scratch, converting it into Berlin's largest pleasure palace. As a result *Haus Vaterland* now provided your average provincial tourist with everything they could hope for from a night out in the metropolis, from food, dance and booze, to scantily clad revue girls – and all under the same, one roof.

Threads of rain glistened in the dazzling electric light that filtered through an open gate at the back of the building. The goods entrance was situated as far away as possible from the busy Stresemannstrasse. A light-coloured delivery van was parked on the street corner with its rear doors open, alongside a dark-red Horch. The Maybach nestled in behind, and the driver moved to open the door for Gräf.

'That'll do, Schröder. I'm hardly the police commissioner.'

'Very good, Sir.'

The slogan *Mathée Luisenbrand, der schmeckt* was visible on the side of the van, and underneath, in smaller letters: *Herbert Lamkau, Spirits Merchant*. Gräf pulled his hat down over his face as the rain grew heavier.

'Don't forget the camera,' he barked at Lange, who was already making a move to find shelter. He hadn't meant to sound so ill-tempered, but he wanted there to be no doubt about who was in charge while the duty inspector was conspicuous by his absence. Lange shouldn't go getting any ideas: so long as he was still completing his inspector training, he retained his old rank of assistant detective. Only time would tell whether he would pass the final examination.

The assistant detective moved stolidly towards the boot of the murder wagon, gave it a jolt, then another, more forceful this time. Still, nothing happened. Gräf knew that the flap sometimes became wedged in the rain. There was a knack to it. Surely, in all the months he had been at Alex, Lange had thought to ask?

Gräf rounded the puddles and approached the goods entrance and the uniform cop standing guard. The rain that had pooled in the brim of his hat splashed on the concrete floor as he lowered his head to fumble for his identification. The cop stepped to one side to avoid getting water on his boots.

'Beg to report: First Sergeant Reuter, 16th precinct, Vossstrasse. We were notified of the corpse by telephone at approximately four thirty-two this morning. I examined the site in person and promptly informed Homicide.'

'Anything so far?'

'Nothing, Inspector, only that ...'

'Detective,' Gräf said. 'The inspector's on his way.'

'Beg to report: no findings, Detective, other than that the man is dead.'

'So, where's the corpse?'

'Up there.'

'On the roof?'

'In the goods elevator. Fourth floor. Or third. It got stuck.'

Gräf looked around. To the left were two plain metal elevator doors. To the right was a concrete staircase leading up.

'We haven't allowed anyone to use the elevators,' the cop said. 'On account of Forensics.'

'Very good,' Gräf said. Such a precaution was by no means a given with Uniform, even though Gennat never tired of lecturing its troops on the fundamentals of modern police work. 'Have there been any issues as a result?'

'Only with the pathologist. When he realised he had to take the stairs.'

'Are there no passenger lifts?'

'Any number, but not back here. Towards the front of the building, in the central hall.'

Gräf sighed and nodded in the direction of the stenographer who, having just joined, was now shaking out her umbrella. 'We need to take the stairs, Fräulein Temme,' he said, and opened the door. He just had time to see Lange finally prise open the boot before starting the trek up to the fourth floor.

A handful of men gazed at them as they emerged from the stairwell. Alongside the uniform cop standing watch was a guard from the Berlin Security Corps; next to him, a man easily identifiable as a chef; then a worker in overalls; and, finally, a wiry, elegantly dressed gentleman whose sand-coloured summer suit bore dark flecks of rain. In the space of a few quick glances, Gräf acquired an overview: behind him the door to the stairwell, on the wall to his left two windows, and on the wall opposite the two elevator doors. The left-hand door was open, revealing a gloomy shaft and a thick wire rope from which the car hung. Being jammed, only the upper two-thirds were visible. The light in the car was still on, illuminating a large pile of plywood crates of schnapps that stood on a wire mesh cart. The name *Mathée Luisenbrand* was branded in ornate lettering on the wood.

Der schmeckt, Gräf thought, removing his identification. *Tastes good*. 'So, tell me what happened,' he said.

Before the cop or anyone else could speak, the man in the

suit jumped in. His unkempt hair was testament to the fact that he had been rudely awakened.

'I just can't explain it, Inspector, it's all so ...'

'Detective,' Gräf corrected. 'The inspector will be here soon.'

'Fleischer, Director Richard Fleischer.' The man in the suit proffered a hand. 'I'm in charge of *Haus Vaterland*.'

'I see.'

'I hope we can handle this unfortunate incident with discretion, Detective. Not to say, speed. We open in a few hours and ...'

'We'll see,' Gräf said.

Director Fleischer looked vexed. He wasn't used to being interrupted, and certainly not twice in quick succession.

'All of our elevators,' Fleischer continued, 'even the freight elevators and dumbwaiters are regularly serviced. The last time was three months ago. After all, we have seventeen lifts in our building and simply cannot allow ...'

'Your freight elevator jammed though, didn't it?'

Fleischer seemed offended. 'As you can no doubt see for yourself, but that isn't what killed Herr Lamkau.'

'Why don't you leave the detective work to us? Is the dead man known to you?'

'He's one of our suppliers.'

Gräf nodded, and gazed towards the elevator car, in which a shadow was moving. Suddenly a lean figure in a white coat appeared next to the schnapps, and a blonde, neatly parted head of hair poked its way out of the car. Although Dr Karthaus measured almost six foot three, it was impossible to make out more than his head and shoulders.

'Well, if it isn't the Berlin Criminal Police.' Karthaus's words rang metallic and hollow from the shaft.

'Dr Karthaus! How is it you always get here before us?'

'I wouldn't complain if I were you. Just be glad it's *me*

15

who's on duty. Dr Schwartz would have refused to climb in here. At his age, he probably wouldn't have managed either.'

'Well,' Gräf said. 'This job makes no allowances for age.'

'You're right there,' Karthaus said. 'Still, I'd rather be working than standing here twiddling my thumbs.'

Gräf went over and peered inside the car. The dead man lay next to his delivery, and was dressed in light-grey shopkeeper's overalls. His face was pale, with blue lips. Above him a red cloth was tied to the wire mesh, its material sodden. The hair, too, was glistening wet, likewise the man's shoulders, where his overalls had taken on a dark-grey hue. There was evidence of a puddle by his head, its remains now trickling out towards the corner of the elevator.

'Been in the rain, has he?'

The pathologist shrugged. 'You'll have to ask Forensics. Let's hope they're here soon.'

'They're on their way.'

'Where's our inspector?'

'Your guess is as good as mine,' Gräf said, gesturing towards the door, where the tip of a camera tripod had emerged from the stairwell. 'First, Lange here will take some photographs. After that you can attend to the corpse.'

Placing the camera and tripod on his shoulders, Lange gazed around curiously. Gräf nodded towards the elevator, and the assistant detective understood.

'Good morning, Doctor,' Lange said, lowering the heavy device into the elevator car. 'Could I pass that over to you?'

Gräf returned to the witnesses. 'Who found the dead man?'

The chef raised his hand like a schoolboy. 'I did, Detective.'

'Herr Unger is one of our head chefs,' prompted Fleischer.

Gräf was growing frustrated by the man's constant interruptions. 'Where were *you* when the corpse was discovered, Herr Direktor?'

16

'Me?' Fleischer hesitated. 'At home of course. Why do you ask?'

'I'm just surprised that a man like you should be here in person at this time.'

'A dead body has been found! I was notified by security, as you would expect, and immediately made my way over.'

'In that case I commend you,' Gräf said, giving a nod of acknowledgement. 'Still, I assume these men were actually on site when the corpse was discovered.'

Guard, chef and worker's-overalls nodded as one.

'Right. Then I'll question you three first. Is there somewhere more private we can talk?'

'You ...ah ...you could use my office,' Fleischer said.

'Good idea. Does it have a telephone?'

'Of course.'

'Then please show me and Fräulein Temme here the way, and round up all those present when the corpse was discovered.'

Fleischer nodded and started off. 'If you would follow me. It's two floors down.'

There was a flash from the elevator. Lange had started taking photographs. Gräf sighed. All he had to do now was find out where the hell Gereon Rath was hiding, then perhaps the day might be salvaged after all.

2

Dawn shimmered grey-blue through the glass roof, displacing the tired light of the electric bulbs. Voices murmured, policemen whistled, the tannoy scratched. The big station clock showed twenty-three minutes past five, and Rath had the feeling that most people were just as tired as him – in spite of the noise they were making. After two cups of black coffee he still felt outside of himself, as if he were hovering above the station observing his body's movements. A tall, dark-haired man in a light-grey summer suit and hat, carrying a platform ticket in one hand and a bouquet of flowers and a red dog lead in the other. A tired man passing through the barrier, with an equally sleepy-looking dog in tow.

It had only occurred to him to buy flowers when he was outside the station. He had seen a light on in the concourse and knocked on the windowpane. The girl had kindly interrupted sorting the freshly delivered flowers to make up a bouquet. Now here they stood on the platform, all dressed up with nowhere to go: a man, a dog and a bouquet of flowers.

Rath stretched, standing on tiptoes to get the blood pumping. Reaching for the cigarette case in his inside jacket pocket, he wedged the flowers under his arm and lit an Overstolz. The truth was he shouldn't be here. He was on standby, which meant he must be contactable at all times.

18

Usually people simply informed headquarters where they could be reached if they didn't want to spend the whole weekend by the telephone. In this way Rath suspected that Buddha Ernst Gennat, the chief of Homicide, had built up a pretty clear idea of how his officers spent their free time, knowing, as he did, the bars, theatres, cinemas, gymnasiums, race tracks and even the women they frequented. It was why under normal circumstances Rath chose to perform his duties from home, as he had done this morning, before ducking out to Bahnhof Zoo. Still, he would only be gone for half an hour, three-quarters of an hour tops. What could possibly go wrong?

Recently, homicide cases had been few and far between – if, that is, you discounted the activities of Communists and Nazis, who seemed to take increasing pleasure in killing one another, ever since the new regime had lifted the SA ban imposed by the Brüning government. Only yesterday there had been gunfights in Wedding and Moabit. The result: one dead Nazi, eight additional casualties. Such cases were handled by local CID forces, if anyone from Alex attended then it would be the political police. Otherwise, suicide was still king. Someone had blown their brains out in Grunewald, while in Bernauer Strasse, a woman had thrown her five-year-old child out of the window before following herself. The usual madness, then.

Rarely had his work in Homicide felt so futile. Rath had always thought that police were there to maintain law and order, but recently it seemed their only role was to pick up the pieces.

There was a scratch on the tannoy and a military-sounding voice announced that the Northern Express would arrive after a delay of approximately ten minutes. Rath flicked his Overstolz onto the platform and reached for another. One more smoke and she'd be here. He felt more and more nervous the longer he was made to wait. It was just him on the platform, no grinning man, no Greta, no one else who might get in the way; two telephone calls had been enough to see to that. He knew that most of Charly's friends preferred to give him a wide berth, or perhaps it was the other way around, he couldn't say for sure. He had never known quite what to make of all these students and lawyers.

Accompanying Charly to the station last autumn, he had felt simply lousy, but now that she was on her way home, he scarcely felt any better. Her single semester in Paris had become two. Though they had exchanged many letters and spoken regularly on the telephone, they had only met once, a few weeks after her departure, and endured a frantic night of lovemaking in a Cologne hotel, before saying their goodbyes. Rath's plan to spend Christmas with her in Paris had been scotched when he hadn't been able to get the time off.

A contract killer was on the loose, a sniper who picked off his victims with a single shot to the heart, before vanishing without trace. A flashy Berlin lawyer had been gunned down in front of the opera house in Charlottenburg and, with only the bullet to go on, Czerwinski, the portly detective, had made a quip about the 'phantom of the opera'. The press had gleefully seized on the name.

The Phantom, as the triggerman was now known in official circles, had gifted police officers a Christmas ban on leave, but Rath had consoled himself with the knowledge that Charly would be returning in mid-February. Perhaps they might even catch the man before New Year's Eve, in which case he could at least decamp to Paris for the Bells.

Sadly, neither came to pass.

They hadn't caught the Phantom, neither before New Year's Eve nor after. The unidentified sniper had continued to strike, and was responsible for at least two further deaths, possibly more, and had become a symbol of failure for the otherwise celebrated Berlin Homicide Division.

As for Charly's return . . . At the end of January, two weeks before she was due home, she had sent a telegram to say that Professor Weyer had extended her contract. Rath had pretended to share her joy and extended his congratulations, keeping his true thoughts to himself. Everything seemed to be going swimmingly in Paris. Fräulein Charlotte Ritter was beginning to make a name for herself in the legal world. In Gereon Rath's world, however, things weren't quite as smooth, and the photo she had left him appeared so unreal it was as if the person depicted no longer existed . . .

. . . but all that was over now. She was coming back, and he had sworn never again to be apart from her for so long, had sworn, finally, to take his life into his own hands.

He threw the stub of his second cigarette on the track bed as the loudspeaker announced the train's arrival. Rath stood up straight, tugged at his suit and gazed into the lights that were gradually emerging out of the dawn, noiselessly at first, until the Northern Express rumbled into the station, hissing and steaming, and filling the air with a loud, metallic squeal. A series of midnight-blue sleeping cars passed, moving ever more slowly until the train eventually came to a halt with a final sizzle of its valves.

It felt as if time had stood still, until the doors flew open and people flooded out, filling the platform with noise and chatter. Rath craned his neck, searching for Charly's slim figure, but it was hopeless in the mayhem. He had to take a step back to avoid being knocked down. Suddenly Kirie barked, wagged her tail vigorously and pulled on the lead with all her might. Rath yielded, allowing her to lead him through the crowd.

Charly was on the platform, and he was so bowled over by the sight of her that for a moment he stood rooted to the spot. Kirie howled as the lead tightened, and gazed up at him in confusion. Charly had scarcely changed but, somehow, he almost failed to recognise her.

Her hair was different, in a shorter, new cut, her dark locks tinged with an unfamiliar, red sheen. Her hat must be new, too, as well as her coat and her shoes. Her appearance contradicted his mental image of her to such an extent that he was overcome by a feeling of estrangement. He shot up an arm and waved the bouquet until, at last, she saw him. When she smiled, the dimple on her left cheek made her a little more familiar. The dog kept pulling, and positively dragged Rath towards her.

Kirie jumped up to lick Charly's face, and Rath was so overjoyed by Charly's laughter that he stood and watched until long after Kirie had settled back into wagging her tail and barking. For a moment they stared at each other without words.

'Welcome home,' he said at last, just to say something, and took her in his arms. He breathed in her scent and, even if her perfume was as foreign as her appearance, underneath he perceived the unmistakable fragrance of her skin, a fragrance that consigned all traces of estrangement to oblivion, reviving countless memories along the way. Not memories, exactly, but something from a deeper place, a place he hadn't even known was there. So much lay in her scent that he felt as if their months of separation had never occurred.

He stepped back to look into her smiling eyes.

'Are those for me, or were you expecting someone else?'

'Marlene Dietrich must have missed the train.'

She rolled her eyes, but smiled. Rath handed her the bouquet.

'Now I'm completely defenceless,' she said, raising both hands. In the left she held a small travel bag, in the right the bouquet of flowers.

'Defenceless is good,' he said, and kissed her. When she reciprocated, he could have fallen on her there and then, but the dog had started to bark and people were looking their way.

'How about we go somewhere more private?' Rath said, and she smiled.

He organised a baggage handler and led Charly to the car where the handler stowed Charly's suitcase and bag onto the dickey seat as Kirie sprang inside. He removed her by the collar, consigning her to the tip-up seat next to the cases.

'She should know to sit in the back when I've got company,' he said, taking his place beside Charly and starting the engine.

'Have you had a lot of company these last few months?'

'So little that Kirie has forgotten her manners.'

Charly didn't seem to notice that they turned off from Hardenbergstrasse as soon as they reached Steinplatz. When he opened the passenger door on Carmerstrasse, however, she looked around curiously. He lifted the dog out of the tip-up seat, then the suitcases, and marched towards the building behind Kirie, who already knew the way, glad that Charly couldn't see his smile. She followed them up the small exterior staircase into a bright, marble-panelled stairwell.

'Good morning, Herr Rath,' the porter said from his lodge.

'Morning, Bergner.'

'What's going on?' Charly whispered, as they stood by the lifts more or less out of earshot. 'Where are we?'

'Patience. You'll see.'

Rath pressed the button and the lift door opened. He didn't have to tell the boy where they were headed, and when they emerged onto the third floor, Charly could scarcely believe her eyes.

He took the key from his pocket and opened up, and Kirie disappeared straight inside. Opening the door wide he set the cases down on the marble floor in the hall, turning away so that Charly couldn't see his grin. Only now had she spotted the brass plate next to the door.

Rath, it said simply. He hadn't wanted to commit himself to an initial. At least not yet.

'I don't believe it,' she said, stepping inside.

'I thought I'd upsize a little,' he said, helping her out of her coat. 'Don't you want to look around?'

She gazed in admiration. Even the hallway was impressive. Bright and modern. Only Kirie, who had settled in her basket and was blinking sleepily, disturbed the picture-perfect image.

'How long have you been living here? Did they make you detective chief inspector, or move you straight up to superintendent?'

He was afraid she might ask something like that. 'Inheritance,' he said, as casually as possible. 'Uncle Joseph.'

That was true, of course, but his godfather, who had died six months previously, hadn't left him much. He thought it best not to mention the cheque that had arrived from overseas three and a half months ago. It might not have carried Abraham Goldstein's signature – the two-thousand-dollar *consulting fee* was made out by *Transatlantic Trade Inc.* – but Charly would put two and two together, which was precisely what he hoped to avoid. No one could know that he accepted handouts from dubious sources, and, further, that he actually believed it was money owed – especially since the Free State of Prussia was in no position to pay him properly. His yearly salary didn't amount to five thousand marks.

He loved Charly's dark eyes all the more when they were wide open like this. He knew how much she adored modern architecture, and had furnished the four rooms accordingly. It wasn't cheap, but the leather, steel and fine wood was sturdy enough to last a hundred years.

He opened the door to the drawing room. 'If you would be so kind as to step this way.'

The morning sun sent its first rays through the window

24

onto a lavishly decked breakfast table of freshly baked bread rolls and coffee. The champagne stood in the cooler, and the glasses were in their place.

Charly seemed genuinely lost for words. 'I...gracious me. Well, how's that for a welcome party,' she said.

'A Berlin breakfast. I'm sure you couldn't bear the sight of another baguette with Camembert.' He gestured towards the one door he still hadn't opened. 'And afterwards, I can show you the bedroom.'

'You old lecher!'

'At your service, my lady.' He realised even the thought of going next door aroused him. Suddenly breakfast didn't seem quite so important.

'Isn't that...' Too late. She had seen the champagne. '...*Heidsieck Monopol*?'

The same brand they had drunk the first time, in Europahaus. When Rath thought that three years had passed since then, his next move seemed long overdue. Pouring carefully, he handed her a champagne glass. The one with the ring.

They clinked glasses. Charly smiled, revealing her dimple. He studied her as she drank. After a moment she hesitated and fished the ring out of the bubbles. She didn't say anything, just stared at the glistening ring as it dripped through her fingers. Slowly she began to grasp its significance.

'Fräulein Charlotte Ritter,' he said, taking her hand. 'With God as my witness, I, Gereon Rath, do hereby request your hand in marriage.'

He gazed into her astonished eyes and realised, for once, that his customary irony was misplaced. 'Charly,' he said, thinking he had never been so earnest before in his life, 'will you marry me?'

She stared at him, in shock almost, or so he thought, and sank onto the nearest chair. 'Phew,' she said. 'That's quite enough surprises for one morning.'

'I thought I'd propose *before* we went into the bedroom. I'm Catholic.'

'That's never stopped you before.'

'Charly...' He was still holding her hand, actually *kneeling* before her now like some romantic suitor from the last century. 'I should have asked you long ago. Only...Paris got in the way. But I'm serious, goddamn it. Will you be my wife?'

She looked at him. 'Don't misunderstand me, but before I respond, I have to...' She broke off and started again. 'Gereon, you realise that it's a very serious question. And even if you *should* have asked it long ago, it's still rather – sudden. I...'

She broke off again, and all at once he knew why he had shied away from this moment for so long; why he had continued to avoid it despite purchasing the ring more than a year ago. The sense of estrangement he had felt at the station came hurtling back. The woman before him wore the latest in Parisian fashion; the Berlin girl of memory was gone.

He let go of her hand and was about to get up, when he felt her taking his head in her hands and kissing him. The erotic atmosphere he had thought destroyed returned, or his erection, at least.

'Is that a *yes*?' he asked.

'Let's not talk. Not now. Later.' He kissed her again and began to unbutton her blouse. 'Take it easy. Didn't you want to show me the bedroom?'

'As you wish, madam.'

'We aren't married yet!'

He lifted her high and carried her through. She was just as soft and warm and feather-light as he remembered. He didn't know if he had made a fool of himself with his proposal, didn't know how she would respond; he only knew that she had brushed the weighty topic aside with a kiss, and now, suddenly, everything was as it had been before.

The telephone rang, but he refused to be perturbed, edging Charly further into the bedroom, where he lowered her onto the bed and kissed her, fiddling with her blouse a second time as she loosened the knot in his tie.

The telephone rang again. Whoever it was, they were stubborn – but Rath was determined to ignore the sound until Kirie's bark drowned it out. Charly grinned and said, 'Perhaps you should take it after all.'

He looked at his watch. A quarter to six. He went over to answer.

'Gereon! Finally! Where the hell have you been hiding?'

Reinhold Gräf. Exactly as Rath had feared. 'I just ducked out to the train station.'

'Just *ducked* out? I've been trying to reach you for ages ...'

'What's happened?'

'Male corpse. *Haus Vaterland*. Potsdamer Platz.'

'Shit.'

'Shit is right. Now, for God's sake get a move on, before along with everyone else Böhm cottons on to the fact that the duty inspector is absent.'

Rath hung up and straightened his tie. He didn't have to say anything to Charly. She was already buttoning her blouse.

27

3

Haus Vaterland overlooked Potsdamer Platz like a marooned pleasure steamer, and in a sense that's what it was. It didn't give a hoot about patriotism, only with fleecing its clients for cash. Behind the building's façade around a dozen restaurants of all kinds waited for custom: a Bavarian *brauhaus*, a Spanish bodega, a Wild West bar, a Turkish café, and more, all with furnishings, menus and entertainment to match. Those who came in just to stare weren't welcome, with would-be patrons obliged to buy food and drinks vouchers at the door.

During his first days in Berlin, Rath had tried to find a home of sorts in the *Rheinterrasse*, but all it offered was oversweet wine and tacky Rhine romanticism. As for Berlin's famous metropolitan flair, an idea propagated mainly by Berliners themselves, *Haus Vaterland* was something of a let-down. Provincial tourists might stop and gawp, but to Rath's mind, the more sophisticated drinking establishments in the west, such as *Femina* or *Kakadu*, had a lot more going for them. The building impressed by its sheer size, as well as its neon strip lights, which dominated Potsdamer Platz at night.

At this hour, however, the marooned pleasure steamer was as deserted as a ghost ship. Only the cars at the goods entrance, above all the murder wagon, suggested that something was afoot. Rath parked his Buick behind an Opel from ED, the police identification service, but remained inside. He took a drag on his Overstolz and blew smoke against the windscreen. Never had he felt so reluctant to work, so begrudging of his profession, as this morning. He had suggested that Charly come along, but she had refused. 'What would people say if we appeared together?' He felt aggrieved by her response, even if he knew she was right.

He stubbed out his cigarette in the Buick's tiny ashtray and got out, determined to get this over and done with as soon as possible and return to Carmerstrasse.

Dr Karthaus, who wore his white coat even outside the dissecting room, stood at the entrance, cigarette in hand, chatting to a uniform cop. The officer saluted as Rath approached; the pathologist nodded his head.

'Good morning, Doctor.'

'Good of you to join us, Inspector. I've been smoking my lungs black waiting. Car trouble, was it? You should get yourself a German model.'

Rath ignored the dig. 'What can you tell me about the corpse?'

Karthaus gave a gentle smile. 'That's the good thing about the Criminal Police – you get to explain everything three times. Come with me and I'll show you. It's upstairs. The undertakers have been positively itching to take it away.'

'Upstairs?'

Karthaus flung his cigarette into a puddle. 'If you would be so kind as to follow me,' he said, and, without waiting for a response, turned and headed inside.

Rath followed the white coat into a large, plain room with two freight elevators and a stairwell, that seemed to be *Haus Vaterland*'s goods reception. Karthaus took the stairs to the fourth floor where two uniform cops and two men dressed in black waited in front of the lift doors. On the floor was a zinc coffin.

'Can we get going?' asked one of the men in black.

'In a moment,' said Karthaus. 'The inspector here needs to look at the corpse.' He gave a sour smile and gestured towards an elevator car hanging a metre too low in its shaft. Two forensic technicians were taking fingerprints from its buttons, as well as from a wire mesh cart loaded to the brim with crates of schnapps.

'An accident, was it?' Rath asked, lighting another cigarette. Even now he felt little interest. Couldn't Gräf have dealt with this on his own?

'Accident?' Karthaus gazed sceptically. 'I'm afraid not.'

Rath climbed down into the car, cigarette between his lips, and the pathologist followed.

The dead man was wearing grey overalls. His eyes were well out of their sockets, gazing wide open as if they had witnessed the full horror of eternal damnation. For a moment Rath had the idea that the freight elevator in *Haus Vaterland* might lead straight down to hell. Instinctively he followed the dead man's gaze, but saw only yellowed plywood.

'So how did he die, if it wasn't an accident?'

The doctor cleared his throat. 'I know it sounds unlikely, but I'm certain the autopsy will confirm my assessment that ...'

'Autopsy?'

'Your colleague has already telephoned the public prosecutor. On my recommendation, of course.'

'Where are my colleagues now?'

'As far as I know, questioning witnesses. Now, as I was saying, unless I am very much mistaken the man here drowned.'

The forensics men continued stoically with their work.

'Drowned?' Rath asked. 'Don't you normally drown in water?'

'Perhaps the corpse was simply dumped here.'

'Doesn't look like it,' said one of the forensics officers.

30

'Not according to the footprints. Everything points to him entering the lift himself.' His colleague secured another fingerprint on the wire mesh cart's steel tubing. 'Besides, he came here in his own van. He wasn't dumped here by anyone.'

Dr Karthaus shrugged. 'We'll know more once the autopsy is complete,' he said.

'Where did you say Gräf was?'

'Questioning witnesses in some office or other. Ask the cops,' Karthaus said and climbed out, seemingly in a hurry to leave. Rath stubbed out his cigarette on the floor, about chest height, and followed.

The undertakers heaved the zinc coffin towards the elevator as one of the uniform cops offered to take him down to his colleagues. Rath followed through the eerily deserted *Löwenbräu*, where the fug of yesterday's beer still hung in the air, and into the vast central hall. From here a multitude of stairways, tribunes, elevators and doors led to the various restaurants and attractions that *Haus Vaterland* hosted across four floors. Normally a hive of activity, now the hall's size made it seem supernaturally calm. Around two dozen men were seated on the stairs, some in kitchen aprons, others in waiter's uniforms or lounge suits, a few more in worker's overalls. If the four or five uniform cops were like dogs guarding a herd of sheep, then Assistant Detective Andreas Lange was their shepherd, manning the stairs with two additional uniform officers.

'Morning, Inspector,' he said. 'Good that you're here.'

'Morning, Lange. What a lot of people!'

'Witnesses. Detective Gräf rounded them up.'

'And all of them saw something?'

'We don't know yet. These workers were on early shift at the probable time of death. Or late shift.'

'All of them?' If Gräf really meant to question each one, they'd be here all day. 'Let's just be grateful this didn't

31

happen last night during the rush. Then there'd be another thousand people on the stairs.' Rath thought of Charly in Carmerstrasse, and his mood darkened further. 'Any findings?'

'Depends how you look at it. We have a dead man, and an unusual cause of death. Otherwise no idea what happened to the poor fellow.'

'Do you really think it's possible that he drowned?'

'If that's what the doctor says.'

'Has he been identified?'

Lange took a document from his pocket. 'Forensics found this in his overalls.'

Herbert Lamkau, Rath read. A driver's licence, issued in October 1919 by the Oletzko district authority. The man's eyes flashed, piercing the photographer with his gaze, a look he must have copied from Kaiser Wilhelm.

'Lamkau. That's what it says on the delivery van too, isn't it?'

Lange nodded. 'Must be the manager.'

'Strange that he should be making the delivery himself . . .'

'Depends on the size of the company. Perhaps he's the only employee.'

'A small-time firm supplying a huge enterprise like *Haus Vaterland*? I don't think so. Try to find out how big it is, and whether Lamkau always made the deliveries himself.'

'Right you are.'

'And tell the ED men to check the lift was working properly. Just to be on the safe side.'

'We've already spoken to the in-house engineer. As well as the chef, who literally stumbled on the corpse. He called the lift up to the fourth floor and almost fell into the car when he opened the door. At the last moment he saw that it was too low in the shaft, and managed to hold on. That's when he saw the corpse.'

'And raised the alarm.'

'Yes. He informed the guard, who alerted us. The engineer says there's nothing wrong with the lift.'

'It doesn't look that way to me.'

Lange shrugged. 'He's assuming someone activated the emergency switch between the two floors. Sometimes when that happens the lift's no longer properly aligned, and doesn't stop on floor level.'

'Hmm ...' A blurred image flickered in Rath's mind. 'That would mean Lamkau activated the switch himself, before he died, wouldn't it?'

'We'll see. ED have taken fingerprints.'

Rath gestured towards the office door. 'Who is Gräf interviewing?'

'The security guard. He was next on the scene, after the chef.'

'Fine. I'm going in.'

Rath knocked and stepped inside. The office was surprisingly small and dark in comparison with the brightness of the central hall, the only source of light a desk lamp with a green shade. Numerous photos of artists hung on the wall behind the executive desk where the detective sat: musicians, illusionists, singers, female dancers. Christel Temme sat with her pad at a small visitor's table, registering the inspector's appearance as stoically as she did everything else. The stenographer was famously unflappable, even during the interrogation of the most callous murderer. She simply noted everything that was said, no matter how appalling or how trivial.

The man sitting on the chair between the two desks was no callous murderer, however, but a gaunt man in his early forties, dressed in the uniform of the Berlin Security Corps, kneading his cap in his hands. Reinhold Gräf rose from his chair.

'Inspector,' he said. It was part greeting, part explanation. The guard started to get up, but Rath waved him away.

33

'Herr Janke works as a security guard here,' Gräf added superfluously.

Rath sat on the edge of the desk and lit a cigarette. Gräf remained standing. Together they gazed down on the man's eyes flitting between them.

'So . . .' the guard began, and immediately the stenographer's pencil could be heard scratching across the page, 'where were we . . .'

'You were about to tell me how you knew the man in the lift was dead, Herr Janke,' Gräf prompted, sitting down when he realised Rath wasn't interested in taking over.

'Right.' Janke nodded. 'So, I went down into the car . . .'

'Did you have to open the door?' Gräf asked.

'Pardon me?'

'The elevator door.'

'No, Unger had already opened it.'

'The chef who discovered the corpse.'

'Right.' The guard squinted from one officer to the next as if sensing a trap. 'So, I went down into the car. The way he was lying there all glassy-eyed . . . I thought straightaway the man's dead. But first I felt his carotid pulse.'

'Why the carotid?' Gräf asked.

'That's . . . what we learned . . . during training. Security Corps.'

Gräf made a note. Rath caught himself looking at his watch. It was all getting too much for him: the guard's long-windedness, Gräf's pedantry, the excruciatingly slow pace of the interrogation.

'What did you do then?'

The guard stole a glance at Rath. 'First I climbed out of the car, and then . . .'

'Thank you, Herr Janke, but we don't need to know every last detail.' Rath slid from the desk. 'I'd like to pause the interrogation for a moment. Would you be so kind as to wait outside?'

34

'Of course.'

Gräf waited until he had left the room. 'Can you tell me what the hell you think you're doing?'

'No need to take down our conversation, Fräulein Temme. If you could wait outside too. Take a little break.'

'I don't need a break, Inspector.'

'We'll call you back in when you're needed,' Rath said, gazing sternly. The stenographer gathered her things and took her leave.

'Damn it, Gereon! First I spend hours trying to reach you, then when you do finally turn up, you have nothing better to do than terminate an interrogation just as it's getting started.'

'Take it easy. I haven't terminated the interrogation, only interrupted it. You can carry on in a moment; our guard here seems very co-operative.'

'What did you want to talk about?'

'First: the people outside – do you mean to question them all *here*? *In person*?'

'I wanted to make a start. Now that you're here, you can decide.'

'In that case, continue questioning the guard but, first, tell the cops outside to take down the personal particulars of every employee waiting in the hall.'

'What do you think we've been doing all this time?'

'If someone saw something, then question them here. If not, these people should kindly proceed to headquarters. In the meantime Lange can supervise Forensics, and we'll take care of everything else next week in the office.'

'Who'll inform the next of kin?'

'Lange can look after that. He has to learn sometime if he's to be an inspector.'

'You're right.' Gräf nodded. 'But that still leaves one question ...'

'Which is?'

'What's *your* role in all of this?'

'That's why I'm telling you now.' Rath didn't attempt to appear contrite. No one would believe him anyway. 'I have to go. I'd be grateful if you could run things in the meantime.'

'Gereon, you know I've never led an investigation.'

'Just do what I told you, then call it a day.' Gräf didn't look exactly thrilled. 'Come on. I'll make it up to you.'

'You've got some nerve.'

'I'll take that as a yes.'

'You're the boss.'

Rath clapped him on the shoulder. 'You'll be fine. Maybe it was all just an accident. There's no evidence of foul play.'

'I know,' Gräf said, 'but it's a mystery. Karthaus says the man drowned.'

'Perhaps he's simply mistaken.'

There was a knock on the door. A man in a light summer suit stepped confidently into the room, took a quick look around, and made a beeline for Rath.

'Inspector? They told me I'd find you here. Fleischer's the name. I'm the director.' They shook hands. 'Good that you're here at last. I hope you won't keep my men much longer. We're well behind schedule. Maintenance is unmanned, the central kitchen's deserted, and our first customers will soon be arriving ...'

'My colleague here will inform you which members of staff we're finished with,' Rath said, gesturing discreetly towards Gräf. 'Now, please accept my apologies, but I have another case to take care of ...'

The director looked annoyed, but before he could say anything Rath had lifted his hat and was gone.

Quarter of an hour later Rath emerged from his Buick on Carmerstrasse, free of the guilty conscience that had accompanied his departure from *Haus Vaterland*. For the

36

first time since returning to live in Charlottenburg, it felt as if he were coming home. He only had to think of who was waiting inside. They would be spending the weekend together again at last.

The area around Steinplatz was a decent part of town: solidly upper middle class, with most buildings possessing a service entrance, and he had rented the modern apartment primarily because of its size. He opened the heavy front door and stepped into bright limestone and glossy marble. No wonder Charly was impressed; she liked the flat, he had seen it in her eyes. It was twice as big as his old place in Kreuzberg, with plenty of room for two – and perhaps more.

Climbing the five carpeted steps to the entrance hall he heard the pitter-patter of doggie paws, and two short barks, and sensed that something was amiss. Kirie's black head peered around the corner of the counter, while the porter looked, embarrassed, over the marble top.

'What's the matter, Bergner?' Rath asked, even though he had already guessed.

The porter cleared his throat. 'I'm afraid the young lady . . .had to leave. She asked me to look after the dog.'

Bergner loosened the lead from Kirie's collar and Rath accepted the dog's wet greeting.

'Did she say where she was going?'

'I'm afraid not.'

Rath's thoughts were already elsewhere as he made towards the lift with Kirie.

Charly's scent hung in the air, making the flat seem that much emptier than before. Kirie was unperturbed, pitter-pattering towards her basket and curling into a ball. Rath sometimes wondered how much sleep a dog could take. Standing at one of the big windows, he looked out, seeing nothing, but aiming a kick at one of the heavy armchairs. Out of anger or disappointment? He couldn't say.

She had cleared the breakfast things and left a handwritten note.

> Forgive me, Gereon,
>
> but I just couldn't wait any longer. I held firm for an hour, but the longer I sat with Kirie in your lovely new home, the more I realised that after so long abroad I first needed to spend some time in Spenerstrasse, in my own apartment - especially since a new chapter awaits on Monday.
>
> Your friendly porter helped me with my luggage and agreed to take charge of Kirie. He seems pretty well versed in that regard, with the dog, I mean.
>
> Now here I am scribbling these lines. My taxi's already waiting below. As for your question, and the ring... Please don't be angry that I couldn't give you an immediate reply. I was very touched by your proposal (after all the years we've known each other!) but such an important question demands a considered response, and, having just stepped off the train after ten months in Paris, I felt as if everything was moving too fast. Our long-awaited reunion, a new apartment and a marriage proposal, all in the space of a single morning - even for a girl from Moabit that's too much at once.
>
> I suggest that we find a more convenient time and place for me to respond. Already I can tell you it isn't a simple case of 'yes' or 'no'. There are a few questions I'd like to ask you in return.
>
> I know it isn't exactly romantic, but there's nothing worse than an overly hasty decision

when so much is at stake. I've already had to
break off one engagement, as you know, and
the last thing I need is a repeat performance.
No hard feelings. Sending hugs.

See you soon
C.

He folded the letter and went into the bedroom. The first thing he noticed was that the bed had been straightened. The ring lay on the bedside table. What did it mean? Did the fact that she hadn't taken it constitute a response? He picked it up and examined it. What was he supposed to do now? Take it to their next meeting, await her response and – perhaps – slip it on her finger? No expert in such matters, he wiped the accursed thing with the tail of his jacket and placed it in his inside pocket, where it seemed destined to see out its days.

He unfolded the letter again, and tried to understand. How did she feel about him? No matter how often he read it, he was none the wiser. He couldn't help thinking back to the moment he had seen her on the platform. To that moment of shock, of being afraid he had lost her, or at least the person he remembered. Until he caught the scent of her hair and skin, and felt his whole body being drawn towards her. He knew she had felt the same way, at least when he'd shown her the flat.

The business with the champagne glass was a crackpot idea. Who on earth had talked him into it? Paul? A colleague from the Castle? Perhaps it was the stupid engagement ring that had driven her away, rather than his lingering too long at the crime scene.

Seeing himself in the mirrored doors of the liquor cabinet he realised he still hadn't taken off his hat. He hung it on the hook and, in the drawing room, chose a record from the pile he had arranged in advance. He put on Ellington's *Mood Indigo*, one of the many discs Severin had sent over from the States in the last few months. He had wanted to play it for her; for them both. The record player was a brand new Telefunken radiogramophone, but that hardly seemed to matter now.

He took the bottle of cognac from the cabinet, along with a glass, and sat in one of the armchairs. The truth was he had bought them for her, after she had pointed out a similar set in the display window of some exclusive furniture store on Tauentzienstrasse. That was back in the days before Paris, with her departure already hanging in the air. At least the chairs were comfortable, even if they didn't look it. He sniffed at the balloon glass and listened to the music, the sad melody of the trumpets, the earthy warmth of the clarinets.

The smell of the cognac soothed him almost more than the music. How he had longed for this moment – even before she had gone away. And now, Herr Rath? It isn't even lunchtime, and you're sitting here pouring yourself a cognac just to get through the day.

4

A restless whimpering roused him from sleep. He opened his eyes to see Kirie wagging her tail. She took a few steps towards the door and turned. Rath sat up. He must have nodded off. An empty cognac glass lay overturned on the carpet. By now Duke Ellington spun inaudibly, the needle striking the groove again and again with a soft, rhythmical crackle.

It was almost two o'clock and the dog urgently needed walking. Rath struggled out of the armchair, shovelled a few handfuls of cold water onto his face and fetched the lead. Kirie positively dragged him outside, down the external staircase and to the first shrub in Carmerstrasse, where she eyed him gratefully as she went about her business. Rath took her for a little stroll across Steinplatz and realised his stomach was rumbling. He found a seat on the terrace of a hotel that modestly termed itself *Pension*, and ordered a beer and a snack. Though the portion was small there were still some leftovers for Kirie, who patiently awaited her chance. Sitting afterwards with a black coffee and a cognac to accompany the obligatory cigarette, Rath knew once and for all that he wouldn't be heading back to his flat. He called the waiter over and paid, bundled Kirie into the car and drove out to Moabit.

He didn't park in Spenerstrasse, but on the corner of Melanchtonstrasse, where two roadside trees meant he could keep an eye on her entrance without being seen from the window. By now, certainty had evaporated. Reading her letter for at least the twentieth time offered no clues. Did she actually want to see him? Should he *really* just go upstairs and ring her doorbell? Perhaps she'd gone for a rest. She'd mentioned how badly she had slept on the train. In which case it would be Greta who came to the door, and that he could do without. He thought back to the year Charly's housemate had spent abroad, when they'd had the flat to themselves. It was almost like being married ...

You'd have been better off staying put, he thought, perhaps she's trying to call you right now. Then he remembered she didn't have his new number. Perhaps, thinking him at work, she'd tried the office, unaware of the extent to which he had neglected his duties on her behalf.

While he was thinking, a young man crossed Spenerstrasse, heading for Charly's front door. Rath hadn't seen him in almost a year, but recognised him immediately. The grinning man. Guido Scherer, Charly's former classmate, now plying his trade in some wretched legal practice in Wedding, but clearly still as devoted to her as ever. Rath couldn't believe it: she couldn't *wait* to get out of his flat, yet here she was hosting that arsehole on her first day back? Perhaps she'd invited all of her friends round for a little reunion, all those lawyers he'd never known quite what to make of ...and of course Gereon Rath, that rough-hewn cop, would only get in the way.

He started the engine and stubbed out his cigarette. At least he knew he wouldn't be going up there now. He accelerated so hard that the tyres squealed, causing the grinning man to turn around before he disappeared inside that shitty little house on Spenerstrasse. Fuck! Rath vented his rage on the gas pedal, racing through the city. At first his only aim was to get out of Moabit, but then, without making a conscious choice, indeed, without even noticing where he was going, he travelled further and further south. Only when, in the shadow of the elevated train, he veered east via Gitschiner Strasse, did he understand that he was headed towards Luisenufer.

Parking on the street corner he let Kirie out, and memories came flooding back, all too many of which, stupidly enough, had to do with Charly. The dog sniffed at a tree on the edge of the play area, almost as if she recognised it, before wagging her tail and gazing expectantly towards her master. The cries of the children romping on the vast expanse of sand reminded Rath of how he had sat on a bench here in the sun with Charly, imagining that one of the children playing was *their* child, the child they shared together. He hadn't said anything, of course, neither that day nor later on – but then he had shared very few of his dreams with her. Kirie went ahead, full of expectation, having traced the same path many hundreds of times before.

A youth in a brown shirt, blonde hair parted wet, approached from the courtyard entrance. On his left arm he wore a swastika armband; tucked underneath was an SA cap. The Nazi gave him a feisty look, but Rath refused to be intimidated. He'd had enough of these brown so-and-sos ever since he'd seen them running wild on the Ku'damm last year. They were worse than the Communists. If the boy wanted a fight, he could have one, so long as he knew he'd wind up in a police cell. For all that, it seemed as though a provocative glance was enough. The youth walked past Rath without saying anything, only to turn around and shoot him a final, wicked glance as he donned his uniform cap.

Nazis were nothing new in this area, even back when a swastika armband wasn't nearly such a common sight. At the same time the Liebigs in the rear building had always kept the red flag flying, without things ever coming to a head. Communists and Nazis sharing the same roof; that, too, was Berlin. In workers' districts especially, Red and Brown often lived side by side, albeit not always as peacefully as here on Luisenufer. As for normal people, Rath had the impression they were getting thinner on the ground, even in the city's more affluent neighbourhoods.

Annemarie Lennartz, the caretaker's wife, was out beating carpets, but paused when she saw who was crossing the courtyard. 'Well, there's a surprise! Nice of you to drop by.'

Rath tipped his hat briefly and pointed towards the rear building. 'Detective at home?'

Annemarie Lennartz looked around and lowered her voice. 'Night shift,' she said, with a knowing expression. 'Didn't get home until lunchtime.'

Rath disappeared inside the rear building and climbed the stairs. Pausing in front of a door on the first floor, he gave a careful knock. He waited a moment, and when still nothing happened, knocked again, violently this time. 'Police! Open at once.'

Someone clattered about inside, and seconds later the door edged open to reveal Reinhold Gräf.

'Gereon!' The detective, hair still wet, and clad in a bathrobe, seemed more irritated than surprised. 'Has something happened?'

'Social call. Not interrupting, am I?'

'I was in the bath, but come on in.' Gräf opened the door wide. 'Make yourself at home. Shouldn't be too tricky.'

Rath followed Gräf into the kitchen where the detective placed a kettle on the stove. 'Coffee?' he asked. 'I haven't had breakfast yet.'

'Wouldn't say no.' Rath took off his hat and hovered in the doorway. Gräf fetched the coffee grinder from the same cupboard Rath had once used. 'Take a seat,' he said, without turning around.

Rath remained standing. 'How was it this morning then?'

Gräf continued pouring coffee beans.

44

'Sorry I had to leave you alone like that…but it really was important.'

Gräf looked at him and turned the crank. For a moment the only sound was the crunching of the grinder. 'If that's an official apology consider it accepted.'

Rath fetched two cups and saucers from the cupboard and placed them on the table, while Gräf busied himself with the kettle and filter. For a moment he tried to think of something to say, but nothing came to mind. He sat at the table and waited for Gräf to join him. The coffee dripped through the filter into the pot.

'You really left us in the lurch this morning, you know that?' Gräf said. 'And don't give me *who's in charge*. You're the one who turned up late to the crime scene. Do you realise how many times I tried to reach you, just to save your skin from Böhm and the rest? Well, more fool me. Because when you *do* show up it seems you've got nothing better to do than piss straight off again.'

Rath nodded without contrition. He had apologised already. Gräf stood up, took the filter from the pot and poured. It was even more watery than usual, but Rath chose to be diplomatic and took an Overstolz from his case. 'I thought I could make amends by shouting you a beer in the *Dreieck*.'

'You're on standby.' Gräf shovelled spoonful after spoonful of sugar into his coffee. 'And I've got night shift at the Castle.'

Rath looked at his watch. 'In three hours.'

'Exactly. I don't want to turn up drunk.'

'One beer. You can use the opportunity to tell me what happened this morning.'

'Gereon, you already reek of booze. Technically you're on duty.'

'It was only a cognac,' Rath lied. 'Just now, after lunch.'

Gräf took a few sips of coffee. 'OK, one beer won't hurt.'

'Not if I say it won't.' Rath grinned. 'Remember who's in charge.'

'Didn't I just warn you about that?'

A short time later the pair sat at the counter of the still deserted *Nasse Dreieck*, probably the smallest and most triangular-shaped bar in Berlin. Before them stood two beer glasses. Kirie had found a spot by their feet, Schorsch, the landlord, having automatically laid out a bowl of water. He had started tapping out the beer before his patrons even ordered, albeit on this occasion the pair declined the schnapps chaser. They clinked glasses. Gräf's mood seemed to be gradually improving. 'Then let me get you up to speed,' he said, wiping foam from his mouth.

'I'm the one who has to brief our superiors, after all.'

'The written report's already in the works. Lange and I were going to take care of the rest this evening.'

'Good. Then give me the abridged version. Did ED find anything?'

'Nothing's confirmed at this stage,' Gräf said. 'There's no sign of a struggle, or of any violence; in fact there's no sign whatsoever of foul play. Though there's nothing to point to a natural death either.'

'We'll just have to wait for the autopsy then.' Rath took another sip of coffee. 'What do you make of Karthaus's suspicion? That the man drowned, I mean.'

'I think he could be right, even if it sounds a little strange. His hair was wet.'

'I didn't notice.'

'Because you were so late. Take a look at Lange's photos and . . .see for yourself.'

'Wet hair.' Rath shrugged. 'So what? It was raining last night.'

'He'd have looked different. His shoulders were wet too, but the rest of him was dry.'

'So, what's your theory?'

46

'On how you can drown in a lift? I don't have one. The red cloth's a puzzle too.'

'Red cloth?'

Gräf gave him a look of mild reproach, and Rath made a conciliatory gesture with his hands.

'All right, all right! I'll look at the photos.'

'The cloth was hanging from the wire mesh cart with the crates of schnapps. It's with ED now.'

'A Communist flag?'

'More like a handkerchief. We'll see.'

Before Gräf could say anything, Schorsch had placed the next round of beers on the counter.

'You really think it's possible to drown in a lift?' Rath asked.

'I don't think anything. The cause of death is a total mystery. If he really *did* drown, it'll only deepen.'

'Perhaps someone just dumped him there.'

'Using Lamkau's van?' Gräf shook his head. 'No, everything points against it. Besides, the perpetrator could hardly have made it past the guard with a corpse.' Schorsch placed a third round on the counter and cleared away the empties. 'That's enough now,' Gräf said.

'One more,' said Rath. 'Rinse your mouth out with a little Odol and the smell will be gone.'

'Sounds like you're speaking from experience.'

Rath raised his glass. 'You have to set an example for young Lange, you know.'

Gräf did likewise. 'The way you set an example for me?'

'Has Lange informed the next of kin?'

'The man left behind a widow,' said Gräf. 'The Lamkaus live next to their offices, out in Tempelhof.'

'How many employees?'

'A dozen, I'd say.'

'So, why did the boss make the delivery himself?'

'That isn't the only question. I've summoned the most

47

important witnesses to the Castle for Monday morning.' Gräf drained his glass and set it to one side. 'It wasn't much good having that director milling about – his men weren't exactly forthcoming in his presence. I think we'll get more from an interrogation.' He slid off his bar stool. 'Perhaps we'll know then why Lamkau was carrying an envelope containing a thousand marks.'

'A thousand marks?'

'In his overalls.'

Rath was about to say something, but, seeing Gräf's face, decided against it.

'ED have it,' the detective continued. 'They're testing for fingerprints.'

'What's he doing with a tidy sum like that?'

Gräf shrugged.

'Well,' Rath said. 'At least we know one thing ...'

'Which is ...'

'We can rule out robbery homicide.'

5

The brass plate on the brick wall bore the inscription *Berlin University Institute of Forensic Medicine*, while a stationary mortuary car prepared visitors for what lay inside. At the external staircase the queasy feeling in Rath's stomach returned; hardly the ideal basis on which to enter the morgue, whose chilly catacombs concealed a range of unappetising surprises.

It had been Dr Karthaus who roused him. He had stupidly kept drinking yesterday evening after Gräf left for his night shift, staying on for a few beers in the *Dreieck*, before taking a taxi home. Arriving there, he was forced to admit that he was still too sober to bear a deserted apartment, especially now that Charly had been and gone. He had dutifully telephoned headquarters at Alex to inform them where he could be reached for the next few hours, before leaving Kirie in the care of the night porter. In the Ku'damm he had abandoned himself to the swing of the *Kakadu* bar and its well-stocked shelves, resisted the advances of an adventuresome blonde, and tried hard not to think of Charly, which, of course, was easier said than done. The cocktails, at any rate, had served their purpose, rendering him insensible enough to return home well after midnight and find sleep at last.

Until he was awoken by the telephone.

'There's something I'd like to show you,' Karthaus had

said, summoning him to Hannoversche Strasse for two o'clock.

Rath fed the dog, but neglected to feed himself, drinking a coffee and showering before setting off with Kirie. Only when he stepped outside did he realise that his car was still parked in Kreuzberg, and started down Hardenbergstrasse towards Bahnhof Zoo.

It wasn't quite two when they reached the morgue. Recognising them, the porter took Kirie's lead, using a bite of his salami sandwich to bring her to heel. 'Doctor's waiting downstairs,' he said, waving Rath through to the cellar, where the pathologists processed their corpses.

Rath kept his eyes on the floor; the black-and-white checked pattern had a soothing effect on his stomach. Stepping through the large swing doors into the autopsy room, he spied Dr Karthaus at his table in the corner, a steaming cup of coffee placed alongside a file.

Karthaus looked up from his notes and furrowed his brow. 'Inspector! You're unusually punctual today.'

'Dead on time.'

The doctor folded his glasses and lit a cigarette. Rath fumbled for an Overstolz, but realised he had left them at home. He stole a glance at the Manoli cigarettes on the desk, but the doctor stood up and led him to a trolley where the contours of a human body could be discerned through a cotton sheet. 'Take a look,' Karthaus said, yanking the sheet to the side almost violently. 'There's something you have to see.'

The corpse still wore the same horrified expression as yesterday morning, but it was paler now, the area around the mouth a deeper shade of blue. The doctor gripped the ashen face and turned it to one side. Using his index finger, he gestured towards a point on the neck around which a small, bluish dot had formed.

'See?' Karthaus asked. Rath nodded, tempted for an instant to lean over the man's neck to get a better view, only to listen to his stomach's advice and trust in the doctor's words. 'A puncture site,' Karthaus continued. 'The injection was administered intravenously.'

'What kind of injection?'

'He didn't get it from a doctor, anyway. I've already checked. Perhaps he was a morphine addict.' The doctor drew on his cigarette. 'Though it's hardly common for morphine addicts to inject through the jugular vein. You'd need a mirror, for starters. Besides . . . if our man here *was* a morphine addict there'd have to be additional puncture sites. But this is the only one.'

'Are you saying that someone administered the injection for him?'

'Everything points that way. Which means we have evidence of external violence after all.'

'A lethal injection?'

'Hopefully a blood analysis will reveal all.'

'So the man didn't drown!' Rath didn't always need to be right, but he savoured it here.

'It's difficult to know for sure.'

'I thought you had completed the autopsy?'

Karthaus nodded. 'The man had water in his lungs. So much, in fact, that it's inconceivable it entered post-mortem. So far, so typical for a victim of drowning. Nevertheless, the level of water aspiration wasn't nearly extreme enough to lead to fatal hypoxia.'

'You'll have to break that down for me, Doctor. I'm no medic, and my Latin isn't up to much either.'

'Hypoxia is derived from the Greek. It denotes a lack of oxygen. Hypoxia as a result of extreme water aspiration is what we would vulgarly term "drowning".' Karthaus looked at Rath like a stern teacher. '*I* suspect, however, that although our man was in danger of drowning, he actually died of respiratory failure. Moments beforehand.'

'What are you saying? Did he drown or didn't he?'

'He drowned a little bit. He definitely inhaled water, a most unpleasant experience, but, most likely, he didn't die as a result. In other words: he stopped breathing before he could drown.'

'Because he was administered poison...' Karthaus shrugged. 'But we're definitely talking murder.'

'We're definitely talking foul play.'

'And here, poor fool, with all my lore, I stand ...'

'I see you know your Goethe, at least.'

'Believe it or not, I graduated high school.'

Karthaus gave a nod of acknowledgement. 'Then no doubt you'll appreciate the value of patience. Once we have the results of the blood analysis, we'll know the cause of death, I'd almost bet on it. This much I can tell you already: we're dealing with a very peculiar case.'

Rath looked at the corpse, the horror in its face. Who had it in for Herbert Lamkau, and why had they tried to drown him, after they'd already administered a lethal injection? 'Thank you, Doctor,' he said. 'Be in touch when you know more.' Rath had reached the door when he turned around. 'There was one more thing ...' Karthaus raised his eyebrows. 'You wouldn't happen to have any aspirin?'

Half an hour later, Rath and Kirie climbed the U-Bahn steps to Potsdamer Platz. The stone figures lining the dome of *Haus Vaterland* made it seem like a neon-signed Roman temple. The enormous complex was the first thing visitors saw as they emerged above ground; only then did the train station and its surrounding buildings come into sight. Things were already happening on the wide perron outside the main entrance. People were actually queuing to be parted from their cash. For the most part they looked like assistant bookkeepers from Königs Wusterhausen out for a wild weekend in the big city – or whatever passed for a wild weekend in their eyes.

Rath ignored the provincials and circled the building. At the goods entrance a few men were unloading sacks of potatoes. Rath observed them for a moment, before strolling inside with Kirie in tow. The left-hand lift was still out of service; the potato men, at least, were only using the right. Rath had almost reached the stairwell when a cry came from behind.

'Hey! What're you doing here? Do I know you?'

Rath recognised the uniform of the Berlin Security Corps. So, they kept watch during the day too. The guard eyed his identification suspiciously.

'CID?'

Rath nodded. 'The murder, yesterday.'

The word 'murder' didn't seem to have any impact. 'What is it you want?'

'To have another look at the crime scene.'

'Did you call in advance?'

'CID never calls in advance.'

The guard looked sour, but waved him through.

Rath climbed the steps, pausing to look outside the lifts on every floor. Kirie was nosing everywhere, but experience taught him to ignore her. Though Bouviers were usually excellent sniffer dogs, Kirie had proved herself to be an exception. On the third floor he came across a man in overalls crouched outside the open door of the lift shaft, screwdriver in hand. Rath surveyed him for a moment, then spoke. 'Is it faulty?' he asked, offering a cigarette. The man accepted gratefully, and Rath gave him a light.

'The door,' the man said, inhaling deeply. 'Why d'you ask?' He had a Berlin accent.

Rath lit an Overstolz and showed his badge. The engineer didn't seem surprised. 'Were you present when the corpse was found yesterday?'

'No, that was Siegmann.'

'Is he here?'

'No, he's on nights this week.'

'What's wrong with the door? Herr Siegmann didn't mention anything about it.'

'Only came to our attention this morning, when someone tried to get out here and it jammed. Most people ride straight up to the kitchen.'

'The door's jammed?'

'Some idiot flicked the emergency switch,' the man said. 'Exactly between the two floors. Then forced the door instead of calling for assistance. Metal's buckled as a result. It doesn't close properly any more.'

'That's the lift where the corpse was found, isn't it?'

The engineer shrugged. 'Could be, but that's no excuse.'

'But you're saying someone climbed out of this car? Where the corpse was found?'

A light came on in the man's head. 'You mean ...'

'It could be how the killer escaped. Have you touched anything?'

'No, but I will. Wouldn't get much done otherwise.'

'Then take a break. See if there's anything else on your list. The elevator door here needs to be examined.'

The engineer seemed to take things as they came, and shrugged his shoulders. 'You'll need to secure this though,' he said. 'So that no one falls into the shaft on me.'

'How about you take care of that until my colleagues arrive? Now, where can I find a telephone?'

'Back that way. The waiters have a common room. I can't be standing around here forever, I ...'

Rath ignored his protests and went through the door. At the end of a row of lockers, in front of which four or five men were getting changed, hung a wall telephone. Rath showed a waiter in full regalia his badge, but the man pretended he hadn't seen him. Clearly he was used to ignoring people but, then again, so was Rath. He pressed the hook down until the connection was interrupted. The waiter was about to protest, but swallowed his words when he saw Rath's face.

Despite ED only operating a skeletal staff on Sundays, he was assigned two men straightaway.

The engineer appeared relieved when Rath re-emerged. 'Can I get back to work now?' he asked.

'Be my guest. So long as you don't touch this elevator.'

The man toddled off and Rath lit another cigarette. His gaze fell on two narrow, high windows that looked onto the outside. One of them was slightly ajar. Kirie followed as he went across. He took out a handkerchief and opened the window fully. Outside was a kind of balcony, a walkway with a stone balustrade that lined the building.

He was about to climb out when he heard someone cough behind him and spun around. Dressed in a light summer suit, looking spruce and freshly coiffed, was Richard Fleischer, director of *Haus Vaterland*. The guard below must have sounded the alarm, or perhaps the engineer had told him he couldn't access the lift.

'Inspector! I must say I'm rather surprised to see you here. What are you doing?'

'My job.'

'Yesterday you hampered business, today you are preventing necessary repair work! Sneaking through the back entrance like that. Who do you think you are?'

'Would you have preferred me to use the front entrance and tell everyone I was from Homicide?'

Fleischer made a face as if he had bitten into a lemon. 'No need to go shouting from the rooftops. It was an accident, after all.'

'Wrong! It now looks as if we are dealing with a premeditated killing. I can tell you already that in such cases CID makes no allowances for operating procedures, nor for your good reputation.'

'But who would want to kill Herr Lamkau on *our* premises?'

'You have no idea?'

'Of course not. You think that one of my employees would beat a delivery man to death?'

'Herr Lamkau wasn't beaten to death.'

A few waiters came past and gazed in bewilderment at their director, standing in front of the freight elevators in conversation with a stranger and his dog.

'Be that as it may.' Fleischer lowered his voice. 'Now, if we must continue this discussion, I would prefer if we did so in my office.'

'I'm afraid I'm to wait here until my colleagues arrive.'

'Your *colleagues*?' The prospect of more police officers descending on his premises hardly filled him with joy.

'Forensic technicians,' Rath said simply, turning to the window once more. 'We have to examine a possible escape route.'

'That takes you to the balcony. You can't get down to the street from there, at most back into the building somewhere.'

Rath offered Fleischer an Overstolz, convinced that smoking together was the best way to dispel animosity or suspicion.

'I get the impression your building is well guarded,' he said, giving the director a light.

'Oh yes, our people are on the ball.'

'Where, would you say, is it possible to enter or leave unnoticed?'

'I would say, nowhere.' Fleischer drew on his cigarette, and gestured with his head towards the open window. 'Unless you're a cat burglar.'

'How many people work here? Two, three hundred?'

'Three hundred?' The director gave a pitying smile. 'There are around four hundred waiters in the service department alone, then in the central kitchen upstairs eighty chefs alongside one hundred and twenty temporary workers. We cater for around a million guests a year. All in all, we have some eleven hundred employees working around the clock. We're almost a miniature city; we even have our own waste incineration.'

'With so many employees, it wouldn't be possible for you to know each one personally.'

'Of course not.'

'How many people were on duty yesterday morning when Herr Lamkau was murdered?'

'You ought to know better than me, seeing as you rounded them all up. Fifty, sixty perhaps, if you count the technical staff, and security. There was hardly anyone from service.'

Their conversation was interrupted when two men in grey overalls emerged from the stairwell. Rath immediately recognised them as forensic technicians and pointed them towards the battered elevator door. 'Take a look at the window over there afterwards. See if you can't secure some fingerprints on the handles and check if there are any marks on the balcony outside.'

The men nodded, unpacked their suitcases and got to work. Rath watched them for a time. 'What do you hope to find?' the director asked at last.

'Information concerning the murderer's escape route,' Rath said. 'Perhaps his identity too.'

'I just hope you don't make too much of a fuss. I could do without the press.'

'Do you have a medical department here?'

Fleischer looked surprised. 'A first-aid room with several mattresses. For emergencies. Why do you ask?'

'Do you keep medicine there? Hypodermic syringes?'

'Naturally. Should I draw up a list?'

'Please. Today, if possible. Have someone you trust check all your medical cupboards. We need to know if anything's missing.' The director nodded like an obedient schoolboy. 'Did you know Herr Lamkau?' Rath asked suddenly. 'Personally, I mean.'

'No.' Fleischer's response was immediate. 'I saw him yesterday for the first time.'

'Were any of your employees privately acquainted with him?'

'Not that I'm aware of, but with such a large staff I couldn't say for certain.'

'What surprises me is that Herr Lamkau made the delivery in person. To say nothing of the time of day.'

Fleischer shrugged and stubbed out his cigarette. 'Owners do sometimes deliver themselves. The timings vary according to how suppliers plan their route. I'm sure Herr Riedel will be able to tell you more.'

'Herr Riedel,' Rath repeated, pulling out his pad.

'Alfons Riedel. One of our buyers.'

'Is Herr Riedel on site?'

'I'm afraid not. It's Sunday. Purchasing is closed.'

'I'll be back tomorrow,' Rath said. 'Please let Herr Riedel know.'

Director Fleischer was still smiling, but it looked as if he had developed a severe toothache.

The Lamkau firm had its headquarters in Tempelhof, beside the canal. The company buildings had an organised look about them, with half a dozen or so newly cleaned delivery vans arranged neatly outside. Rath drew up alongside one of the vehicles as it gleamed spotlessly in the sun. In comparison, his dull, dusty Buick, which he had since collected from Kreuzberg, was like a street urchin that had wandered into a group of confirmands. The vehicles were similar to the van discovered yesterday outside *Haus Vaterland*, which was still in the hands of Forensics. Some advertised Lamkau's liquor dealership and *Mathée Luisenbrand*; others promoted *Danziger Goldwasser* or *Treuburger Bärenfang*.

Rath got out and took Kirie by the lead. Walking to the residential building, he realised the hairs on her neck were

58

standing on end. She issued a soft *yip*. 'Easy, old girl,' he said. 'Easy.'

Then he gave a start himself, for behind him he heard loud barking and the rattle of a chain unfurling at rapid speed. He turned around and saw a whopping great brute making straight for him. Instinctively he took a few steps to one side. Just as the dog reached him, the chain tightened and held the beast in check. The barking didn't stop, however, as the guard dog threw its entire weight against the choker, and continued rasping at the visitors. In the meantime Kirie issued her own response, so that the Sunday afternoon peace and quiet was now well and truly destroyed.

The front door opened and a maid looked at him. She had to shout to make herself heard above the din.

'How can I help?'

'First, you can stop me being eaten.'

'I'm afraid Nero doesn't listen to me. And his master is sadly ...'

'Dead. I know.' Rath showed his badge. 'My condolences. I'd like to speak to his wife. Is she here?'

The girl gestured towards the company buildings. 'She's in the office next door.'

'How do I get there without being torn to shreds?'

'By giving Nero a wide berth.'

Rath proceeded to do exactly that and finally gained the premises, consisting as they did of a warehouse, in front of which the delivery vans were parked, and a simple little office wing at the building's head. The guard dog stopped barking when it realised Rath was beating a retreat. It seemed the company premises were outside its jurisdiction. A brass plate hung next to the entrance, glistening in the sun, as spick and span as everything else around here. The glass door stood half open and Rath went inside. The office wing appeared neat and tidy, with a slight smell of alcohol.

Inside, a woman with greyish blonde hair sat at a desk,

leafing through a muddle of opened and closed files. Bills, contracts, orders, staff lists. A gust of wind and the chaos would be complete.

The woman was so engrossed she didn't look up until Rath knocked on the open door and showed his badge.

'Edith Lamkau?' he asked. She nodded. 'Rath, CID. My condolences on the death of your husband. Please excuse our disturbing you again.'

The widow Lamkau nodded and gazed at the files she held in her hands. She seemed to be somewhere else entirely, the very picture of despair.

'What a mess,' she said.

'That's an awful lot of paperwork,' Rath added sympathetically.

She nodded, and gazed with a wounded expression at the litter of files on the desk before her. They, rather than the death of her husband, seemed to be the cause of her despair. 'What the hell am I meant to do with all this? Orders, bills ... Then all these people asking what's going to happen. Somehow word on Herbert's death has got about quicker than news of our latest promotions.'

'Don't you have someone who knows their way around the business, and can help you out?'

'Herbert looked after everything himself. No one could have known that he ...'

She let the papers drop, breaking into a sob so suddenly that Rath gave a start. He remembered the lily-white cotton handkerchief in his jacket. Edith Lamkau dabbed gratefully at her wet eyes.

'Frau Lamkau,' Rath said, when she had composed herself again. 'In the meantime, our suspicions that your husband died an unnatural death have been confirmed.'

'Oh God! Did someone kill him?' Rath nodded awkwardly. 'Who?'

'That's what we're trying to find out, Frau Lamkau. It's

the reason I'm here.' He pointed outside, to where Nero had barked again. 'You're well guarded here. Was your husband afraid? Did he have enemies?'

She shook her head. 'Herbert was only concerned with our safety. There have been a number of break-ins here recently.'

'In your husband's overalls we found an envelope containing a thousand marks. Can you explain where it came from?' She shook her head. 'Did your clients settle their accounts in cash?'

'Some maybe. I don't know.'

'Then there must be an invoice for this amount somewhere. Do you know which clients your husband visited yesterday? Is there a journey log? A list of suppliers?' Edith Lamkau didn't seem to know anything about her husband's affairs. Perhaps they weren't all above board. 'How about I send a few men over tomorrow to look after your papers?' Rath said.

She smiled gratefully. 'You'd do that?'

'But you have to promise to forget about all this. Just make sure you lock the door when you leave.'

'Of course. Gladly!' Edith Lamkau looked as if a burden had been lifted from her soul.

6

Dear Gereon,

Back in Berlin, yet here we are still writing to one another...you're harder to pin down than the police commissioner!

My darling, I'd have liked to see you again before our paths inevitably cross tomorrow at the Castle. I assume that for the time being our old agreement still holds. No one should realise just how collegial our relationship is. It'd mean a lot to me, you know ... It's my first day tomorrow, and there are already more than enough people who think there's no room for women on the police force. Let's not give them any further ammunition by being over-familiar on duty. You know how quickly the Castle's rumour mill can be set in motion.

Aside from that I think it's important we meet as soon as possible. I still owe you a response, after all.

Forgive me for abandoning Kirie, but she seemed rather well acquainted with your friendly porter, and I didn't want to kidnap her, even if I'm certain she'd have come willingly. The thing is I just had to get out of your flat. I hope you understand, and that you're not *angry with me. I'm not made to spend hours waiting for a man - that's something you'll have to get used to.*

In the meantime, I've settled nicely back into Berlin life. You wouldn't believe how many people have visited already. Old Krause from the grocery store round the corner snapped at me as though I'd never been away - 'you touch it, you buy it'. Nice that Berlin's so pleased to have me back.

A thousand hugs

C.

Rath folded the letter and placed it back in its envelope, took it out and read it again. A quarter past seven. One more cigarette and it would be time to head over to the conference room. He sat in the Buick by the railway arches, watching his colleagues streaming into the Castle from all sides. He lit an Overstolz and opened the side window.

He swallowed another aspirin from the bottle, washing it down with a slug from his silver hip flask. It felt as if the cognac did more for his headache than the pill. Lack of sleep coupled with too much alcohol was a deadly combination, but last night the bottle had been his only consolation.

From the moment the night porter pushed the envelope across the counter, he knew it was from her, tearing it open in the lift going up. Reaching his apartment, he fetched a bottle of cognac and, still in his coat, slumped into an armchair and began to read, not knowing how to feel.

He didn't know how many times he had read the letter since, only that he still didn't understand. She wasn't made to spend hours waiting for him? Was that a 'no' to his proposal? *Berlin* was pleased to have her back, was she referring to another man, or just old Krause? All right, she hadn't forgotten him, but did she really have to emphasise how many people had already been to visit . . .

Even now, with a slightly clearer head, he couldn't decipher the letter's meaning, but her words seemed more positive, friendlier somehow. The best thing, however, better than any single word, was that the letter smelled of Charly. He could still smell her this morning in among the odour of paper and rubber lining, and realised it was the thing he had missed most last year. Sniffing the note a final time, he returned it to its envelope.

Kirie, who was crouched on the passenger seat itching to be released, issued two short barks. 'You're right, old girl, time to go.'

They made a detour via Alexanderplatz, so that she had a chance to pee before entering the station. The enormous building loomed as sombre as a medieval castle, hence the name given to it by employees: the Castle. Once upon a time, the red brick of police headquarters had held sway over Alexanderplatz, but the various new additions had since relegated it to second place. The police commissioner, who had previously enjoyed a clear view from his private office on the first floor, now had to content himself with the windows of Alexanderhaus, in which the *Aschinger* restaurant had also found its new home.

Rath's office on the first floor was still locked. He ought to have remembered that his secretary, Erika Voss, didn't arrive until eight. He had no choice but to bring Kirie into the conference room. It was already busy, with the meeting due to start in a few minutes. He pushed through the crowd, as far as possible towards the back. A few colleagues were amazed to see him with Kirie on her lead, but what else could he do? He could hardly tie her up outside.

'Are they introducing the new police *dogs* as well?' an officer asked. The bystanders laughed, and Rath forced a grin. To his astonishment, he brought the nervous-seeming

64

Kirie to heel with a sharp 'sit', as the cadets started filing in: the latest batch of candidates for inspector. Lange was third, followed at the end of the line by Charly and another female officer, with Bernhard Weiss taking up the rear. Even though he had known she'd be here, his heart started beating faster. Despite wearing an unremarkable mouse-grey ensemble, she still contrived to look stunning, and Rath felt as if all eyes were on her. For a moment he actually thought the male officers were whistling, although nothing of the kind occurred. Seeing them gawp like that, he felt the old rage returning and gritted his teeth until it passed.

The cadets took their seats, out of sight in the front row, as Dr Weiss climbed on stage and the whispering subsided to a murmur. The deputy commissioner waited until the final coughs had abated.

'Before we turn to happier affairs, allow me to say a few words on the current situation,' he began. Owing to his thick spectacle lenses, it always felt as if Bernhard Weiss were looking you straight in the eye. 'It is no coincidence that, in the two weeks since the SA and SS have been allowed to display their uniforms and march again, the situation has become spectacularly worse. This weekend alone political confrontations in Wedding and Moabit resulted in five casualties and a death, and that is merely in Berlin.'

'Wasn't the dead man an SA officer, gunned down by the Reds?' a colleague whispered, careful to ensure he couldn't be heard up front.

'There were good reasons for the uniform ban,' Weiss continued. 'Deprived of it, SA men could be seen for what they are: a brutal gang of thugs. In their uniforms, however, they don't regard themselves as criminals. Indeed, some even presume to act as police officers. More and more often, SA members are taking the liberty of carrying out house searches in Communist apartments. There are reports from Friedrichshain that an SA troop stormed an ice-cream parlour and attempted to carry off all members of the Reichsbanner, as though it were a police raid. Fortunately, our colleagues were able to intervene in time.

'Such behaviour, ladies and gentlemen,' Weiss said, casting a friendly glance towards the front row at the word *ladies*, 'must be nipped in the bud. We cannot allow the mob to rule the streets, whether they are dressed in red or in brown.'

Weiss paused, and a few colleagues began to clap. The applause soon died, making it more awkward than if there had been none at all.

'Sadly,' he continued, 'the new government's policies seem to have emboldened the National Socialists to carry out such initiatives. For two weeks now, since – not to put too fine a point on it – the lifting of the SA ban, the safety on our streets has been severely compromised.'

'I always thought the police were apolitical,' grumbled an officer in front of Rath. 'He's sticking his neck out a little too far for my liking. We *do* work for the government after all.'

'We answer to the Free State of Prussia, not the German Reich,' the man behind him hissed. 'And no one would deny this government's missing a few screws.'

'At least it *is* a government. Prussia doesn't have one any more, at least not a functional one.'

'Oh, shut your mouth, would you!'

'Shut *my* mouth!'

Before the dispute could escalate, two colleagues pulled the men apart, at which stage the noise and grumbling reached Weiss's ears. He gazed sternly into the room and it ceased. The two officers who had nearly come to blows contented themselves with exchanging angry glances.

When all was silent again, Weiss continued. 'Now let us move on to the real purpose of our meeting. Please welcome the new cadets, who will henceforth be serving as your colleagues in CID.'

He reached for a list and read the names of the new recruits, each one dutifully approaching the stage as they were called, until all stood in line at the front. Most grinned nervously. Lange blushed, but Charly, who stood next to a blonde woman, smiled self-assuredly into the horde of male officers. Rath thought her smile a little over-friendly.

The deputy preached the usual sermon, stressing the importance of treating the novices with consideration and offering assistance when it was required, before closing with the same joke he always made: 'Remember that, in years to come, one of these men could be your superior.'

The officers laughed obediently, even if most of them had heard it all before. No one expressed surprise that Weiss had chosen to exclude the two women. The fact was that, even if Charly and her colleague did make a career for themselves, they would never get out of G Division; nor, irrespective of their capabilities as police officers, would they ever issue orders to men, at least not in the Castle. 'On this occasion it gives me particular pleasure,' Weiss said, when the polite laughter died, 'to introduce two female cadets, who will be augmenting the ranks of G Division.'

So, that was what Charly's future with the Berlin Police had in store: G Division, the women's branch of CID, who dealt mainly with youth crime and female offenders. There was no doubt she'd have been better deployed in complex murder investigations, but they wouldn't be seeing her in Homicide, unless she started working as a stenographer again.

'I'd like to teach those honeys a thing or two,' Rath heard someone mumble, recognising the voice. 'That brunette's a sight for sore eyes, isn't she, eh, boys?'

Rath craned his neck but couldn't make out the man's face. He felt the same helpless rage as before, especially since the remark was greeted with subdued laugher. Couldn't the bastards keep their mouths shut? But, of course not. The police was a boys' club; women had no place here. Rath was suddenly glad Charly would be working with other women, rather than troublemakers like this.

He had stopped listening, but by the ever louder murmuring the meeting had been adjourned. He joined the throng of colleagues drifting slowly towards the exit. Reaching the door, he realised that Kirie had started pulling on her lead. 'To heel,' Rath hissed, but she whimpered and pulled even harder.

Seeing a mouse-grey ladies' hat a few metres ahead he realised what was up: the bloody dog had recognised Charly's scent. Now she was wagging her tail like crazy, pulling harder and harder on her lead so that Rath could barely keep hold. Suddenly she issued a brief *woof*, as loud as it was reproachful, as if to say: *let me at her*!

All eyes turned to Kirie and her master, Charly's included. Rath saw how she grinned, only for her grin first to freeze and then disappear altogether when she realised what was happening. Kirie was almost upon her, there was no holding her back. She was full-grown now, no longer the sweet, little furball she'd once been. Charly couldn't bear to see her suffer any longer. She stepped towards her, stroked her and let her lick her hands.

After an extensive greeting Kirie settled down again, allowing Rath to regain control. 'Tut, tut,' he said, wagging his index finger and ordering her to sit. He now stood directly opposite Charly, hardly daring to look in her eyes. He saw her dimple, then the curious glances of those standing by. Half of CID had witnessed Kirie's passionate greeting. This wasn't how he and Charly had envisaged their first meeting at the Castle.

'Apologies,' Rath mumbled, now fixing her in the eyes. 'It won't happen again.'

'Didn't she lead us to the cinema killer back in the day?'

Rath nodded, grateful for her presence of mind. Charly

had worked on the case herself. The fact that the pair had known each other at least since then was common knowledge, in A Division anyway. 'You've a good memory, Fräulein Ritter,' he said, lifting his hat. 'Delighted to have you back on board, though it's a shame Homicide must do without you.'

With that he made his way towards the door, fighting the temptation to turn around. He couldn't have looked Charly in the eye a moment longer, forced to pretend like this. Kirie made no more trouble, following her master dutifully outside.

'You've got that one well-trained,' a colleague said, giving Rath a poke in the side as they left the room. 'You should give us a loan some time.'

Rath forced a smile, and proceeded down the long corridor quicker than in all his years of service. The way was lined with doors, and he was glad to reach his office at last. Once inside Kirie made a beeline for the two bowls Erika Voss kept ready. It was she who had persuaded him to adopt Kirie, whose previous owner had been murdered. 'Detective Gräf has already left to provide the weekend summary,' she said. 'He asked about a report: *Haus Vaterland*. Do you have any idea where it could be?'

Morning briefing was a ritual first established by Detective Chief Inspector Böhm. CID officers exchanged notes on current investigations, breaking free of the confines of their individual teams. An outside view could kick-start cases that had become stalled, and on several occasions links had been made between apparently isolated fatalities. Of the senior homicide officers, Rath was the only one not to make it to the small conference room on time. All eyes turned as he entered.

Detective Gräf was in the middle of listing all deaths that local CID forces had reported to headquarters over the weekend. He had a fatigued air about him. Though there was little of note, Ernst Gennat, the chief of Homicide, listened spellbound. The superintendent never missed a detail, and often he had resolved homicide cases by recalling seemingly irrelevant items. Other times, he made connections that escaped everyone else.

Rath was only half listening to what Gräf said. There had been a fatal shooting at Stuttgarter Platz in Charlottenburg, probably politically motivated, which Section 1A had already taken on, to go with the dead Nazi in Wedding Weiss had mentioned earlier. The political police dealt with such cases on an almost daily basis. A corpse in Grunewald had turned out to be suicide, and been passed over to the local precinct. In Schlosspark Bellevue a man had killed his wife with a shaving knife. The 21st precinct had initially assumed the case, but now it had landed at Alex. Detective Chief Inspector Wilhelm Böhm had commandeered Henning and Czerwinski, two officers Rath often worked alongside, who had originally belonged to the *Phantom* troop. He was considering how he could reclaim the pair when he heard his name.

'Since Inspector Rath is now here,' Gräf said, 'perhaps he should tell you about the *Haus Vaterland* corpse from the early hours of Saturday morning.'

Rath moved towards the front with a small file wedged under his arm. He didn't look inside; most of what he had to say wasn't in there anyway. He briefly summarised their findings in *Haus Vaterland*, before moving onto Dr Karthaus's discovery. 'It looks as though we are dealing with a violent death, even if there are no outward signs of force save for the injection to the jugular vein, which was most likely administered by a third party. An extremely peculiar case, not least because of the circumstances surrounding the death itself.'

Ernst Gennat, who had earned the nickname *Buddha* in part because of his impressive physique, now spoke. 'If I've understood you correctly, the body displays all the hallmarks of drowning, yet there is some doubt as to whether this is the actual cause of death.'

'Correct, Sir. Assuming *I* have understood Dr Karthaus correctly.' A few officers laughed. Most of those present had experienced the pathologist's use of latinate terms. Lange and Gräf were unsmiling. 'The written report is still pending but we hope for a more concrete indication of the cause of death from the blood analysis. For all that, it's strange enough already. What we have here is a simulated drowning that took place in a freight elevator.'

Gennat nodded thoughtfully. Something seemed to be bothering him, but he said nothing more, leaving Rath to continue with his report. He mentioned his discovery by the third-floor elevator, and his suspicion that the perpetrator most likely stemmed from the *Haus Vaterland* workforce. 'I'm assuming the offending party was still inside when police arrived. Security pays close attention that no one unauthorised enters or leaves the building. According to the duty guard, no one was seen leaving after the murder. We have a list of around fifty people present on Saturday morning, all of whom will be subjected to a detailed interrogation. Perhaps we'll find a motive.'

'What about the thousand marks?' Böhm asked. 'That's your motive right there.'

'If that were true, then surely they'd have been taken,' Rath replied, winning another few laughs. He savoured Böhm's sour expression.

'Not necessarily,' Gennat said. 'Detective Chief Inspector Böhm is right. Carrying so much cash in a blank envelope is highly unusual. Money can always be a motive, not just in a robbery homicide.'

'Of course, Superintendent. Sir.' Rath cleared his throat. 'Needless to say, I also looked into this anomaly. The widow Lamkau can't explain the money in her husband's pocket, although admittedly she has little knowledge of company affairs. We'll be going through the paperwork today to see if there's an explanation.'

'If that's the case, you could have spared us a needless joke at your colleague's expense.'

Gennat concluded the meeting. Moments later chair legs began scraping over the stone floor. Despite knowing it would be futile, Rath approached to try and reclaim Henning and Czerwinski, who had been withdrawn from the *Phantom* troop.

'You haven't made any progress there for weeks,' Buddha said. 'Leave it for the time being. Take Gräf and Lange, and focus your attentions on the dead man in *Haus Vaterland*. Perhaps you'll have more success there.'

'With respect, Sir, I could use some more men.'

'I'm afraid I can't spare you any. Homicide is up to its ears at the moment.'

'What about the cadets?'

Gennat considered for a moment. 'I'll see what I can do.'

'Thank you, Sir.'

His team was already waiting when he returned to the office. Erika Voss had made coffee, and both Lange and Gräf held steaming mugs in their hands. The pair had dark circles under their eyes.

'Coffee for you too, Inspector?' Erika Voss asked.

'Thank you,' Rath said, as she set it down, heading into the back room with the two officers.

'One more thing, Erika,' he said, before closing the connecting door. 'Put a call through to Pathology and ask Dr Karthaus if he's completed the Lamkau blood analysis. Then ask ED if our colleagues from Forensics have found any hypodermic needles in *Haus Vaterland*.'

'Good of you to share what you did yesterday,' Gräf said, no sooner than Rath had closed the door.

'I stopped by. You weren't home.'

'Then you ought to have at least left a message in the office. If you're going to go about pinching files.'

'Surely you're not annoyed that I acted on new information from Pathology?' Rath placed the file on the table. 'Well, from now on, we'll be working alongside each other. As a three.'

'That's it?' Gräf asked.

'The Phantom case has been temporarily shelved, and Gennat can't spare us any men for the corpse in *Haus Vaterland*.'

'Do you have any idea how many interrogations we need to get through today?'

'We'll just have to share them out between the three of us.'

Gräf sighed. 'Christ, Gereon! You know sometimes you're a real pain in the arse.'

7

No matter how hard Charly tried, no matter how determined she was to commit herself fully to her first day on the job, she couldn't concentrate. Gereon's look just now as Kirie jumped on her...she couldn't get it out of her mind. There was sadness there, a strange uncertainty which couldn't just be from Kirie forcing them into an unexpectedly public meeting. They desperately needed to speak to one another, that much was clear. Their weekend, indeed their whole reunion, had been a disaster. She had spent all Sunday trying to reach him, but his number still wasn't in the telephone book, and there was no one at the Castle she could have asked without arousing suspicion. She'd had no choice but to take Greta's bicycle out to Steinplatz where the friendly porter told her that Herr Rath had left the building moments before. The first time, she believed him; the second time she began to suspect that Gereon was feigning absence. She left him a letter, the second one since her return, hoping he would call her at least, but he had done no such thing, even though he knew he wouldn't be able to speak to her in the conference room this morning...and what on earth had he been thinking, bringing Kirie?

'What do you think? They could be from Wedding?'

'Hm?'

Charly looked up into the face of her blonde colleague. Karin van Almsick had no experience of police work, having come to Alex from the youth welfare department, which was as much information as they had managed to exchange between the conference room and the offices of female CID, where Superintendent Friederike Wieking gave them a stern welcome. Ernst Gennat led the Homicide division with considerably more warmth. After the briefest of introductions, Superintendent Wieking tasked them with the first item of drudge work: a band of girls had been robbing passengers on deserted underground trains, keeping police guessing for weeks. There was nothing to go on but for a few vague witness statements. Seven hold-ups, each following the same pattern, had already been placed on file, though the descriptions of the perpetrators diverged wildly. The only thing witnesses could agree on was that there were two or three girls involved, and that they used knives to threaten their victims.

'From Wedding?' Charly parroted unthinkingly.

Karin van Almsick didn't seem to notice. 'The attacks all occurred on the C Line,' she said. 'Most of them in the north. That's something, isn't it?'

Charly shrugged.

'What do you think? Should we mention it to Wieking?'

'What?'

'Issuing a warrant for these girls up in Wedding. Wieking will want to hear from us, won't she?'

Her colleague's zeal was starting to get on Charly's nerves. On the other hand, she could sympathise. She ought to have been capable of the same. 'I'm afraid I haven't got that far yet. Maybe we should exchange ideas after lunch.'

'Or during.'

'Or during.'

Karin clearly hoped to make friends, and Charly didn't want to seem cold, especially since, as a trained lawyer, it could easily be construed as arrogance.

She made a renewed attempt to concentrate on the file in

front of her, but, even on the first page, realised she wasn't processing any of its content. She tried again, but all she could see were Gereon's sad eyes; his face two days ago, as he tried to hide his disappointment. She should have guessed. After all, she had known he was planning to propose at *some* point, but the timing had thrown her. Ever since last summer, she'd known he had bought a ring. To think, she could have spent all those months in Paris imagining being married to Gereon Rath, and to some extent, at least at the start, she had – but work and life in a new city had taken over, and before long any such notions had vanished.

Travelling back to Berlin, her thoughts had mostly concerned her new career in CID. Marriage was the last thing on her mind. Couldn't the stupid bastard have waited a day or two before ambushing her like that?

Realising what was happening, she couldn't help but grin. She had finally achieved her aim of joining CID, not as a stenographer this time, but as a candidate for inspector. And what had she spent her first day doing? Thinking about Gereon Rath, instead of concentrating on the case she had been assigned. She snapped the file shut. 'I need to make a quick telephone call,' she said to Karin.

Her colleague shrugged. 'Of course.'

'In private, if that's OK?'

A broad grin spread across her colleague's features. 'What's his name?'

Charly couldn't help but smile too, even if she was in no mood to share confidences. She raised a finger in warning. 'Curiosity killed the cat.'

Her colleague stood up. 'I wanted to go across to Robbery Division anyway, and ask if they had any similar cases on file.' She gave a brief wink.

Charly smiled back, despite being irritated by the suggestive wink. She waited a moment for the door to click shut – Karin van Almsick seemed just the type to eavesdrop

– and plucked up the courage to dial the extension she knew all too well.

'Voss, Homicide. Inspector Rath's office.'

Shit.

'Ritter, G Division. Inspector Rath, please,' she said, trying to sound as businesslike as possible.

'The inspector isn't here, I'm afraid. Can I take a message?'

'Not necessary. I'll try again later.'

Charly hung up. Goddamn it! Was it really so hard to talk to someone when you worked in the same building? Had she asked her colleague to leave for this? Again she turned to the file in front of her, but again her mind wandered until the telephone rang, and she gave a start. Had he simply been feigning absence, only now to call her back?

'Ritter, G Division,' she said, heart pounding.

'Gennat here!' The beat of her heart slowed again. 'I wanted to take the opportunity to wish you all the best at the start of your training year.'

'Thank you, Superintendent,' Charly said politely, trying not to sound too disappointed. She thought the world of her former boss, worshipped him even, and knew that an accolade like this was no given, even if she found herself incapable of enjoying it.

'I think I speak for all of A Division when I say we are very sorry that you are no longer with us in Homicide.'

'I'm sorry too, but I'm afraid there's nothing that can be done about CID's organisational structure.'

'Quite,' Gennat said. 'Not even I can help you there.' He cleared his throat before continuing. 'But I *can* make you an offer, Charly. If you agree then I'll speak with your superior officer. If I know Frau Wieking, she's unlikely to object.'

'What sort of offer, Sir?'

When he told her, Charly was glad she'd sent Karin van Almsick away after all.

8

The interrogations had eaten into their lunch hour. Against expectation, Gennat had failed to provide any additional troops, not even a cadet. With no time for a proper break or to discuss their findings, Rath paused at the *Aschinger* on Leipziger Strasse for a Bratwurst and red cabbage. The interrogation marathon had confirmed what they already knew, the only item of note being that one of the witnesses failed to show up.

Rath had sent Gräf and Lange out to the Lamkau office in Tempelhof. 'Lamkau's widow is expecting you. Take a look at the company papers, most recent bills and so on. See if you can't find some explanation for the thousand marks in Lamkau's overalls.' With that he had not only dispensed of his colleagues, but kept his promise to Edith Lamkau.

Arriving at *Haus Vaterland* he was glad to have eaten en route, since he met Alfons Riedel, the spirits buyer, in the afternoon hurly-burly of the *Rheinterrasse*. Behind a glass pane, the end wall of the saloon displayed a huge, illuminated Rhine panorama: Sankt Goarshausen complete with moving trains and ships. Riedel sat in a quiet corner of the restaurant before an array of bottles, testing the quality of various digestifs. 'Yes, yes. Lamkau.' He nodded. 'A tragic business.'

Rath ordered a coffee from the waiter who had led him over. 'You knew him personally?'

'More professionally, I would say.'

'But you've shaken his hand? Spoken to him?'

'Naturally.' Riedel sniffed calmly at the glass he'd just filled.

'We found a large quantity of cash on his person, the source of which is still unclear. Could it be that Lamkau made the delivery in person on Saturday morning because there was an outstanding balance here in *Haus Vaterland*?'

'Kempinski pays by cheque or banker's order. Not in cash!' Riedel sounded almost indignant.

'So, is there an outstanding balance between *Haus Vaterland* and the Lamkau firm, or not?'

'Kempinski,' Riedel said. 'I don't just buy for *Haus Vaterland*, but Kempinski too.'

'Right. So does the Kempinski firm still owe Lamkau?'

'I'm not directly responsible for company accounts, but no, not as far as I know.'

'Then can you explain why he had so much cash on him?'

Riedel shrugged. 'Perhaps he'd just delivered somewhere else. I don't know how other companies settle their accounts.'

'We're surprised the company owner should've made the delivery in person on Saturday.'

Riedel looked around, as if afraid someone might be listening. 'One shouldn't speak ill of the dead,' he said at length. 'But you're bound to hear it at some point.'

'Hear what?'

'His delivering in person might've been a gesture of ...' There was a pregnant pause. '...goodwill. The Lamkau firm has a little ground to make up.' Rath pricked up his ears as Riedel gestured towards the bottles in front of him. 'This is all high-quality stuff. No such thing as rotgut at Kempinski. Our clients know that, and so do our suppliers.'

'What's that got to do with Lamkau?'

'A recent delivery was tainted. Several crates of the stuff. Not *Luisenbrand*, like it said on the label, but cheap hooch.

79

A layman might've fallen for it, but an expert – impossible.'
Riedel sniffed at a glass of light pomace brandy. It wasn't
hard to believe the man was an expert in all things alcoholic,
and not just because of the colour of his nose.

'You're saying Lamkau tried to palm you off with low-
grade hooch?'

'Who knows? He may not make the stuff himself, but he's
the sole distributor of *Mathée Luisenbrand* across Central
Germany. Either way, this sort of thing shouldn't happen.'

'But it did.'

'Yes. Which is why the Lamkau firm stood to be removed
from our list of suppliers. In fact I had invited Herbert
Lamkau to a meeting today.' He looked at his watch. 'He
ought to be sitting exactly where you are now.'

Suddenly everything in the room went black, and a
murmur passed through the crowd. Behind the glass pane
there was a flash of lightning, followed by a peal of thunder,
and rain started falling over the miniature Sankt Goar.
Cries of astonishment suggested the majority of diners had
never been here before. Rath doubted there was anyone
who would watch the show a second time.

'*Im Haus Vaterland ist man gründlich, hier gewittert's
stündlich,*' Riedel said with a shrug.

A reference to these simulated hourly storms, the tired
slogan was designed to entice potential customers. Riedel
made it sound more like an apology. Rath waited until
the noise had died and lit a cigarette. 'This meeting. What
would it have been about?' he asked, waving the match out.
At the same moment the lights came back on.

Riedel took a sip from one of the glasses before him,
taking notes on the individual drinks. 'Staying on our list
of suppliers,' he said.

'What happens now that he's dead?'

'I can get hold of their other products easily enough. It's
only *Luisenbrand* the firm has sole distribution rights to.'

'What about *Danziger Goldwasser*?'

'Lamkau isn't the sole distributor there.'

'So, if the Lamkau firm had been dropped, who would supply *Haus Vaterland* in their place?'

'Do you know, honestly, I haven't given it much thought, but *Luisenbrand* isn't the only decent Korn about.'

Rath tore a sheet from his notebook and passed it across the table. 'Write me a list of potential alternatives and their suppliers.'

'You think it's a competitor who has Lamkau on their conscience?' Riedel shook his head. 'I can't imagine it.' He wrote down a few names and Rath briefly surveyed the list. He didn't recognise any of the companies on it.

'Let's get back to your meeting with Lamkau,' he said, stowing the paper in his pocket. 'What could have persuaded you to change your mind?'

'An apology.' Riedel held a glass containing a yellow-gold liquid against the light. 'A reasonable explanation as to how it could've happened. And, naturally, a guarantee there would be no repeat. That would have been enough.'

'Perhaps the odd banknote might have helped.'

'What do you mean?'

'You have a lot of power here. In the whole Kempinski firm, in fact. Surely the odd supplier has tried to bribe you?'

'In my position, you can't afford to be susceptible.'

'But a thousand marks? Wouldn't that make you more ...susceptible?'

Riedel laughed loudly. 'A thousand marks? You must be joking. The quantities Lamkau supplied, how d'you suppose he'd recoup a sum like that?'

On the way up to the fourth floor Rath noted that both freight elevators were back in commission, before reaching the heart, or rather the stomach, of *Haus Vaterland*. There was so much equipment on display the central kitchen felt more like a small factory. Inside, Rath found a line of gas stoves: huge cauldrons, big as bathtubs, full of steaming soups and sauces, numerous coffee machines, stirring machines, slicing machines, mixing machines, potato-peeling machines and mincers. Set slightly apart, an enormous metal structure went about its business, a kitchen-hand loading a never-ending supply of trays and dirty crockery onto its conveyor belt. Everything hissed and scratched and rattled and clanked and jangled and turned, while countless staff scurried between the glistening technology snipping vegetables, stirring pans, tenderising meat or loading trays of food onto the little paternoster.

Directly above the time clock at the entrance hung several job advertisements. *Dishwasher, kitchen-hands wanted; office worker wanted (knowledge of shorthand and experience of commercial kitchens desirable)*. Rath flagged down a boy pushing a crockery trolley. 'Where can I find Herr Unger?' he asked. 'Apparently he's the head chef.'

The boy nodded towards a large window before wheeling his trolley on. The window was more like a glass wall, and belonged to a small office. Inside, a man with a chef's hat sat behind a desk, making entries in a thick notebook. Before him were shelves of files. Here, too, vacancy notices hung by the window. Rath gave a brief knock and entered.

For a chef Manfred Unger was surprisingly thin. He seemed less than pleased at the interruption. 'What are you doing here? The entire kitchen is closed to unauthorised personnel.'

The room reminded him of a shift supervisor's office at Ford. The large viewing window made it possible to keep a close eye on the kitchen. 'Manfred Unger?'

'Who's asking?' Rath reached for his badge, and the chef stood up. 'So that's what this is about! Don't you see I can't come to the station now?' He gestured towards the milling mass that was the kitchen. 'We're in the middle of a rush.'

'Who said anything about now?' Rath looked at his wristwatch. 'You ought to have been there four and a half hours ago.'

'When it was even busier. If no one comes to relieve me, there's nothing I can do.'

'I'm not sure you understand the gravity of being issued with a summons.'

'What summons? On Saturday your colleague *requested* that I come to the station this morning. I'm afraid it wasn't possible.'

'I'm not here to argue, Herr Unger, but I'd advise you to make a little time for me now, otherwise things could get nasty.' Unger sat down. 'You do realise you're an important witness in a murder inquiry . . .'

'A murder inquiry?'

' . . .and refusing to co-operate can very quickly turn a witness into a suspect.'

'Inspector, as I've just explained . . .' Unger gestured beyond the viewing window, a hint of desperation in his eyes.

'I just wanted to make those things clear. Now, am I right in thinking you do have a little time for me?'

'Of course.'

Rath lit a cigarette before taking his notebook from his pocket. Examining the point of his pencil, he asked his first question. 'It was you who found Herr Lamkau?'

'I've already explained everything to your colleague.'

'But not to me.'

'It scared me half to death, seeing him there like that. I almost fell on top of him.'

'What were you doing by the lifts?'

'Pardon me?'

'Why did you push the button?'

'Why do you think? I needed to get something from downstairs.'

'What did you need to get?'

'How should I know? I imagine it was something to eat.' Unger laughed, but fell silent when he saw Rath's expression.

'Aren't the cold store and stockrooms up here?'

'Most of them, but not all.'

'Surely you don't often go *down* to fetch goods? It would mean serious disruption.'

Unger looked rattled. 'What are you getting at? What does this have to do with a murder inquiry?'

'Leave me to worry about that. You wanted to fetch something, but have forgotten what?'

'I never had the chance, did I, not when your people showed up. Talk about serious disruption. They were here for hours.'

Rath made a lengthy note. Not because there was much to write, but as an unsettling tactic. Unger had spent the whole time fidgeting on his chair. His legs hadn't stopped moving for an instant. Time and time again he craned his neck to look out of the viewing window into the kitchen. What he saw only seemed to make him more nervous. Rath was about to ask his next question when he sprang to his feet, opened the door and issued a volley of instructions.

'Friedhelm! Get the pot roast out of the oven, for God's sake! Carsten, if you're not finished with that chicken ragout soon, I'll come out there personally and light a fire under your arse. And where the *fuck* is the mash? The first orders will be here in less than an hour! Now get a move on!'

'*Im Haus Vaterland ist man gründlich, hier gewittert's stündlich,*' Rath murmured.

'Did you say something?' Unger closed the door and returned to his desk.

'Herr Lamkau ...' Rath cleared his throat. 'Did you know him personally?'

'The spirits man? Why should I? I'm a chef.'

'I was only asking, Herr Unger.'

84

'Of course.'

Again the thin man squinted through the window. Rath wasn't sure if it was their conversation or the lack of kitchen supervision that was making him so uneasy.

'Is there anyone here who did know Herr Lamkau?'

'No.' The chef shook his head.

'Herr Riedel perhaps?'

'Who's that?'

'A colleague of yours. Spirits buyer at Kempinski.'

'Yes, I know the one.'

Rath made another note, before continuing with his questions. 'Apparently he had some trouble with a batch of spirits . . .'

'There's always issues with suppliers. We don't have much cause for spirits in the kitchen. For seasoning perhaps, or if something needs to be flambéd.'

'So you didn't hear anything about the tainted schnapps? *Luisenbrand*. A whole consignment apparently.'

'Come to think of it, that does sound familiar. Though we absolutely never use Korn.'

Unger was still gazing out of the window. His mind seemed elsewhere. Suddenly he sprang to his feet and ran to the door. 'What the hell is that?' he screamed at an unfortunate who had just carried an enormous plate of roast beef past the window, and now froze mid-motion. 'Who the fuck's going to eat *that*? It's overcooked! Pink! It has to be *pink*! Only place that's good for is the pig pail!' Unger struck out, and there was a clatter as the plate landed on the tiled floor. 'Now clean it up!' he said, face the colour of beetroot. 'I want to see you in my office!' He slammed the door and returned, still breathing heavily as he took his seat.

'I hope we'll be finished here soon,' he said. 'You see what happens when you take your eye off the ball.'

Rath stubbed out his cigarette and stood up. 'That's it for now,' he said, looking through the window to where three kitchen-hands in white aprons were scooping roast beef up from the floor. 'Sorry to have caused so much trouble. Next time just come to Alex when we ask, and this sort of thing won't happen.'

Rath drove to Hannoversche Strasse from Potsdamer Platz, arriving at the morgue half an hour early. Dr Karthaus wasn't in the autopsy room, so the porter sent him up to the first floor. He heard a typewriter clattering behind the office door, and knocked. The clattering ceased as he entered and gazed into the eyes of Karthaus and his secretary. The doctor squinted over the rim of his reading glasses and glanced at his watch.

'What are you doing here? Did I give your secretary the wrong time?'

'Punctuality is the politeness of princes,' Rath said.

'In my estimation, arriving too early is far *worse* than arriving too late. Or is this a way of compensating for your legendary tardiness?'

'Don't make such a fuss, Doctor. You were more or less on my way – so, here I am.'

'Then you must simply be *dying* to hear my assessment.' Karthaus turned to his secretary. 'Wouldn't want to disappoint such scientific curiosity, would we, Martha? Pack your things. We'll pick this up tomorrow.'

With that the doctor swept out of the room and down the stairs, white coat flapping in his wake. Rath struggled to keep pace. Karthaus didn't say another word until they had passed through the swing doors into the autopsy room. 'You do realise that was your hotly anticipated written report I was working on?'

'So?'

'I was hoping to have it ready for you by this afternoon. Now you'll have to wait for the internal mail tomorrow.'

'I prefer my reports to be delivered orally.'

The pathologist shook his head as he sat behind a messy desk and offered Rath a rickety wooden chair. He straightened his reading glasses. 'So,' he began. 'The results of the blood analysis.' He glanced at a sheet of paper, then reached for another. 'I've found evidence of an unusual substance in the dead man's bloodstream.'

'Unusual in what respect?'

'It's something you might expect to observe in the South American jungle. It's called tubocurarine.'

'Tubo . . . what?'

'Curarine. We have the Indians from South America to thank for it. Savages in the Amazon jungle hunt with a blowpipe, killing their prey with a deadly arrow poison, curare. The stuff paralyses the musculature, affecting a victim's breathing. The speed depends on the dosage.'

'Are you saying we should be looking for an Indian? Why don't we start in the *Wild West Bar* in *Haus Vaterland*?'

'You can spare me the unhelpful jokes. Now, let me finish.' Karthaus actually seemed offended. 'There are different forms of the curare poison, one of which is tubocurarine . . .'

' . . . which you found in the dead man's bloodstream.'

'Right. The interesting thing is that it is currently being trialled in modern medicine for use during surgical procedures . . .'

'A poison?'

' . . . as a muscle relaxant during operations on the abdomen and thorax. Believe it or not, by loosening the muscles, tubocurarine makes a number of subsequent procedures possible. You just have to administer the correct dose. And, of course, monitor the patient's breathing.'

'Then our dead man was given an incorrect dose.'

'Difficult to say, but since we are searching for a cause of death, and, despite the symptoms, drowning can be ruled out, I would say our man died as a result of respiratory paralysis.'

Rath nodded thoughtfully. 'That means someone thrust a syringe into Lamkau's jugular vein, which first put him out of action, then killed him.'

Karthaus nodded.

'And while all this was going on,' Rath continued, 'this same someone tried to drown the poor bastard? That doesn't make any sense.'

'Maybe he only tortured him. Water torture has been used since the Spanish Inquisition. The guilty party believes they are drowning and suffers mortal terror.'

'How does it work?'

'The *tormenta de toca*? First the guilty party is held fast, then a cloth is placed over their mouth and nose while water is poured over it.'

'How much water?'

'A few litres are enough. You just have to make sure the cloth stays wet. The gag reflex takes care of the rest.'

'You're frighteningly well informed, Doctor. Should I be concerned?'

Karthaus was unmoved. 'The history of criminal interrogation is fascinating stuff. Particularly from a medical standpoint.'

'I see.' Rath resisted the urge to shake his head. With his gaunt figure and sunken cheeks, Karthaus really did give him the creeps. He felt more at home with the easy-going Dr Schwartz and his macabre humour. 'Something I don't understand ... Torture is about extracting information from your victim. Why would you administer an anaesthetic beforehand? A lethal one at that?'

'Anaesthetic isn't quite right,' Karthaus said. 'Tubocurarine doesn't act as an analgesic. It paralyses your musculature, but you remain fully conscious and sensitive to pain. Even if you can't move, can't even speak, in fact.'

Rath gave a shudder. 'I just hope something like that doesn't happen in theatre.'

'You'll laugh,' Karthaus said, making a deadly serious face, 'but it already has. Unfortunately the patients couldn't say anything during the procedure, because they were completely paralysed at the time.'

'Knock it off, Doctor. Lucky for me I've never had to go under the knife.'

'No invasive procedure is devoid of risk, a fact any colleague will confirm.' Karthaus shrugged again. 'At least I can open up my clients with peace of mind.'

There was no trace of irony in the doctor's voice.

9

He was too late, damn it! Had he learned of Lamkau's death sooner, none of this would have happened, but they hadn't telephoned him until this morning. They must be going out of their minds in Treuburg, but what else could he do? The green Opel arrived just as he was about to drop in on the widow to offer his condolences. You could tell the pair who got out were cops from a hundred metres, so he had continued down Ordensmeisterstrasse as if it were part of his beat, inwardly cursing the bastards as he went.

With any luck they wouldn't find anything, but he couldn't be sure. After all, these were Gennat's boys, homicide detectives from Alex. The kind that didn't miss a thing.

Goddamn it!

He'd wait until the cops had disappeared then take a look himself. Perhaps Lamkau had managed to hide the book. If he was smart he'd have chucked it long ago. Still, he couldn't be that clever, otherwise he'd have survived all this. Whatever this was. They still weren't sure, even if the death notices were plain enough. Somebody knew; the question was, *who*?

There was movement on the other side of the road. The cops were returning to the Opel, laden with cardboard boxes. It was exactly as he'd feared. They were taking everything back to Alex to sift at their leisure.

'Why can't Rath look at this himself,' he heard one say. 'What are we, bookkeepers now?'

'That's clearly what the widow thought. It felt like she expected us to put her papers in order.'

'Well, more fool her.'

They heaved the boxes into the car and went back inside, accompanied by the sound of the great mutt Lamkau had acquired after Wawerka's death. For a moment he was tempted to take a look, but the car was parked in the courtyard next to the delivery vans, and would be visible from the office. Besides, the cur would sound the alarm. He resolved to stay where he was, in the shadow of an advertising pillar. The men emerged several more times to load boxes before driving off.

He briefly considered going inside to the widow, even if it was no longer necessary. The two officers had been kind enough to say where the documents were headed.

10

Erika Voss was still waiting to finish for the day. Through the open door Rath could see Lange's and Gräf's desks were already deserted, in their place were around a dozen cardboard boxes full of files. 'Detective Gräf said to tell you that examining the Lamkau accounts proved trickier than expected,' she explained. 'They seized a number of papers instead.'

Rath nodded and hung up his hat. Kirie pitter-pattered towards him and sniffed his hands.

'And a lady telephoned a few moments ago,' she continued, looking at a sheet of paper. 'From G Division.'

'Very good,' Rath intoned casually. 'Did she say what it was about?'

'No. She said she'd call back.'

'Any news from ED?'

'Afraid not. Herr Kronberg says the report will be ready for tomorrow.'

With that, Erika Voss was gone. Rath gazed after her. Under normal circumstances, he'd have accompanied her, perhaps even driven her home, but the prospect of his deserted, oversized flat filled him with dread.

He went into the office and heaved one of the boxes onto his desk. Didn't look like company papers. The overzealous Gräf appeared to have purged Herbert Lamkau's private desk. Or perhaps it was the equally overzealous Lange.

Kirie pattered over and let Rath ruffle her fur as he sifted through the contents. A few letters, a passport with a few foreign stamps, mainly Poland and the Free City of Danzig. A thick black notebook, containing endless columns of figures he couldn't make head or tail of, and, right at the bottom, a pile of gazettes. *Alkohol*, read the title on the first, *General Magazine for the Spirit, Korn and Compressed Yeast Industries. Official Organ of the German Association of Brewing and Distilling*. Another was called the *Spirit Industry Magazine, Mouthpiece of the Association of Spirit Manufacturers in Germany*. Rath shook his head. What a country to be a boffin!

There didn't seem to be anything else private in the remaining boxes. A glance was enough to tell Rath it wasn't just the last few months his colleagues had seized, but several financial years. The widow Lamkau would have her work cut out.

He was about to light a cigarette and look at some of the more recent files, when there was a tentative knock at the door. Kirie sprang to her feet and pricked up her ears. Perhaps it was Kronberg, here to share some of ED's findings. Ever since his wife had died, Kronberg, too, was prone to working overtime. 'Yes!' he said.

The door slowly opened and a young woman appeared in the outer office. Kirie made a beeline for her. 'Superintendent Gennat sent me, Sir.'

Rath couldn't believe his eyes. She gazed at the floor like a convent girl, but perhaps it was only to conceal her grin. 'Truth be told,' the convent girl continued, 'I'm not due to report until tomorrow morning, but I thought I'd come and introduce myself. To save you from alarm.'

He couldn't help it. The moment he'd seen who it was, he'd felt a tingling sensation. 'Let's have a look at you then. Unfortunately the others have already called it a night.'

'*Unfortunately*?' She closed the door behind her and

stepped inside, gaze still firmly fixed on the floor. Gently, he took her chin and tilted it upwards so that she was finally looking him in the eye. Then he kissed her, and felt her kiss him back. 'But Sir,' she said.

The fact that she was still in character only aroused him more.

'Why don't you come into my office,' he said sternly, observing her for a moment from behind before following. He shooed Kirie into the outer office, where she sulkily lay in her basket. Once inside he closed the door and they looked at each other. It seemed she could read his mind.

'We can't,' she said, even before he leaned over and kissed her on the nape of the neck, the point that always made her grow weak. Her heavy breathing gave the lie to her protest. 'Not here!'

'You are a CID cadet, Fräulein Ritter, and I am your training officer.'

She sighed when he kissed her again. 'Gereon, cut it out!'

He turned her around and looked at her. 'For once, will you just do as I say. At least while we're on the job!'

'Yes, Sir!'

'In the upper desk drawer is a key. Take it and lock the door. Just in case.'

She did as bidden. 'And now, Sir?'

He had already pulled the curtains. He carefully unbuttoned her blouse, kissing the soft skin above her clavicle, working his way slowly down, button by button. Charly breathed heavily and sighed. 'I'd forgotten how much you enjoy delayed gratification,' she said.

'Only up to a point,' he said.

He surveyed her as she stood before him and decided that point had been reached.

11

He stood outside the police station and gazed up at the offices of Homicide, whose corridors he had visited years before. A crowd of officers left the building, signalling the end of the day shift. He remained in the shadow of the railway arches until the two men emerged. Keeping a low profile was easy in the throng at Alexanderplatz, and he was certain they hadn't recognised him. They probably hadn't even seen him.

He smoked a cigarette before leaving his post, knowing that he could enter the building without passing the porter's lodge. There was no one in the atrium save for two uniform cops at the gate. You just had to say hello and look as if you had business and no one took any notice. He strode determinedly towards the stairwell and climbed the stone steps to the first floor, reaching the glass door on which the word HOMICIDE was printed.

There wasn't a soul up here, the clatter of typewriters had long since faded. After passing a line of names and doors, including that of the famous Gennat, he found the one he had been searching for.

Detective Inspector Gereon Rath.

He felt for the picklock in his pocket, which he had fetched from Kreuzberg, and looked around. The corridor was still empty. He listened at the door. Silence.

Then out of the corner of his eye he saw movement. The glass door opened, and a reflection flitted briefly in the corridor, a slender young woman. He turned away from the door and continued down the corridor, trying not to move too quickly, resisting the temptation to turn around. There was no way she could have seen him standing outside the door, she was just some dim-witted secretary doing overtime. He saw a toilet and went inside. The stalls appeared to be empty. He opened one, bolted the lock and sat on the toilet seat, listening to the drip of a tap and what he thought was the sound of a door closing. For a long time there was silence, but still he waited before venturing outside.

The corridor was empty. He had no idea whose secretary it was, but hoped it wasn't Detective Inspector Rath's. That he, of all people, should be doing overtime . . .but no, or his colleagues would never have left when they did. No one reacted when he knocked, and he was about to remove the picklock from his pocket when he realised the door was unlocked. He replaced the false key, knocked a second time and, when still no one answered, opened the door.

The outer office was deserted, but just then he caught sight of the black dog looking at him, head tilted to one side. The thing had probably been staring at him this whole time, curiously, guilelessly, neither growling nor gnashing its teeth. He beat an orderly retreat, realising he'd made the right choice when, before he'd even closed the door, the cur issued two short, loud barks.

He looked around but no one had entered the corridor in the meantime. Everyone had finished save for the late shift; the late shift and those imbeciles still clocking up overtime, like Detective Inspector Rath.

What a stroke of luck he hadn't bumped into him, only his mutt – who couldn't speak.

The incident had him break out in a sweat. On the way out he took the stairwell at the opposite end of the corridor to avoid crossing Homicide again.

At least now he knew where to look.

12

'You still haven't given me a response,' Rath said, as they shared an Overstolz. 'Or was that it just now?'

He pulled back the curtains and allowed daylight into the office, not knowing how long they had lain skin to skin on his 'overtime' sofa, dreaming and out of breath. Kirie had barked once or twice, fetching them back to reality, reminding Rath that she was waiting for him outside. They put on the rest of their clothes.

'You seduced me, you cad,' she said, taking a drag on the cigarette.

'I thought it was *you* who seduced me.'

'Then we're equally culpable.'

'Agreed, Your Honour. Now, how about that response?'

She took another drag and passed him the Overstolz. 'Not now,' she said. 'And not here.'

'I know a nice restaurant in Friedrichstadt.' He could have eaten a horse.

'Gereon,' she said. 'Not now.'

'Then when?'

'Soon. Right now I don't have the time.'

He looked at his watch. 'At nine, then? Ten?'

'You're incorrigible!' She gazed out of the window, as if her appointments diary was hovering in the sky above the court building. 'Ten's too late, but nine should be fine.' She smiled.

'Splendid, then let's go to *Femina*. Make sure you put on your dance dress.'

'Then I really do have to go.' She grabbed the cigarette for a final drag. 'I'm late enough as it is.' She kissed him, giving him an angry look. 'You and your delayed gratification.'

With that she turned the key. No sooner had she opened the door than Kirie came bounding in. 'You two ought to wait a while,' she said. 'Late as it is, I don't want to risk being seen together at the Castle.'

'Well, don't be upset if Kirie takes it personally.'

She shrugged and left. He gazed after her pensively, and only when he saw that Kirie wore a similar expression did he break into a grin. Half an hour later, after taking Kirie for a short walk in Tiergarten, he was back in Carmerstrasse, albeit much earlier than planned. He felt almost indecently cheerful as he marched up the steps with Kirie in tow.

'Evening, Bergner,' he said in passing.

'Evening, Herr Rath.'

He relished the porter's greeting, which sounded a little like *Evening, Herr Kriminalrat*. Evening, Superintendent. For the first time in a long time he caught himself thinking about rank and promotion as he took the lift up. Superintendent might be a distant dream, but by now detective chief inspector was surely overdue. It felt like forever since he had been in breach of his duties – at least, it would feel like forever to his superiors. His status as husband and, hopefully, family man, could significantly increase his chances of promotion. Assuming Charly said 'yes', it wouldn't hurt to make their engagement public in the Castle as soon as possible. Perhaps they might even persuade Gennat to act as witness ...

Arriving upstairs, he slung his hat on the hook and let Kirie off the lead. He went into the living room, opened a window, lit a cigarette and gazed out. The fresh summer breeze and evening atmosphere only improved his mood further. For once he felt at peace with the world.

The telephone rang. Was it Charly already? He still had to get changed.

'*Apparatebau Rath, Rath am Apparat,*' he answered, rolling his 'r's' and stressing his 't's'.

'Are you ever going to grow up?'

'Paul?'

Paul Wittkamp was Rath's oldest friend, the only one left from his Cologne days. When he'd moved to Berlin, nearly all his supposed friends had turned their backs on him. In truth it had started even before that, when the Cologne press were hounding him and his colleagues began avoiding him in the canteen; when his fiancée, a good match from an equally good Cologne house, broke off their engagement. Only Paul had stayed loyal. Since then Rath had met a great many people in Berlin, but Paul remained his one, true friend, even if they only saw each other once in a blue moon.

'Fräulein Heller left a note saying a Herr Rath from Berlin had been in touch.'

'I need your advice.'

'There was me thinking you needed a best man. She's back now, isn't she?'

Paul had already made Charly's acquaintance. In fact, it was he who'd urged Rath to marry her, over two years ago. Since then the prospect of their marriage came up at every turn.

'We Prussians are slow on the draw.'

'Funny, I'd never realised. How long is it now?'

'You know very well.' Rath was pleased Paul couldn't see his grin. 'Things might be moving quicker on that front than you think, but right now what I need is your professional advice.'

'Do you want me to recommend a wine? I'm afraid Wittkamp don't supply bachelors with burgeoning drink problems.'

'But you do supply Kempinski?'

'For two years now. I remember my Berlin visit very well. Cost me a grazing shot and a few bruises. Managed to get you out of trouble *and* land my contract with Kempinski on the side.'

'Just how important is that contract with Kempinski?'

'Very. Not only in terms of revenue, but reputation. Once upon a time you could be a purveyor to the court, to the Kaiser or King. Now you can supply Kempinski. The name means something, not just in Berlin.'

'Is it hard to get in there?'

'Let's just say, other clients are easier. For Kempinski quality is the most important thing, and then the price.'

'Can Kempinski buyers be bought?'

'Pardon me?'

'Can you jog their goodwill? I don't know, with gifts for example.'

'I don't know how you think these things work, but I've never done anything of the sort.'

'I'm not saying you have. I'm just asking if it's a possibility.'

'Fundamentally, anyone can be bought. But if the quality isn't right, no Kempinski buyer would be interested. The supplier would be out on their ear right away.'

'Supposing the quality wasn't up to scratch just once, and you were in danger of being out on your ear, might a gift help then? Provided you swore blind it would never happen again?'

'Gereon, listen, I don't know if I can help. I don't know what desperate people do. I can't predict how Kempinski buyers might react.'

'But it could drive you to despair, losing your Kempinski contract ...'

'It could certainly ruin your good reputation. Provided, of course, you had one in the first place.'

13

The *Femina-Bar* was at the top of Nürnberger Strasse, right by Tauentzienstrasse, in a large, modern premises with an apparently endless, elegantly curved façade. Nowhere was Berlin more fashionable than here. A man in a red-gold uniform opened the taxi door and helped Charly out, while Rath pressed a note into the driver's hand. Already he knew the evening wouldn't be cheap. A few hundred metres further towards Wilmersdorf was where he had lodged with the widow Behnke, three years before. Back then the *Femina* had still been a construction site.

Charly stood next to the taxi and smiled, looking stunning in her midnight-blue dress and light summer coat. Rath was glad he'd purchased a new dinner suit. He offered his arm, and she took it in hers, and how amazingly proud he felt to be strolling with her through the night, following the gold-braided porter as he led them to the entrance, a row of modern glass doors, a wide, inviting strip of warm, bright-coloured light, above which the rest of the façade was lost in darkness, broken only by ribbons of neon: *Femina, das Ballhaus Berlins*. Berlin's ballroom.

It was the hottest ticket in town, but he wanted to show her that she was worth it, that she meant more to him than money could buy. In the taxi they had barely exchanged a word. Rath had the feeling that Charly was at least as nervous as he was, although he didn't know if that was a good sign or a bad.

The porter opened one of the glass doors. Unseen by Charly, Rath thrust five marks into his hand, upon which the man entrusted them to a colleague in the lobby, who in turn led them to the cloakroom, where he was likewise rewarded with five marks. All the while Rath took pains to ensure that Charly saw no money exchanging hands. After relieving them of their coats, the man accompanied them to a large lift. As they stepped into the car Rath couldn't help thinking of Herbert Lamkau's dead eyes.

The lift took them up to a huge ballroom with a wrap-around gallery, the imitation gold Rococo offering the perfect contrast to the modern façade. Another five marks guaranteed a front row seat and an unusually obliging waiter. Rath was glad when they finally sat down. He was starting to run out of change.

The first dancers began moving to the sounds of the jazz band, who played flawlessly despite their stiff appearance. Rath ordered champagne to start while Charly studied the menu. Apparently she was hungry. He watched her eyes widen as she whistled quietly through her teeth. 'You must be feeling flush!' she said, placing it to one side.

'It's a special evening.'

She threw him an enigmatic glance. All of a sudden he felt overcome by the insecurity which had dogged him these last few days.

The champagne arrived and they clinked glasses. 'What are we drinking to?' he asked. 'To us?'

'How about we start with tonight, and your bulging wallet,' Charly said, revealing her dimpled smile. At that moment he knew she had long since made up her mind, and that her answer would be more complex than a simple 'yes'. They were silent for a time as they browsed the menus.

'So, you want to marry me,' she said at length, fumbling

103

a Juno out of her handbag, the trailing vestiges of a smile still on her face. 'Do you have any idea what you're letting yourself in for?'

'I think so,' he said, and opened his cigarette case. 'I mean, we've been practising long enough.'

'Marriage means more than performing your conjugal duties,' she whispered across the table.

'Keep talking like that and I'll jump on you right here.'

'Seriously, Gereon. How do you envisage our everyday life?'

Here they come, he thought, the complex Charly-style questions, and even though he'd been expecting them, he still didn't have any answers. How could he? He didn't *envisage* his everyday life or his future, he just wanted to live them, with her by his side.

'It'll be like a fairy tale,' he said, drawing the words in the air with his cigarette: '*And they lived happily ever after.*' He held his lighter first to her Juno, then to his Overstolz. 'What about you? How do you envisage our everyday life?'

Charly's response came promptly. 'I know I don't want to spend the whole day in the kitchen looking after our hundred kids, just waiting for the master of the house to return so I can serve him dinner and pamper him.'

'What a picture. But who said anything about a hundred kids? I'd settle for between one and three . . .'

She laughed. 'Oh, stop being such a silly clot! I'm not saying I don't *ever* want kids! Just that I want a career first!'

The waiter came to take their order. The table held nothing like the romantic atmosphere Rath had been hoping for. Somehow it felt as if they were negotiating a contract, rather than deciding to spend the rest of their lives together out of love.

Charly waited until they were alone again. 'Don't

misunderstand me, but I know there are lots of women who'd like to work, who are forbidden from doing so by their husbands, and I've no desire to join their ranks.'

'What do you mean "forbidden"? All I'm saying is I earn enough to support us both.'

'Gereon, listen to me, I'll work for as long as I please, there's nothing you can do about it. If you should ever try, I'll divorce you on the spot!'

He could have embraced her, the way she sat there looking so indignant. He lifted his glass and grinned. 'Let's drink to that.'

'Pardon me?'

'Well, if I've understood correctly, you've just said "yes". If we can't drink to that, what can we drink to?'

For a moment she looked bewildered, only for her dimple to reappear. 'No flies on you pigs, are there?' She reached for her glass, and they clinked before she took his hand in hers and gazed at him through her brown eyes. She was worth every grey hair she'd already given him, as well as those that were still to come.

'Seriously, Gereon,' she said. 'These things are important to me.'

He nodded. No one had said it would be easy with Charly, but that's not what this was about. 'I promise,' he said and smiled. 'I'll never prevent you from working. But...that doesn't mean I don't want kids with you...at some stage.'

She smiled, revealing her dimple again. 'We can have a hundred as far as I'm concerned, but I must warn you: I can only have girls. And they'll all be exactly like me!'

'Lord have mercy! Perhaps we should reconsider after all.'

'No chance. Now, give me that ring!'

He took the little case out of his inside pocket and opened it. 'If I could ask for your hand, Fräulein Ritter.'

She stretched out her hand and skilfully he eased the

ring onto her finger. It was a perfect fit. 'You've done this before,' she said.

'I thought you knew.' He raised his glass. 'To us. To the best engagement I've ever had!'

She inspected the ring from a distance. 'You're lucky it's so pretty, otherwise I'd be throwing it straight back in your face. The effrontery.'

'No can do. It's official now.' Rath took the champagne from the cooler and poured. 'But I want to hear it from you, just once.'

'Hear what?'

'What do you mean "what"? That little word. "Yes".'

'I thought that didn't matter until the registry office.' She smiled.

There was a commotion. It must have been going on for some time, but up till that point the music had mercifully drowned it out. Now the piece was finished, however, a man could be heard screeching into the applause.

'If I want a beer, then it's your job to get me one, fancy pants!'

Rath turned around. The waiter stood at most three tables away, wine list in hand, trying to pacify a beetroot-coloured customer who seemed determined to kick up a fuss. His companion, a full-figured beauty, was clearly ill at ease. The waiter spoke at a civilised volume, meaning Rath could only catch the odd snippet. '...I'm sorry...', '...you have to order wine here...', '...beer is only served in the gallery...' Then the loudmouth started again, with the whole room listening this time.

'Are you trying to tell me what I can and can't order? I'm the customer here, so bring me a goddamn beer! Or do I have to make you?'

In the meantime two elegantly dressed, well-built men had approached. The waiter discreetly took his leave to see to the other guests, while they quietly persuaded the

106

troublemaker to start looking for his cloakroom ticket. The loudmouth still wasn't ready to accept defeat. He sprang to his feet, thrusting a hand from his shoulder. 'I won't stand for it, not in a goddamn Jew restaurant! You can't treat a German like this!'

He was wrong, of course. As discreetly as possible the strongmen ushered the hothead out of the room. 'Someday you'll be in for a surprise,' he ranted, before being bundled into the lift. 'You Jews!' he yelled as the doors closed. 'Think you're better than the rest, but you're wrong!'

His companion gazed around in embarrassment, then took her handbag and stood up.

By now the musicians had finished turning their pages. The band started up again, and the guests, who had listened to the exchange in silence, resumed their conversations. The dancers swayed as before, as if nothing had happened.

'Maybe *that's* a possibility,' Charly said.

'Pardon me?'

'Anti-Semitism. *Haus Vaterland* is a *goddamn Jew restaurant* too, to borrow that delightful man's turn of phrase.'

'As a motive for murder? I'm not sure. When people like that curse the Jews, they don't mean it seriously. It's like getting worked up about a "Jew club" winning the German league. It's just a manner of speaking.'

'It's anti-Semitism. I was angry Bayern Munich won instead of Hertha, too, but you don't catch me talking about a "Jew club".'

'There you are, talking about work again.' Rath grinned. 'You know, you can tell *you're* a pig too. We aren't on duty again till tomorrow morning.'

'Doesn't quite work calling a female CID officer "pig", does it?'

'What should I call you then? A sow?'

'No animal names until we've been married at least ten years.'

107

'As you wish, honey bear.'

'Buffoon!'

Rath grinned. 'What will Gennat make of it when he hears?'

'Make of what?'

'Our engagement.'

'Let's keep it to ourselves while the *Vaterland* investigation is ongoing.'

'And go public as soon as it's closed.'

'It's a deal.' Charly stood up. 'Now if you don't mind, I'd like to dance.'

'Before dinner? I didn't hear anything about it being ladies' choice.'

'You're engaged now. You'd better get used to it.' With that she stretched out a slender arm and waited for him to lead her to the dance floor.

14

Erika Voss's typewriter clattered on the adjoining desk, but if Charly covered her ear when making a call everything was fine. Gereon had assigned her a spot on the visitor's table in the outer office with his secretary and Kirie. The dog had taken it better than Erika Voss, who seemed personally aggrieved that she should curl up under Charly's table. The secretary had been just as surprised by the noisy greeting Kirie afforded the new girl, but accepted both with a shrug. Only when Charly asked to use the telephone did she give a slightly venomous look.

'So long as you answer when it rings,' she said.

Charly offered a disarming smile, and Gereon's secretary left her in peace. Sitting at this wobbly table, she was scarcely able to believe her luck.

Who'd have thought she'd be working for Homicide again? Certainly not her. A transfer like this was exceedingly rare, hence the looks when she appeared at A Division's morning briefing. She had revelled in her colleagues' surprise, before taking her place with the *Vaterland* team and Gereon Rath.

From time to time she'd asked herself whether Gennat suspected her relationship with Gereon was more than simply professional. But then he wouldn't have allocated her to him. Or would he?

At any rate, neither of them had let on during briefing or back in the office. They greeted one another politely, as usual, when their paths crossed. It was a strange feeling after yesterday evening, and last night. She had stayed over, but they'd travelled to Alex separately, he in the Buick, she on the BVG. She'd arrived on schedule; he a little behind. Then, for the second time that day, she'd bid him good morning, this time using the polite form of address.

She had to take care that she didn't get things muddled with her new colleagues. She was on first-name terms with Reinhold Gräf, whom she'd known for ages, but not with Andreas Lange, although they'd worked together before. With Gereon, of course, she was also on first-name terms, but not in the Castle. It was pretty complicated. As for Erika Voss, she had absolutely no idea. Under normal circumstances she'd have gone for 'informal', but wasn't that a little too pally? Shouldn't a candidate for inspector keep her distance from a secretary?

Resolving not to worry too much she focused on the task at hand. Gereon had started her off on a piece of drudge work, of course, since he couldn't display a preference. She was to canvass suppliers for a paralytic poison called tubocurarine, which had been used to kill the man in *Haus Vaterland*. Reinhold Gräf had provided a long list of addresses where the drug was stocked: South American researchers and institutes for tropical diseases, as well as a few hospitals. Setting to work on her telephone marathon, she was sceptical that someone who'd employed the poison as a murder weapon would have access by legal means. They'd either have stolen it, or got it from someone who'd acquired it illegally themselves.

After two hours she finished working her way through Gräf's list with her suspicions confirmed: no thefts, no unexplained dwindling of supplies; curare reserves all intact.

Erika Voss was still hammering away while giving her new colleague the silent treatment. No doubt Charly had made a rookie error in finishing something she'd been given to keep

110

her temporarily occupied, but now wasn't the time to think about that. She wanted to do something meaningful, and not just sit around. There was no option but to disturb the gentlemen's club, and request a fresh assignment.

Erika Voss reclaimed her telephone with an expression faintly reminiscent of a smile, as, address list wedged under her arm, Charly knocked on the connecting door, entering to find Lange and Gräf engaged in conversation over a box of files, some of which lay open on the desk. Gereon was on the telephone, and merely raised his eyebrows when he saw her. She hardly took any notice and felt a perverse delight in effecting to ignore him, only to discreetly stroke his hand as she passed. On no account could she think about what happened last night in this office, otherwise she'd have dragged him by the tie into the nearest broom cupboard.

She stood before the desk with the files and cleared her throat. 'No joy. We can rule out hospitals and South American researchers.' Gräf and Lange both looked up. No doubt they had been hoping to keep her occupied until at least lunchtime. Before they could say anything, she continued. 'I suggest we concentrate on known illegal sources of supply.' Hearing no opposition, she continued. 'Perhaps I should speak with Narcotics?'

Reinhold Gräf was staring at her goggle-eyed, and she almost burst out laughing. 'Finished already?' he said disbelievingly, looking over her list. 'You didn't find any irregularities?'

'None. They all checked their stocks and called back. We've no reason to disbelieve them. They're all reputable establishments.'

'I see,' Gräf said. 'And now you want to look into the disreputable ones.'

Gereon finished his telephone conversation and stood to cast his eye over the list. 'Good work, Fräulein Ritter,' he said, 'and good thinking about Narcotics, but you don't have to go through the proper channels right away. It can be rather painstaking here at headquarters.' He gestured towards the wall, and the obligatory portrait of Hindenburg. 'A few doors along from us is Detective Inspector Dettmann. He joined the department from Narcotics two months ago. Perhaps he has an idea. People say he knows his way around the streets. If that doesn't work, then you can always make it official.'

He spoke the last sentence in such paternal, schoolmasterly tones that it was all she could do to keep her facial muscles under control. At that moment Erika Voss poked her head around the door.

'Inspector,' she said, avoiding Charly's gaze. 'Superintendent Gennat says he can see you now.'

'Tell the super I'll be along in five minutes.'

She disappeared, and Charly smiled at Gereon. 'Thanks for the tip, Sir. Detective Inspector Dettmann. Where did you say his office was?'

'If you wait a moment, I'll take you there myself. I have to see Gennat anyway.'

He could have skipped the explanation, she thought. It sounded overeager and a little forced. Still, her colleagues didn't seem to notice anything. She nodded as submissively as one would expect from a female cadet.

Lange and Gräf returned to the files as the pair exited the office. Erika Voss didn't look up from her typewriter, but Charly was certain she had registered them leaving together.

'I'm just showing Fräulein Ritter here the way to Dettmann's office,' Rath said. 'Then I'm off to see the super.' Erika Voss nodded, refusing to be distracted from her work.

With a stoical expression, Rath closed the door behind them. Outside their gazes met for an instant, whereupon Charly noticed something else. 'Oh,' she said. 'Is that my doing?'

Rath looked around. Fortunately the corridor was empty. A few people stood at the other end by the glass door, too far away to see anything, save, perhaps, for a man and a woman lingering slightly too long outside an office door.

'You'd better show me the way to Dettmann's,' she whispered. 'Stay here any longer and it'll look like we're sharing a tearful goodbye.'

'We need to think of something, Charly, and fast. Things can't go on like this.'

'Maybe you should try thinking a little *harder* about work.'

'Shouldn't be too tricky with Gennat.' He paused and gestured towards a door. 'This is Dettmann here. Not necessarily the friendliest, but he spent almost ten years with Narcotics. If anyone can tell you about sources of supply, it's him.'

'Right you are,' she said. 'Everything OK down there?'

'Much better,' he said, kissing her so suddenly that she started. But it was no good, she couldn't help herself. Afterwards she looked up into his boyish grin and turned around. The officers by the glass door had disappeared, and the corridor was deserted once more.

'Opportunity makes the thief,' Gereon said, disappearing in the opposite direction, where Gennat had his office. He was right: they had to think of something.

Detective Inspector Harald Dettmann's office was only two doors down from Gereon's. She took a quick glance at her pocket mirror to check her lipstick, before knocking and entering cautiously. Dettmann's outer office was empty but the connecting door was open, and she went through. A wiry man in his late thirties with thinning hair sat at his desk; a second desk in the room was abandoned. He looked up.

'Detective Inspector Dettmann, I presume.' Charly stepped inside, still in high spirits.

'The very same,' Dettmann said and stood up. 'Come on in.' He sat casually on the edge of the desk. 'With whom do I have the pleasure?'

'Charlotte Ritter, CID cadet. My apologies. I thought you were at briefing this morning.'

'I was busy.' He looked her up and down. 'Did I miss anything?'

'Well, I'm currently working on a homicide case and ...'

'A homicide.' He lit a cigarette. 'Didn't know G Division dealt with that sort of thing.'

'I've been assigned to the *Vaterland* team, led by Inspector Gereon Rath,' she said, as businesslike as possible. 'We urgently need information about a substance called tubocurarine. As well as any illegal sources of supply here in Berlin.'

'I see.'

'I was hoping you might be able to help.'

'Why doesn't Rath come to me himself?'

'Inspector Rath entrusted *me* with the task, so it's *me* you'll have to make do with.'

'Don't they teach you cadets to speak to Narcotics in such cases? I'm a homicide detective.'

What should have been a harmless chat between colleagues was already going badly wrong. Still, Charly persevered. She wouldn't let herself be ground down; she hadn't grown up in Moabit for nothing. 'Call it an unofficial request,' she said with a smile, but Dettmann remained impassive. 'Before I go to another department ...I thought, between colleagues ...'

'I see. Between colleagues ... Is this some sort of joke?'

'Pardon me?'

'Do I look like a bloody typist?'

'I don't understand ...'

'You were Gennat's stenographer, weren't you? And since you take me for a colleague ...'

114

'I'm no *typist*, as you'd have it, but a CID cadet. A candidate for inspector in G Division, currently seconded to A Division! And I won't stand for this much longer.'

'You won't stand for this much longer? Well, I say!'

Dettmann looked her up and down, shamelessly ogling her legs. 'Listen to me, lady,' he said quietly, leaning so far forward she could smell his aftershave and bad breath. 'I don't know who you've been *blowing* around here, Böhm or Buddha, but I do know one thing: you can't tell me what to do.'

Charly couldn't believe her ears. 'What did you just say?'

'I don't know what it is you heard, Charlotte.'

'Since when did I give you permission to use my first name?' In fact, Dettmann had been using the informal mode of address throughout.

'Your permission? I don't need your permission to do anything. Is that clear? Certainly not in my office. Now, why don't you go back to your women's division? Maybe they'll let you order them about. Beat it, I have things to do.' He returned behind his desk, not deigning to give her another glance.

She stood open-mouthed, baffled. Her initial impulse was to go over and give the bastard a smack, but common sense told her it was unlikely to be a good career move. Instead she stood gasping for air like a fish out of water.

'Was there something else, Fräulein Ritter?' Dettmann smiled so brazenly she was rendered speechless once and for all. 'I thought we were finished here.'

He had reverted to the formal mode of address. Seeing him grin like that, Charly knew, at that moment, that Harald Dettmann would point-blank deny uttering the shameless insults he had just said to her face. And who would believe a female cadet against a veteran detective inspector? Besides, according to the pin on his lapel, Dettmann was a member of the Schrader Verband, the Association of Prussian Police

Officers; he'd have to be caught stealing silver spoons from the commissioner's office to be knocked from his perch.

Charly didn't want the grinning Dettmann to enjoy her frustration. She turned on her heel, accidentally slamming the door as she returned through the outer office without knowing where she was headed.

The incident seemed more and more unreal the longer she thought about it. As if it had been a dream, although her anger told her in no uncertain terms that it had really happened. Worse than that was her sense of shame. Somehow it felt as if *she* were the one who ought to be ashamed at Dettmann's impertinence. Yes, she actually felt ashamed, and when she realised this, she only grew angrier.

Finally, without realising how she had got there, she found herself in the female toilets, built to accommodate the numerous secretaries and stenographers who worked in A Division. Fortunately, there was no one else here; the large washroom was empty, and would only fill up when the women came to fix their lipstick during lunch hour. She locked herself in one of the stalls, sat on the toilet seat and gave way to tears of rage. She couldn't help it. She kicked against the cubicle door, but it brought nothing but a loud bang and a painful foot.

Dettmann, the fucking arsehole!

The thing that annoyed her most was that he'd managed to hurt her quite so much, just when she'd begun to think of herself as a fully fledged member of the Berlin Police. Now she had been fetched back to earth. The simple fact was that, as a woman in CID, she was nobody. Any inspector with a career-enhancing union membership and a dirty mind could say what the hell he liked, to her face, without fear of the consequences.

15

Rath sat on the worn green sofa in Gennat's office before a veritable mountain of cakes, contemplating a slice of nutcake whose dryness more than compensated for its lack of size. Gennat helped himself to a slice of gooseberry tart as his secretary, Trudchen Steiner, entered with a pot of freshly brewed coffee. Rath gratefully accepted.

'That was some performance you gave this morning,' Gennat said, skewering a slice of tart with his cake fork. Rath had provided an update on the *Vaterland* case, as the investigation had been dubbed internally, and Buddha was particularly impressed by the results of the blood analysis. 'Have you made any progress with your search for this Indian arrow poison?'

'Fräulein Ritter is on top of it. So far we've been able to rule out hospitals, university institutes, and all known South American researchers in Berlin. Fräulein Ritter has suggested that with the help of Narcotics we now focus our attentions on illegal sources of supply.'

'How is she getting on? Are you satisfied?'

'Very.' Rath hurriedly swallowed his cake. 'Fräulein Ritter is a quick and reliable worker.'

'Isn't she just? She'd be a real asset to A Division. Sadly I can only loan her from Superintendent Wieking on a case-by-case basis.' He shook his head. 'I suppose I should be glad there is a women's CID at all.'

'Besides the sequence of events,' Rath continued, 'the thing that concerns us most is motive. With that, we're back to the thousand marks found on the victim.'

'Still no explanation?'

'The *Vaterland* accounts aren't settled in cash. Gräf and Lange are currently in the process of reconstructing Herbert Lamkau's final rounds. We still don't know why he decided to make his deliveries in person on the morning in question.'

'But you have your suspicions?'

'It's possible the money was intended as a bribe for some-one in *Haus Vaterland*, one of the buyers perhaps. Lamkau was in danger of losing his most important client, but above all his reputation. Supplying Kempinski . . .is like being a purveyor to the court.'

'So, where's the motive? The recipient of a bribe would hardly have recourse to murder.'

'Perhaps it was blackmail.'

'Then why was the money still in Lamkau's overalls?'

'There are some inconsistencies that need ironing out,' Rath said. 'It's clear there were some shady deals going on behind the scenes at *Haus Vaterland*. Perhaps there still are. It's conceivable they could be linked to Lamkau's death.' He replaced his plate on the table. 'We can also safely assume that Lamkau's killer was still in the building when the police arrived, meaning it's someone already on our list of names. We've had no luck with the interrogations so far, but . . .'

Having only just dealt with his nutcake, Rath looked on in horror as Gennat now shovelled a slice of Sachertorte onto his plate.

'Thank you, Sir,' he said, failing to preface the line with a 'no'.

'Please continue.'

'Since we are dealing with a limited group of people, it might be worthwhile checking the employees in question for specialist medical knowledge, acquired before their time at *Haus Vaterland*, or outside of work. With the Red Cross or wherever.'

'Because of the deadly injection, you mean?'

Rath nodded. 'According to Dr Karthaus it isn't at all easy to inject through the jugular vein. And how many people know their way around tubocurarine?' He picked up a forkful of Sachertorte and decided to repeat his request for reinforcements. 'What I could imagine in this situation, Sir, is an undercover operation. We could smuggle someone into *Haus Vaterland* to keep an eye on our suspects.'

To Rath's delight, Gennat nodded. 'Good idea.'

'I'm glad you think so, Sir.' Rath was still balancing cake on his fork. 'Perhaps you could spare me a colleague or two ...'

'I'm afraid staffing issues won't allow that.'

'The problem is,' Rath said, 'that both Lange and Gräf – and myself too, of course – have already visited *Haus Vaterland* in our capacity as CID officers, and would be recognised immediately. Quite apart from the fact that we lack the knowledge and skills to work in a commercial kitchen.'

'Detective Roeder used a fake beard to avoid being recognised.'

'Detective Roeder is no longer with the police force.'

Erwin Roeder had quit his post a few years back to pursue a career as an author. The sort of costumes favoured by the self-proclaimed 'arch investigator' would barely have passed muster at the Cologne Carnival.

'You're right,' Gennat said. 'A fake beard would be no good to us here.'

'You're certain there's nothing you can do? A single officer would be enough. Couldn't you pull some strings with the other departments?'

'I've already given you Fräulein Ritter. That's the best

I can do.' Gennat sounded unusually short. Rath chose to focus on his cake. 'And when I think about it,' Buddha continued, 'she could be just what you need. Am I right in thinking that so far Charly's been confined to desk duty?'

Rath was still working his way through his Sachertorte, and was happy to stay quiet for the time being. This wasn't how he'd pictured things, but Gennat seemed set on the idea.

'A woman would create the least suspicion,' Buddha said. 'No one would imagine they were dealing with a police officer. Besides, Charly has worked undercover before. Very successfully I might add.'

'If at great personal risk.'

'There's always personal risk, but Fräulein Ritter can look after herself. It was you that suggested an undercover operation in the first place!'

True, Rath thought, *but only because I needed more men.* 'Yes, but ...'

'But what? Go away and have a think about how you're going to smuggle her into *Haus Vaterland*. The operation is hereby approved.'

Rath wondered what Charly might say when he suggested she apply for one of the positions in *Haus Vaterland*, but he could see from Gennat's face that there would be no going back. Buddha reached for the tray of cakes, skilfully dismembering a second slice of gooseberry tart while Rath made further inroads into his Sachertorte. It was an unwritten rule that you should always finish your plate in Buddha's office; he was said to view leftovers as an insult.

'There was something else I wanted to discuss,' Gennat said. 'Something just between us. It concerns the possibility that we might be dealing with a serial killer.'

The phrase 'serial killer' made Rath sit bolt upright. The press were already breathing down his neck about the Phantom murders, and he could do without such scrutiny here. *Serial killer*. Gennat himself had coined the phrase, and usually it spelled trouble. The papers were quick to strike when investigations stalled, citing police incompetence and sowing fear among the population, which could all too quickly get out of hand.

Buddha gestured towards the table with his fork, on top of which lay a journal. Rath recognised the cover of the *Kriminalistische Monatshefte*, a periodical for which Gennat wrote now and again, most recently about Peter Kürten, the *Vampire of Düsseldorf*, a serial killer who had eventually fallen into police hands by chance.

'Listening to you yesterday morning,' Buddha continued, 'I couldn't help thinking of an article I read in the *Monatshefte* a few weeks back, in which a similarly strange case was described.' He took the periodical from the table and put on his reading glasses. 'I looked it up again, and I must say the similarities between our case and the . . .' He peered through his spectacles ' . . .Wawerka case from Dortmund are quite astonishing. Here, too, we have a victim who drowned in an enclosed space.'

'Lamkau didn't drown.'

'Maybe Wawerka didn't either. Who knows if forensic pathology is up to scratch in Dortmund. Either way, I couldn't help thinking of it when you spoke yesterday.' Gennat pushed the magazine across the table. 'Have a look for yourself.'

Rath laid his plate on the table, praying that Buddha wouldn't cut him a third slice, and picked up the journal. *Perhaps I should read this sort of thing more often*, he thought, feigning interest. 'Have our colleagues in Dortmund had any more luck?'

'I'm afraid not. The case is with the wet fish.' *Wet fish* was Castle terminology for cold case. 'But the similarities are striking. I didn't want to make a big deal of it at briefing. Some officers are rather closer to the press than they ought to be.' He looked Rath in the eye, knowing his inspector had links there too. 'If the papers should catch the phrase "serial killer", then all hell will break loose. But I don't have to tell *you* that.'

'No, Sir.'

'Anyhow, we can't allow them to make a fuss, especially when we still don't know if we're on the right track. I would therefore ask you to pursue this with discretion.'

'Doesn't the distance mitigate against your theory? Berlin and Dortmund are more than five hundred kilometres apart.'

'Four hundred and ninety, if you take the Reichsstrasse. Six and a half hours by train.' Gennat was unmoved. 'But you're right. Normally a serial killer operates in a more confined radius. Even so, we now have two cases that could go together, and perhaps there are more. Perhaps there are links we're still not seeing, geographical or otherwise.'

'And if it really is one and the same perpetrator, maybe they don't come from Berlin at all, but Dortmund.'

'Or elsewhere. Perhaps it's a travelling salesman who strikes wherever he stops for the night.'

'Then we should check if there have been any similar incidents in Prussia.'

'My thinking exactly, Inspector.' Gennat polished off his second slice of gooseberry tart, and look sated for the time being, a sure sign that the audience was over. 'I've already notified police headquarters in all major cities, as well as the State Crime Bureau and Gendarmerie. That way we'll hear of anything, even if it happened out in the sticks.'

'Thank you, Sir.' Rath rolled up the periodical and got to his feet. 'One more thing,' he said from the door. 'The dead man from Dortmund – did he have links with the catering industry? Or was he found in a lift like Lamkau?'

'He was a miner at the Zollern Colliery, found on site, dead in his bed.'

16

At least Rath didn't have to say anything right away. When he returned to his men, Charly still hadn't materialised. No one had heard anything from her since they'd left the office together around an hour before, but there was no way her talk with Dettmann could have lasted this long. He lit a cigarette and wondered whether he would have to give her a public dressing-down, if only to show his colleagues there were no favourites. He couldn't overlook the fact that she had failed to inform the team of her movements. Had she paid Narcotics a visit? She ought to have left that to him. His colleagues would hardly have taken a male cadet seriously, so God alone knew how they'd react to a woman.

'How'd it go with Buddha?' Gräf asked.

'Superintendent Gennat regrets not being able to supply us with additional officers, but would like a CID employee to work undercover in the *Haus Vaterland* kitchen.'

Gräf was unimpressed. 'We're supposed to scrub vegetables now?'

'I wouldn't be averse, providing we get to keep the wage,' Lange said. 'With our salaries, we need all the help we can get.'

'It can't be any one of us,' Rath replied. 'Our faces are known there.'

'That leaves only Fräulein Ritter,' Lange said.

'Exactly who Gennat suggested!'

'Poor Charly!' Gräf couldn't conceal a grin. 'Finally gets a job with CID and still winds up in the kitchen.'

Rath found this less than amusing, since he was the one who had to break the news.

'At least she knows her way around the kitchen,' he heard Lange say. 'You wouldn't be able to use a man there. Unless you know anyone who can cook?'

'One more thing,' Rath said, in a tone that silenced the two jokers. 'Gennat thinks we might be dealing with a serial killer.'

The phrase could choke any light-heartedness at police headquarters.

'What?' Gräf said disbelievingly, but with a hint of cheer still in his face. 'You're not serious. Where else is our killer meant to have struck?'

'Somewhere out in the Ruhrgebiet.' Rath pointed to the journal he had placed on the table. 'Buddha came upon the case in the *Monatshefte*. I'm sceptical myself.'

'You're suggesting we ignore a tip from on high?'

'I'm suggesting we don't rush into anything. We're under express orders to investigate discreetly. First I'd like to read the article properly. We'll talk about it after lunch.'

Gräf nodded. 'My stomach's already rumbling. There's beef liver in the canteen today.'

'Count me in,' Lange said. 'How about you, Gereon?'

'Liver's not for me.' Rath stubbed out his cigarette. 'Ask Erika if she wants to join you. I'll get something from *Aschinger*.'

With his colleagues gone, Rath leafed through the journal to the article in question. *Mysterious drowning*, the headline ran, *sequence of events unexplained*. As was often the case in the *Monatshefte*, the article was written in matter-of-fact, almost bureaucratic German, no livelier than the language used in police statements, albeit underscored by a pseudo-academic, schoolmasterly tone. He remembered now why he read it so rarely.

The man from Dortmund gazed innocently from the page: Hans Wawerka, found dead in his bed on Easter morning.

The investigation left the reader in no doubt that the miner had suffered a violent end, even if questions persisted everywhere else. The pathological report had ruled death by drowning, although whether it was simply a near-drowning, as Gennat suspected, was of secondary importance. Of greater interest was the fact that the Dortmund pathologist had also discovered a puncture site, likewise in the jugular vein, but neglected to pursue the matter, or, at least, failed to perform a blood analysis. Gennat's suspicions regarding the competence of Prussian CID forces outside Berlin were clearly based on more than just arrogance. Could they establish the presence of tubocurarine in a three-month-old corpse? He would have to ask Dr Karthaus. Either way, it was time to dig the poor bastard up.

He looked at the article and again at the photo. Wawerka was dead, with water in his lungs and a puncture site on his neck, but everything else, as with Lamkau, was a mystery. There were no signs of a struggle or, indeed, of any suspects that were still alive. A Communist newspaper vendor, with whom the dead man had been in conflict, could be ruled out, since he had been killed the day before in an apparently politically motivated arson attack on his kiosk.

Hans Wawerka had just turned thirty-three, and lived alone in a small attic apartment in Dortmund-Bövinghausen. He was a miner at the Zollern Colliery, and a reclusive bachelor. Herbert Lamkau, on the other hand, was in his mid-forties, a successful businessman and father.

The photos gave even less away. Wawerka had the powerful physique of a worker, tall and muscular, whereas Lamkau was what some might call a 'weakling'. Only the determination in his eyes, staring out from his driving licence, testified to his strength. In contrast, Hans Wawerka gazed almost naively into the camera lens.

They were as different as chalk and cheese, and yet they had suffered the same fate, one in Dortmund, the other in Berlin. Were it not for the striking similarities between the pathological reports, Rath would never have suspected the two deaths were linked. The article in the *Monatshefte* concentrated primarily on the mysterious aspects of the case though, like their Berlin counterparts, the Dortmund officers had neither a lead nor a convincing explanation. Something else the cases shared.

By the time Rath had finished his last Overstolz, Charly still hadn't appeared, but he couldn't put it off any longer. Kirie desperately needed walking and, besides, he had to buy more cigarettes.

'Come on,' he said, reaching for hat and lead.

After a lap of Alexanderplatz, where the new tram tracks were being laid, he purchased a Bockwurst from a street hawker outside the train station. While Kirie ate or, rather, devoured the sausage, he turned his thoughts to Charly.

Disappearing for lunch wasn't a good look at the Castle, no one knew that better than Charly, who had always warned him against it. All the more strange, therefore, that she hadn't reappeared. Should he be worried? But, then, what could have happened? She'd probably just run in to Wilhelm Böhm, and the DCI had taken his one-time favourite stenographer out to lunch.

To his great surprise, everyone was back in the office when he returned half an hour later. Erika Voss was on the telephone, and Charly sat at her table studying a file as if nothing had happened. She seemed strangely pensive, almost absent, when she greeted him. If her coolness were merely an act, she was making a damn good fist of it. It was in marked contrast with Kirie, who, no sooner than she was untied, licked Charly's hands and curled up under her table.

When he rounded them up in his office, she still seemed a little remote. 'We missed you, Fräulein Ritter,' he said, sternly. 'Were you successful, at least?'

Charly looked as if she were about to start bawling. Surely she must know all this was just a front; a role that he, like her, was obliged to play.

'I was in Narcotics,' she said.

'Then Dettmann couldn't help?'

She made a gesture that might as well have been a shiver as a shake of the head, and stared right through him. Her list of known drug traffickers wasn't especially long, and two were in jail.

'Detective Gräf will look into it,' he said, passing the list on. 'A pretty dubious bunch. No kind of work for a woman.' He was afraid she might think he was being condescending, but she barely reacted. 'I have a different assignment for you,' he said. 'Superintendent Gennat would like us to carry out an undercover operation in *Haus Vaterland*.' He cleared his throat, thinking how much he'd like to wipe the smirk off Reinhold Gräf's face. 'In short: I'd like you to present yourself for work in the central kitchen tomorrow. There are a few vacancies. We might even be able to smuggle you in without the help of management – the fewer people who know about the operation, the better ...'

Against expectation, Charly's face brightened. Finally she seemed to be with them. 'Good idea,' she said. 'They'll never take me for a police officer.'

Rath leafed through the *Monatshefte* until he found Hans Wawerka's face. He showed it to the room and briefly recapped Gennat's theory for Charly's benefit.

'Isn't there usually a sexual dimension to serial killers' crimes?' she said. 'I don't see one here.'

She was on the ball again. He stubbed out his cigarette. 'Correct, Fräulein Ritter, but that doesn't mean we should rule out the possibility. There have been a number of serial killings that haven't been sexually motivated. I need only remind you of the cinema killer. Perhaps there's a link between Wawerka and Lamkau we're not seeing. We should continue to pursue all avenues. Given the mysterious circumstances, we should concentrate on the motive. That's still the quickest route to the perpetrator. Once we get them, they can explain the "how".'

Lange and Charly nodded, but Gräf looked as if he had been struck by lightning. When he finally moved, it was only for his mouth to form a question. 'What did you say the dead man was called?'

'Wawerka.' Rath checked the journal. 'Hans Wawerka.'

Gräf turned white as a sheet.

'What's the matter?'

Gräf didn't respond, but proceeded to his desk where he rummaged in one of the boxes he had seized from the Lamkau office. He returned to Rath's table with two envelopes. 'Here,' he said, fumbling for a yellowed death notice that someone must have cut from the newspaper. 'From Lamkau's private desk. It was among the other letters. Sorry it took me so long to twig.'

Rath looked at the thin paper and couldn't believe his eyes. A simple death notice, probably the cheapest available. No bible quotation, just a few words:

We mourn the loss of our faithful colleague

JOHANN WAWERKA

* 14th December 1898 Marggrabowa
† 27th March 1932 Dortmund-Bövinghausen
The staff of the Zollern II/IV Colliery

17

The new *Aschinger* was brighter than its predecessor in the former Königstadt Theatre, whose demolition could be observed through the large windows of Alexanderhaus. Despite the light, something of the old building's ambience had been retained. Most importantly, however, the menu – and the prices – were the same, meaning the Alexanderhaus branch was as busy as its previous incarnation, perhaps more so, for the new building attracted curious passers-by. It certainly took them long enough to find a table.

Rath was happy to be alone with her again after the chaos of the afternoon. The discovery that there was a link between Lamkau and the second victim had sent a rush through the group. Gräf was crestfallen that he hadn't thought of the death notice sooner, and wouldn't be consoled.

Rath had sent him to work through Charly's list of drug traffickers, before dispatching Lange to Edith Lamkau in Tempelhof, and requesting that the forensic technicians from I Division join him in his office. Lamkau's drawers had contained a second letter, with a further death notice, this one mourning the loss of a certain August Simoneit, who had died aged forty-seven on 11th May in Wittenberge – though not, it appeared, in violent circumstances.

He had asked Charly to investigate the circumstances surrounding the third man's death, though this proved trickier than anticipated. There had been no police inquiry, nor was Simoneit's name known to the local CID. It was a poor return, especially since Charly had appeared determined to prove how good she was, something neither Rath nor the others had ever doubted. The only person who had any doubts was Charly herself, and Rath couldn't help wondering if it went deeper than her inability to trace the source of tubocurarine.

The presence of Erika Voss made it impossible to clarify matters at the Castle, but he hoped it was some comfort for Charly to know that his own inquiries had also stalled. Herbert Lamkau hadn't received the first death notice from the Zollern Colliery, either from management or the works council, and Rath had failed to get hold of the investigating officer in the Wawerka case, reaching only his secretary. Lange, too, had returned from Tempelhof empty-handed. The widow Lamkau had known nothing about the death notices, and been equally flummoxed by the names Wawerka and August Simoneit.

Charly would just have to get used to the fact that most of what they did in CID was a waste of time.

At long last he had sent his team home, only to intercept Charly outside the train station and invite her to *Aschinger*. Somehow it felt more like he had ensnared her, as if, without his intervention, she'd have simply gone back to Spenerstrasse; as if, after a single day, she had completely forgotten about their engagement. On the way to *Aschinger* she had only wanted to discuss work.

Now they sat at the window, Kirie curled up under their table, gazing out at the ruins of the Königstadt Theatre, and the last, forlorn-looking, pieces of wall. A solitary washbasin stood roughly ten metres above the relieving arch. He was considering his opening gambit when Charly broke the silence. 'The question is why?' she said, and it wasn't clear if she were speaking to him, or to herself.

'Pardon me?'

130

'Why make such heavy weather of it?' She turned from the window. 'There must be some reason to first paralyse, then drown your victims. Or, at least, let them think they'll drown.'

Rath didn't want to talk about work.

'Perhaps he's trying to tell us something. Like with these death notices. It's a message.'

'A message for whom? The police?' Rath was shorter than he intended, but she didn't seem to notice.

'Then we'd have got them too. No.' She shook her head. 'It's a message for the victim, saying their time is up.'

Why was she pretending everything was fine? He couldn't take it any longer. 'What happened today?' he asked.

She looked surprised for a moment. 'What do you mean, "what happened?"' Her smile was so artificial it could have been glued on.

'You don't stop by the office after visiting Dettmann, you spend an age with Narcotics, and who knows what you're up to during lunch. And then, wham, you're back at your desk making a face like your goldfish has just died. It isn't normal.'

'Do you mind telling me what passes for normal at police headquarters? You, of all people?'

'I just want to know what happened. I was worried. You should have come back when you realised Dettmann couldn't help. I'd have been better off talking to Narcotics. Did they mock you, or make some stupid remark? Don't take it personally, they do the same with all new recruits.'

She was about to say something but stopped suddenly. When he saw her face, Rath started. There was something in her gaze that shook him to the core. Something numb, something dead. Her otherwise warm, brown eyes looked frozen. He knew his Charly. She only looked like that when she was losing her temper, or trying desperately to conceal her feelings, but there was no outburst, nothing.

131

She stared at the table as if trying to pull herself together.

'Sorry,' he said, as gently as he could. 'I didn't mean to sound harsh, I'm just worried. What's the matter?'

'Nothing,' she said, but her voice told a different story.

'Charly! Has something happened? Is it about how I was today?' She shook her head. 'All that bossing you around was just a front. You know that, don't you?' She nodded, still incapable of getting the words out. 'Tell me what's wrong. You're really scaring me here.'

She shook her head as if trying to jerk her face awake.

He took her by the hand, as if asking her to dance, only there was no dance floor or music. Even so, she stood up and he took her in his arms. 'What's the matter, girl?' he whispered in her ear. A silent sob heaved through her body. 'It's OK,' he said, stroking her head, and, when she wouldn't stop: 'It's OK, it's OK,' repeating it over and over like an incantation.

Finally the shaking stopped and she prised herself loose. She looked at him through mascara-smudged eyes before lowering her gaze and disappearing inside the ladies' toilet. When she returned to the table, tears dried and face newly made-up, she managed to tell him what had happened.

18

Hackhackhackhackhack.

Movements so quick they were almost impossible to follow, and with that the latest onion was chopped into tiny pieces.

'There, d'you see? Hold it like this, and Bob's your uncle. Keep the knife pointing down, bish bash bosh, and mind your fingers when you flip it back.'

The red-headed boy couldn't have been more than eighteen, but he chopped with such speed and precision he could have been in the circus. Charly had rarely felt so clumsy. She tried to hold the knife and onion the way he had shown her, and soon realised she was making progress, even if she was still a long way off his greased-lightning pace.

'There you are.' He had been assigned to her by the head chef, Unger. 'By the time you get through this lot, it'll feel like you've been doing it your whole life.'

This lot must have been a good fifty kilograms of onions, an absolute mountain at any rate. Charly had never seen so many in her life. The boy gave a wink of encouragement and left her to it.

She set about her task with a plucky grin. The tears started immediately, but she was loath to follow his advice – 'just keep your peepers closed' – for fear she'd be heading home bereft of her fingers. Besides, her eyes only burned more when she closed them. She decided to let the tears flow, and tried to work out what she was doing through the watery haze.

The interview with Unger was the highlight of her day so far, although he had spent the entire time ogling her legs. He had dictated a small sample text but had failed, so far, to actually use her shorthand skills.

'You can start immediately,' he had said, giving her a vexed look when she reached for her pad. 'No, no. It's kitchen work for the moment. I'll get someone to train you up.'

She had put her pad away and asked to make a telephone call, meeting Unger's furrowed brow with a friendly smile. 'My mother. She'll worry if I'm not home for lunch.'

Unger pushed the telephone across the desk. 'It'll cost you twenty pfennigs. To be deducted from your wage.' He left to fetch the apprentice.

She had been looking forward to a few words in private with Gereon, but got Erika Voss instead. The inspector was elsewhere. Moments later Unger returned with the redhead in tow.

Thinking back to last night: it had helped to finally tell someone, even if recounting the incident made her feel small and dirty again. Despite having nothing to reproach herself for, it had felt like a confession. As if Gereon had actually absolved her of sin. At once she felt her anger return, that same, helpless rage. For a moment he'd said nothing, just sat there looking at her, incensed.

'Why didn't you defend yourself? Give that arsehole a piece of your mind?'

'Gereon, it sounds as if you're blaming me. Haven't you ever been rendered speechless by someone's sheer *audacity*?'

'Sorry. You know I have.'

She had watched his eyes fill with anger and made him promise not to mention anything at the Castle, neither to Gennat nor anyone else.

In spite of everything, it had turned into an enjoyable evening. Somehow she had managed to laugh again, properly laugh through her dried tears. They had made themselves comfortable in Carmerstrasse, in the huge apartment she still wasn't convinced Gereon could actually afford, at least not with his salary payments alone. Perhaps his Uncle Joseph *had* left him something. The family had money, she had seen as much during her visit to Cologne the previous year.

They had drunk a little wine before retiring to the bedroom, where Gereon was so tender she almost burst out laughing. 'I'm not made of china,' she said, finally.

'Now wouldn't that be a thing,' he replied, before throwing caution to the wind. Soon, asleep in his arms, she was no longer thinking of Dettmann. That much, at least, Gereon had achieved.

She surveyed the mound of onions before her. It was as if a wicked magician had cast a spell not only on them, but on the large clock hanging above the office window, halting the passage of time. These onions would keep her busy the whole day, making it impossible to have a poke around, let alone discreetly. Unger's face appeared behind the glass wall-pane, casting disapproving glances whenever she paused for breath. At least her tears were abating, or perhaps she simply had no more to shed.

If all they had her do was chop onions, she would never work out what really went on here, either in public or behind closed doors. *Haus Vaterland* was a huge complex with hundreds of employees. The kitchen alone was bigger than most Berlin restaurants. She reached for the next onion. At least she was getting a little practice in. As for the rest ... perhaps she'd have to accept that she'd never make the perfect housewife, despite her mother's best efforts. Not that she wanted to be one anyway.

19

Rath could have handled Böhm's report being as dull as the technical summaries of ED Chief Werner Kronberg, but not the presence of Harald Dettmann in the row in front, wearing the sort of smirk he'd have happily wiped from the man's face. Dettmann usually skipped morning briefing, often on the flimsiest of pretexts, but today, of all days, he was present and grinning like a Cheshire cat. It was unbearable.

Rath had arrived at the station weary and several minutes late, and not just because Charly had spent the night. In point of fact, they had gone to bed relatively early, or at least *Charly* had. He, on the other hand, had spent the night watching her or staring at the ceiling, unable to get her story out of his head. She was right: she couldn't mention anything to Gennat or her direct superior, Wieking, since that would make things official. If, as he'd intimated he would, Dettmann denied both his outrageous behaviour and his even more outrageous remarks, then she would be pigeonholed as a resentful liar out to discredit male officers. And *that* would only serve to confirm existing preconceptions. Most Castle workers regarded female CID as superfluous, but deploying a woman in Homicide was nothing short of a catastrophe.

Now they were in the conference room, with Harald

Dettmann smiling cheerily in their midst. The bastard must have felt like a million dollars.

Rath had taken his seat scarcely able to follow Böhm's report, but twigging, nevertheless, that the detective chief inspector had as good as solved the shaving knife murder in Schlosspark Bellevue. At least the Bulldog was doing something to improve A Division's detection rate, in contrast to Inspector Gereon Rath, whose desk housed a growing number of unsolved cases. Perhaps now there was a chance that Henning and Czerwinski would be stood down from Böhm's command and assigned to the *Vaterland* team.

A twitch of Gennat's eyebrow told him he was up next. He walked to the front and summarised the latest findings in the *Vaterland* case.

'We have three starting points. First, the anaesthetic agent tubocurarine, whose source of supply we are hoping to isolate . . .' He glanced towards Dettmann, who looked as though it was the first he'd heard of it. 'Thanks to the help of Narcotics officers, we have managed to draw up a list containing the relevant addresses of known drug traffickers, which Officers Gräf and Lange are working through as we speak.' Dettmann displayed the same languid interest as everyone else in the room.

Rath realised he had paused for slightly too long, and continued. 'Second, is the prospect of irregular goings-on at *Haus Vaterland*, in which Lamkau, our victim, could be involved. This is backed up, among other things, by the thousand marks we found on his person. In order to gather more information here, a covert operation is underway as of this morning.'

He didn't give any further details.

'The third starting point for our investigation,' he continued, 'is something we discovered only yesterday afternoon. We were able to establish a link between the *Vaterland* case and a second, apparently identical, death in

Dortmund. The victims appear to be connected, although we cannot, at this moment, say how. We found the death notice of the Dortmund victim in Herbert Lamkau's possession, as well as that of another man, the circumstances of whose death remain a mystery.'

He finished his report and, for once, Gennat saw fit to praise the work of his team. He reclaimed his seat, assuming morning briefing was over, and that Buddha, as was customary, would close with a few words. Not on this occasion.

'Gentlemen,' the superintendent began, 'there is still no mention of it in the press but you'll know by midday at the latest. Shortly before midnight last night, there was a fatal incident outside the *Lichtburg* multiplex in Wedding. The victim was killed by a precision shot to the heart that took half his chest with it. Despite our immediate intervention, the killer has vanished without trace.'

Though Gennat named no names, everyone in the room knew what it meant. The Phantom had struck again.

Too late for the mornings, but the midday and evening editions would take great pleasure in breaking the news. The headlines would carry the name *Phantom* once more and refer to the fact that, despite more than six months of investigations, police still hadn't made an iota of progress. One or two articles would mention the name *Gereon Rath*, citing him as the officer who had been chasing the Phantom in vain all these months.

In the room, all was silent. With increased public scrutiny, everyone knew that the next few days would be tough, whatever case they were handling. As the officer in charge of the Phantom case, Rath was surprised they hadn't tried to make contact with him last night, though the reason soon became clear enough.

'The *Bellevue* case is now closed, save for the final report,' Gennat continued, 'meaning that Detectives Henning and

Czerwinski can rejoin the disbanded *Phantom* troop, which is hereby resurrected under new leadership.'

Most officers in the room were aware that Rath had been in charge, and turned to face him. He put on a brave face, as if he'd known all along.

'I have chosen to place the case in new hands,' Gennat explained. 'With Inspector Rath making great strides in the *Vaterland* case, it would seem churlish to dissolve his team at this moment in time.'

The superintendent gazed kindly towards him, but he felt as if he were being pilloried. Looking at the floor, he feigned boredom, and wondered who would be taking over. Wilhelm Böhm, most likely.

'Through happy coincidence,' he heard Gennat continue, 'we were fortunate yesterday that an experienced colleague found himself in the vicinity of the crime scene, enabling us to initiate search measures in and around the area with immediate effect. Two suspects were apprehended and are awaiting questioning. I intend, therefore, to pass the case onto the man whose courageous actions may finally have gained us an advantage in our fight against this unscrupulous killer. Please step forward, Inspector Dettmann, and outline the particulars of yesterday's incident.'

Rath thought he had misheard, but no, a few seats away, Harald Dettmann rose from his chair and strolled forward, a small file wedged under his arm.

He had to make every effort to stay seated, and the longer he listened to Dettmann recounting his heroic deeds with that unbearable strain of *faux* humility, the angrier he became.

The Phantom's latest victim was a drug dealer, a figure 'not unknown' to Dettmann due to his 'many years' of service in Narcotics. Dettmann provided this characterisation of the victim to stress that his was not a loss the world should mourn. The man had emerged with his girlfriend from the picture palace's late showing and been dropped by a single shot outside Gesundbrunnen Bahnhof. His girl had been unharmed, but the force of the shot had thrown the man to the floor and shredded his chest.

After Dettmann's report Gennat concluded the meeting, with Rath among the first to leave, preferring to take his anger to the sanctity of his office. Perhaps, he told himself, it was better to be rid of the accursed Phantom case, but the manner of it, and the fact that it was Dettmann who would reap what he and his team had sown, made it hard to take.

'No interruptions,' he barked at his secretary as he disappeared inside his room and slammed the door. No sooner had he sat down than Erika Voss poked her blonde head around the door. 'Didn't I make myself clear?'

Erika Voss refused to be intimidated. 'Why not take your anger out on this,' she said, handing him a file. 'Just in from Dortmund. Our colleagues there sent a car especially. With best wishes from Detective Chief Inspector Watzke. To Superintendent Gennat too.'

'Thank you,' he grumbled, accepting two thick lever arch files.

'There you are, you see!' Erika Voss said and smiled. 'By the way, Herr Watzke telephoned while you were at briefing.'

'And?'

'He'll try again at lunch. He has an appointment at court this morning. And Fräulein Ritter said to tell you she got the job. Stenographer-cum-kitchen maid, as you said.'

'Wonderful. Thank you, Erika. You're a gem.' He opened the first lever arch file. 'But I really did mean *no* interruptions.'

'So you don't want coffee then?'

He smiled for the first time since entering the Castle that morning. 'You win,' he said, 'but close the door on your way out.'

Smelling as though it had been freshly brewed, sometimes he thought his secretary made the best coffee in the whole of police headquarters. Either way she certainly knew how to make him happy. He lit a cigarette and took a sip before burying himself in his work.

After two hours he had gone through both files and made a whole raft of notes. He might not have unearthed any fresh insights, but experience told him the devil was in the detail. He took the Lamkau file from the shelf and placed it alongside the Dortmund papers on his desk. There were still two Overstolz in his cigarette case. He lit one and compared the dead men's personal details again.

Herbert Lamkau, born 1890 in Tilsit, married, two children, with a business registered in Tempelhof since 1925; no prior convictions and ...

...Hans Wawerka, born 1898 in Marggrabowa, a Zollern Colliery employee since 1924. Unlike Lamkau, Wawerka had been placed on police file two years before, following a politically motivated bar brawl that escalated. The incident had led Dortmund homicide detectives to their sole suspect, a Communist who had fallen victim to an arson attack and subsequently been eliminated from inquiries.

Erika Voss knocked on the door. 'Apologies, Inspector, two things. Herr Kronberg just called. The Forensics report is as good as finished.'

'At last. What was the second thing?'

'I'd like to take my break. If you don't need me.'

'Go, but it isn't that I don't need you.' He took out his wallet and gave her a two-mark coin. 'Can you do me a favour and look after Kirie? Buy her a few Bouletten from *Aschinger*. Treat yourself to a coffee while you're at it. I need a few more minutes for my own peace of mind.'

He lit his final cigarette and got to thinking. The two dead men were linked to one another, but how? Why had Herbert Lamkau been sent Hans Wawerka's death notice?

It wasn't clear from the files. Perhaps he had overlooked some connection between these two very different men? What on earth was it that bound them together? He took a long drag on his Overstolz, as if the truth were concealed somewhere inside the cigarette.

20

No amount of scrubbing could get rid of the onion smell from Charly's hands. Even her cigarette tasted of them, but at least she was on her break.

After what seemed like an eternity, her red-headed mentor had reappeared, cast a sceptical glance towards the still imposing mound of onions, and ordered her to lunch; she had a quarter of an hour. 'Then get back to it, and see if you can't up the tempo.' She almost threw in the towel.

With strictly no smoking in the kitchen, the longer she was made to wait for her break, the more feverish her anticipation became. Now she was standing on the fourth-floor balcony, with a cigarette that smelled of onions. Imagine having to do this your whole life . . .

There was no such thing as a joint break at *Haus Vaterland*. Lunch was the busiest time of day. Vast quantities of food went out, and, clearly, most of the recipes contained onions.

She stood on the south-eastern side of the building, and gazed at the sea of houses, in the middle of which the great hall of Anhalter Bahnhof appeared like a ship floating bottom up. Europahaus seemed almost within touching distance. The tower block was where she had spent her first evening with Gereon, more than three years ago. He had hurt her more than any other man but, even though she'd wished him to hell, they were together again after a year, and now they were engaged. She didn't know if he'd make a good husband, but she did know she didn't want anyone else.

Could a police marriage really work? There couldn't be many who had tried. They might even be the first.

Don't get ahead of yourself, Cadet! You aren't a police officer yet, and you've a job to do here first.

She looked at her watch. Only ten minutes left, and she still didn't know where to start. So far she hadn't observed a thing. Save for the fact that Unger had a permanent overview, and spent more time making calls and looking out of his poky little office than he did in the kitchen.

A door opened and a man stepped onto the balcony. His skin was as dark as the night; he wore a checked flannel shirt and red necktie, trousers with loose threads and a gun belt. On his head was a Stetson at least as big as Tom Mix's. A cigarette dangled from his mouth.

A black man dressed as a cowboy. Charly thought she had seen him in the *Haus Vaterland* programme on a previous occasion and wondered if there really were black cowboys in America. She hadn't seen any in the films.

Only after lighting his cigarette did he look up. He seemed surprised to see her, to see anyone here outside, and greeted her with a casual tip of his hat. Just like a real cowboy.

'Any objection to my joining you?' His German was slightly accented, but Charly couldn't place it. She raised her hand in a welcoming gesture and he joined her by the balustrade. 'I've never seen you here before,' he said.

'It's my first day.'

'What are you doing?'

She gave a lopsided grin. 'To tell the truth, I thought I was here as a stenographer, but so far all I've done is chop onions. Are you American?'

'No, German.' The cowboy grinned, showing his white teeth. 'From Dar es Salaam, German East Africa. I even fought for Kaiser and Fatherland.'

'You're an askari?'

'Husen's the name.' He proffered a hand. 'Bayume Mohamed Husen.'

'Charlotte Ritter.' Husen had a pleasantly firm handshake. 'How is it that an askari winds up playing a cowboy in Berlin?'

'You'd need longer than a cigarette break. Here's the abridged version: I'm in Berlin because I'm owed money.'

'By *Haus Vaterland*?'

Husen laughed. 'No, the other *Vaterland*.' He described a curve with his arms, as if taking the whole world in his embrace. 'Germany still owes me my pay.'

'That doesn't explain how you became a cowboy.'

'A man has to live. I wait tables in the *Turkish Café* or the *Wild West Bar*. The main thing is to be exotic. Aren't too many Negroes in Berlin.'

Charly stubbed out her Juno on the balustrade. 'Do you often come here to smoke?' she asked.

'If it isn't raining. I need to get out. It feels like a prison in there, despite all the landscape murals.'

'I know what you mean. If I have to spend another day chopping onions ...'

'You'll be fine. People get used to anything.' Husen stubbed out his cigarette too. A Turkish brand, she noted, not American. 'Why don't you come and see me in the *Wild West Bar* once you finish,' he said. 'I'll stand you a whisky ...'

'Do you have *Luisenbrand*?'

'It's hardly the classic western drink, but it shouldn't be a problem for Joe. The *Wild West Bar* has the best selection of liquor *Haus Vaterland* has to offer.'

'Joe?'

'Our barman. It's Johannes, actually. But then my name's not Husen either. It's Hussein.'

'We'll see,' Charly said. 'If I haven't turned into an onion myself by then.'

'Ma'am ...'

The way Mohamed Husen tipped his hat really did remind her of Tom Mix.

21

All was quiet as Rath stepped outside his office. Most colleagues had already left for lunch; only a uniform cop and two plain-clothes officers remained in the long Homicide corridor. He was about to close the door when he heard the clatter of a typewriter, loud as machine-gun fire in the midday silence. He guessed which office it was coming from. He looked inside. The outer office was empty; the clattering came from further back. In the main office he found Inspector Harald Dettmann sitting in front of a typewriter, removing a sheet from its drum. In the absence of his secretary he was obliged to operate the machine himself.

'If it isn't Inspector Rath,' he said, with eyebrows raised.

'Afternoon.'

Dettmann placed the sheet neatly on a pile of typewritten pages. Rath had forgotten that he wasn't just an arsehole, but a pedant to boot.

'What is it?' Dettmann asked, placing the stack of papers under a puncher. Rath made out a few sentences and concluded it was nothing to do with the Phantom. It looked like the full report on the Tiergarten case. Gennat had requested the report at briefing on Monday. The old excuse about a poorly secretary wasn't much cop now that

Detective Inspector Dettmann had been assigned the most high-profile case Gennat had to offer. There was a crack as the puncher went about its business. There must have been twenty sheets in the pile.

Rath planted himself in front of the desk. 'A real pain when your secretary's off sick, isn't it? You realise how much work they do.'

'Takes longer to write than type up.' Dettmann eyed him suspiciously. 'What do you want from me, Rath? Pining for your old case? I've already assembled my team, and it doesn't include you.'

'Did you manage to get anything out of the two suspects?'

'Why do you want to know?'

'No reason. I'd just be surprised if either of them's the Phantom.'

'Interrogations are ongoing.'

'So what are you doing here?'

'If you looked at your watch, you'd know that we're almost an hour into lunch break. Which I'm using to complete my Tiergarten report for Gennat and the public prosecutor.'

'Very commendable, I'm sure. So, it's true then?'

'What the hell do you want, Rath?'

'You know, sitting like that you *do* actually look like a typist. How many words a minute?'

Dettmann seemed to finally grasp what he was talking about. 'Has someone been telling tales?'

'That was what you asked, wasn't it? *Do I look like a bloody typist*? And I'd say: yes, you do.'

'So the dirty bitch actually squealed!' Dettmann shook his head. 'Don't believe everything you hear. These women get the wrong end of the stick. So, police talk can be a little rough. You've got to be able to take it if you want to mix with the big boys. If I were you I'd never have invited a

148

little minx like her onto my team in the first place, but you must ...'

'Shut your face,' Rath yelled, and Dettmann was so surprised that he did as bidden. 'You arsehole,' Rath said, leaning both arms on the desk. 'If you insult Cadet Ritter again; if you so much as even *look* at her sideways, there'll be trouble, do you understand?'

'It's like that, is it?' Dettmann looked Rath up and down. 'What is this? You're her guardian now, are you? What's the poor thing been saying?'

'You know exactly what I'm talking about. This isn't about specifics. It's about the principle. Not what bastards like you say about a female colleague, but that you don't transgress a second time. In thought, word or deed.'

'This is all getting a bit Catholic for me.'

'Have I made myself clear?'

Dettmann shook his head in disbelief. 'I can hardly believe what I'm witnessing here. Inspector Rath, the avenger of tramps and sluts!' Dettmann made an O with his mouth. 'Did she have to blow you for this? Or just look at you out of those doe-eyes?'

Rath was centimetres away from Dettmann's face. 'I'm warning you. Watch what you say!'

Almost imperceptibly Dettmann took a step back. 'You're *warning* me? Stop making a fool of yourself! What are you going to do? Should I be frightened?' He was grinning again. 'Ah yes, of course. How could I forget? Apparently you enjoy beating up colleagues.'

'Only the arseholes ...' Rath paused. 'Come to think of it, that might just put you in danger.'

'Very funny. You really want to risk another round of disciplinary proceedings? Go ahead, I won't put up a fight.' Dettmann gestured towards the point of his chin. 'Come on. What are you waiting for? But you'd better clear your desk straight after, because it'll mean the end of your career.'

Rath stepped back. 'You think I'm going to get my hands dirty on someone like you?'

'Well, well, it seems there's a first for everything.' Dettmann looked Rath up and down. 'I understand, you know. A girl like that might make me go weak too. Have you pulled her across the desk yet? I'm sure none of the boys round here would begrudge you it. Wouldn't say no myself, either. But all *I* got from Buddha were Henning and Czerwinski.'

While Dettmann was still speaking, Rath felt for the inkwell on his desk, fixing the bastard in the eye as he gradually emptied the contents over the pristine, freshly typed Tiergarten report. Only when the ink dripped from the edge of the desk and created an ugly pattern on his summer trousers did Dettmann realise what was happening. He sprang to his feet and stepped back so frantically that his chair tipped over and he stumbled backwards.

He stared at the mess in disbelief.

'Are you fucking mad?' There was no sign of his grin now.

'Oops,' said Rath, replacing the empty inkwell on the desk. 'How clumsy. I'm afraid those trousers are done for.'

Dettmann's attention turned to the ink-soaked pages, which he had most likely spent hours typing up. 'You piece of shit,' he said, pulling the report from the desk, which worsened the mess. 'It hasn't even been copied yet!'

'You'll just have to write it again. Take comfort from the old journalist's rule: you're always quicker second time around. I'd think that's true of police reports too.'

'I'll kill you, you bastard!'

Rath raised his hands. 'Then go ahead. I won't put up a fight.'

Dettmann stood, breathing heavily, holding the desecrated report and staring at Rath, who tipped the brim of his hat and made for the door. 'I almost forgot,' he said. 'I'd like to offer a formal apology for the trouble I've caused. I'm truly, truly sorry. I can be a real klutz sometimes.'

The inkwell came flying, but he had already closed the door. He couldn't remember the last time he'd gone on his break feeling this good.

22

He had done it: the book was in his possession. You just had to be patient and wait for the right opportunity.

For two days he had marked time but, now, at last, he had been rewarded.

He had been observing the wanted posters near the glass door, fingers already searching for the false key in his trouser pocket, when he saw the inspector disappear inside the next office without locking his door.

Talk about good fortune. It meant he could do away with the picklock, and avoid the risk of being caught fumbling with a police door.

Yesterday there had been a twenty-minute window during the lunch hour when no one else was around, but he knew that might not always be the case. Indeed, he wasn't alone now, but it was clear the two men standing close by had only agreed to meet here on their way to the canteen, and were soon gone.

So, calm as you like, he made for the door in question, taking one final look around before venturing inside. This time there was no barking dog; this time he could enter unopposed, and saw the cardboard boxes the two officers had seized from Lamkau's premises spread across the chairs and floor.

He didn't need long to find the book. A quick look inside told him he had the right one. With any luck, they wouldn't have deciphered its meaning yet. Cops were ignorant when it came to figures, the ones that worked in Homicide anyway.

Still in the outer office, he stowed the book in his waistband and, after making sure the coast was clear, emerged back into the corridor.

Now he just needed to reach the stairwell. He almost jumped out of his skin when he heard steps behind him and, turning his head slightly, saw Inspector Rath trailing in his wake, gaining on him the whole time. By the time he reached the stairwell door the inspector had caught up. But there was no firm grip on his neck, no 'What were you doing in my office?'

Instead, all he received was a friendly 'Afternoon', as the inspector overtook him on the half landing and continued cheerily down the stairs.

23

Rath was returning from his break when he heard Erika Voss say: 'That's him now.' She pressed her hand over the mouthpiece. 'Dortmund.'

He nodded, ruffled Kirie's fur, hung his hat on the hook and went through to his office. It was empty, meaning Lange and Gräf were still investigating the tubocurarine lead.

'One moment, please, I'll put you through,' Erika Voss said, and the telephone on his desk began to ring. He closed the door, fetched both the Wawerka and Lamkau files, and placed his notes alongside them on the desk. Only then did he pick up.

Detective Chief Inspector Watzke from Dortmund was helpful enough, but he couldn't say much that wasn't already in the Wawerka file.

'Was the man known for being violent?' Rath asked. 'As this business with the fight suggests.'

'It's the only incident we have on file. Truth be told it was no more than a harmless bar brawl which led Wawerka to my colleagues at Lütgendortmund. Otherwise the man's clean. We had a good look into his past, even asked our friends in Treuburg, but there too Hans Wawerka was considered a law-abiding citizen.'

'Why Treuburg?'

'His home town. It's where he lived and worked before moving to Westphalia to earn his keep.'

'Treuburg, you say?' Rath was confused. He leafed through the file. 'But . . .in the file it says . . .wait a moment . . .' At last he found the relevant information. 'It says he was born in Marggrabowa.'

'I assume you've no interest in East Prussia?'

'You must be joking. I wouldn't be seen dead there. I'm a Rhinelander.'

'Well, Marggrabowa and Treuburg are one and the same city.'

'A city with two names?'

'Marggrabowa changed its name four years ago. Its inhabitants wanted to pay homage to the fact that, during the 1920 plebiscite in Masuria, only two citizens voted for Poland. The rest remained loyal to Prussia and the Reich.'

'I must say, you know a hell of a lot about East Prussia.'

'My father hails from Königsberg. He didn't want to be seen dead there either, and eventually moved west.'

Watzke didn't sound too upset, but Rath sensed he had put his foot in it. 'No offence intended,' he said. 'I really don't have anything against East Prussia, it's just that I haven't had much to do with it until now. Let me get this straight. Today: Treuburg; before that: Marggrabowa.'

'You'll find it in Brockhaus. It's the capital of the Oletzko district.'

Watzke didn't stop there, but Rath was no longer listening. A word his Dortmund colleague had said echoed in his mind. He had stumbled across it recently, he didn't know where, but he knew it was something to grab at, a link, a piece of common ground, information that was contained in the files, information that he had already read. He thanked his colleague for the telephone call and hung up before rummaging through the two murder files on his desk, searching feverishly, leafing through each individual page, each individual document, scanning his memory bank.

At length he held Lamkau's driving licence in his hand,

and the feeling that he had a concrete lead became a certainty, even before his gaze or, rather, his mind alighted on precisely what it was that Watzke had said. It was three words printed on Lamkau's passport photo.

Oletzko District Authority.

His instincts had been correct. He had found it, goddamn it. The connection he had been seeking for days.

24

Edith Lamkau was amazed to see the police again so soon. 'I told your colleagues yesterday. I don't recognise these men, and I don't recognise these death notices.'

'Your husband seems to have known them,' Rath said. 'Or one of them, at least. Hans Wawerka.'

She shrugged. 'We weren't at his funeral.'

'Take another look at the photo.' He showed her the police photograph from the Dortmund file. 'Perhaps you saw Herr Wawerka somewhere. Perhaps he came to see your husband...'

The widow recoiled in disgust, as if the photo had halitosis. She gestured towards the numbered chalkboard Wawerka held in front of his chest. 'Is he a criminal? Why would someone like that come to see my husband?'

'Your husband's from East Prussia, isn't he?'

She nodded. 'A Tilsiter. He always joked about that. Tilsiter cheese, you know?' She smiled, but with the memory came the tears.

He waited until she had composed herself and finished dabbing her face with a lily-white handkerchief. 'And Marggrabowa?'

'Pardon me?'

'Does the name Marggrabowa mean anything to you?'

'You mean Treuburg?'

'It's where your husband learned to drive.'

'That's right. He lived there for a few years before moving to Berlin. Worked for the Mathée Korn distillery. Somewhere out near Luisenhöhe.'

'They're the ones that make *Luisenbrand*, aren't they? The label your company distributes.'

'*Bärenfang* too. It's an East Prussian specialty.'

'So, your husband still had links to his former employer?'

'We retained the sole distribution rights for Berlin and Brandenburg. It's a pretty lucrative business.'

'Might your husband's death change all that?'

'I hope not.' She gave him a look of reproach. 'Your colleagues seized all our company files from the last few years. I hope they're returned soon, so we can continue as before.'

'Who would take charge? You claim you don't have any idea.'

'I've advertised. I'm looking for a managing director. Besides which, Director Wengler has promised to help.'

'Director Wengler?'

'He owns the Luisenhöhe estate. As well as the distillery.'

Rath made a note of the name. 'Back to Marggrabowa, Frau Lamkau ...'

'You mean, Treuburg ...'

'Whatever. I suspect your husband knew Herr Wawerka from his time there. Are you sure he never mentioned the name to you? When he spoke about the old days for instance?'

'I've told you already. He never mentioned him.'

'Was Wawerka an old colleague, perhaps? From the distillery?'

'Inspector, I don't know. Can't the police find that sort of thing out for themselves?'

'Funnily enough, that's exactly what I'm trying to do.'

Edith Lamkau was taken aback by her own hostility, and adopted a more reasonable tone. 'What is it about this

158

Wawerka?' she asked. 'Why's it so important if Herbert knew him or not?'

'If I could tell you that, Frau Lamkau,' Rath said, 'it would be a major step forward.'

He left her blank-faced and goggle-eyed, and returned to the Castle. He had been hoping Edith Lamkau might remember something when confronted with the magic word 'Marggrabowa'. Well, too bad.

Before setting out for Tempelhof he had telephoned the police in Treuburg, with equally disappointing results. Wawerka had kept a low profile in his former home town, low enough not to appear anywhere on file. The same went for Herbert Lamkau, who had learned to drive in the same Masurian district capital where Hans Wawerka had spent his formative years. That didn't prove a thing, of course, but Rath would eat his hat if the two victims hadn't known each other.

Erika Voss had a whole stack of messages for him when he returned to the office. 'Superintendent Gennat wishes to speak with you urgently,' she said, looking at her notes. 'Then Detective Gräf telephoned about this drugs business, and Fräulein Ritter has also been in touch.'

'Cadet Ritter,' Rath corrected, as he hung up his hat.

Erika Voss made as if she hadn't heard, blowing strands of blonde hair from her eyes. 'Oh,' she continued. 'ED want you to call them back. I didn't note that one down. They only telephoned just now.'

'Well, you can't say I'm not in demand. What did Fräulein Ritter want?'

'*Cadet* Ritter would like to meet in order to submit her report. She can't telephone too often, she said, otherwise people will start taking notice.'

'She shouldn't be telephoning so often anyway. Tell her that next time. I'll call her tonight at home. What about Detective Gräf?'

159

'No luck so far. He thinks he'll be through the list by tonight. Should he and Assistant Detective Lange return to the office after that?'

'Of course – unless they've requested holiday leave.'

He went through to his office and sat by the telephone. 'Could you put me through to ED,' he called through the door. 'After that I'll need the Mathée distillery in or just outside Treuburg, Masuria.'

Erika Voss did as bidden and moments later Rath had ED on the line. Kronberg took the call himself.

'Inspector, that was quick. I have something for you.'

'The written report on the evidence from *Haus Vaterland*?'

'With you early tomorrow morning. We've got a lot on right now, what with the Phantom . . .'

'That's fine.'

'No, it concerns the death notices you submitted yesterday,' the ED chief said, not without a hint of pride. 'We know which newspapers they're from.'

'Excellent. Fire away.'

'So . . .' Kronberg began, as ponderous as ever. Rath could picture him at the other end of the line donning his reading glasses and painstakingly unfolding a sheet of paper. 'The Simoneit death notice is from the *Volkszeitung für die Ost- und Westprignitz*, from 14th May this year. The paper is published in . . .'

'. . . let me guess: Wittenberge,' Rath said. He couldn't stand the ED chief's long-windedness. 'And no doubt the Wawerka death notice comes from a Dortmund paper.'

'Correct. *The* Dortmund paper, in fact. *Die Dortmunder Zeitung*. From 2nd April.'

He made a note.

'So,' he said. 'Many thanks.'

'The letters in which the death notices were contained, on the other hand,' Kronberg began, and Rath could tell by his voice that he had saved something special for last. 'Were both dispatched from Berlin.'

'Meaning the person who sent them lives here?'

'That's a possibility. The other possibility is that he wants us to *think* he lives there.'

'If he's that clever. Have you taken any fingerprints?'

'We found a few on the envelopes, but they're not clean. My men are still comparing; though I don't hold out much hope.'

'What about the prints from *Haus Vaterland*? Any luck there?'

'We've managed to account for most. They're either from staff or the deceased.'

'Which staff?'

'A good dozen. You'll find the names in the report.'

'It would be good if I could have it soon.'

'Listen, Inspector, we only got the sheets on Monday. Almost fifty of them. We're not miracle workers, you know.'

'It's just that we're under a little pressure here, Herr Kronberg. The killer could strike again at any time.'

No sooner had he hung up than Erika Voss poked her blonde head around the door. 'Do you have the number for the distillery?' he asked. She nodded. 'Then put me through, please.'

'Gladly, Inspector, but perhaps you should wait a little.'

'Why?'

'It's . . .while you were on the telephone . . .Superintendent Gennat has been in touch again.'

'And?'

'I think you'd better head over . . .'

He looked at her face and knew she was right.

25

There was no cake, which ought to have given Rath pause, but, aside from that, everything was as normal: he sat on the green sofa, Gennat in his armchair, and Trudchen Steiner poured the coffee.

Buddha seemed interested in the latest developments in the *Vaterland* case. 'Looks like the trail leads towards East Prussia?'

'You already know?'

'Lamkau is from East Prussia, which is where he gets his *Luisenbrand*; the dead man from Dortmund is an East Prussian, likewise our man in Wittenberge.'

'Him as well?'

Gennat pushed a thin file across the table. 'August Simoneit. Police registration documents from Wittenberge.'

'Requested by Fräulein Ritter,' Rath slipped in. 'They got here quick.'

'Official mail.' Gennat slapped the file cover with the palm of his hand. 'The man came to the Elbe in September 1924. From Marggrabowa.'

'You mean, Treuburg.'

'That's right. Treuburg. I see you've done your homework.'

Rath omitted to mention Detective Chief Inspector Watzke's help. 'Everything seems to point to Treuburg,' he said instead. 'According to his driving licence, Herr Lamkau lived there before moving to Berlin.'

'So, that's why you went back out to Tempelhof?'

'Yes, Sir. I wanted to question the widow on her husband's past. Lamkau and Wawerka must have known each other from Treuburg, and this Simoneit is clearly the third in the trio.'

'Let's hope there isn't a fourth.' Gennat stirred his coffee. 'We need to find out what connects these men. It could be our way to the motive.'

'I think so too, Sir.'

'If all three were in Treuburg less than ten years ago, that's where you should begin.'

'I've already spoken with our colleagues there. None of them have police records.'

'You're not seriously proposing to leave inquiries to that bunch of amateurs! The Treuburg Police!'

'I can hardly transfer my whole team to East Prussia! Fräulein Ritter is working undercover in *Haus Vaterland* at your behest, Sir. Meanwhile Lange and Gräf are still looking for this tubocurarine, which might prove just as important.'

'You don't have to decamp there en masse.'

'We're not exactly overcome with resources as it is.'

Gennat looked annoyed, but before he could say anything there was a knock, and Trudchen Steiner appeared in the doorway. 'The inspector is here now, Sir.'

'Tell him to come in.'

The superintendent didn't bother to say *which* inspector should come in, but the discussion on East Prussia and the make-up of the *Vaterland* team appeared to be over. It was soon clear why. In the door frame stood the figure of Harald Dettmann.

'Let's skip the introductions,' Gennat said. 'Please take a seat, Herr Dettmann.'

Dettmann did as bidden, and threw Rath a hostile glance. *Who's been squealing now, you arsehole*, Rath thought,

163

placing his cup back on its saucer. It made him feel more battle-ready.

'I asked Herr Dettmann here to submit his final report on the Tiergarten case,' Buddha began. His face gave no indication of what he was thinking. 'So that he can commit fully to the Phantom investigation.'

Gennat looked at Rath, but the inspector preferred to remain silent. By now he knew Buddha well enough to appreciate this must be serious. Even so the force of Gennat's ire took him by surprise.

'What were you thinking, rendering an important report – the work of two or three days, no less – illegible like that?'

'I didn't mean to.'

Dettmann sprang to his feet, scarlet with rage. 'You didn't mean to? Of all the brass neck!'

Rath remained calm. He knew Dettmann was already in the red. 'There was this inkwell. It was very precariously placed ... I'm truly sorry.'

'Herr Dettmann, please take a seat,' Gennat said. 'Let's discuss this like grown men.' He turned to Rath. 'What were you doing in Dettmann's office in the first place, Herr Rath?'

'The Phantom investigation,' Rath said calmly. 'My colleague here had taken on my old case, and I wanted to ...'

'That's a bare-faced lie!' Dettmann shouted. A look from Gennat was enough to make him see reason.

Rath was now ahead on points. 'I wanted,' he continued, 'to offer my support. But I'm afraid before I could do so ... well, you know the rest. Herr Dettmann was so incensed that I was barely able to get a word in.'

'What? The cheek of it! He's just manipulating the facts to suit his own agenda.'

'Inspector Dettmann! I must ask you to control yourself. You've already told me your side of the story, now let

Inspector Rath tell his.' Buddha turned to Rath again. 'Inspector, if things happened the way you say they did, then I must say I'm surprised you didn't offer to help clean up. After all, you were responsible for this *mishap*. You should have apologised.'

'I did, in fact, if memory serves,' Rath said. 'Even so, I chose to leave Herr Dettmann's office after he launched the inkwell at me.'

'Is this true?' Gennat asked.

'It's all lies. Inspector Rath had no intention of apologising, let alone helping me to clean up. Or ...' He gave Rath a fierce look. ' ...rewrite the report.'

Rath was unmoved. 'I've no objection to our enlisting Forensics, Sir. I'd be willing to bet there are still traces of ink on the door.'

'I think we'll leave Herr Kronberg out of this one,' Gennat said. 'Let's settle this among ourselves. Now, Herr Dettmann, did you throw the inkwell at Rath here?'

'Yes, but ...'

'Good,' Gennat said, and Dettmann fell silent. 'You've both had a chance to tell your stories. Now, I'd like you to shake hands and make peace. This is Homicide, not some kindergarten.' Neither inspector made any move to offer the other his hand. 'Do I make myself clear?'

Rath stood up, and at length Dettmann, too, laboured out of the worn upholstery. The men shook hands. Dettmann's eyes flashed with rage, but he said nothing. Rath withstood his furious gaze and offered a friendly smile.

'I'd like to apologise again for my clumsiness.'

Dettmann said nothing, but his handshake grew firmer, and became almost painful as he looked daggers at his rival. Suddenly, he let go, murmured a goodbye and left the office.

Rath was about to follow suit, when Gennat held him back. 'I haven't finished with you, Herr Rath. Take a seat!'

Gennat scrutinised him closely, stirring his coffee while

Dettmann left the outer office. 'I hope you don't expect me to believe that story.'

'Sir, it's the . . .'

'For God's sake, man, don't give me that rubbish!'

Rath gave a start as, for the second time that afternoon, the normally composed Gennat raised his voice. He couldn't remember Buddha ever shouting like this. 'You think I don't know when someone's playing me for a fool? There are plenty who've sat here who can lie a damn sight better than you. So, how about you stop telling tales!'

'I . . .'

'You gave Dettmann the official version, but now I'd like to know what really happened.'

'I'm sorry, Sir.' For once, Rath was contrite. 'You're right. I did it intentionally.'

'All because I took the case away from you and gave it to Dettmann? I have my reasons, believe me.' Gennat shook his head. 'I just hope your next act of revenge isn't to set my office on fire. Or indeed the whole building.'

'The Phantom wasn't the reason.'

'Then what *was* it? If there can ever be a reason for doing something like that!'

'I'm afraid I can't speak about it.'

'Well, you better had, otherwise things could get pretty nasty around here.'

'With respect, Sir, things can get as nasty as you like, but discretion demands that I remain silent. All I'll say is that it has to do with Dettmann's behaviour towards a female colleague.'

'There aren't too many ladies in our Division, and Fräulein Ritter is more than capable of looking after herself without you playing her knight in shining armour. This *is* about Charly, isn't it?'

'I don't want to speak about it.'

'My dear Rath, this is fatally reminiscent of another

episode. When our old friend Herr Brenner wound up in hospital...'

'Those were false certificates. Brenner was never in hospital.'

'Be that as it may, but when you beat him up, and survived the subsequent disciplinary proceedings with no more than a slap on the wrist...that was about a female colleague, too, wasn't it?' Rath fell silent. 'Inspector, your private life has nothing to do with me. Except when it impinges upon your performance at work.'

'I...I wa...I wanted to make it public. But at the same time, I didn't want this colleague to suffer any consequences.' He gazed uncertainly in Gennat's direction, but Buddha appeared to have regained his equilibrium. 'I...' Rath cleared his throat. 'Fräulein Ritter and I have been...engaged...for two days now.'

Gennat actually seemed to be smiling. His face gave nothing away, but his eyes were laughing. He stretched out his oversized paws. 'Well, then, congratulations,' he said. 'My compliments, Inspector.'

'Thank you, Sir.' Rath shook the chief's hand, surprised at how easy it had been. The only person he felt guilty about was Charly. They had intended to wait...

'Then Herr Dettmann besmirched the honour of your bride-to-be. In what way?'

'With respect, Sir, if Fräulein Ritter hasn't discussed the matter with you, I'd prefer to respect her confidence. I've already said too much.'

'All right, all right. I won't insist further. Did anyone witness the incident in Dettmann's office?'

'It was just us, Sir.'

Gennat nodded. 'With any luck, you'll be able to bypass disciplinary proceedings. Perhaps it really was your *clumsiness* that made a mess of the report.'

The hint of a smile flickered across Rath's face, but he

managed to suppress it, in favour of time-honoured grateful humility. 'Thank you, Sir.'

'I wouldn't be too hasty. Dettmann isn't your only problem. The powers-that-be take a dim view of privately involved colleagues operating as part of the same department.'

'I'd like to stress again how important it is that Fräulein Ritter doesn't suffer any professional disadvantage. I know how much she enjoys working in Homicide, and I ...'

'Don't worry about Fräulein Ritter. She won't suffer any consequences on your behalf. Heaven forbid. No, Charly will continue to work on the *Vaterland* case until it's resolved. I'm glad that G Division has placed her at our disposal.' Gennat shook his head. 'In fact, I have a different solution in mind. One that might help defuse the tension with Inspector Dettmann.'

26

No matter how hard she scrubbed she couldn't get rid of the accursed onion smell. Every bone in her body ached and her eyes were puffy and swollen. My God, what a sight she was!

She couldn't go to Carmerstrasse looking like this, not with her onion hands, and her hair and clothes still reeking of dripping. *You've got a lot to learn, Charlotte Ritter*, she thought, *if you're serious about this marriage business. You have to be able to let your husband see you like this.*

But then was she – serious about this marriage business?

Despite saying 'yes' to his proposal, she still wasn't sure. She didn't see how it could fit with the life she envisioned. The truth was, she wasn't entirely clear what kind of life that was, only that she wanted to do things differently from her mother, who had stayed at home and been unhappy. She knew that much – and that she wanted to work. As well as having children, and a home. The trouble was, no one could tell her how to go about it.

There was a knock on the door.

'Will you be out soon? I need to use the bathroom *too*.'

'Be done in a few hours . . .'

The door opened, and Greta poked her head inside. 'What's the matter, my little kitchen fairy? Have you turned into a pumpkin?' Charly held out her dripping wet hands. Greta sniffed and pulled a face. 'Have you tried toothpaste?' she asked.

'Bad breath isn't the problem.'

'No, seriously. Give 'em here.' Greta took Charly's hands, squeezed Chlorodont on them, and rubbed her palms together. 'Ancient remedy – you'd know if you'd ever chopped onions here.'

Charly rinsed the toothpaste sludge with tap water. Her hands now smelled of mint, but no longer of onion. She gazed in the mirror; her eyes were starting to look normal again too.

She wondered if Gereon would even be home. She had tried the office again in the afternoon, but only reached his secretary, with whom, of course, she couldn't leave a message. From everything Erika Voss had said, it sounded as if he were out pursuing a fresh lead, but Charly couldn't be sure. Perhaps that was the point.

Despite itching to leave work, she had accepted the black waiter's invitation and called into the *Wild West Bar* on her way home. Mohamed Husen, the African cowboy, was delighted, and stood her a *Luisenbrand*.

'That's the stuff,' she said, placing a hand over her glass when he made to top her up. 'Doesn't taste very American, mind.'

'If this really were America, there wouldn't be any bourbon either. In fact there wouldn't be any alcohol at all. It's illegal over there.' Husen gestured discreetly towards a band of unruly drinkers. 'That's why the Yanks love it here so much. They drink anything, Korn, vodka, brandy. The main thing's the alcohol content. If you ask me, Prohibition's only made people want to drink more.'

'I'm surprised you have any time for me.'

'I'm taking my cigarette break inside.' He took out his cigarette case and offered one to Charly, who accepted.

Mohamed Husen seemed pretty well informed, having been at *Haus Vaterland* two years now. He even knew there had been issues with the *Luisenbrand*. The Yanks in the *Wild West Bar* hadn't noticed, but Riedel, the spirits buyer, who often took a glass here, had discreetly raised the alarm, upon which the waiters had proceeded to gather up all offending bottles. Three of the seven in the *Wild West Bar* alone were tainted. All in all, around two dozen held cheap hooch instead of high-end schnapps.

The patrons in the *Wild West Bar* kept looking furtively in their direction. At first Charly thought that she was imagining it, and ascribed the feeling to the paranoia that affected agents during a covert operation. But she wasn't imagining anything, the explanation was sitting next to her at the bar. She couldn't be sure if it was Husen's exotic appearance or his cowboy outfit, or the simple fact that a German girl was sharing a table with a black.

Mohamed Husen didn't turn a hair. He was probably used to it, Charly thought, examining her tired face in the mirror and fixing her lipstick. Either way, if they spoke again they'd have to go somewhere else. They were simply too conspicuous in the *Wild West Bar*. If the waiters here started gossiping, the rumours would soon reach the central kitchen, and Charly would be out of a job.

Sitting, at last, in a taxi to Gereon's flat in Charlottenburg, she considered what she could actually tell him about *Haus Vaterland*. That she had met a black man in the *Wild West Bar* and attracted the attention of everyone inside? No, it would be enough to tell him about the tainted *Luisenbrand*. She asked the driver to stop in Carmerstrasse and paid as she got out. She gazed down the street towards Steinplatz, and looked at the house fronts. It still didn't feel like home, but she was looking forward to seeing Gereon and Kirie and spending the evening together.

The porter greeted her casually as she passed his lodge, and the lift boy brought her to the third floor without having to be asked. Perhaps it did feel a little like home after all and, after a day like today, there was nothing she needed more than the feeling of coming home.

171

She rang the bell, inspecting her fingernails as she waited and realising that, although she had rubbed her hands with toothpaste, she had completely forgotten to brush her teeth. She would almost certainly still smell of alcohol. Damn it! There was a crash, and then she heard his steps. The door opened. Gereon was in hat and coat, and Kirie seemed to be elsewhere, otherwise she'd have greeted Charly long ago.

'You just got home too?' she asked.

He shook his head. 'On the contrary.'

She didn't understand what he meant until she registered a large suitcase in the hallway. 'What's going on?' she asked, trying to locate a smile. 'Engaged two days, and you're leaving me already?'

'Something like that.' He forced a smile. 'I'm afraid I have a confession to make . . .'

27

The scissors are sharp; they need only touch the newsprint and it falls to pieces. Carefully, you cut around the double black border. It should remain intact, you don't want to destroy it.

O Death where is thy sting? O Hell where is thy victory?

You wonder whether it was the widow who chose Corinthians or the funeral parlour. But what does it matter?

For as much as it has pleased Almighty God in his unfathomable wisdom to take unto Himself my beloved husband, suddenly and unexpectedly departed from his busy life.

Such a death notice reaches many people, but still only those who read the newspaper in which it appears. You, on the other hand, ensure that the right people set eyes on it; people the widow doesn't know, of whose existence she can barely even conceive.

Herbert Lamkau
* 5th January 1890
† 2nd July 1932

It appeared in the *Kreuz-Zeitung*. A Prussian like Lamkau, you ought to have guessed. The man in the kiosk was about to complain at your leafing through so many newspapers one after the other for the third day in a row, but bit his tongue when you produced your wallet, and looked at you strangely as you straightaway purchased two copies. Still, he said nothing. That is the wonderful thing about Berlin. No one is surprised by anything.

You still have one more task to take care of in this city, and then, finally, you will be able to take the long road back. Back into the past.

To the day when your old life ends.

There is nothing you can do. You relive it over and over again. It was a beautiful day, that much you still remember, until the moment it was destroyed and the world shattered like thin glass.

A glorious Sunday morning, the city decked out in bunting and flags. But the peaceful surface is deceptive; underneath is hatred. You meet the hostile glances they cast in your direction with a smile. You smile because you believe in the future; you don't know that your life is already at an end – the moment you step out into the street and blink in the sunlight.

PART II

Masuria

7th to 13th July 1932

If you ask what people are like here, I have to say: like everywhere! The human race is a monotonous affair. Most people spend the greatest part of their time working in order to live, and what little freedom remains so fills them with fear that they seek out any and every means to be rid of it.

Johann Wolfgang Goethe,
THE SORROWS OF YOUNG WERTHER

28

The engines roared in Rath's ear, an infernal noise, but it took an age before the plane started moving. Suddenly, he felt a jolt and soon they were gathering speed. Instinctively he gripped the rests with his hands, until a glance outside told him they were being taxied across the strip.

Charly had told him that flying was different from a tower or scaffolding: he wouldn't have any problems with his vertigo. Statistically speaking, aeroplanes were actually safer than trains and motorcars. That was all very well, but right now he was scared, *scared*, goddamn it – and they weren't even airborne!

Her reassurances had proved in vain as they waited alongside twelve others, mainly businessmen, for the Königsberg night flight to be called. 'Perhaps you'll see an elk,' she said, as if his trip to Masuria was some kind of holiday.

He wasn't sure if she was being comforting or sarcastic but, whatever, she wasn't in the best of moods. On the journey to Tempelhof they had barely exchanged a word, and what little they had said had been ill-tempered. No doubt she had pictured their first week of engagement differently. She certainly couldn't have imagined one of them would be leaving so soon.

The journey passed in silence until they reached the Yorck Bridge and he came clean about Dettmann. What choice did he have? Sooner or later, it would have got out, and, besides, now that they were engaged, he had resolved to be more honest. With Charly, at least.

'You have to learn to control yourself,' she said.

'Maybe, but the arsehole still deserved it.'

Then he saw that, despite her best efforts to look stern, she was stifling a grin, and he knew once and for all that he'd done the right thing. A few days in exile seemed a fair price and Gennat was right, someone had to make the journey east, so why not him? After all, it was his investigation. Perhaps the flying was part of his punishment. Buddha had certainly been keen to scotch any notion that he might drive there himself.

'Have you any idea how long that will take? You need a transit visa to pass through the Corridor, and the Poles won't exactly welcome you with open arms, especially not when they see you're a police officer.'

'Don't we have an agreement with the Polish Police?'

'You'll be dealing with customs officials, not police officers.'

Buddha had refused to budge, Rath's ticket was already on the desk, and all other arrangements had been made. Gennat handed him the travel documents. 'You're expected first thing tomorrow morning at police headquarters in Königsberg. Report to Superintendent Grunert; he'll assign you a vehicle.' First thing tomorrow. Suddenly Rath realised how keen they were to be rid of him. 'You're not due at the airport for another six hours. See that you pack something warm. Masuria can be very cold, even in summer.'

Before he could head home to follow Gennat's advice, Rath visited Deputy Commissioner Weiss for a letter of introduction that called upon all officers of the Prussian Police and Gendarmerie to provide Detective Inspector Gereon Rath of Berlin with any assistance he might require. While Rath skimmed the text, Weiss took the opportunity to launch into one of his political sermons. 'I want you to appreciate the significance of your presence there as a Prussian officer.'

'Yes, Sir.'

'Do you know why the Brüning government stepped aside?'

'I'm afraid I'm not interested in politics, Sir.'

'Well, you should be, Herr Rath. You should be! Everything we do is political, whether we like it or not.'

'With respect, Sir, I see things differently. My job is to fight crime.'

'Things are delicate in the East. The farmers are having trouble with the landowners and many have left the country. The Brüning administration has been a disaster. In April, the Masurians hailed this Hitler – a man who has only just finagled himself German citizenship – as if he were the saviour of East Prussia, and already the Nazis are talking of a "Masurian awakening". You know how they glorify everything and exploit it for their own propaganda.'

'What are you trying to say, Sir? That they're all Nazis in East Prussia? Should I invest in a swastika brassard as camouflage?'

'The opposite. I want your presence in East Prussia, and in Masuria especially, to be an advertisement for Prussian democracy ...'

'Not German democracy?'

'You are welcome to try, of course, but I fear there is no longer such a thing. The Reich might still be a Republic in name, but in reality it is simply biding its time until the Kaiser can be re-installed – or a military dictatorship proclaimed. Ever since Hindenburg appointed that schemer, von Papen, as chancellor.'

At some point Rath switched off. He had no interest in all this political bickering. Like Weiss, he was no fan of the self-proclaimed Führer and his SA thugs, but then so what? You didn't have to vote for him. He caught himself

179

wondering when he had last visited the polls. At the presidential elections he had stayed at home. Hindenburg, Hitler or Thälmann – what sort of choice was that?

He gazed out of the window. In the headlights he could make out the grass of Tempelhofer Feld. It was only hours since Weiss had sent him on his way, and now he was clattering across the airstrip. They had told him a Junkers G31 was a highly reliable craft. Luft Hansa had been flying to Königsberg for six years, but it was a mystery how this droning, rattling, old crate would get off the ground, let alone stay airborne. It felt as if it might disintegrate at any moment. His forehead was slick with sweat.

He unfolded Weiss's letter, but his concentration failed and he soon gave up. A glance out of the window told him they were still on the runway.

His neighbour on the other side of the aisle appeared more at ease, burying his head in a paper as though on a train. Rath gazed at the article and tried to take his mind off things. *Polizei überlastet. Die Folgen von Demonstrationsfreiheit. Right to demonstrate leaves police feeling the strain.* The topic should have interested him, but the words blurred before his eyes. He was still thinking about all the strange noises the plane was making.

By now they seemed to be accelerating. He was jolted back in his seat, and, all of a sudden, realised they must have taken off, despite not being able to see anything for the darkness outside. Somewhere beyond there appeared a blaze of lights, and he recognised the brightly lit colossus that was Karstadt on Hermannplatz, and the network of streets: a spider's web of light that took his breath away. They were flying, they were actually flying! The question was, for how long.

The paper on the other side of the aisle rustled gently and Rath stared into the red-cheeked face of a portly man in his mid-forties. 'Your first time?' the man asked.

'Hm?'

'You realise you don't *have* to hold onto the armrests. You're not going to fall out of the plane.' The man laughed, but he wasn't being spiteful.

Rath looked down at his hands on the armrests. His knuckles had gone white. 'You're right,' he said. 'Trains are fine; and I've even done the odd transatlantic crossing. But I don't like this at all.'

'Never mind, you can rest easy. As long as you have your parachute, you're safe.'

'My parachute?'

'You mean you don't have one?' The man made a horrified face.

'No!'

'Well, then ...' The man burst out laughing. 'Just a little joke. No harm meant.'

Rath tried to smile. 'What business do you have in Königsberg?'

'Wood.' The man leaned across and stretched out a hand. 'Hillbrich, furniture manufacturer. Yourself? What brings you East?'

'Crime.' He shook Hillbrich's hand. 'Rath, CID.'

'Police? I can sleep easy, knowing my pocket watch is safe.'

Rath forced another smile as, somehow, the monotonous drone of the engine calmed him. He looked out of the window, realising he felt no vertigo. All he could see were a few scattered lights like stars on the ground. He had no idea where they were.

'What do you think?' he asked. 'Will we land on time?'

Hillbrich looked at his watch and shrugged. 'I think so,' he said. 'As long as those dirty Polacks don't gun us down.' There was a moment's pause before Hillbrich clapped him on the shoulder. 'Just joking, old boy. I've flown to Königsberg hundreds of times, Danzig too, without any problems. You're better off flying than passing through that accursed Corridor, where the Poles treat you like a criminal.'

This was going to be fun. Rath resolved not to smile for the remainder of the flight.

Shortly afterwards, the steward prepared the sleeping cabins. He wasn't convinced he'd get any sleep, but accepted the offer, if only to avoid having to listen to any more jokes. The gentle rocking, which had filled him with dread moments before, now achieved the opposite effect. He closed his eyes, thinking of Charly, and soon his thoughts turned to dreams.

29

She stared at the ceiling, unable to sleep. Goddamn it!

She was in her own bed at Spenerstrasse, even though Gereon had left her both the Buick and the key to his flat. Still, the last thing she had wanted was to stroll past that same porter again, who stood guarding the stairwell in Carmerstrasse like some kind of Cerberus!

God knows, she had pictured tonight differently. How had it ended like this? A consoling arm would have been nice, a degree of sympathy, perhaps even a little pampering after the day she'd had. Even now she still saw onions, nothing but onions, as soon as she closed her eyes. She'd probably dream of them too, assuming she fell asleep at all.

She'd wanted to tell him about her mission on the German onion front, about how she had spoken to someone with information about the *Luisenbrand* scandal, but Gereon hadn't been the slightest bit interested in her day. Instead, everything had revolved around him: his encounter with Dettmann and his punishment as a result. When he casually mentioned that he'd confessed to their engagement, she could have slapped him. Given, however, that they were racing up the Tempelhofer Berg on Belle-Alliance-Strasse, she decided not to risk it.

'You did *what*?'

'Charly, please! There was no other way. Buddha cornered me. I'm sorry.'

'We had an agreement!'

'He congratulated us. You don't stand to lose anything. I'm the one he's sending to East Prussia.'

'You think I'm happy about my fiancé being dispatched to the middle of nowhere? You didn't even leave me the dog!'

'You have to work tomorrow. Erika will look after her.'

'Does *she* know we're engaged?'

'Of course not.' He looked at her with his puppy-dog eyes. 'Come on, Charly. At some stage everyone's going to know. That's the point of getting married. So the whole world can see we're together.'

'Is that right?'

'Yes, that's right!'

After that they'd reverted to silence.

By the time they pushed the luggage trolley towards check-in, her anger had abated. Thinking about what Gereon had done to Dettmann, she took a kind of mischievous pleasure in the image. For once he had done the right thing, damn it, no matter how stupid it might have been. Well, sometimes doing the right thing *was* stupid. Perhaps, on some level, he had accepted his banishment for her sake, and that was deeply flattering – more so than she cared to admit. She despised male posturing, but even so it was wonderful knowing he had defended her, perhaps even avenged her a little.

Did Gennat really hope to gain anything by this East Prussian operation? Perhaps it was more important that Gereon be removed from the line of fire; that way there was no risk of Inspectors Rath and Dettmann duelling at first light.

Things could certainly have turned out worse. Another disciplinary hearing and Gereon Rath could kiss goodbye to his police career, just when he was on the verge of marrying and starting a family. Now that *would* be stupid, even though she had a career these days too. She looked up at the ceiling and smiled at the idea of her returning home, exhausted from work, to find her husband in an apron and brandishing a wooden spoon. What a crazy idea! Not to say unrealistic: Gereon's culinary skills were even more questionable than her own – and that was saying something.

As far as the cooking went, they'd both have been better off finding a new partner ...

She heard the apartment door opening and Greta giggling quietly. She seemed to have brought her latest crush home, a lodger with a strict landlady who didn't allow female visitors. It wasn't the first time he had stayed over. Would the two of them make it? Would Greta even want them to? She was a permissive sort, so permissive it was sometimes frightening. Charly still hadn't told her friend that she was engaged. She knew that she wouldn't be in favour, either of Gereon, whom she'd always given the cold shoulder, or, indeed, the concept of engagement itself.

Still, at some point, she'd have to confess. Admit that she couldn't stay much longer in Spenerstrasse. Even now, just thinking about it, she felt the wrench of separation. She and Greta had lived here more than four years, with a couple of breaks, and for the most part it had been good. Why did life have to be so complicated?

She closed her eyes, picturing a mound of onions, only this time she fell asleep.

30

Königsberg Police Headquarters bore no comparison with its Berlin counterpart, feeling almost homely in style. If anything, the modern train station on the other side of the road was more monolithic. Despite the strong Luft Hansa coffee, Rath felt tired as he climbed out of the taxi and heaved his case up the stairs.

They had landed at Devau Airport in Königsberg half an hour earlier, but he had been awake since the stopover at Danzig two hours before. Taking off for a second time, he had gazed upon Danzig centre and the mighty Marienkirche, even winding down the window to locate the Crane Gate among the toy houses, and let in a little fresh air. He could get used to this flying business.

At headquarters, he soon found his way to the relevant office. Behind the desk sat a fat, excessively jovial man with thin glasses and thinning hair. The superintendent had clearly been expecting him, for no sooner had he entered than a secretary placed a tray of fresh coffee on the table.

'Welcome to Königsberg,' he said, stretching out a hand. 'Grunert, Superintendent Wilhelm Grunert.'

'Gereon Rath. Detective Inspector.'

'Yes, yes, I know. They announced you at reception.' Grunert gestured towards the visitor's chair, and Rath sat down.

'So, you're off to Treuburg, Superintendent Gennat tells me . . .' Grunert poured coffee.

'Yes, Sir. We have a lead in a homicide case.'

Rath took a sip: a clear dip in quality compared with the plane, but police coffee was supposed to wake you up, not taste good.

'You're looking for the killer here?'

'His victims.' Rath lit a cigarette. 'Three men from East Prussia; the killer is most likely in Berlin.'

'Then let's hope you catch him soon. A serial killer?'

'Seems that way.'

'One who has it in for East Prussians?'

'Former East Prussians. Treuburgers, who'd been living in West or Central Germany for years.' Rath smiled. 'Nothing to fear so long as you stay in East Prussia.'

Grunert's secretary must have smelled the cigarette smoke, and entered with an ashtray for Rath.

'Very well,' Grunert said, rubbing his hands. 'Then let's get you on your way. If you set off now, you should be in Treuburg by midday. I've taken the liberty of letting the local police know. I thought you could discuss the matter over lunch.'

Rath felt uneasy. How many people knew he was here? All he needed now was a red carpet and brass band. 'Many thanks, Superintendent.'

'We've arranged a car for your onward journey.'

'Then I'll just need a decent map. I'm afraid I don't know my way around here.'

'No need. I've something better.' The superintendent picked up the receiver and pushed a white button under the dial. 'Fräulein Sieger,' he bellowed into the mouthpiece. 'Please send Kowalski in.'

Moments later a gaunt young man with straggly blonde hair entered. There was something odd about his appearance. It took Rath a moment to realise there were still bits of toilet tissue clinging to his face and neck from his morning shave.

'Where culture ends, there Masuria begins,' Grunert declared and laughed. The youth remained impassive. 'Assistant Detective Kowalski here is a local, and will serve as your companion.'

This was all he needed! He'd been looking forward to a solo journey through the expanses of East Prussia, but now they'd assigned him a chaperone. Rath took his place next to the dour Kowalski on the narrow front seat of a pitch-black Wanderer W10 which had seen better days. From 1926, he estimated, which made it significantly older than the vehicles belonging to the Berlin motor pool. He'd never have thought he'd find himself longing for a green Opel.

As Assistant Detective Kowalski steered through the dawning city, past the castle and over several bridges, he wondered if it had been Buddha who'd requested his presence, or perhaps Superintendent Grunert. Either way, he wasn't sure whether the man was there to provide assistance or surveillance, but at least he was a local.

He lit a cigarette and debated whether he should draw Kowalski's attention to the lingering evidence of his morning shave but decided against. By now most of the tissue had fallen away, save for an isolated wisp that clung stubbornly to the young man's chin. He blew cigarette smoke through his nose so that Kowalski couldn't hear him sigh and gazed in the opposite direction. They passed a low city gate and a park, allotments and suburban houses as the city began to fray into the countryside.

He was prepared to endure his driver's silence up to a point, but as the cigarettes and kilometres mounted his patience began to wear. An hour after they'd set off from Stresemannstrasse neither of them had said a word, which was more than any self-respecting Rhinelander could bear.

'I've worked with East Prussians before,' he began, after clearing his throat. Kowalski nodded silently while overtaking a horse and cart that sagged under its load. Rath lit his next cigarette and fell silent. It occurred to him that Stephan Jänicke was dead and Helmut Grabowski in prison, making his two East Prussian colleagues unlikely conversation starters. He gazed out of the window onto a sleepy avenue that meandered through the countryside past a still lake surrounded by woodland and wheat fields. 'It's pretty here,' he said. 'The region, I mean.' Again Kowalski nodded. 'So, you're from Treuburg?' Another nod. 'Is it as pretty as here?'

'Prettier.'

Rath didn't know if he could chalk Kowalski's response up as a success, but at least the man had said something. He stubbed out his cigarette. They passed through a little town. *Wehlau, Reg. Bez. Königsberg*, the sign said. *Wehlau, Administrative Region of Königsberg*. A pair of storks had built their nest on a telegraph pole near the entrance.

'So why did you leave, if Treuburg's so pretty?'

'I was transferred.'

'Do you know the Mathée firm? *Luisenbrand*?'

Kowalski looked at Rath reproachfully, as if he took him for a drinker, nodded and again focused on the road. 'It's part of the Luisenhöhe estate,' he said.

Now it was Rath who turned his head, gazing at Kowalski in astonishment. 'A *proper* estate? With a Junker and all that?'

Kowalski shook his head. 'It used to belong to the von Mathée family, Huguenots ennobled by Old Fritz himself. But they went bankrupt during the great inflation, or something.'

'How about now?'

'Mathée's old managing director took it on.'

'Wengler? Director Wengler?'

'That's the one. Made a truly model company of it, the distillery especially. *Mathée Luisenbrand* is distributed all over the world. People are very proud of it in the Oletzko district.'

It was Rath's turn to nod. All it needed was a little patience, and these East Prussians became positively loquacious.

31

The Treuburg marketplace was enormous. So enormous, in fact, that there was a tree-covered hillock in its centre. The church sat regally at the summit, its spire towering above the trees. At the foot of the hillock were a few houses, the town hall, and, next to it, a school and the fire station. 'The largest marketplace in Germany,' Kowalski announced, and Rath believed him. It was so large that, at first glance, it appeared to be something else. It was as if time here had stood still: smart, gabled houses lined its four sides, road traffic was still dominated by horse-drawn carriages, and a few sheep must have escaped their pen, or perhaps simply belonged in the centre.

Kowalski braked and, within seconds, the official car of the Königsberg Police was mobbed by children squinting through its windows. No red carpet or brass band, but it wasn't exactly what Rath would call a discreet entrance. He rolled his eyes. All he needed now was for the local press to take his picture, and invite him to sign the town's Golden Book.

It was not yet twelve. 'Shouldn't they be in school?' he asked.

'Summer holidays,' Kowalski said, stepping on the accelerator. The children jumped aside and grew ever smaller in the rear-view mirror until the W10 left the marketplace. Kowalski continued to a little river and crossed a bridge, passing another church and eventually reaching a large brick building overlooking the shore. *Oletzko District Administrative Office*, the sign bearing the Prussian eagle read. Rath got out of the car and stretched his aching limbs before following his aide-cum-chaperone inside.

They passed through an anteroom occupied by a bespectacled girl, reaching the office of a portly man who wore an old-fashioned moustache and blue uniform.

'Our visitor from Berlin,' the uniformed officer said, after Kowalski made his report. 'We weren't expecting you so early. Please, take a seat!'

Rath sat on the visitor's chair and admired the view from the window behind the desk: lake glistening in the midday sun, boats pitching and tossing, the whitewashed diving platform of the public baths, dark green treetops on the far side of the shore. Feeling as if he were on holiday he lit a cigarette. 'Did we speak yesterday on the telephone?' he asked. 'Chief Constable Grigat?'

'That's right. Erich Grigat. Welcome to my humble abode. It isn't often we have visitors from the capital.'

'You're in charge of the Treuburg Police?'

'De facto, let's say. *De jure*, of course, the police chief would be Landrat Wachsmann, the district administrator. But I am his highest-ranking officer.'

'Nice view you've got here. My office looks out onto the suburban railway and district court. There's soot everywhere because of the trains.'

'It's worth making time for our little town. The lake, the new park with the war memorial.' Local pride was etched all over Grigat's face. 'Have you seen our marketplace? The biggest in the whole of Germany! Seven hectares.'

Rath nodded and drew on his cigarette. 'Very impressive.'

Grigat fetched a file from the drawer. 'I've taken the liberty of doing a little digging and, lo and behold, the three names you passed on yesterday were all registered here in the district at one point.'

192

'Two were born here in fact,' Rath said. 'Do you have their addresses?'

'It's all in here.' Grigat tapped the file. 'Let's discuss it over lunch. I've booked us a table at one in the *Salzburger Hof.*'

'Don't put yourself out on my account.'

'I eat lunch there every day. Besides, it's also your hotel. I've taken the liberty of reserving a room for you.'

The round-the-clock service was starting to get on Rath's nerves, but in the meantime he bowed to his fate. 'Many thanks,' he said, looking at his watch. 'That's still a bit away. If you don't mind, I'd like to get to my room and freshen up a little. I spent last night in the plane and still feel a little washed-out.' He stubbed out his cigarette and stood up. 'We'll talk at one.'

'Of course.'

Rath looked at the file. 'You don't mind if I take this? That way I can read up a little before lunch.'

Grigat made a face as if he minded very much. Then his smile returned. 'Of course.'

A little later, Rath and Kowalski stood at the reception of the *Salzburger Hof.* Kowalski deposited Rath's suitcase by the counter and made to leave.

'Where are you staying?' Rath asked. He wouldn't have been surprised if the assistant detective had gestured towards the back seat of the car.

'My uncle lives just around the corner. Goldaper Strasse. I'll report back at one if I may, Sir.'

'Of course. Go to your uncle. I won't need you again till two.'

Shortly afterwards Rath stood gazing out of his first-floor window. They had given him a balcony room overlooking the Treuburg marketplace; it even came with private bathroom and running water, the hotelier had proudly informed him at reception. Despite his suitcase still being unpacked, he flopped down onto the bed, exhausted by Masurian hospitality, and glad at last to be alone. He dozed for a while, before a glance at his alarm clock told him it was time: only half an hour until his lunchtime meeting with Chief Constable Grigat.

He went into the bathroom and shovelled cold water on his face until he felt halfway revived. He sat by the window with Grigat's file.

The information gathered by the Treuburg Police was sparse but there were no gaps. All three men had indeed lived for a number of years in Treuburg, or Marggrabowa as it was known then. August Simoneit and Hans Wawerka had never left their home town before the summer of 1924, when both packed their things and headed west, the one to Wittenberge, the other to Dortmund.

Herbert Lamkau had come to Marggrabowa a few years after the war and initially registered as living at the Luisenhöhe estate. After that he had lived on Lindenallee, likewise until 1924.

Before the war, Simoneit had lived in a village called Krupinnen, which was also part of the Oletzko district, registering his address at Legasteg in Marggrabowa following his return from battle in 1918. Wawerka, meanwhile, had always lived in the Schmale Gasse, in the town centre.

Rath decided to wait until after lunch to look at the three addresses and the Korn distillery. After that he had to find out what happened in the spring of 1924. What had prompted the three men to leave town in the same year? He felt certain that if he could answer these questions, he'd find the link between them – and, perhaps, the reason they were murdered.

He lit a cigarette, stepped onto the little balcony and gazed down at the square. So, this was Germany's largest marketplace, as everyone was at pains to tell him. Right now it was the probably its most deserted too. The vast expanse lay desolate in the midday heat. Children would be at home eating lunch with their mothers, and even the sheep had disappeared. A lone group of young men wearing brown uniforms and swastika brassards emerged from the little wood by the church and marched across the square. In Berlin the presence of brownshirts inevitably denoted a threat. On the sunlit Treuburg marketplace, against a backdrop of pretty gable houses, there was something almost idyllic about it, as if a group of SA officers on their way to lunch was just another aspect of small-town life. This impression was reinforced when the blue uniform of Chief Constable Grigat emerged from an alleyway into a cordial exchange that ended when the policeman touched his shako in military salute.

In Berlin it would have been unthinkable for a police officer to greet Nazis in this way. Rath stubbed out his cigarette on the wrought-iron balcony railing and remembered his audience with Bernhard Weiss. Was Erich Grigat a Nazi? Not officially, of course, otherwise he would have had to quit his post. Still, an officer couldn't be prevented from harbouring political sympathies. Rath reflected that one or two of his Berlin colleagues might pull on the brownshirt as soon they were permitted.

He went inside, took the file from the table and made his way downstairs. Grigat was already seated when he entered the dining room.

'Afternoon,' the constable said, looking up from the menu.

He returned the greeting and sat down, placing the file on the lily-white table cloth. 'So, what can you recommend?'

'Seeing as we're in East Prussia, you might want to try the Königsberger Klopse or buttermilk blintzes and caraway meatballs. It's all there.' Grigat leaned over the menu as if protecting a secret. 'I'd take the roast pork and potato dumplings.'

'I can get that in Berlin.'

'But not like here.'

Grigat was right. The meat, which was served by a young girl following a starter of beetroot soup, was mouth-watering, and there was plenty of it.

'Did you manage to get some reading done?' Grigat asked, pointing at the file.

'There wasn't much to read. The most intriguing thing is why all three left Treuburg in the same year.'

'No idea. There's no information about that.'

'Can you remember any of them? Personally, I mean.'

'Sadly not.' Grigat swallowed and dabbed at his mouth with a serviette. 'I only moved here in the autumn of '29 but you can always ask around. You've got the addresses; perhaps someone here can remember them.'

'Precisely what I had in mind. I can take a look at your lovely town while I'm at it.'

'If you need any help, just say. I could place a man at your ...'

'Not necessary, thank you. I have Herr Kowalski.'

'Of course. Where is he, by the way?'

'At his uncle's.'

'Your companion has relatives here?'

'Actually, he's from here himself.'

'Then you should ask him. Perhaps he knows what happened in '24.'

Rath nodded. Not such a bad idea, although he wondered how old Anton Kowalski would have been eight years ago. He was probably still at school.

At last they conquered the mountains of flesh. The blonde girl cleared the plates and, without being asked, served two bowls of a golden yellow mixture topped with raisins.

'Masurian *Glumse*,' Grigat explained.

'*Glumse*?'

'What you'd call *Quark*. Tastes like cheesecake without the biscuit.'

Erich Grigat was right, it tasted good. Even so, Rath felt as if he'd endured a lengthy meeting with Buddha. Grigat, however, couldn't get enough. He sat rubbing his hands. 'You wanted to try something East Prussian? How about a *Pillkaller* to finish?'

'I don't think I've got room for anything else.'

'To help with digestion.' Grigat grinned, hands already raised. 'Hella? Can you bring us two *Pillkaller*, please!'

Moments later the girl returned. She wore long blonde pigtails, the sort of hairstyle that had long since gone out of fashion in Berlin. She balanced two large glasses of Doppelkorn on her tray, a slice of liver sausage on top of each, spread thick with mustard. Rath found the sight alone disgusting.

'Put the sausage on your tongue, pour the schnapps over it, then swallow,' Grigat said, and demonstrated.

This ritual was even less appealing. The thought made him decidedly uneasy, but Grigat's expectant face left him no choice. Time to grit your teeth and get on with it! The result was a horrible sludge that didn't taste quite as bad as expected.

'And now we repeat, a dozen or so times.' Grigat laughed when he saw Rath's horrified expression. 'Don't worry,' he said. '*Pillkaller* is more of an evening thing. When you want to get drunk but don't have much in your stomach.'

Rath resolved to give Chief Constable Grigat a wide berth this evening, if not for the remainder of his stay in Treuburg.

32

The houses on Legasteg were small, with low roofs. Bed sheets lay on the low meadows, bleaching in the afternoon sun. The tired, sluggish river; the crooked little houses – at first glance it appeared idyllic, but poverty was plain to see. Rath knocked on the door of August Simoneit's former address and waited. There was no bell, neither here nor anywhere else on the street. Probably, most houses had no electricity.

He heard floorboards creaking before the door opened. At first he could hardly make out the man standing in the dark hollow of the entrance hall. 'Good afternoon,' he said. 'Please excuse the interruption.'

'We're not buying.'

'I'm not trying to sell.' Rath showed his identification. 'CID, Berlin. I have a question.'

'Berlin?'

The man stepped into the sun to take a closer look at the badge. Rath saw a thin, wrinkled face, with blonde hair that was now mostly white. 'It concerns August Simoneit,' he said. 'He used to live here. Do you remember?'

The man looked at him through suspicious eyes and shook his head before closing the door. It wasn't rude; he didn't slam it, just closed it without another word.

Taciturn and lightning-fast. Rath remembered how they used to joke about the odd Westphalian officer who strayed into the Rhineland during his years in Cologne.

He knocked again and waited. After a time, the man opened the door again and looked at him inquiringly. He didn't have a photograph of Simoneit but took pictures of the other two men from his jacket. The man at the door inspected them thoroughly. 'Do you recognise either of them?' Rath asked. 'They used to live in Treuburg.'

The man shook his head. 'Don't know them,' he said, and promptly closed the door a second time.

Rath gave up. It really wasn't unfriendliness; the people here were just taciturn. It was how they communicated – or didn't, as the case might be.

It was the same story in the Schmale Gasse, where Wawerka had lived before moving west, only here a woman came to the door – and she proved even more taciturn than the man at Legasteg. Her contribution consisted entirely of headshakes, nods and suspicious glances. She had never heard of a Johann Wawerka.

Unlike the previous two streets, Lamkau's address on Lindenallee was perfectly presentable, a neat, solidly middle-class little home with a well-maintained garden. Rath stood at the garden gate and, for a moment, considered entering the grounds. He rejected the notion. He felt himself being watched. The whole neighbourhood was probably just waiting for this stranger in the fancy suit to do something illegal so that they could call the police or, better still, reach for their shotguns.

Assmann, the enamel sign read. Rath noted the name and made his way back to the marketplace. It was gone three, but the sun was still beating down. At least the shadows were starting to lengthen, and a few shops had their awnings down. An advertisement on one of the houses gave him an idea. *Fahrschule Emil Hermann*. A driving school. He rang the bell and asked the instructor about a certain pupil.

'Lamkau? When would this be?' Another suspicious Treuburg resident.

'A good ten years ago.'

The instructor, a well-fed man in his fifties, scratched his chin in careful consideration, but all it yielded was a regretful shrug, and an isolated sentence. 'Nope, no idea.'

'Perhaps you have a telephone book?'

Herr Hermann led him through a kind of classroom into his office at the back. As soon as Rath saw the so-called telephone book, he knew it was no use. The sum total of Treuburg's telephone subscribers, from Adomeit to Zukowski, fitted on a single page hanging from the wall. He had intended to take a note of any Wawerkas, Simoneits and Lamkaus with a view to tracking down potential relatives, but the only thing he found was the number of a certain Dietrich Assmann, the man who lived at Lamkau's old address. At least *he* had a telephone, unlike the Lamkaus, Simoneits and Wawerkas of this town.

After making a solitary entry, he clapped his notebook shut. 'One more thing,' he said, once driving instructor Hermann had accompanied him to the door. 'The Luisenhöhe estate and Mathée Korn distillery... What's the best way to get there?'

Emil Hermann looked him up and down. 'It's about half an hour on foot,' he said, at length. 'Or you can take the light railway to Schwentainen. It stops at Luisenhöhe. Doesn't go too often, mind.'

'Thank you.'

Rath returned to find his unsolicited colleague and chaperone exactly where he'd left him: in the catacombs of the district administrative office, surrounded by a mound of files and card boxes. 'Found anything?'

'You should know that Prussians are slow on the draw,' Kowalski replied.

Rath had asked him to scour the archives for mention of the three names. 'You find anything that links them, you let me know right away.'

Kowalski had been unable to recall anything specific that had happened in Treuburg or Marggrabowa in 1924. 'But that doesn't mean anything. I was at the village school in Markowsken; it wasn't easy keeping up with the world outside.'

Perhaps he wasn't quite so taciturn after all, at least not in comparison with his fellow East Prussians, but his failure didn't bother Rath particularly, since the main reason he'd left him trawling through the archives was to buy himself a few hours' peace. 'Then spend the afternoon looking through the case files from the district court. Maybe you'll find something there,' he said. 'Focus on 1924 again.'

Kowalski nodded, less than thrilled. 'How about you? Any luck?'

'I'm certainly getting to know Treuburg.' Rath lit a cigarette. 'I'm going to drive out to the Luisenhöhe estate. Could you pass me the keys ...'

Kowalski looked reluctant. Evidently his superiors weren't banking on him handing over the car without a fight. 'Why don't I drive you there? I know the way. It's why I'm here after all.'

'Don't worry, I'll be fine.' Rath gestured towards the dusty mound of files. 'You're of more use to me here.'

'You know,' Kowalski said, 'I'm not even sure I'm *authorised* to lend you the car ...'

'It's a Prussian police vehicle, right?'

'Right.'

'What does a Prussian assistant detective say when a Prussian detective inspector requests the use of a vehicle?'

'He says: "Yes, Sir!", Detective Inspector, Sir.'

'There we are.' Rath gave a satisfied nod and stretched out his right hand for the keys.

The black Wanderer handled well enough, and Rath enjoyed steering through the countryside unaccompanied. The truth was that he preferred working alone; somehow it

allowed him to think better. He took the B road to Schwentainen, but quickly realised it was a mistake. A farmer on a
hay cart sent him back to Treuburg, where he was to take the
road to Lyck. He reached the railway line within ten minutes
and, shortly after that, the stop with the lightly rusted sign.
LUISENHÖHE. With its high chimneys, the brick distillery
appeared more like a factory than an estate building. The
name *Mathée* was printed on the pediment in the same
ornate writing as on the *Luisenbrand* bottles; below, in much
smaller, simple block letters was the rubric *Brennerei Gut
Luisenhöhe*. Luisenhöhe Distillery. A low, modern annexe,
behind which two large copper storage tanks glistened in the
sunlight, marked the boundary of a paved square, upon which
two trucks containing barley malt waited to be unloaded.

The quantities that must be produced here! This was no
provincial operation distilling cheap schnapps for Treuburg
and its outlying villages.

Rath parked the car in the courtyard and spoke to the
nearest worker. 'Where can I find the boss around here?'

'You mean the operations manager or the managing
director?'

'Director Wengler,' he said, displaying Lamkau's driving
licence photo. 'Or anyone who can tell me about this man.
Herbert Lamkau.' The worker looked at the photo briefly
and shrugged. 'He never put in an appearance here? Lamkau
was a distributor, a pretty important one too, I might add.'

The worker gestured towards the top of the hill. 'Director
Wengler has his office up there in the estate house.'

'Many thanks,' Rath said. 'Wait a minute...1924...
That was the year Herr Lamkau left town, along with a few
other men. I suspect something happened here that forced
their hand. Any idea what it might be?'

Again the worker shrugged, but this time Rath sensed he
was lying; the man knew exactly what had happened eight
years ago.

A shaded avenue led up to the estate house, which wasn't nearly as ostentatious as he had imagined: more large villa than small castle. He parked in front of a stoop, and no sooner had he got out of the car than a man in a suit descended the steps. Either they were permanently on guard here, or the distillery worker below had telephoned up to the house.

'Good afternoon,' the suit said, sounding excessively polite. He had the air of a bookkeeper.

'Herr Wengler?'

'I'm afraid Herr Wengler is away on business; we're not expecting him back before evening.' The man stretched out a hand. 'Fischer's the name. I'm Herr Wengler's private secretary. With whom do I have the pleasure?'

'Rath, CID.'

The secretary didn't look overly surprised. 'What can I do for you, Inspector?'

Rath showed him the driving licence photo. 'I need some information about this man,' he said. 'Herbert Lamkau. A business associate of Herr Wengler's.'

'I'm afraid I'm not responsible for Herr Wengler's business affairs. But I could make you an appointment to see him.' Fischer pulled out a little black book and leafed through it. 'You're in luck. There's a small window tomorrow morning at eleven o'clock.'

'You're in luck too.' Rath handed the secretary his card. 'Tell Herr Wengler I'll be with him at ten.'

33

The day had begun with a mound of carrots that needed peeling, a doddle in comparison with chopping onions. Then, immediately after lunch, Unger had summoned Charly to his office. The head chef had a pile of correspondence to deal with, and, after dictating various letters, had left her to type them up.

Working quickly, she used the opportunity to rummage through Unger's drawers. The window glass prevented a systematic search, but she managed an overview as she feigned looking for paperclips or envelopes.

She didn't strike lucky until the filing shelves, where, right at the top, she stumbled on a folder marked *Complaints*. After skimming the copies inside, she surmised that they were letters of complaint sent by Unger on behalf of the Kempinski firm. It was unappetising stuff. One was a complaint addressed to *Fehling Foods* about a venison delivery overrun with maggots, another concerned a pallet of rotten eggs from *Friedrichsen Eggs and Poultry*.

Hearing the door open behind her she returned the folder to the shelf, and looked around to find Manfred Unger ogling her legs.

'What is it you're looking for, Fräulein Ritter?'

'I'm finished with your correspondence and thought I might file the copies.' She dismounted her stool.

'No need to go up there.'

He took a folder from the shelf in front of her. +++ *Korrespondenz 1932* +++ the cover said.

'Another classic case.' Charly laughed.

'A classic case of what?'

'Failing to see the wood for the trees.'

She opened the folder and returned to the desk. Luckily, she really had finished her typing. Unger regarded her benevolently as she reached for the punch and began filing the copies. He didn't seem to have noticed anything. 'You just need to sign,' she said, placing the originals in front of him.

He tore his gaze away and turned to signing correspondence that was perfectly harmless compared to what she had just found. 'If you could take these to the post office and then call it a night. You'll find envelopes and stamps in the flat drawer at the top.'

She nodded demurely. She already knew where they were kept, but there was no reason for Unger to find out. 'Many thanks, Herr Unger.' At the desk she began folding the letters and placing them in their envelopes.

Unger gazed at her legs for a final time before disappearing inside the kitchen. It seemed like there was a lot going on today; he was everywhere issuing instructions, but still glanced periodically in her direction.

Did he suspect? Surely not but, even so, she didn't dare reach for the *Complaints* folder a second time. She had seen enough, even if she hadn't found anything addressed to Lamkau. Gereon's hunch appeared to have been borne out. The letters were odd, not so much for their sharpness of tone as their ambiguities. Despite reading no more than two or three, she had noticed straightaway that they weren't letters of complaint. They were letters of extortion.

34

The lounge was filled with smoke despite the early hour. Two men stood at the bar speaking in hushed tones; three others sat at a table playing skat, noisy only when they revealed their hands. By the window, a solitary old man in hard-wearing corduroy slacks and woollen pullover crouched over a glass of schnapps. A wiry, bespectacled man in his mid-thirties dressed in a coarse linen suit with elbow patches ate a light supper on his own. Rath nursed his beer at the only other table, hoping that Chief Constable Grigat avoided this dive, and that no one else decided to stand him a *Pillkaller*.

The risk seemed slight as, so far, the patrons had scrupulously ignored him. Only the man in the linen suit had looked up as he entered the lounge, appraising him openly through wire-framed spectacles. The most from anyone else was the occasional stolen glance. He had planned to have a drink at the bar and engage in conversation with the landlord and his locals, but the suspicion he'd met on entry made him plump for the window instead.

Assistant Detective Kowalski had offered to accompany him, but, after releasing him from the district archive, Rath had sent him on a bar crawl of his own, to do a little nosing around his compatriots, and to leave the 'Herr Inspector' in peace.

The wall of silence since he'd started asking about

Lamkau, Simoneit and Wawerka made him suspicious. This wasn't simply East Prussian reticence, more like a conspiracy everyone was in on. The contents of Grigat's police file were sketchy at best, and Kowalski had spent the afternoon trawling through the archives in vain. Rath didn't know if he should trust him.

There was nothing for it but to keep chivvying the stubborn fools until one of them offered more than a shrug. There was no doubt his mere presence was getting to them. He didn't have to ask any questions.

He lit a cigarette and raised his by now empty glass. At least the landlord wasn't ignoring him, and began tapping out a fresh beer. That was the kind of reserve he could deal with. He had taken his evening meal in a pretty little restaurant by the lakeshore, eschewing the *Salzburger Hof*, and with it Chief Constable Grigat. Kowalski had given him the name of the bar here; '*Pritzkus's* is where the ordinary folk meet,' he had said, and it was true. Ordinary folk, who didn't take kindly to strangers.

He placed the photos of Lamkau and Wawerka on the table as the landlord approached with his beer. 'Do you recognise either of these men? Herbert Lamkau, Hans Wawerka. Or does the name August Simoneit mean anything to you?'

'It's possible they drank here from time to time. Must've been a good while ago though.'

'Eight years.'

'Back then my father was still in charge.'

Rath dared to hope. 'Would it be possible to speak to him?'

The landlord shook his head. 'I'm afraid we buried him two years ago.'

'I'm sorry to hear that,' but the landlord had disappeared to take the skat players' latest order.

He stood up and took the two photos over to the old

man, who sat alone with his schnapps and a fat cigar that didn't seem to get any shorter. The man didn't look like he was expecting company, let alone conversation. Rath showed him the photos all the same. 'Good evening. I'm looking for someone who can tell me about this man.' The old man puffed on his cheroot. 'Herbert Lamkau. Does the name mean anything to you? Or this man here. Johann Wawerka.' Silence. 'They lived here, eight years ago. You're old enough to remember them. How about August Simoneit? I don't have a photo of him, unfortunately.' The man mumbled something incomprehensible without removing the cheroot from his mouth. 'Pardon me?'

The man removed the cigar and repeated what he'd just said. He spoke loudly and clearly, but Rath didn't understand a word. Whatever language he was using, it wasn't German.

'I'm sorry,' Rath said, taking his photos and standing up. 'I didn't realise you were Polish. I thought you were from here.'

The man glared at him, and conversation at the surrounding tables ceased. Suddenly, he started so violently from his chair that his drink overturned, his eyes sparkling with rage.

'Ne jem Polak,' the man said, genuinely outraged, 'jestem Prußakiem.'

Rath raised his hands in a conciliatory gesture. 'Easy now, easy! I'm not sure what you thought you heard, but I don't have anything against Poles.'

The man wouldn't be appeased. Already alarmingly close, he took another step towards Rath and emitted a Babylonian torrent of words, accompanying the outburst by slamming his fist on the table. Rath took a step back. He'd never have guessed the residents here, whether Polish or German, could say so much in one go.

Some of the patrons were amused, others got to their feet. Rath didn't imagine they'd be on his side if things turned nasty. He doubted whether they had actually been privy to the exchange; more likely, they were simply spoiling for a fight, glad to show this big-city type what they thought of him.

He should have brought Kowalski after all! In any low dive in Berlin he could resolve this, but here, without a local by his side, he felt helpless. He was debating how identifying himself as a police officer would play when the man in the linen suit and wire-framed spectacles stood up, placed his serviette next to his roast potatoes and said something to the old-timer and the men beside him.

Rath could have sworn that he, too, was speaking in Polish. After his experience with the old man, however, he resolved to keep his counsel, standing with his fists inwardly raised, waiting to see what would happen.

Glasses man seemed to have found the right words, even if Rath hadn't understood them. The men laughed heartily and clapped the old-timer on the shoulder. He returned to his schnapps, which the landlord refilled, and the men, who moments before had been itching for a fight, did likewise. One of them said something to his neighbour and pointed at Rath, and they burst out laughing again.

He turned to face his saviour, who took him by the arm. 'Come on,' he said. 'Leave Pritzkus here a few marks for your beer and for Adamek's Korn, then get your hat and coat. It's best we go elsewhere. Who knows how long the mood will hold.'

Rath did as bidden, remembering his cigarettes from the table, and the pair exited the lounge. 'Thanks again,' he said when they reached the marketplace. 'Things could have got nasty in there.' He opened his cigarette case, and offered an Overstolz.

'No problem,' the man said, lighting up. 'Strangers rarely venture inside *Pritzkus's*. You have to do your bit to prevent misunderstandings.'

'No kidding. I don't have any Polish.'

'That wasn't Polish Adamek was speaking.'

'I still didn't understand a word.'

'It was Masurian,' the man continued. 'A variant of Polish, maybe, but the people here are proud Prussians. They don't consider themselves Polish.'

'I'm Prussian too,' Rath said. 'Rhine-Prussian.'

'A "Booty-Prussian" then. These people are Ur-Prussians. They've always been great patriots, even in times when no one spoke German apart from the parish priest and estate owner.'

'Some of them still don't seem to have learned any German.'

'Old Adamek understands everything, believe me. He just feels more at home in his native language, especially after a few schnapps. But he's a Prussian patriot through and through.'

'Yes, I realise that.'

'Forget about it, it's over now. But you should be more careful about using the word *Polish*, especially here in Treuburg, where people are proud of the fact that only two votes were cast for Poland in the entire district.'

'You know your stuff.'

'It's my job.' The man stretched out a hand. 'Rammoser,' he said. 'Karl Rammoser. I'm the teacher over at the village school in Wielitzken. A good place to contemplate the vagaries of the passage of time.'

'Rath, CID Berlin.'

'Delighted. But there's no need for introductions. News here travels fast.'

'In that case, since we're already acquainted, let me stand you a beer.'

'Gladly.'

'Then you can tell me what kind of Prussian *you* are. Going by your name, I'd say Alpine-Prussian. But as far as

I know, Old Fritz only occupied Silesia, not Tyrol as well.'

Rammoser nodded. 'Alpine-Prussian,' he repeated. 'First time I've heard it – but it rings true. Or, at least, true enough.'

A short time later they sat in a more welcoming bar, suggested by Rammoser. 'A Rhine-Prussian like you won't stand out quite so much in the *Kronprinzen*. It's even open to holidaymakers.'

Indeed, it looked like there were a few eating their supper on the adjoining table. From Berlin, judging by all the big mouths, from father down to youngest daughter. Still, anything was better than the *Salzburger Hof*, where staff would keep Chief Constable Grigat informed of Rath's every move. 'It's nice here,' he said. 'Why would you go to *Pritzkus's*?'

'Because,' Rammoser raised his glass, 'it's cheap and the food's good. How much do you think a Prussian village schoolmaster earns?'

'You're speaking to a fellow comrade-in-suffering,' Rath said, likewise raising his glass. 'To Prussia and its destitute officials.' The men clinked glasses. 'Rammoser doesn't sound very Prussian to me. Are you from Bavaria?'

'Try telling my father he wasn't Prussian. He'd have challenged you to a duel.' He set his beer glass down. 'No, my family came to Prussia from Salzburg two hundred years ago, like many other Protestants who were expelled at that time.'

'Then you're a refugee, a kind of Huguenot?'

'Something like that,' Rammoser said. 'You wouldn't believe how many nationalities have been subject to Prussian rule down the years. Germans, French, Dutch, Silesians, Lithuanians, Jews, and, of course, Poles. And they all consider themselves Prussian. More Prussian, at any rate, than some Rhinelander looted from Napoleon's bankruptcy assets.'

'So that's why the old man reacted so sensitively. I thought he was Polish.'

'Do you know what bound the Poles across the generations, even when they no longer had a nation to call their own? It wasn't language, but religion. And do you know why twelve years ago nearly all Masurians voted for Prussia? In spite of the language?'

'Religion.' Rath felt as if he were back at school.

'Correct,' Rammoser said. 'The Masurians have lived under Prussian rule for years. They're Protestant through and through, as well as being Prussian patriots. Ordinary people here have always spoken Polish – or Masurian, which is a Polish dialect, as opposed to a German one. We, the teachers, are responsible for the fact that the younger generation speaks German. But at home, with their grandparents, I'd be willing to bet that most still speak Masurian.'

'So they are *kind* of Polish, then?'

'That's a delicate subject since the 1920 plebiscite. No one wanted to be suspected of harbouring Polish sympathies, least of all the Masurians.' He lowered his voice. 'There were some pretty ugly scenes. Beatings, broken windows, arson attacks and worse. Some people here turned into real Pole-bashers. The relationship's been poisoned ever since. Not that the newly created Polish state was entirely blameless, of course; if they'd had their way they'd have annexed all of East Prussia. They would still. At least, that's what people around here think, and they're wary as a result. You have to understand that old Adamek probably thought you were trying to insult him.'

'If he really wants to be German, then perhaps he should speak the language.'

'First, he doesn't want to be German, but, above all, Prussian. Second, after five or six Doppelkorn Adamek only speaks Masurian – but that doesn't make him any less German. Any claims to the contrary, and you'll have me to deal with!'

'I wouldn't dare.' Rath grinned. 'But tell me one thing. What did you say to Adamek and the other men just now?'

'You really want to know?'

'At least why they laughed like that.'

'Well, now . . .' Rammoser cleared his throat. 'I told them they shouldn't take you so seriously, that you're just a poor, stray *Zabrak* who knows no better.'

'A poor, stray what?' Rath asked, before waving the teacher away. 'Actually, forget I asked. I can work it out for myself.' He took a drag on his cigarette. 'So, in other words, you exposed me to ridicule.'

'It never hurts to be underestimated.'

'Well, if that's the case, then thank you.'

'At your service.'

Rath fetched the photos from his bag. 'I only wanted to ask Adamek about these men. You don't happen to know them?'

'Is that Lamkau?' Rammoser asked. 'What's happened to him?'

Rath felt mildly euphoric. At last, someone who knew who Lamkau was. 'He's dead,' he said.

'No great loss.'

'Careful. You'll make yourself into a suspect.'

'I knew I shouldn't have said anything.'

'What have you got against Lamkau?'

'He was one of Wengler's thugs. I wouldn't like to say how many people he put in hospital.'

'Wengler? Director Wengler?'

'That's right. Gustav Wengler. The owner of the Luisenhöhe estate.'

'He had a band of thugs?'

'That's old hat. It was a long time ago.'

'Doesn't surprise me, given how he snaffled up the estate during inflation.'

'Wengler, a profiteer from inflation? Who told you that?'

'I heard it somewhere,' Rath said.

Rammoser was thinking about something. 'Do you have a torch, Inspector?' he asked suddenly.

'I think there's one in the car.'

'Let's go.' Rammoser drained his glass. 'I have to show you something. Perhaps then you'll understand that things here aren't quite so simple.'

'When are they ever?' Rath said. Arriving at the car he located the torch and stowed it in his pocket. 'Where to?' he asked. 'Wouldn't we be better off driving?'

Rammoser shook his head. 'It isn't far, five minutes perhaps. Besides, you're not exactly sober.'

The marketplace was still lit, but when they entered the appropriately named *Stille Gasse – Silent Lane* – everything went pitch black. A few lights were visible from the windows in the distance, otherwise nothing. Rath switched on the torch. They walked uphill for a time, before the beam of light fell on a circular brick wall.

'The water tower,' Rammoser said. 'We're almost there.'

Rath now knew roughly where they were. The Treuburg water tower was easier to locate than the church steeple. Rammoser opened a wrought-iron gate, which gave a slight squeak. Somewhere in the dark an owl hooted. Then the light fell upon a gravestone. 'Are we . . .is this the . . .?'

'Treuburg Cemetery,' Rammoser said. 'The Protestant one. The Catholics are buried down by the lake.'

'I didn't think there were any Catholics in Treuburg.'

'Well, there's you, Inspector.'

'I hope I don't wind up in the cemetery. Even if it is by the lake.'

'I might have prevented it today. But you need to mind your step.'

'Which is why you've dragged me *here*, in the middle of the night?'

'Something like that. So that you come to a greater

understanding of our region and its people, and don't put your foot in it again.' Rammoser came to a halt. 'So,' he said. 'Here we are.'

Rath shone the torch where the teacher pointed to reveal a family grave. Simple, Doric columns flanked a large marble slab with a French inscription: *Passant! Souviens-toi que la perfection n'est point sur la terre, si je n'ai pas été le meilleur des hommes. Au moins ne suis-je pas au nombre des méchans!*

Rath could make out the name *Friedrich von Mathée*, as well as those of other family members buried here. 'The owners of the Luisenhöhe estate,' he said. He couldn't help but whisper, as if the deceased family members might be listening from beyond the grave.

'Correct. But it's two lives I wanted to draw your attention to. Pass me the light.'

Rath handed over the torch, and Rammoser manoeuvred the beam of light until it rested on the names. *Anna von Mathée*, Rath read, * 15th August 1902 † 11th July 1920.

'Is that the daughter?' he asked.

'Yes,' Rammoser said. 'His only one.'

'She died on the day of the plebiscite.' Rath shook his head. 'What kind of story is this?' Suddenly he felt completely sober.

'A tragic one. Anna von Mathée was Gustav Wengler's fiancée. She was murdered on the day of the plebiscite.'

'Murdered?'

Rammoser nodded. 'It was a doctor of all people, a registrar at the local hospital. He raped her, then drowned her in the lake.'

'That's terrible.'

'Most of the people around here wouldn't have begrudged Wengler killing the man. Especially given the anti-Polish sentiment at the time.'

'The killer was Polish?'

Rammoser shrugged. 'It was hard to say in those days. He was certainly Catholic, and he sympathised with the new Polish state.'

'So now he's languishing in a Prussian jail.'

'Not any more.'

'Pardon me?'

'Anna's killer died trying to escape. People around here regard it as a higher form of justice.'

'And it was this sorry tale that turned Gustav Wengler into a Pole-basher, as you put it?'

'Wengler could never stand the Poles, even before the murder, but a Pole-basher – that was Herbert Lamkau. He and his men beat the living daylights out of anyone they thought was Polish.'

'The way you tell it, there aren't any Poles here. Even the ones who speak Polish.'

'Back then it was enough just to be Catholic, or favourably disposed towards Poland. If you're looking for people with a reason to hate Herbert Lamkau, you'll find plenty here.'

'Could it be that someone wished him dead? One of his victims perhaps?'

'I wouldn't go that far, but there won't be many shedding a tear. On either side of the border.'

'Including you?'

'I got into a tangle with him once, around the time of the plebiscite, when things were pretty heated here. Still, that's long forgotten now. I was away for a few years training as a teacher, and by the time I returned Lamkau had gone.'

'I'm afraid I don't follow,' Rath said. 'You excoriate Lamkau, while at the same time standing up for his master, Wengler. Is there a point to this story?'

'There is no story, and I'm not standing up for anyone. God knows I'm no fan of Gustav Wengler, I just want you to understand what was happening here after the war. The present can only be understood through reference to the past.'

216

Rammoser was starting to sound like a teacher again. The beam of light drifted back onto the name Rath had just read.

Friedrich von Mathée * 23rd November 1847 † 2nd May 1924

'Gustav Wengler was the designated heir of the Luisenhöhe estate,' Rammoser continued. 'Friedrich von Mathée only had the one daughter, and he wanted her to marry his trustee. His sons all fell in the war.'

'Gustav Wengler was the estate's trustee?'

'He'd have inherited it anyway, but took over from old Mathée prior to his death because of debt issues. That's where all the local gossip stems from – not least because he's made a pretty penny since.'

'No doubt he'd have preferred a living bride.'

'And no doubt it was her death that made him seek refuge in his work. He made the Mathée name great in memory of his murdered fiancée, whom he never got to lead to the altar.'

Rath realised he was shivering. It had grown cold. 'Let's get back to the *Kronprinzen*,' he said. 'I could use a drink after that. As well as some light, and a little company.'

When they returned to the marketplace there was almost no light from the houses, and the street lamps were out. Rath lit the way with the torch. The light caught an advertising pillar on the corner of Bahnhofstrasse, startling two figures armed with a wall brush and bucket who immediately took to their heels.

Rath almost cried 'Stop! Police!', but managed to restrain himself. 'Who was that?' he asked.

'I'd wager it was Albrecht and Rosanki.'

'Who?'

'Our local Communists. You mustn't think you only have them in Berlin.'

'I fear we have more than two.'

217

Rath approached the advertising pillar and found three election posters arranged neatly alongside each other, still damp with paste. The other posters were untouched, even the Nazi ones: no graffiti moustaches, no torn corners. 'I thought we'd caught them at sabotage, but they were only putting their posters up.' He shook his head. 'I'm wondering why they ran if they weren't doing anything wrong.'

'If you were a Communist trying to put up election posters in Treuburg, you'd know,' Rammoser said. 'It isn't much fun running into Wengler's boys on the job.'

'Wengler's boys? Does he still have a band of thugs? I thought the plebiscite settled all that.'

'The plebiscite didn't settle anything,' Rammoser said. 'It's just that Wengler's thugs wear uniform now, and put up posters themselves. The ones with the swastikas.'

35

Rath was awakened by a fearful clamour and hullabaloo, as if a thousand people were cheering a boxing match while the Town Musicians of Bremen performed at maximum volume.

The reality wasn't so different. Still a little dazed, he padded towards the window and pulled back the curtain to see that the peaceful Treuburg marketplace of yesterday had been transformed into a madhouse. Cows and horses, geese and hens, sheep and pigs; animals were being sold everywhere, their din merging with the cries of the market barkers. East Prussian constraint, it seemed, was just a state of mind.

He sloped into the bathroom and felt his head as, slowly, the memories returned. Rammoser, the village teacher. The night-time excursion to the cemetery. The stories about Herbert Lamkau and Gustav Wengler. The drinking. One beer had turned into two, and before long the first *Luisenbrand* had been ordered. He had stopped counting after that.

'This is the stuff Wengler made his fortune on,' Rammoser said, as they toasted the first schnapps. That was their final word on the subject, though they continued to drink the *stuff*, ordering round after round to chase their beers.

Rath had thought little of it, since he wasn't the one who

had to cycle six kilometres home. As it transpired, he had greater problems crossing the marketplace and climbing to his room on the first floor than Rammoser did with his trusty bicycle, which he had left against a street lamp. He swung himself onto the saddle without so much as a wobble.

'Stop by the schoolhouse in Wielitzken sometime,' he had said.

Thinking back, Rath felt strangely elated. More than being the first decent informant he'd found, Karl Rammoser was also a nice guy. True, he wasn't technically from Treuburg, but maybe that was an advantage. Maybe it was the fact that he didn't belong that made him so effusive.

Rath looked at his watch: time for breakfast if he didn't want to be late for the distillery. He used cold water for his fatigue, and aspirin for his headache. Luckily, he had remembered to pack a tube in Berlin.

Kowalski sat waiting in the lounge, this time minus the shaving tissue. He stood to attention. 'Good morning, Sir.'

'Morning, Kowalski. Any luck yesterday evening?'

'A few witnesses.'

'Any insights?'

'Afraid not, Sir. Only that all three worked at the Luisenhöhe distillery.' Kowalski fumbled in his jacket pocket. 'Witness addresses. Question them yourself if you like.'

Rath stowed the list in his pocket. No sooner had he sat down than the girl who served him lunch yesterday appeared with the breakfast tray. Hella, if he remembered rightly. She pulled a face as if to say: *I'm only doing this because my parents are making me*. 'Thank you,' he said, savouring the smell of fresh coffee.

'Would you like anything else, sir?

'Perhaps some coffee for my colleague.' Kowalski shook his head. 'Don't you want to sit down?'

'Thank you, Sir. I prefer to stand. What are my orders

for today? Can I assist with questioning? Or drive you somewhere?'

'I can drive myself. Continue with your work in the archive. You're bound to hit on something.'

'Yes, Sir.'

'Take a look at the newspaper archive as well. I assume there's one here in Treuburg?'

'Of course.'

Rath placed the lily-white serviette on his lap. 'Once you've finished going through the case records, head over there. Perhaps today will be the day.'

Kowalski appeared slightly offended. He wouldn't have pictured his days in Treuburg swallowing dust. Indeed, no doubt he already *had* his instructions, but was too Prussian to defy his senior officer's command. He gave a smart salute and had already reached the door when Rath thought of something else. 'One more thing, Kowalski...'

'Yes, Sir?'

'Do you speak Masurian?'

'A little.' Kowalski appeared embarrassed by the admission. '*Groska*, for example, means grandmother. And *Grosek*, grandfather. Why do you ask?'

'Just wondering.'

'My uncle speaks fluent Masurian, and my grandparents spoke nothing but.'

Rath nodded and dismissed him. After a first cup of coffee he felt ready to take on some solids. The bread rolls here were something else, and the quince jelly must be home-made.

'Hella?'

Was that her name? Either way she came over. She was a pretty girl, blonde and suntanned, but the braided pigtails made her look like a country cousin. A different haircut, a little make-up, a fashionable dress, and even Berlin men would crane their necks for a glimpse.

221

'Would you like anything else, sir?'

'No, thank you, everything's fine.' He pressed a one-mark coin into her hand. 'Haven't had a breakfast like this in a long time.'

'Thank you, sir.' Her smile knocked him dead, perhaps because it came so unexpectedly. Clearing the table, she brushed against his arm.

'Lots going on today,' he said. 'Outside, I mean.'

'Friday is market day.'

She curtseyed, disappearing with her tray and her smile into the kitchen. He tore his gaze away from her rear and stood up. It was time to go.

Friday was indeed market day, and it took a long time to crawl through the milling mass of animals and people in the car. Somehow, Rath managed to reach Bahnhofstrasse without running over a pig. In front of the advertising pillar on the street corner, a group of young brownshirts were in the process of tearing down the Communist placards from last night. No one took exception, although Rath debated whether he should intervene. As matters stood, going by the market had cost him ten minutes already. He wouldn't make the time up now, no matter how fast he drove.

At five minutes past ten he parked outside the Luisen-höhe estate house. With no one to receive him he rang the doorbell. A liveried servant opened and raised an eyebrow. 'Director Wengler is expecting me,' Rath said, showing his card.

Director Wengler was in no rush. Rath spent the next five minutes waiting in the hall, until the servant returned and bade him enter the drawing room, where the waiting began again. He felt as though he were at the doctor's surgery. On the table were journals he recognised from Lamkau's estate: *Alkohol* and the *Spirit Industry Magazine*. He leafed through the pages and smoked, but it wasn't until after finishing his cigarette that the door opened to reveal, not the arrogant servant this time, but the equally glib Herr Fischer, Wengler's private secretary.

'Good morning, Inspector. Director Wengler will see you now.' Rath looked at his watch. Half past ten.

The office looked down the valley onto the great brick chimney of the distillery and, in the distance, the Treuburg water tower. The furnishings were caught between Prussian Junkerdom and modern office. On the spacious desk was a black telephone next to an old-fashioned inkwell complete with fountain pen and card index boxes. On the wood-panelled wall was an oil painting of hunting scenes. Behind the desk hung two portraits in valuable, old-fashioned frames. One showed a grey-haired man with a stern, aristocratic gaze, and the other, far more elaborately rendered, a young woman. In sharp contrast with these oil paintings was a plain, but no less striking graphic detailing the distillery's revenue curve since 1920. The curve was on an upward trajectory, particularly in the last few years, despite the economic crisis. Perhaps, even, *because* of the economic crisis. The worse people felt, the more they drank.

Beneath the graphic, advertising placards for *Luisenbrand* and *Treuburger Bärenfang* stood against the wall. Rath recognised the motif from Lamkau's office in Berlin: the bear with the bottle. It was well done, and it looked as if the *Bärenfang* was to be the Mathée firm's next money-spinner.

Gustav Wengler cut a wiry figure, not at all the obese managing director Rath had expected. He stood as his guest entered behind the overzealous private secretary.

'Inspector. Please come in. My apologies for the delay. Urgent meeting.'

'I think you'll find this equally urgent.'

Wengler laughed. 'Fischer, would you fetch the inspector something to drink. Coffee? Tea? Water? Or perhaps you'd prefer schnapps? There's no shortage!'

'Thank you, I'm on duty, but coffee would be nice.'

Private Secretary Fischer disappeared. 'I'm familiar with your schnapps. It's available in Berlin, you know.'

'But that isn't why you're here,' Wengler said. 'Or has someone used my Korn as a murder weapon?'

'How do you know there's been a murder?'

'I fear I may even know the victim.' Wengler's face grew serious. 'You're a police inspector from Berlin, where my best salesman has just been killed. I can put two and two together.'

'So, you know ...'

'Edith Lamkau told me a few days ago. The poor woman!'

'Yes, Frau Lamkau is having a rough time. She said you were going to help her ...'

'Insofar as I can.' Wengler looked at him. 'So, Inspector, what are you doing here?'

'Looking for answers. Trying to find out why Herbert Lamkau had to die.'

'You're hoping the answer will lead you to the killer?'

'That's usually how it works.' Rath gazed pensively out of the window at the thick clouds rising from the chimney; the distillery seemed to be in full swing. 'Do *you* know why he had to die?'

Wengler shook his head. 'I'm afraid I can't help you there.'

'Then perhaps you could tell me a little more about Herbert Lamkau the man. Before he moved to Berlin and began distributing *Luisenbrand*, he was employed here by you.'

'That's true. Herbert was my operations manager at the distillery.'

'Did he perform other tasks for you?'

'What do you mean?'

'Beating up Poles, for instance?'

'Herbert wasn't always in control of his temper.' A deep wrinkle formed at the bridge of Wengler's nose and his eyes

224

flashed. 'Have I understood you correctly? You're implying that he engaged in violence at my behest?'

'I'm just telling you what I've heard.'

'Then you've been talking to the wrong people. You shouldn't believe everything you hear.'

'Perhaps I'm talking to the right person now?'

'Herbert Lamkau was no angel, and he made no secret of the fact that he couldn't stand the Poles. Yes, there were times twelve years ago when emotions were running high and he became physical. But to imply that he did so at my behest is simply outrageous!'

There was a knock and a girl appeared with the coffee. The private secretary would consider actually *serving* it beneath his dignity.

'Is it possible that one of these Poles, one of these people Lamkau manhandled, has sought revenge?'

'Anything is possible, Inspector, but why wait twelve years?'

'Lamkau skipped town eight years ago. Do you know why? Things were clearly on an upward trajectory here.'

'You can say that again!' Wengler gestured towards the sales curve behind him. 'Since I took over, we've increased production by almost 500 per cent. I wouldn't like to say how many public officials live off the money we pay in taxes.'

'You don't have it so bad yourself. I mean, you're an estate owner. People say it was inflation that brought it into your possession . . .'

'*People* say?' Wengler tapped a cigarette out of a silver case and looked at Rath indignantly. 'Where on earth did you hear that?' Rath remained silent, having drawn Wengler out of his shell.

'Friedrich von Mathée,' Wengler began, lighting a cigarette without offering one to Rath, 'was an honest soul and a loyal patriot, but he had no idea about money. The dear man invested almost his entire fortune in war bonds, encumbering the Luisenhöhe estate with massive debts.'

'And you helped him ...'

'I was the superintendent here and worked as managing director of the distillery. Which I took over after the war. I was to inherit the estate.' Wengler struggled to get the words out. 'I was Herr von Mathée's future son-in-law, but sadly my fiancée ...Anna ...passed ...before we could be married.'

'I see,' Rath lit an Overstolz. 'So, you took on the estate before your father-in-law's death.'

'Otherwise it would have belonged to the bank.'

'How did you manage to write off his debts?'

'I had a little luck.' Wengler took a deep drag on his cigarette. 'Inflation certainly played its part.'

'Your schnapps must have helped too.'

'It did.' Wengler gestured out of the window towards the chimney. 'The distillery didn't always look like this. I built a new bottling plant and storage tanks. Today *Luisenbrand* is famous all over the world.'

Rath gave a nod of acknowledgement. 'Not to say, a licence to print money.'

'*Luisenbrand* is a success story, but you mustn't think it comes with the territory here in East Prussia. Since we were cut off from the Reich, everything has become that much harder. Especially where agriculture is concerned. How much do you think the Prussian state collects in spirit duty when you're no longer categorised as a small-scale producer?'

'Which you no longer are.'

'It isn't just your salary we're financing with our taxes, Inspector. You can't blame us for Prussia's liquidity problems.' Wengler sounded more conciliatory now. 'Why do you need to know all this? It has nothing to do with Herbert, or your murder inquiry.'

'A man has to pass the time somehow. But let's get back to Herr Lamkau. How would you assess his character? I need you to be precise.'

'Herr Lamkau was one of my most capable employees. Operations manager, as I said, and he kept things here shipshape. No idling on his watch. People respected him.'

'How about on the streets? Was he similarly . . . respected?'

'I don't know why you're still on about that. Herbert Lamkau was of impeccable character. People always wag their tongues when someone runs up against the law – even if nothing was ever proven.'

'Runs up against the law?'

'You don't know?' Wengler shook his head as if to say: *a fine inspector, you are*! 'I shouldn't speak ill of the dead, but you're bound to find out sooner or later. A few years ago, Herbert Lamkau was accused of selling moonshine as *Luisenbrand*. To this day, I still don't know if it was him or one of his employees. Naturally I had no choice but to fire him, to salvage the reputation of our brand.'

'You assigned him sole distribution rights in Berlin all the same. Wasn't that reckless?'

'Oh, I challenged him, believe me, but Herbert swore he had nothing to do with it. I offered him compensation, and he started afresh in Berlin, where no one knew him.'

'With some success.'

'With a great deal of success. Thanks to his dedication we've achieved market dominance throughout Central Germany.'

'You're convinced he was innocent?'

'Who can look into another person's mind? Even if he was guilty, I was certain he wouldn't try again, not after all that fuss. Mistakes like that you don't repeat.'

'That's just it,' Rath said. 'Exactly the same thing has occurred in Berlin. Didn't he pass on Kempinski's complaint?'

Gustav Wengler was flabbergasted. 'Kempinski's complaint? It's the first I've heard of it.'

Now Rath was surprised. If Lamkau hadn't passed on the complaint, there was every reason to suspect he *had* been making moonshine again. He placed the photo of Hans Wawerka alongside Lamkau's driving licence.

'What about this man here? Do you know him?'

'He looks familiar. Who is he?'

'Johann Wawerka.'

'Hänschen! Of course! He's changed a bit since I knew him. He was a labourer at the distillery.'

'And August Simoneit?'

'Simoneit? He was my top fitter. He kept the distillation plants in good nick, let me tell you. You hardly needed to ...' Wengler paused. He seemed to have a premonition. 'What's happened to these men?'

'They're dead. Perished the same way as Herbert Lamkau. We think their deaths are linked.' Wengler gazed, deep in thought, at the smoke from his cigarette. 'Now I know they were colleagues here at the distillery.'

'I'm afraid I can go one better ...' Rath was all ears. 'Wawerka and Simoneit were both involved in the moonshining scandal.'

36

The District Office Cellar Archive was deserted when Rath looked in around twelve. On the reading table was a pile of case files bearing the seal of the Marggrabowa District Court. He leafed through them. All docket numbers ended in '24' – probably an entire year's worth. Had Kowalski got through them already? How many could there be, in a place like this? He examined the pile, wondering whether he should take a closer look when a voice interrupted his thoughts. 'Herr Rath! How are things?'

Chief Constable Grigat stood in the door with his legs apart, thumbs hooked on his uniform belt, a broad smile under his shako.

'No cause for complaint.'

'I'm on my way to the *Salzburger Hof*, if you'd care to join me? We could talk over lunch.'

'Thank you, but I have an appointment already.'

'Well, then, how about tonight? I take supper in the *Königlicher Hof*. They have a terrace that gets the evening sun.' Chief Constable Grigat appeared to structure his day around mealtimes, and to choose his restaurants according to their cardinal point.

'Perhaps it could be arranged ... I'm looking for Assistant Detective Kowalski. You haven't seen him, have you?'

'If I understood him correctly, he was on his way to the newspaper office.'

229

'Because he found something?'

'I'm afraid he didn't say.'

At the marketplace a few men were clearing the remnants of the weekly market: cabbage and salad leaves that lay on the pavement, horse droppings and cowpat. Rath had hoped to park outside the offices of the *Treuburger Zeitung*, but the space was taken by an Adler sedan. Its owner, a businessman, was discussing advertising rates with a female employee. Rath interrupted. 'Where can I find Assistant Detective Kowalski?'

The woman nodded towards the back without breaking her flow.

Kowalski greeted him with what, by his standards, amounted to euphoria. 'You were right, Sir! About the paper, I mean. There was nothing in the files, but here...'

Rath drew a headline in the air. 'Moonshining scandal,' he said. 'The good name of the Mathée firm besmirched. Operations manager and two employees arrested.'

Kowalski looked at the papers in confusion. 'You already know?'

'Director Wengler was very forthcoming.'

'Even though the distillery was caught up in the affair?'

'You'd be amazed what a sound interrogation technique can yield.' He grinned. 'The fact that proceedings were discontinued made it easier for Herr Wengler to divulge.'

'Discontinued,' Kowalski said. 'That may be, but it was in the papers for weeks. I've gathered all articles related to the case. You can see for yourself.'

For the most part the articles confirmed what Wengler had said. The director himself was quoted on numerous occasions, stressing that the Luisenhöhe distillery had nothing to do with the scandal. In fact, it was a victim, since the bottles containing the tainted schnapps all carried the *Luisenbrand* label. *We will do everything in our power to assist police in their inquiries*, he had said.

'There must be *something* about this in the files,' Rath said. 'Even if proceedings were discontinued, there was still an investigation.'

'I've been through the whole of 1924. Two or three cases involved moonshining, but nothing compared to this, and none mentioned *Luisenbrand*.'

'You're sure you've seen them all?'

'Chief Constable Grigat had everything from 1924 sent over.'

'Grigat?' Rath asked.

'Yes.'

Rath took the pile of newspapers and made for the door. 'Come with me,' he said, when Kowalski gave him a questioning look. 'Come with me!'

Erich Grigat was eating his dessert when they entered the *Salzburger Hof* dining area. Kowalski stayed by the door while Rath went over. Grigat looked up, making a surprised face. 'Ah, Inspector! Did you have a change of heart?' He gestured towards his pudding bowl. 'You're a little late. I'm afraid I'm just finishing up.'

'I'm not here to eat,' Rath placed a yellowed front page of the *Oletzkoer Zeitung* on the table. He slammed his fists on the dusty paper. 'This caused quite a stir in your town eight years ago.' He read from the report. '*Marggrabowa. Three men have been taken into custody today for their part in the Luisenbrand moonshining scandal. As has been previously reported, the bootlegged alcohol, the consumption of which has been deemed extremely hazardous, was stowed and marketed in original Mathée Luisenbrand bottles. The men in custody are all distillery employees, and include the operations manager. Police continue to investigate.*'

'What's this got to do with me?'

'*Police continue to investigate,*' Rath repeated. 'Lamkau, Simoneit and Wawerka were under investigation in the spring of 1924, and I have to get it from the papers!'

231

'Why the fuss? The most important thing is you know now.'

The greedy constable's composure riled Rath even more than the missing police file. With some effort, he controlled himself.

'For two days you have known that the Berlin Police is trying to establish a link between these three men,' he said. 'You give me a paper-thin file that contains little more than their names and have Kowalski here plough through any number of case files, all of which are irrelevant. But the decisive file concerning the *Luisenbrand* scandal . . .' – He beat down on the paper again. – ' . . .is strangely nowhere to be found.' He took a deep breath and smiled. 'That's why the fuss.'

'I'm sure there's an explanation,' Grigat said, dabbing at his mouth with a serviette. 'Assistant Detective Kowalski requested all case files from the year 1924, and I had them sent over.'

'Except clearly you didn't . . .' Rath took a deep breath. 'You're in charge of the police here . . .'

'In the whole Oletzko district!'

'Which means you ought to be able to supply case files in their entirety!' Rath shook his head. 'What a fucking mess!'

'Moderate your tone, Inspector!' Grigat placed his serviette on the table and stood up. His moustache twitched. 'You're forgetting yourself, and who you're speaking to. The Oletzko District Police will not stand for it, you are not my superior!'

'No, you're right there.' Rath rummaged for the letter he hadn't wanted to use. 'Dr Bernhard Weiss in Berlin is my superior. He's counting on me to solve a murder, and he's counting on *you* to assist me in my inquiries.'

'What more do you want? I've done exactly as your Dr Weiss requested. I had a file put together on the men in question, granted you and your colleague access to our records and prepared a workstation for you complete with telephone. I've given you every possible assistance, and even raised the prospect of *additional* support. It's you who hasn't taken advantage of it!'

'I don't need support. What I need is a better organised regional police authority and district court.'

'Now, listen here, Inspector!' Grigat turned red. 'We don't have many police officers in Treuburg and the Oletzko district. Here in town I have a handful at my disposal, as well as two secretarial staff. Outside of Treuburg there are a dozen gendarmerie posts and the Border Commissariat in Gross-Czymochen, and that's it. When things get tight – if someone's sick or on holiday – then we call in reinforcements from Goldap or Lyck. We can't always go by the book, as you can in Berlin. We have to take things as they come: to identify unroadworthy vehicles and conmen alike; attend to registry tasks as well as criminal records. Files relating to an age-old case are the least of our worries. Apart from that, the archiving of case files is the responsibility of the district court and public prosecutor's office, not the regional police authority.'

Rath decided to backpedal. Warring with the local authorities was no help to anyone. 'You're right, Constable. My apologies. I've no intention of arguing with you. You cannot be held responsible for every foul-up that occurs in Treuburg. In all likelihood, as you say, the error lies with the court.'

'I'm glad you see it that way, Inspector.' The man's moustache ceased twitching.

'Now,' Rath said, managing a smile, 'let's find out why that moonshining file was never delivered.'

'Now?' Grigat made the sort of horrified face that was the trademark of dyed-in-the-wool public officials everywhere. 'On a Friday afternoon?'

*

233

The district court building was located next to the district office, and most employees seemed to have finished for the weekend. Only the porter remained when Rath looked in with Grigat and Kowalski.

'Afternoon, Feibler,' Grigat said.

The dishevelled old man in the porter's lodge stood to attention. 'Sir!'

'Anyone in Registry?'

'No one, Sir!'

'We need to look inside. It's urgent. You have a key, don't you?'

The porter's gaze flitted suspiciously between them. As a good Prussian, he was loyal to Grigat, but unsure of his companions.

'I'm afraid I'm not authorised to give out files, Sir.'

'That won't be necessary,' Rath interrupted. 'We are concerned about the whereabouts of a particular document. Once we establish that, we'll proceed through the proper channels.'

The porter eyed him suspiciously but lifted the wooden barrier and exited his lodge. He led them into a chilly, windowless room secured by a steel door. 'Year?' he asked.

'Twenty-four,' Rath said.

'I see. Then we'll have to check the archive. Right at the back.'

Once inside, the porter switched on the light. 'Inventory's here,' he said, gesturing towards a thick tome, but they didn't need the inventory to locate the shelf. Two racks above floor level had been cleared. Rath crouched to look. Nothing: neither on nor behind the shelves.

'Like I told you,' Grigat said. 'I had everything sent over.'

'Then the file must be somewhere else.' Rath went over to the inventory and traced down the index of cases from 1924 to find: *Lamkau. Infringement Against Reich Alcohol Legislation*. He took out his notebook and recorded the

234

docket number and archive shelf mark. Soon he was back in front of the empty shelf. 'The file must have been here,' he said, looking at Kowalski. 'Are you sure you haven't overlooked something?'

'Believe me, Sir, I looked through everything, page by page.'

Rath turned to the porter. 'There must be some index documenting which files have been removed?'

'Of course, but the inventory won't help you. The withdrawal register's back the way we came.'

'Let's take a look inside then.'

'I don't know if I'm authorised ...' the porter began, but Rath cut him off.

'Listen, I'm not sure if you've realised, but the three of us, we're the good guys. We're not here to make your life difficult.'

The porter looked at Grigat inquiringly.

'He's right, Feibler. Let us look inside.'

No one could accuse the registry office of being disorganised. Under today's date was a record of one hundred and seven case files, complete with docket number and archive shelf mark. Grigat wasn't lying. Rath compared the sequences against his notebook but found no match.

'Someone must have taken the file.'

He leafed back through the withdrawal register, paying attention only to the final two numbers. Most dated from 1930 or later, but then, little by little, older cases began to appear. Rath had already gone back a few pages when his finger alighted on a sequence ending in '24'. He checked his notebook. A match!

Case file II Gs 117/24 had been withdrawn almost three years ago.

'Date of withdrawal, Monday, 30th September 1929,' Rath read. 'By a *PM Naujoks*.' He looked at the porter. 'Is it normal for case files to be out this long?' The man with the uniform cap shrugged. 'Goddamn it!' Rath said. 'Someone must know!'

The porter winced at every word, but Grigat's thoughts were elsewhere.

'Naujoks?' he asked. 'Polizeimeister Robert Naujoks?'

'You know the man?'

'I wouldn't say "know". Robert Naujoks was my predecessor here. He took early retirement.'

'He's the one stashing these case files?' Rath was surprised. 'I don't know about you, but I picture *my* retirement differently.'

'Naujoks was a strange bird.' Grigat gestured towards the date in the register. 'The 30th of September must have been his final day on the job. I started exactly one day later.'

37

Robert Naujoks was younger than Rath expected, in his late fifties. The former police constable had chosen to spend his retirement outside the Oletzko region, in a garden settlement in the district capital of Lyck, about thirty kilometres south of Treuburg, and situated, likewise, on a lake. It seemed lakes were a necessary condition of Masurian town life.

The Lycker Lake had a small island that was connected by bridge to the mainland, and it was this island that Naujoks viewed from his study window as he sat smoking his pipe. There are worse fates, Rath thought, as he and Kowalski were shown to their seats.

'So, you're interested in the *Luisenbrand* affair,' Naujoks said. He wore braces over his shirt, and in his cantankerousness was slightly reminiscent of Wilhelm Böhm – despite being ten years older, white-haired, and without a walrus moustache.

'We're interested in Herbert Lamkau, August Simoneit and Johann Wawerka,' Rath said. 'A chunk of whose past is contained on your shelves.'

'The file you mentioned on the telephone? Why these three? Are you investigating them?'

'I'm investigating whoever is responsible for their deaths.'

Naujoks's eyebrows gave a twitch. 'They're dead?'

237

'Yes.'

Excepting his eyebrows, Naujoks remained motionless.

A maid served tea. Robert Naujoks was clearly a bachelor, a status common among police officers. Rath wondered if there might be a reason, realising, in the same moment, that he hadn't contacted Charly, hadn't even sent a postcard since arriving in East Prussia.

He took a sip of tea. 'I used to know a Naujoks in Cologne,' he said. 'We were altar boys together, a long time ago. You're not related?'

Naujoks looked at him blankly. 'I'm Protestant.'

Like Böhm, the man was impossible to engage in relaxed conversation. 'Why did you take the file?' Rath asked, 'on the day of your retirement?'

Like a stony monument to police investigators of the old school, Robert Naujoks sat on his leather-upholstered armchair and stared blankly out of the window. Only the occasional glow of tobacco from his pipe bowl gave any indication that he was still alive.

Naujoks took the pipe from his mouth and leaned forward. 'Do you know that feeling? When a case just won't let go?'

Rath, who knew all too well, nodded his response. 'They're the ones you'd do anything to close,' he said. 'Damn nuisance for your private life when the work follows you home. It can swallow you up.'

'That's just it. My case isn't closed. Proceedings were discontinued at the behest of the public prosecutor.'

'You were called off?'

'If you like.' Naujoks looked out of the window. 'Though I'm no dog.'

In some ways he was not unlike a bulldog, albeit one distinguished by years of service. He manoeuvred his body out of the leather chair with surprising ease, and fetched a thick lever arch file with the reference number II Gs 117/24 from the shelf. He placed it on the table. 'Here it is,' he said.

Rath opened the cover. Photographs of Lamkau and Wawerka gazed back and, for the first time, Simoneit's face was there too. The trio might not have inspired confidence but they didn't look like hardened criminals either. Simoneit appeared almost delicate, unlike Wawerka, who was a great hulk of a man. Only Lamkau's face had something nasty, something devious, about it.

'A trio of moonshiners,' Rath said, looking at Naujoks. 'Hardly a spectacular case, even if a prominent distillery was implicated. What is it that won't let you go? The fact that you couldn't prove anything?'

He knew the investigation had stalled, having read the newspaper articles in the car on the half-hour journey over. It was even alleged that a distilling kettle with Lamkau's prints had been taken from the evidence room. In other words, not the retired constable's finest hour.

'The answer's in there,' said Naujoks.

'And *my* answer? Why the three men were killed?'

'I'd need more information about their deaths.'

'None of them died well. They were paralysed by Indian arrow poison and drowned. We still don't know the exact cause of death. But ...'

'Indian arrow poison?' Naujoks raised his eyebrows.

'Two died in their beds, one in a freight elevator, but what it has to do with moonshining beats me. Apart from the fact that Lamkau was clearly at it again in Berlin, this time with a prominent business.'

'It wasn't just moonshining, Inspector,' Naujoks said, knocking out his pipe. 'We also investigated a fatality.' He stood to retrieve a second folder. 'And I believe the two cases are linked.'

A little later, Rath and Kowalski sat in the car heading northeast. Kowalski steered with the same pensive expression he had maintained in Naujoks's parlour, but somehow this was different. Rath couldn't have said just how, but he was starting to understand that Masurian silence was a multifarious beast.

'Something on your mind?' he asked.

Kowalski took a moment before he began. 'I didn't want to say anything in the presence of Chief Constable Naujoks, Sir.'

'What didn't you want to say? Do you think he killed our trio?'

'No.' Rath had meant it as a joke, but Kowalski shook his head, deadly serious. 'There could be someone with a motive.'

'Who?'

'Did you see Naujoks's reaction when you mentioned the Indian arrow poison?'

Rath nodded.

'Perhaps I should tell you the story of the Radlewski family ...'

Martha Radlewski was the fatality Naujoks had touched upon, a notorious drunk found dead in her shanty on the outskirts of town. Next to the body was an almost empty bottle of the tainted *Luisenbrand*. Naujoks believed she had died from methanol poisoning, but was alone in this view, and somehow the investigations were never merged. Noting the abnormal size of Martha Radlewski's liver, the pathologist had expressed astonishment that she'd made it to forty-nine, and attributed her death to alcohol abuse in general, rather than the tainted Korn.

Naujoks had said nothing about a Radlewski family, but why would he? The files attested that Martha Radlewski had died alone and destitute, a long-time slave to the bottle.

'If there's a story, then why didn't Naujoks tell it?'

'Perhaps he doesn't know,' Kowalski said. 'Though

240

he must do – everyone here does. I'd guess his silence is a means of protecting someone. Perhaps he regards these deaths as a kind of belated justice and doesn't want to voice his suspicions.'

'You know who he's trying to protect?'

Kowalski nodded. 'The Kaubuk.'

'The what?'

'The Kaubuk. A kind of bogeyman that generations of Masurian parents have used to scare naughty children. Only, here in the Oletzko district, he's real.' It was the first time Rath had heard Kowalski say so much in one go. 'His name is Artur Radlewski.'

Kowalski didn't finish until they'd reached the Lyck road and were filtering into Treuburg.

The story was among the strangest Rath had ever heard. An oddball had lived in the forests around Treuburg since at least the outbreak of war. He dressed like an Indian in leather and hides, hunted with a bow and arrow, and lived on whatever nature could provide. He had fled home as an adolescent and was supposedly Martha Radlewski's son.

'You think he's avenging his mother's death?'

Kowalski shrugged. 'When you mentioned the Indian arrow poison, I couldn't help thinking of the Kaubuk. Naujoks too, I'd be willing to bet.'

'So, which forest do we find him in, this Kaubuk? Or Radlewski, I should say.'

'I've no idea where his hideout is. People say it's on the moors, somewhere only he and his dog know, though it's possible he doesn't live there any more. The story is from my childhood, and I haven't been in this part of Masuria for years.' Kowalski shrugged. 'I don't know, it was just an idea.'

'The man would certainly have motive, but why wait this long?'

'Perhaps because he had to find our trio first, and go

west, into the cities. Not easy when you look like an Indian. Who knows how long it'd take to get used to civilisation again after all these years?'

'Supposing Radlewski junior has left the wilds to avenge his mother. Do you think Naujoks might be holding something back?'

'Unlikely. He was just as surprised as me when he heard about the arrow poison.'

'Would Artur Radlewski be capable of making such a thing?'

'All I know is he's supposed to live like an Indian. I've never seen him myself.'

'Is there someone who could tell me more?'

'My uncle perhaps. Or we could ask in Wielitzken, which, to my knowledge, is where the Radlewskis lived. Perhaps there's someone who knew him as a child.'

'Let's head to your uncle's now.'

Kowalski had just steered the Wanderer onto the Treuburg marketplace when Rath's gaze alighted on the advertising pillar. Above the sorry-looking remains of the Communist placards, someone had scrawled *Rotfront verrecke* in red ink. Red Front Die. Most likely someone dressed in brown, thought Rath, cheered on by the good citizens of Treuburg.

Kowalski parked the car on Goldaper Strasse and the two of them got out. *F. Kowalski, Shoemaker* the sign on the house front said.

'On you go and ask,' Rath said.

'You're not coming in?'

Rath shook his head. 'You question your uncle; I'll try my luck in Wielitzken.' He gestured towards the front door. 'Find out what he has to say about the Kaubuk, and submit your report in the morning. And, please, not a word to Grigat. I don't know how far we can trust him. We'll talk tomorrow.'

Kowalski nodded, proud to have been taken into Rath's confidence. 'Yes, Sir. You know, it's strange ...'

'What is?'

'Whenever I misbehaved as a child I was afraid the Kaubuk might come and get me ...' Kowalski grinned. 'Well, now it's the Kaubuk's turn to be afraid.'

38

Rath pulled over by a gas station on Lindenallee, just behind the town mill, and skimmed through Robert Naujoks's files while the attendant checked the oil level and tyre pressure. The ex-chief constable might not have been entirely honest with them, but he'd gladly parted with both documents he'd swiped on the day of his retirement, the second of which, previously housed at Lyck District Court, concerned the Radlewski investigation, a lead they might otherwise have missed.

At first glance the files were of little use. The pathology report mitigated against Naujoks's theory that the cases were linked. It was true that he had arranged a chemical analysis of the confiscated hooch, which had yielded potentially fatal levels of methanol, but despite the various bottles in circulation, Martha Radlewski's death in 1924 was an isolated incident. Perhaps Naujoks had been gripped by an obsession, but if Artur Radlewski had drawn the same conclusions there was no question he'd have motive.

Kowalski's story about the Kaubuk who lived like an Indian in the forest seemed outlandish – it wasn't even clear if the man was still alive – but it was something like a lead. They had found someone with a plausible motive for killing the three moonshiners. Rath wondered if the tainted booze might not have claimed other victims whom neither Naujoks nor the deceased trio knew anything about.

Either way, at some point proceedings against Lamkau, Simoneit and Wawerka had been discontinued. Had Gustav Wengler smuggled his employees out west because he feared they could be avenged? By Radlewski? Had he, Radlewski, gone unsighted for so long because he'd been killing people in Berlin, Dortmund and Wittenberge? Or was the Kaubuk long dead himself?

He had to learn more about this strange Masurian Indian. He waited for the attendant to finish cleaning his windscreen, then paid and asked for a receipt. Heading south, signposts informed him that the Polish border was only sixteen kilometres away.

He reached Wielitzken after a few minutes via a ramrod-straight road that took a sharp curve just before the village. The schoolhouse was a low, elongated building near an ancient wooden church that was set back from the road in a slightly elevated position and hidden behind a few old trees.

After first trying his flat, he found the schoolmaster in his spacious classroom. On his desk in front of the blackboard was a fragile mini-laboratory of tubes and bottles. In a large glass vessel a cloudy-brown liquid boiled and bubbled away, while a second, smaller glass vessel collected drop after drop of a glassy distillate.

Rammoser was sniffing at a test tube when Rath entered. He looked up in surprise. 'Inspector! Good of you to stop by. Finished for the day already?'

'Sorry to interrupt. Are you preparing a lesson?'

'More of a hobby. During the holidays I have the run of the classroom.'

'Looks like you'd have made a good chemist.'

'I doubt it.' Rammoser laughed and waved the test tube. 'Fancy a sniff?'

The scent was extremely familiar.

'You're ... distilling schnapps.'

245

'Correct.'

'That's illegal!'

'Come off it,' Rammoser said. 'Where there's no complaint, there can be no redress. Lots of people are at it around here.'

'Some of them have died.'

'Do you think I'm making some cheap rotgut? The recipe is from my father.'

'Your father was a master distiller?'

'My father, God rest his soul, was a village schoolmaster, like me. In the same village, in this very school. A man with a *thirst* for righteousness.'

'All right. I've no intention of impugning your father's good name, or of locking you up ...'

'That would be a thing, after I saved your skin yesterday.'

'...although I am here on duty.'

'Shame. I was about to offer you a taste. You won't find schnapps like this anywhere on the market.' Rammoser held the glass towards him. 'Go on, have a sip. Then you'll see why I bother.'

'As long as you guarantee I won't go blind.'

'You won't go blind, that much I can guarantee.' The teacher grinned. 'But after that, you're on your own.'

'Then perhaps I will take a glass.'

'I thought you were on duty?'

'I've done too much overtime already. This can just as easily be a private conversation.'

Rammoser switched off the flame and turned a few valves. 'Come on, let's go next door. Erna can make us a little something for supper. We can have a drink while we wait.' He went over to the naughty corner and picked out a bottle from the line of corks.

Moments later they sat in the cosy lounge of the teacher's apartment, a bottle and two glasses arranged in front of them on the table. Rammoser hadn't been exaggerating.

The pear schnapps was unbelievably mild, imbuing Rath's body with a pleasant warmth.

'You need it sometimes,' Rammoser said. 'The winters here are long. This is the coldest region in Germany.'

'Didn't feel that way today.'

'It isn't always so humid. There's a storm brewing. When it breaks, things will be cooler again, but you didn't come here to discuss the weather.'

'I came to discuss Artur Radlewski. Apparently, he's from here?'

Rammoser shot him a glance that held surprise and suspicion in equal measure. 'What's Artur got to do with all this?'

'It could be related to the death of his mother. Did you know him?'

'My father taught him, actually, before the war. Highly intelligent, but very reserved.'

'No wonder, given his family history,' Rath said. 'Mother an alcoholic ...'

'His mother wasn't the issue,' Rammoser interrupted. 'I don't know what you've heard, but back when Artur still lived with her, she never touched a drop. It was her husband who drank. Not only that. Friedrich Radlewski was a brutal bastard who beat his wife black and blue whenever the mood took him. Who knows what else he did in front of the child, or how often the boy tried to help his mother and took a beating for his troubles.'

Rammoser took a sip of schnapps.

'From time to time,' he went on, 'my father would appeal to Radlewski senior's conscience but, next day, little Artur either failed to attend school, or had apparently fallen from the hayloft. As time went on, he grew more reserved, and sought refuge in books about Indians. It was all he cared about, and my father supplied him with what titles he could, starting with Karl May, but soon enough Artur wanted to read other things, travelogues, the truth about the North American Indians.'

'Even back then he wanted to be an Indian . . .'

'He needed an escape, and my father helped him find it. I still remember how he once went all the way to Königsberg to source books for him. Since he couldn't get him away from his father he wanted at least to encourage him. Perhaps he thought little Artur was planning to emigrate to America. I don't know.' Rammoser paused to top up their glasses. 'Do you have any cigarettes?'

Rath laid his case on the table. 'Help yourself.' Rammoser lit an Overstolz, and Rath did likewise.

'Anyway,' Rammoser continued, 'the day came when Father cursed himself for having supplied the boy with so many books: the day they found a bare-skulled, bloodied Friedrich Radlewski dead outside his shanty. Someone had scalped him while he was still alive. His wife lay unconscious inside, covered in bruises. At first, they thought that Martha was dead too, but she was still breathing. There was no sign of Artur. Neither of him, nor his books. He must have been fourteen or fifteen at the time.'

'My God, what a tragic story.'

'No one mourned Fritz Radlewski. Most people were glad the bastard was in the ground.' Rammoser looked at Rath. 'Old Radlewski was rotten to the core. Some people are pure evil.'

'You don't have to tell a police officer that.'

'As a teacher, you have a duty to see the good in people but, if I've learned one thing in all these years, it is this. Most people are capable of good and evil, but there are some who are evil through and through. It doesn't matter if they're ten, fifty or a hundred years old.'

Rath nodded pensively. 'Perhaps you're right, but you can't lock people up for being *evil through and through*.'

'Friedrich Radlewski beat his wife half to death,'

Rammoser continued. 'She couldn't even leave the hospital for his funeral. She needed months to get back on her feet.'

'And Artur? He became the Kaubuk?'

'You've heard his nickname? I think it's a poor fit.' Rammoser took a drag on his cigarette. 'Artur remained missing. He was under suspicion, and the Landgendarmerie spent several days looking for him in vain. At some point, a travelling salesman claimed to have seen a figure in the forest behind Markowsken, flitting through the trees at supernatural speed. Suddenly other people started describing strange encounters in the forest, over by the border.'

'Which is where he lives to this day, terrifying women and children?'

'He doesn't terrify anyone, he avoids people.' Rammoser topped them up again. 'In the beginning, he must've slipped into the villages fairly regularly to stock up on essentials. A goose would go missing in Urbanken, the grocer's in Willkassen might report a paraffin lamp stolen; an entire toolbox vanished from the sawmill. In Markowsken, Kowalski senior had five rabbits pinched from his sheds. The most anyone ever saw was a shadow. That this elusive being could only be a spirit, could only be the Kaubuk, was a given for most people.'

'Turns out it was no more than a common thief.'

'Or someone trying to survive in the wilds.' Evidently Rammoser felt obliged to defend Radlewski. 'Most people thought as you did. When the thefts continued they threatened the Landgendarmerie, saying if the police couldn't find him, they'd start looking themselves, but then war broke out, the Russians rolled in and people had other things to worry about. At some point, the thefts ceased.'

'Perhaps Radlewski didn't survive the war?'

'The thefts might have ceased, but there were other mysterious goings-on in the forest. On one occasion a cow elk carcass was found with its hide missing, along with the best bits of meat. And there were any number of traps; primitive certainly, but immaculate in their design.'

'Radlewski's handiwork?'

'No one knows for sure, but there are fewer and fewer who remember the old stories. The last sighting was years ago, and for most people he has become a kind of mythical figure, a ghost. Others claim Radlewski has long since died or emigrated.'

'You don't think he's dead. I can see it in your eyes. You think he's still out there in the forest.'

Rammoser smiled for the first time since he'd started telling Artur Radlewski's story. 'There are no flies on you, Herr Rath.' He poured another glass of moonshine, and Rath realised he was becoming drunk. A pleasant feeling, it somehow brought him closer to this foreign world. He felt at one with himself, suddenly at home in Masuria, as if he had spent his whole life here.

'You're right,' Rammoser continued. 'I don't think Artur is dead. I think he's become so skilled at concealing himself and covering his tracks that no one's quick enough to see him.'

'Like an Indian.'

'Precisely.'

'What makes you so sure?'

'Let me tell you a different story . . .' Rammoser lifted his glass. 'Here in Treuburg we have a lending library, and every couple of months a few books inexplicably vanish. No one's ever discovered how, but the fact is they do. Every so often three or four titles will just go missing from the catalogue, as if by magic. Even more strangely, on the same morning these books are marked absent, the librarian will find a different pile on her desk, containing titles stolen in the previous weeks. Books about Indians, every last one.'

Rath couldn't help but laugh. 'Well, it is a lending library. You think a person who has withdrawn from civilisation is capable of reading so many books?'

Rammoser shrugged. 'I'd say he *must*. If he doesn't want to die of loneliness.'

39

Lange wore such a look of consternation that Charly felt duty-bound to ask what was wrong. Until she realised it was her.

'Have you been crying?' he asked as he stood to greet her.

She couldn't help but laugh. 'No,' she said. 'Chopping onions.'

In fact, she'd started in the salad kitchen today, which was considerably more enjoyable. Just as she struck up a conversation with the girl on the adjoining table Unger drafted her in for more onion chopping. Apparently, he wasn't too keen on his employees making small talk.

Lange straightened her chair like a gentleman of the old school, and she sat down. *Café Schottenhaml* on Kemperplatz was the sort of place they could pass themselves off as an amorous couple if one of her new colleagues should make an unexpected appearance. In truth, it was unlikely: *Schottenhaml* was modern, tasteful and elegant, no place for kitchen staff.

'I just thought ...your eyes ...'

'You're right. We look like we're in the middle of a tearful separation.'

Lange went red. 'The main thing is that no one thinks we're police officers.'

Charly opened her cigarette case. 'What's the latest

from East Prussia?' she asked, as casually as possible. 'Has Inspector Rath been in touch?'

Lange shook his head. 'Not yet, but he's only been there two days.'

'But he's definitely arrived?'

'The Treuburg Police have confirmed as much. A Chief Constable Grigat seemed curious to know what we were doing. Inspector Rath doesn't seem to have been especially forthcoming.'

'Isn't Böhm expecting a report?'

'Poor old Rath still doesn't know Böhm's taken over the case.' Lange grinned. 'Otherwise he might have been a little more conscientious.'

Or not, Charly thought, once he knew Böhm had been parachuted in again. 'Have you made any progress with the tubocurarine lead?' she asked.

'I'd say by now we've looked into all known sources of supply in Berlin. Still no luck.'

She couldn't help feeling reassured that her colleagues hadn't made much progress either. It meant the fault didn't lie with her or this business with Dettmann.

'Perhaps he's making the tubocurarine himself,' she said. 'Perhaps we should ask an expert what you'd need to cook it up.'

'Precisely what Gräf's doing tomorrow.'

'Of course.' Charly nodded, ashamed of her wiseacring. The waiter appeared, they ordered and Lange changed the subject. 'So, what do you have for me? Have you seen anything?'

'Not much. Chopping onions makes it rather tricky.'

'You poor thing.'

'I had more luck the day before yesterday. I managed to look inside a folder full of complaint letters. They were pretty harsh. Some of them sounded more like extortion.'

'You think Rath was onto something?'

'I still haven't managed to work out if Riedel and Unger know each other, but Unger seems pretty wary. It's possible that suppliers are being blackmailed.' She fetched a note from her pocket. 'I haven't found any correspondence with the Lamkau firm yet. If there was anything, it would most likely be in Riedel's office, but how I'm supposed to get in there beats me . . .' She passed the note across. '. . .I do have two addresses. Perhaps you should try and find out what kind of trouble they had with *Haus Vaterland* – and how they were able to smooth things over.'

Lange pocketed the note. 'Excellent,' he said. 'Thank you.'

'I'm afraid that's it. Today I've been mostly concentrating on my home-making skills.'

'How long do you think you'll be able to continue undetected?'

'Not too much longer, I hope, otherwise I'll need a new pair of eyes.'

'Well, just get through tomorrow, then it's the weekend.'

'For you maybe.' Charly forced a smile. 'Unger's already asked if I can work overtime on Sunday.'

Lange nodded as the drinks arrived.

'There was one more thing,' Charly said, once the waiter had taken his leave. 'I've met someone who seems to know the ropes.'

'Go on.' Lange took out his pencil.

'He knows Riedel, he says. The spirits man Unger is most likely in cahoots with. I've arranged to have a drink with him, tomorrow after work.'

'With Riedel?'

'No, with this waiter. A Negro from German East Africa.'

'A Negro? I hope you're not taking any unnecessary risks. Should I have someone tail you?'

Charly shook her head. 'If you really want to help, you could always chop some onions yourself!'

40

Yippee, yoohoo. Run, Julius, run and I'll catch you! I've got you! Julius, I'm faster than you. I'll run, I'll race, I'll zoom. And I'll catch you all. Eeny, meeny, miny, moe, catch a tiger by the toe . . .

Rath stared at an image of two happy children with satchels playing tag. A textbook, clearly. A primer. He tried to order his thoughts, but only when he sat up and rubbed his eyes did he realise where he was.

Morning sunlight filtered through a small window onto a skeleton hanging beside a desk. But for the rolled-up maps in the corner and a portrait of Hindenburg on the wall, it could have been a doctor's surgery. The Wielitzken village school staffroom, he remembered now. A woollen blanket slid to the floor as he rose from the sofa.

The primer was open on a side table. He snapped it shut and looked at the cover. *Der fröhliche Anfang. Happy Beginnings*. He recalled a similar book from childhood and reflected that some things never change. The smell of coffee wafted into the room, and he traced the aroma back to the teacher's apartment, where Karl Rammoser sat at breakfast, reading the paper. The *Treuburger Zeitung*. Of course.

'Morning, Inspector.' Rammoser was full of beans. 'Coffee? Erna's just brewed some fresh.'

Rath nodded. 'First I need to pee.'

255

'You know where.'

He made his way across the yard.

Erna. By the time the housekeeper had served supper last night, he was already experiencing problems with his balance. Their aperitif had stretched to half a bottle, and Rammoser's pear schnapps packed quite a punch. 'I don't think you should drive again tonight, Inspector,' he had said. 'Erna can make up the sofa in the staffroom.'

Erna proceeded to do just that, while the pair resumed their discussion. The problem was that Rath couldn't for the life of him remember what they had discussed. With the reappearance of the bottle, the *real* drinking had begun. Incredibly he didn't have a hangover, though the gaps in his memory troubled him. In the outhouse he washed his hands and splashed cold water on his face.

Coffee awaited him on return, and it did him the power of good. He would have liked a cigarette, but, out of consideration for Rammoser, made do with the bread basket. 'Late one last night . . .' he said.

The teacher shrugged. 'You had a lot of questions.'

'Occupational hazard.' A loud gong sounded behind him. He turned and saw a magnificent grandfather clock, then the dial, and hands. 'Damn it,' he said. 'Half past eight already. Is that clock right?'

'I hope so. We use it to set the school bell.'

'I need to make a telephone call.'

'Then you'll have to go to the post office.'

A little later Rath stood in the small, shadowy post office and waited as an old man conducted an important, or at least lengthy, telephone conversation. The branch had only one booth.

After two minutes it didn't look as if the conversation would ever end. He returned to the counter and gestured towards the black Bakelite device on the desk. 'It must be possible to make an outside call on that.'

'Not without authorisation.'

'Here's my authorisation.' He showed his identification.

The girl from *Salzburger Hof* came on the line. 'Hella? Hello!' he said, not realising how stupid he sounded until it was too late. 'Inspector Rath from room twenty-one. Is Assistant Detective Kowalski with you?'

'Herr Kowalski has been here over half an hour. You weren't in your room this morning.'

'Take the man a coffee and tell him I'll be there in a quarter of an hour.'

When he returned to the school Rammoser stood outside the building, a leather bag under his arm. 'Let me guess,' he said. 'You need to go into town.'

'I'm sorry. No time for breakfast.'

'All is forgiven,' Rammoser said. 'So long as you take me with you.'

'How will you get back?'

'By train.'

Rath opened the car door and cleared the case files from the passenger seat. 'Take a seat.'

Rammoser gestured towards the folder. 'Anything on Marta Radlewski's death in there?'

'Only the circumstances; nothing on her life, or why she turned to drink.'

Rammoser climbed in with his leather bag. 'A tragic irony, don't you think? No sooner is she rid of her drunk of a husband than she takes to the bottle herself.'

'What a life . . .' Rath started the car. 'I mean, what choice did she have? When you consider how her husband died; and her only son vanishing to live like an animal in the forest.' He accelerated onto the road.

'Like an *Indian* in the forest,' Rammoser said. 'You think that Artur Radlewski is avenging his mother's death? Because he believes she died as a result of the tainted *Luisenbrand*? Even though it happened years ago?'

'I don't think anything, but I'd like to speak to him.'

'That could prove tricky. I'd be willing to bet Artur hasn't spoken a word to anyone since vanishing.'

'Then he'd better start once we find him.'

'Finding him could prove trickier still.'

'We'll see.' On Bahnhofstrasse in Treuburg, the fire brigade were using ladders to put up black-and-white garlands. 'What's going on here?' Rath asked.

'Preparations for Monday.'

'For the marksmen's festival?'

'Plebiscite anniversary. The most important celebration of the year.'

'You mean the plebiscite of 1920.'

'Yes. You'll be aware of the result, above all here in the Oletzko district.'

'Yes, sir. Two votes for Poland.'

'Very good.' Rammoser smiled, but it was a pensive smile. 'Two out of almost thirty thousand counted. The young Polish state did its best to win the Masurians over. It even established an Agitation Bureau here in Marggrabowa, all in vain. The only upshot was that the Heimatdienst knew whose windows to smash at night.'

'Who?'

'The Marggrabowa Homeland Service. I told you last night. They campaigned for Prussia.'

'Yes, of course.' Rath searched his memory but found nothing. 'You don't think much of them?'

'Don't get me wrong, I voted for Prussia too, but even then I didn't like the way the Homeland Service sowed hatred against anything foreign, hatred against anything Polish; hatred and violence.' Rath pulled over by the *Salzburger Hof*. The schoolmaster wasn't finished. 'For hundreds of years,' he said, 'people in Masuria co-existed peacefully alongside one another. Then suddenly, after the war, hatred was all the rage. Not least because of people like Wengler and Lamkau.'

258

'Were they part of the Homeland Service?'

'Stick around until Monday, and you'll see Gustav Wengler in his element as Homeland Service Chief and acclaimed keynote speaker.' Rammoser looked around as if someone might be listening. 'As for Lamkau, you already know what I think. He and a few others did Wengler's dirty work for him.'

'By smashing Agitation Bureau windows.'

'Worse. Countless people were injured. I've already mentioned the beatings, but don't go thinking it stopped there. On one occasion a barn was set alight, over in Kleszöwen. It was a miracle there were no fatalities.'

'Are you telling me Lamkau waged a systematic campaign of fear and terror against Polish sympathisers here in Oletzko?'

'I just want you to know what kind of man you're dealing with.'

'A Nazi?'

'There weren't any Nazis back then, but brutal bastards who thought human life was worthless . . .they existed all right.' Rammoser opened the car door. 'Thanks for the lift, Inspector.'

With that, Karl Rammoser was gone. Rath gazed after him a time before exiting the vehicle himself. Entering the lounge he found Assistant Detective Kowalski sitting dutifully before his coffee. 'Morning, Sir.'

'Morning, Kowalski.' Rath took a seat and waved Hella over. She approached with the coffee pot and poured, even offered a smile as their eyes met. He lit a cigarette.

Kowalski seemed restless. 'What is it?' Rath asked. 'You look like you've seen the Kaubuk. Or perhaps you've caught him already?'

'We have a witness, Sir.'

'A witness?'

'Someone who knows the Kaubuk.'

259

'Personally?'

'My uncle claims old Adamek saw the Kaubuk last year. Out in the forest somewhere.'

'A taciturn sort, isn't he, this Adamek? Does he even speak German?' Kowalski looked at him blankly. 'Doesn't matter. You can always speak Masurian if need be.'

The journey took less than five minutes by car. Old Adamek lived in a small, one-storey building on the edge of town, more shanty than house. They knocked, but no one answered. Rath realised that the door was unlocked, pushed it open and stepped into the dark hall. 'Herr Adamek,' he called. No response. 'Herr Adamek? CID. We've a few questions we'd like to ask.'

Wilhelm Adamek wasn't home. Rath looked around. The decor was spartan. A table, two wooden stools, a pot-bellied stove. The only decoration on the wall was a framed photograph of Hindenburg, upon which an Iron Cross, Second Class was pinned. He opened a door that led to the back.

'Shouldn't we be going, Sir?' Kowalski seemed uncomfortable with his curiosity.

'I just want to make sure Adamek isn't lying dead in his bed. Or sleeping off his hangover.'

The bed was empty.

'Sir, he isn't here. We'll come back another time.'

'Strange bird, this Adamek, isn't he? Does he live alone?'

'His wife died a long time ago, my uncle says. During the war, when the Russians were here. They wreaked havoc in our district.'

'You were a child back then. Do you remember?'

'The fighting lasted nearly a year. In Markowsken too. For nights we couldn't sleep for fear; days were punctuated by the rumble of artillery fire.'

Rath was about to heed Kowalski's advice and leave, when he saw something that roused his curiosity. 'Just a moment . . .' On a stool by the bed was a mound of dirty washing.

'I thought we wanted to question Adamek. You're sniffing around like he's a suspect.'

'Who knows,' Rath said, lifting the flannel shirt that had attracted his attention. 'Perhaps he is.' He gestured towards the red-brown stain covering almost the entire right side. 'Unless I'm mistaken, this is dried blood. Lots of it, too.'

The assistant detective opened his mouth to say something when a dark shadow appeared in the door behind him. Rath heard a dull thud as Kowalski hit the ground like a sack of potatoes.

Seconds later he gazed into the double barrel of a shotgun and the inert, unshaven face of Wilhelm Adamek. The only sound was that of the hammer being cocked.

41

The place smelled of blood. Hardly the ideal start to the day.

An employee in white overalls led Andreas Lange along a cold storage hall, in which bloody, skinned cadavers hung from the ceiling, then through a room in which more white overalls stood at large tables hacking the corpses to pieces. Lange toyed with the idea of choosing a salad at lunch. The office was at the far end of the building. He wondered if there was an alternative access point.

Fehling Foods had its headquarters in Tegel, on the northern outskirts of the city. Franz Fehling was an elderly man with a neat white beard, who appeared more respectable than an evangelical pastor, and spoke just as unctuously. 'I'm surprised the police are bothering with this. It was over a year ago now. Besides, I thought all disputes between the Fehling firm and Kempinski had been resolved. I am *more* than surprised that Kempinski think it necessary ...'

'Kempinski don't think anything,' Lange interrupted. 'The Berlin Criminal Police are here of their own accord.'

'I'm afraid I don't understand.'

'You don't have to. It'll be enough to answer my questions.' It was a line he had from Rath. More often than not it had the desired effect. Clearly, Franz Fehling wasn't immune. Arrogant and upstanding moments before, almost imperceptibly the man's shoulders began to drop. 'How long have you supplied Kempinski?'

'Almost ten years, and our turnover is constantly increasing. Wild game is becoming ever more popular, at least where fine dining is concerned.'

Lange made a few notes. That, too, could put an interviewee on edge. Especially when you took your time. 'Did you receive any similar complaints before May 1931? From Kempinski? Or other clients?'

'Every so often one receives complaints . . .'

'Of course.'

'But not as grievous as these . . .' Fehling shook his head vigorously. 'Twenty kilos of fallow deer, and the whole lot crawling with maggots. To this day I can't explain how it happened.'

'I'd think it was the flies laying their eggs.'

'Oh, knock it off!' Fehling was shouting now. 'Have you any idea how strict the regulations are? We take a sample from each batch. There wasn't the slightest contamination. It wasn't until *Haus Vaterland* that the problem showed, and then the sheer scale of it . . . an absolute catastrophe.' He shook his head.

'Did you trace the origin of the fallow deer?'

'The meat came from a breeding farm near Soldin. In the New March.'

'A breeding farm? I thought you shot game in the forest.'

Fehling seemed put out. 'It stands to reason that in a city of four million the demand for game cannot be met by local hunting preserves alone. Besides, it's easier to treat the meat, and you don't have to pick out shotgun pellets before you start.'

Lange made several more notes. Fehling squinted nervously at the pad, but unless he was clairvoyant, he might as well give up. No one could read Andreas Lange's handwriting, sometimes not even Lange himself.

263

'Is that how it's usually done? Keeping game as livestock and then slaughtering, rather than shooting it?'

'Define "usually". The end customer shouldn't necessarily be aware.'

'What about the intermediate customer?'

'Meaning?'

'Kempinski.'

'The kitchen would know. There are no issues there. Our meat isn't any worse than wild game. If anything, it's better.'

'Except when it's overrun with maggots.' Fehling fell silent. The subject clearly made him uncomfortable. 'How,' Lange continued, 'did you manage to persuade the *Haus Vaterland* kitchen to keep using your firm as a supplier?'

Fehling's eyes flitted this way and that. 'Naturally we . . . Well, naturally the first thing we did was recall the spoiled product. And waive our fee.'

'I should think so.'

'Even though we weren't aware of any fault!'

'You never considered that the maggots might have got into the meat at *Haus Vaterland*?'

'Yes, but . . . it doesn't usually happen that fast. They take a while to hatch. Someone would've had to deliberately . . .' He waved the idea away. 'They noticed the next day.' He looked at Lange. 'So the buck stops with us.'

'I assume that Kempinski is an important client?'

'Of course.'

'A client you wouldn't want to lose, and no doubt it was important that news of the scandal didn't reach the public.'

'I don't know what you're driving at.'

'I'm just trying to work out how important it was for you that this matter be resolved, *discreetly* . . .'

'Of the utmost importance!'

' . . . and how much you were willing to invest to make it happen.'

Fehling no longer looked comfortable behind his desk. 'I don't know quite what it is you're insinuating, but I'd like you to leave my office now. I have work to do.'

Lange left his card on the desk. 'Perhaps you were, how shall I say this, *pressured*. If you ever want to talk, there's my number.'

He stood up, turning a final time to see Fehling reading his card. 'One last thing,' he said. 'Experience tells me that blackmail never ends. Once you've been squeezed the first time, it just carries on. The threat lingers in the air, and there's nothing you can do. A nasty feeling.' He put on his hat. 'A simple confession often works wonders.'

42

Rath stared into the darkness of the double barrel, not daring to move. He had raised both hands, one of which still held the bloody shirt. Old Adamek didn't breathe a word. Kowalski groaned from the floor.

He decided to put an end to the silence. 'We not intruders,' he said. 'We police. Myself and colleague.' He gestured towards Kowalski with his chin. The assistant detective was slowly coming round.

Adamek opened his mouth, and this time didn't speak Polish, or even broken German. There was a light, singsong quality to his Masurian accent. 'What are you doing in my home? Do you have a search warrant?'

Rath forced a smile. 'We wanted to question you. The door was open and we ...'

'Have you been sniffing around?'

'I just wanted to check you weren't in bed.'

'You're trespassing.'

He hadn't expected old Adamek to have such command of the Penal Code, or, for that matter, the German language. 'I've explained why we're here. Now, perhaps you could explain why you floored my colleague and are holding me at gunpoint.'

'Because I thought you were intruders.' The man refused to lower his gun.

'Well, now you know we aren't.'

Kowalski sat up and felt his head. He needed a moment to grasp the situation, then said something to Adamek that sounded like Masurian-Polish. The man responded in kind, weapon trained as before. There was a brief back-and-forth until Wilhelm Adamek finally lowered the shotgun. Rath put his hands down.

'Would you like a tea?' Adamek asked. Rath nodded, and the old man vanished inside the lounge.

'What did you say to him?' he asked.

'That no one cares if he's been poaching in the Markowsken forest or anywhere else. We won't be bringing charges for that, or this little episode here.' Kowalski pointed towards the blood-encrusted shirt. 'Why don't you put it back with the other dirty things, otherwise he'll think we're collecting evidence against him.'

'Adamek's a poacher?'

'Any five-year-old will tell you that, but no one's going to report him. Everyone gets something out of it. He supplies the entire catering trade in Treuburg. Besides, he's a war hero who fought against the Russians; people don't forget.'

'Goddamn it,' Rath said. 'The things I'm expected to turn a blind eye to. Two days I've been here . . .it's worse than Berlin!'

'Look on it as an exercise in trust-building.'

'Is that what they teach you at police academy these days?'

'Sir, don't make any trouble, otherwise we won't get anything more out of him. Don't forget we're here for the Kaubuk. Besides . . .' Kowalski gestured towards the back of his head. 'I'm the one who's borne the brunt of our truce.'

'Let's have a look.' Rath inspected the cut, which was still bleeding slightly. 'That's going to leave a nasty bump. Make sure you keep it iced.'

Wilhelm Adamek soaked a cloth for Kowalski, which he served with the tea. They sat at the table in the lounge. He didn't say anything about the bloody shirt, or Kowalski's bump, or anything that had occurred in the last quarter of an hour. He hadn't said a single word since his Masurian-Polish exchange with Kowalski.

'Apologies again for bursting in like that, Herr Adamek,' Rath began. It took some willpower, but Kowalski was right: they had to win Adamek's trust if they were to get anything out of him. 'We were acting in good faith. We're here because we want to speak to you about Artur Radlewski.'

'The Kaubuk...' Adamek nodded, waiting for their questions.

A Rhinelander, Rath thought, would have declared himself satisfied with this conversational gambit and talked a blue streak; he would have positively effervesced with information and told them anything that came to mind, and more besides.

Clearly Masurians were more like Westphalians, which was no doubt why they felt so at home in Dortmund, Bochum or Gelsenkirchen. Rath imagined he was dealing with a Westphalian. An East Westphalian, at that.

'You know something about the Kaubuk?' he asked. Adamek nodded, but still said nothing. 'You've seen him?'

Another nod.

'Where?'

'In the forest.'

Rath could tell this exchange was going to test the limits of his patience. 'Can you be a little more precise?'

Adamek nodded again. Rath was about to probe further when the old-timer continued. 'Out by the border. Less than a year ago.'

'When, exactly?'

Adamek considered. 'Before Christmas, I think. There was snow lying.'

'Can you describe the man?'

'He had a bow and arrow, as usual. Tanned; long hair, dressed in leather and hides.'

'Like an Indian,' Rath said, more to himself than Adamek.

'Like the Kaubuk.'

'You're certain it was Artur Radlewski?'

'It isn't the first time I've seen the Kaubuk.'

'You've come across him before?'

'He lives out there. Spend enough time in his forest, and you'll run into him every once in a while. I'm the only one around here who ventures that deep. Most people don't like to, because of the moors. They can be treacherous if you don't know your way around.'

Look at the man go! Rath felt proud at having persuaded him to open up like this. 'But you. You know your way around?' Adamek gave him a look of reproach, or contempt, perhaps, it was hard to tell. 'Could you take us to him?'

Now the man's gaze held plain suspicion. 'Why?'

'We urgently need to speak with him.'

'He doesn't speak with anyone.'

'We'll see about that. The police have their methods ...'

'You won't find him. He isn't there.'

'Pardon me?'

'Hasn't been there all winter.'

'How do you know that?'

'Because there was no smoke from his hut, all winter long.'

'You know where his hut is?'

'No.'

'But you just said ...'

'I said, I didn't see any pillars of smoke over the moor.'

'But you know Radlewski lives in a hut, and lights fires.'

'How else would he survive the winter?' Adamek looked at Rath as if he had taken leave of his senses.

'And last winter he wasn't there.'

'That's what I just said.'

Adamek must take him for a real windbag. 'Could you take us there? To this hut?'

The old-timer looked at Kowalski, who shrugged, then back at Rath. 'Not right there, but I could take you close.'

'Fine,' Rath said. 'Take us close. We'll manage the rest by ourselves.'

'I wouldn't advise it, the area's dangerous. Lots of moorland. I wouldn't advise anyone to go there. Besides, you won't find him. He isn't there.'

'Perhaps he's returned.'

'He wasn't there this morning.'

'This morning?'

'Where do you think I've just come from?'

'How do you know he isn't there? He won't be lighting any fires in July.'

'I can feel it.'

'Pardon me?'

'I can feel if there's someone else in the forest. I can't explain it.'

Rath gave up. 'It's some time since you saw Artur Radlewski. Do you think you could still describe him?'

'I already have. Long hair, tanned, leather and hides ...'

'I mean his face. How he'd look if he cut his hair, or wore a suit.'

For the second time Adamek gazed at Rath as if he were a sandwich short of a picnic. 'If you think it would help, but I can't imagine the Kaubuk ever cutting his hair.'

43

The post office was the largest building in the marketplace, diagonally across from an advertising pillar newly covered by Communist posters. Rath didn't have to wait long for a booth. Grigat had provided him with a desk and telephone in the district administrative office, but he preferred to sacrifice his loose change. Having now dispensed of Kowalski, he had no wish for the company of the meddling police constable.

Overzealous Kowalski had been itching to hunt for the Kaubuk, but Rath ordered him back to his uncle. 'Go and see to that head of yours. Have a lie-down. You might be concussed; a little rest couldn't hurt.'

'Fresh forest air would do just as well.'

'If Artur Radlewski is behind these murders he'll be somewhere in Berlin, clean-shaven and freshly coiffed. The one place he won't be is his forest retreat.'

'If he's finished the job, why shouldn't he have returned?'

'Old Adamek doesn't think he's there, and he was in the forest this morning. Besides, we don't know that Radlewski *has* finished the job.'

'We should still take a look at his hideout.'

'We will, as agreed with Adamek. All in good time. First I need to call Berlin and submit my report. I won't forget your contribution, Kowalski. You have a good nose.'

Kowalski was embarrassed by the praise. 'It was thanks to my uncle, really.'

'Give him my regards.'

After Kowalski was gone, Rath lit a cigarette and thought things through in peace. He did his best thinking alone; in fact, it was something he could do *only* when free of distraction.

He fetched the two files from the rear seat and skimmed them again. Martha Radlewski was forty-nine years old when she died, and hadn't seen her only son in over ten years. Had the Kaubuk still cared about his mother and, if so, how had he learned of her death and the circumstances surrounding it?

At length he snapped the folder shut and crossed to the post office, but his mind was still racing as he waited to be connected with Berlin. The library! The district library. What had Rammoser said about the books that had been stolen at regular intervals, and then returned? An idea started to form as the operator returned him to the present. 'Caller. Your connection with Berlin.'

'Thank you.'

A switch flicked and the Berlin exchange came on the line. He asked for Reinhold Gräf's extension. The connection was astonishingly good. Too good, as it proved.

'Homicide, Detective Chief Inspector Böhm,' a voice barked down the receiver.

Rath was so taken aback that, for once, he forgot to identify himself. 'Isn't that Detective Gräf's extension?'

'Who's speaking, please?'

'Rath here, Inspector Rath.'

'Our man in Masuria.'

'I was hoping to speak with Detective Gräf. Or someone else from the *Vaterland* team.'

'If it's work-related, and I hope very much that it is, then you'll have to make do with me.'

'It's about the *Vaterland* case, and I ...'

'Talk to me. I'm leading the investigation.'

'I'm sorry, you're what?'

'Superintendent Gennat asked me to take over. The *Bellevue* team has been dissolved, and you requested reinforcements.'

He couldn't believe it. Gennat had parachuted Böhm in again. *Böhm*, of all people! If this was punishment for spilling ink over Dettmann, he'd sooner have taken his chances with a disciplinary hearing. 'I'm sorry, Sir, I'm just a little surprised.'

'You only have yourself to blame, Inspector. If you'd made contact sooner, you'd have been in the picture long ago. But for Chief Constable Grigat's telephone call, we wouldn't even have known you'd arrived safely.'

'With respect, Sir, I didn't see any reason to make contact until there'd been a breakthrough.'

'I'm all ears.'

Switchboard cut in. 'Caller? Your conversation will be terminated in thirty seconds. If you wish to continue, please insert ten pfennigs.'

He wedged the receiver against his shoulder and rummaged in his wallet for change, cursing inwardly. On top of everything else he had to fritter his money away on Böhm.

'Are you in a public telephone booth?' Böhm asked.

'Yes, Sir.' At last he'd found a few coins.

'Didn't Chief Constable Grigat provide you with an office?'

'He did, Sir, but I'm out in the field. Do you want to hear this or not?' He knew he was being bold, but didn't care. Böhm could shove it up his arse.

'Tell me,' Böhm said simply.

So Rath told him, in as few words as possible, everything he'd learned about Lamkau and his dead, bootlegging goons. He finished by listing possible murder motives, and saying which theory he thought most likely.

273

'What was the man's name again?' the Bulldog barked. No doubt he had forgotten his notepad.

'Radlewski. Artur Radlewski.'

'Residence?'

'No fixed abode.'

'A tramp?'

'More like a wood sprite. An Indian. Here, they call him the Kaubuk.'

'An Indian? What do you mean?'

'Apparently this Radlewski lives like an Indian out in the forest. He's read just about every book going on Native Americans.'

'Hmm.' Böhm seemed pensive. 'Is it possible that he's read somewhere how to *manufacture* tubocurarine? It's an Indian poison, after all.'

'Perfectly possible, Sir.'

'It looks as if the poison is home-grown. We've canvassed all sites in Berlin where it can be obtained. There's none reported missing, nor has any been procured illegally.'

'Then we need to find out how to make it.'

'You don't say, Inspector. Detective Gräf is currently speaking with a university expert on that very subject.'

'Either way we should put out a warrant for the man ...'

'Inspector,' Böhm thundered. 'I'm the one leading this investigation, not you.'

'Does that mean you're *not* going to put out a warrant?'

'Of course I am. Stop twisting my words. Have you a photo of the man?'

'Just a description.' He relayed what Adamek had told him.

'You think there's more?'

'That's all I have.'

'I mean, is there anyone else Radlewski could hold responsible for his mother's death?'

'Not according to the file.'

274

'What about this *Luisenbrand* business? Could it be that Radlewski has it in for the principal there too?'

'Director Wengler?'

'Or others who worked at the distillery in '24. Get a list together, and listen for rumours connecting anyone else to the scandal. If we know where these people live, we might be able to predict where the killer will strike next.'

'Yes, Sir.'

Rath hung up before having to insert more coins. What the hell was going on? Here he was more than eight hundred kilometres away from Berlin, and Böhm was still ordering him about.

He sifted through his remaining change and asked to be put through to Berlin on two further occasions, once to Carmerstrasse, and once to Spenerstrasse. No one picked up, which was hardly surprising since it was not yet midday. Still, his conscience was eating away at him. Despite meaning to call, something unexpected had come up on both evenings so far. If, that is, you could define 'something unexpected' as getting drunk with a village schoolmaster who was on summer holidays and had nothing better to do. Perhaps it was better Charly didn't find out; at the very least he owed her a decent excuse.

When the time came, he'd have an exciting tale about roaming the forest in search of a Masurian Indian. It might not sound entirely plausible, but the truth rarely did.

Remembering how Charly furrowed her brow when listening, he realised how much he missed her. Yet here he was, holed up in a one-horse town at the arse-end of nowhere; the fringes of civilisation. That was how it was starting to feel, anyway, and not just when people here spoke of their forest, that expanse of woodland that was said to stretch all the way into Russia and beyond.

It was time to clear out. He just had to take care of Böhm's list and see that he boarded the next train to Berlin.

44

The Oletzko District Library occupied two rooms in the district administrative office: a large room with the bookshelves, and a small room in which a woman of perhaps forty sat behind a desk.

Exactly Rath's idea of a provincial librarian, she wore glasses and her favourite colour was apparently grey. When she turned her head, he saw that even her dark-blonde hair, combed severely back, was tied in a tight bun. The view from her office window was spoiled by the presence of two massive tenement blocks located on the shore. Rath's police badge induced a frenzy of activity.

'Yes, the books ...though it's by no means certain it was Artur who took them ...'

'I'm assuming he did,' Rath said. 'If it's any consolation, I don't plan to charge Artur Radlewski with larceny. Nor am I interested in why nothing was reported. I just want to know what he's been reading recently.'

She gave a shrug. 'Well, recently ...nothing.'

'What do you mean?'

'That he ... That for around half a year no books ...have gone missing.'

'Since December 1931?' The librarian nodded. That fitted with Adamek's statement. 'Is this sort of thing common?'

'I've been working here more than twelve years. Since

then he's . . .it's only happened twice. On both occasions all the books that he . . .that went missing were returned.'

'You're not worried something could have happened to him.' She shook her head artlessly, blushing when she realised she was giving herself away. 'And most recently . . .I mean, last December, he returned everything then, too?' She nodded. 'You've been a great help, Fräulein Cofalka.' He smiled and handed her his card. 'I'm staying in the *Salzburger Hof*. Please notify me immediately if any more books go missing. If Herr Radlewski is anywhere in the vicinity, I need to be told.'

She took the card and nodded again. 'He hasn't done anything wrong, Inspector. Artur is a good man.'

'You know him, don't you?'

She lowered her head in embarrassment, as if he had extracted her deepest secret. 'Yes,' she said. 'I knew him when we were children. We went to the same school, over in Wielitzken.'

'With Rammoser senior . . .'

'That's right.' She looked at him in astonishment, surprised a detective inspector from Berlin should know old Rammoser.

'A final request, Fräulein Cofalka. The books Radlewski was interested in – can you arrange them for me?'

The librarian smiled for the first time. He took it as a good sign. 'That won't be too hard. They're all from the same shelf.'

There were around two dozen books in all. Without exception they were concerned with Indians and their culture. To his surprise the shelf contained considerably more non-fiction texts than adventure novels. Equally astonishing was the variety of titles on offer. No need to embarrass Fräulein Cofalka here, he already knew the reason why. Evidently the librarian had a soft spot for Artur Radlewski. Perhaps the forest dweller was the great,

277

unrequited love of her school days, even of her life, and it wasn't hard to imagine her thoughts turning to him with each new acquisition. The titles alone gave no indication of whether the books might contain poison recipes. Someone would have to take a look inside.

'I'd like to take these out,' he said, gesturing towards the shelf.

'All of them?'

'All of them.'

'I'll have to make out a membership card,' she said, rummaging in one of the card boxes.

Rath placed his identification on the table. 'I think this will do.' She hesitated for a moment, before helping him load the books into a cardboard box.

He was about to leave when he spied a table next to the entrance, on top of which was today's edition of the *Treuburger Zeitung*, secured against theft by a long, thin chain. 'Is this always here?' he asked, chin pointing towards the front page.

'Not for loan, but you're welcome to take a look.'

'But the paper's here at night?'

'Yes. It stays there until morning, when I lay out the new edition.'

'So it's possible that during his night-time visits, Artur Radlewski also read the paper?'

'I wouldn't put it past him.'

'Can you remember roughly when in December Artur returned those books?'

She knew the exact date.

Kowalski was astonished to find Rath outside the door. 'I wasn't expecting you so soon, Sir.'

'How's the head?'

'Better already.'

'No concussion?'

'Luckily for me.'

'Good,' Rath said. 'I have a task for you.' Kowalski looked at him expectantly. 'Go to the newspaper's administrative office, and look at the editions for 9th December 1931, as well as the 8th and 10th to be sure. See if you can find anything that might've lured the Kaubuk out of his forest.' Kowalski's face fell in disappointment. 'After that,' Rath continued, 'you'll need to use your local knowledge. Berlin's asking if there could have been others involved in the moonshining scandal of 1924. Names that don't appear in the case file or newspapers. Do some asking around, and see what the Treuburg rumour mill churns out.'

'You think the Kaubuk isn't finished?'

'I don't think anything. Detective Chief Inspector Böhm from Berlin wants us to ask around, so that's what we're going to do. Böhm is leading the investigation.' Kowalski nodded eagerly. 'When you've finished that,' he pressed the box of books into Kowalski's hands, 'you can spend tonight looking through these. Should make for ideal bedtime reading.'

'What are they?'

'Books read by Radlewski. I'd like to know if any contain instructions for making poison.'

Kowalski nodded, took the box inside, and returned moments later carrying his hat. Rath dropped him outside the newspaper office and drove onto Luisenhöhe. Regrettably, Herr Director Wengler wasn't home, the liveried servant informed him, barely a note of apology in his voice. Fischer, the private secretary, was likewise unavailable. The servant couldn't say where the two men were; couldn't, or didn't want to.

Rath tried the distillery. The secretary in the operations manager's office looked as if she were preparing to go home. 'I'm afraid Herr Assmann isn't here,' she said.

'Herr Assmann? Doesn't he live on Lindenallee?'

She arched her eyebrows. 'Yes, but you won't find him there. Herr Assmann is away on business. Danzig, then Berlin.'

'When's he coming back?'

She looked in her appointments diary. 'It says here: Berlin until further notice.'

'Until further notice . . . What's he doing in Berlin?'

'I'm afraid I don't know, but I can give you the name of the hotel he's staying in.'

'Not necessary. I just need a list of all employees who worked at the distillery in the spring of 1924.'

'I think,' the secretary said, 'I should call Herr Assmann after all.'

'You do that,' he said. 'Do whatever it takes, but I'll need the list this afternoon, let's say by five.' He smiled at her. 'If it isn't ready by then, I'll be obliged to return for a third time, with a warrant.'

The secretary looked horrified, and began dialling with her index finger. Somehow he felt pleased to have upset her plans. 'Berlin,' he heard her say as he exited the office. 'Südring, seven-four-zero-three.'

A number in Tempelhof. He remained in the hallway listening. The secretary asked for a room number. So, the operations manager was staying in a hotel in Tempelhof, where the Lamkau firm had its headquarters.

'Herr Assmann,' she said. Evidently she took no pleasure in disturbing her employer. 'Please excuse the interruption, but I've just had an Inspector Rath here . . .'

45

It was the sort of dive Charly would never have set foot in unaccompanied. It didn't even have a name, at least none that was printed above the door or on either of the grime-covered display windows. Not far from Potsdamer Platz, it was a completely different world. Mohamed Husen held the door for her and cleared a path through the drinkers. A number of them looked up briefly when they entered, but she soon realised no one was interested in the white woman with her black companion.

Perhaps that was why Husen had suggested the place. At lunch today he had been smoking on the balcony dressed as a *Sarotti Moor*. 'A colleague dropped out at the *Turkish Café*,' he explained. She pitied him his fate, but Husen didn't seem to mind the ever-changing outfits; if anything it gave him pleasure. He took the whole business in good humour.

Now he was dressed like an ordinary European, wearing a grey suit and elegant bowler hat, which he hung on the stand. He led her to a table by the long wall at the back, where they could talk in peace over coffee and cigarettes.

'Not an ideal spot to take a lady,' he said, offering her a Muratti, 'but the coffee's better than in *Vaterland*, and no one's going to shoot their mouth off if we're seen together.'

'That'd be the last thing I need.' She showed her ring. 'I'm engaged.'

Husen laughed. 'I'm *married*, but you're right. That

281

doesn't stop people's imaginations running away with them. Particularly where colleagues are involved.'

There was smoke everywhere, and all sorts of negotiations were being brokered at the tables. She couldn't vouch for their legality, but Husen was right. No one was looking at them. 'How are you settling in?' he asked.

'I'm afraid I'm not made for kitchen work.'

He looked at her. 'Stick at it, and you can work your way up to waitress. You'll earn more money, and there are tips.'

'I've never waited tables.'

'You learn quickly. If a vacancy pops up somewhere I'll let you know. Maybe you'll be lucky and won't have to dress up.'

Talk about career prospects, she thought, but even so, she was grateful for his concern. 'Thank you,' she said. 'That's kind.'

The waiter arrived with their coffee.

'Waitressing's pretty easy, you know,' Husen said, once the man was gone. 'Set down your plates and cups, pour a few drinks. Then it's all maths and remembering the right table.'

'We'll see,' she said. 'My training's as a stenographer, but I guess these days you have to be flexible. You mentioned recently that you know this spirits buyer ...'

'Chief Red Nose?'

'Maybe he needs an office hand?' she asked. 'He must have more correspondence than a head chef.'

'Which is why he'll have one already. I'm afraid you're too late.'

'Perhaps you could put in a word for me, if a position became free.'

Husen took a drag on his cigarette. 'I'm afraid I don't know him that well. I just know that he enjoys a drink at the *Wild West Bar*, and that ... Goddamn it!' He broke off mid-sentence and hid behind the menu.

'What's the matter?' she asked.

'Speak of the devil...' Husen spoke so softly she could barely hear him. 'Riedel's here.'

'Who?'

'Chief Red Nose,' she heard him whisper behind the menu. 'He's just come in. What's someone like him doing in a place like this?'

'He won't have anything against two colleagues having coffee together after work.'

'If he sees us together, *Vaterland* will be full of exactly the kind of rumours we want to avoid.'

'So what?'

'I need my job. And you don't want to lose yours either.'

'Then what do we do?'

'We leave, but separately. You go first. He won't know you yet, unless he's been in the kitchen recently.'

'Why would he have been?'

'Because he's Kempinski's main buyer. He orders the hard stuff for Unger too.'

'I've never seen him upstairs.'

'Good. Then off you go. We'll meet outside.'

She stubbed out her cigarette and stood up. She didn't want Mohamed Husen losing his job on her account.

She only knew Alfons Riedel from Gereon's description, but, in a place like this, the red nose and slightly outmoded attire immediately stood out. He hung his hat and coat next to Husen's bowler, granting her at most a fleeting glance as she retrieved her coat from the stand. Reaching the door she recognised a face through the large window pane, and made a beeline for the telephone booth that stood against the wall.

In the reflective glass of the booth she saw the face look left and right before entering, apparently reluctant to set foot in such a disreputable establishment. The man stood in the dining area, looking around. Manfred Unger, head chef and target of her covert operation in *Haus Vaterland*.

She took the receiver from the cradle and pretended to make a call. Instead of rummaging in her pockets for change, however, she took out her little make-up mirror and opened it. Yes, Unger was making straight for Riedel's table. The two men knew one another, Gereon had been right. Rather well, if their cheerful manner was anything to go by.

She watched Husen remove his hat from the hook, nod briefly at Riedel, who barely accorded him a glance, and make for the exit. As he reached the door, two men jostled past him into the smoky lounge. She wouldn't have noticed them hovering by the entrance with their backs to her were it not for the scarcely perceptible twitch of the chin with which one of them gestured towards Unger and Riedel's table. She watched as they sat next to the would-be blackmailers. She'd have given anything to eavesdrop, but there was no way she could simply appear at an adjoining table.

Was she actually going to witness a pay-off? The new arrivals had removed their headgear, and now she waited for one of them to discreetly place an envelope under his hat and slide it across the table. Or, perhaps they were accomplices, and this blackmailing business was somehow linked to a Ringverein?

She was wrong on both counts. One of the new men might have been lanky and a little gaunt, but as soon as she saw the pair's faces she knew they hadn't come to make a payment. Their eyes brooked no argument; men like this wouldn't be blackmailed.

Not that Unger and Riedel seemed to have realised. There was a brief argument, during which the spirits buyer affected a manner of superiority, only to pause mid-flow and puff out his cheeks as if gasping for air. He sat at a slight angle, stock-still, not daring to move, his head increasingly the colour of his nose. The man opposite leaned forward slightly and continued speaking, unperturbed. He had one hand under the table, and though she couldn't see exactly what he was doing, she knew it must be painful. All of a sudden Unger appeared in a rush to get up, but the second man pressed him back in his chair. She almost pitied the blackmailers.

Without warning, Riedel, who had turned a deep shade of purple, began nodding, and now Unger, too, wagged his head eagerly. The synchronised display made for a ridiculous sight, but the two strangers appeared satisfied, put on their hats, and exited the lounge as swiftly as they had entered.

The whole thing had lasted barely five minutes. Among the remaining patrons, it appeared no one had seen anything. Even if they had, this wasn't the sort of place you got involved.

Unger and Riedel remained at the table. The waiter brought two beers and two schnapps, which must have been ordered sometime before, and Riedel, whose head was still red as a beet, drained the Korn using his left hand. He held his right hand tight to his body as if afraid the fingers might fall off. Unger raised his glass almost as if to propose a toast, only to give a start as Riedel scolded him.

Charly was startled by a knock on the glass. A man wearing his hat at an angle banged a coin against the pane. 'Are you putting down roots here, woman? If I don't get on that phone soon, there'll be hell to pay with my old lady.'

She hung up and left the booth, but before stepping onto the street, she took a final glance at the two men, who appeared completely at a loss, stricken somehow. Unger drank his beer and gazed into thin air, and she couldn't be sure he wasn't looking in her direction. She turned her head away and left the café. Now she just had to think of a reason for leaving Mohamed Husen waiting so long. She no longer had so many questions for the African waiter, and, those she did have, were very different from a quarter of an hour before.

46

Rath reacted badly when the servant at the Luisenhöhe estate tried to fob him off again on Sunday morning. 'Listen here! If you don't want to be responsible for the Prussian Police carrying out a house search in your esteemed Herr Wengler's residence, then I suggest you tell me where I can find him. Today!'

Clearly it was the first time the arrogant pizzle had been spoken to like that. He gasped for air. 'One moment, Sir. I'll see what I can do.' The liveried servant vanished behind a door.

Rath was certain he wouldn't have to make any inquiries as to Gustav Wengler's whereabouts. Most likely he was simply counting to sixty in his head. As expected, after about a minute the man re-emerged. 'I've been informed that Director Wengler is at the festival site in town.' He sounded more nasal than a hundred Frenchmen. 'However, he is very busy . . .'

'I thought the plebiscite anniversary was tomorrow?'

'Preparations.' The man now spoke exclusively through his nose. 'Director Wengler is, after all . . .'

'I know. Chief of the Homeland Service.' Rath enjoyed interrupting the smug bastard. 'So, where's this festival site of yours?'

The man threw him a glance that implied you had to be a particularly unworthy species of insect not to know where the festival site was. 'Hindenburg Park, by the district war memorial.'

'Where is that?'

'On the road out to Goldap, by the lake.'

Rath headed back towards town. People here were starting to get on his nerves. He longed for Berlin, all the more since finally managing to get hold of Charly yesterday evening in a prosaic exchange during which they had mostly discussed work. Her Cinderella-like existence in the *Haus Vaterland* kitchen was starting to bear fruit. Messrs Unger and Riedel were indeed involved in blackmail, which had apparently brought them into conflict with the underworld. Perhaps they'd hit upon someone who'd paid his protection money, and was now receiving a service in return. Bagmen didn't like it when people got in their way. It now seemed increasingly unlikely that the business had to do with Lamkau's death, but Rath was pleased Charly had a lead which would net her a few points with Gennat, not to say her actual boss, Friederike Wieking.

As for himself, he had at least partially completed Böhm's list of tasks, having collected the employee names from the distillery yesterday afternoon. Ready on time, as promised, the list was neatly typed and devoid of spelling errors. He'd have gladly had its author accompany him back to Berlin.

The cars lining the road ensured that Hindenburg Park was easy to find. Rath pulled over and strolled across the site, which was a mix of sports grounds and parkland. Flags fluttered on all available poles, black-and-white, and black-white-and-red; but nowhere the red-black-gold of the Republic. Everywhere you looked was a hive of activity; next to the athletics field a marquee was being erected, on the side of which were advertising slogans for *Treuburger Bärenfang* and *Luisenbrand*. Next to it was a carousel, and sausage, tombola and gingerbread heart stalls, even a shooting gallery – a veritable funfair stretching across the main path. Meanwhile the ubiquitous slogans for Mathée firm products left visitors in no doubt who was funding – and profiting from – the whole shebang.

The war memorial at the end of the park looked like a church that hadn't been completed: an apse with no altar or roof, a semi-circle of rubble stone with lancet windows affording wonderful views of the lake. The monument was decked with flowers and garlands, while the platform, which was accessed by a rubble perron, housed a similarly adorned lectern, above which members of the fire brigade were fixing a banner. *Prussia and the Reich Semper Fidelis*. Rath couldn't shake the impression that the *Oletzko District Fire Department* had acquired its ladder truck not so much to extinguish blazes as to help decorate public festivals.

At the foot of the memorial a handful of men were erecting the stage. In the meantime Gustav Wengler had appeared on the plateau, surveying the workers beneath him like a military general. Alongside him was an entourage of three men, one of whom Rath recognised instantly. Chief Constable Grigat stood gazing self-importantly from underneath his shako, moustache combed, uniform ironed, and hands folded behind his back. The other two wore formal dark suits and top hats. Even from afar they looked like senior public officials.

Rath climbed the steps and Wengler extended his arms as if to greet an old friend. 'Ah! Our visitor from Berlin!'

'You're a hard man to pin down, Herr Wengler.'

'Chief Constable Grigat says the same about you.' Wengler gestured towards his companions. 'Might I introduce: District Administrator Wachsmann, Mayor Maeckelburg – Inspector Rath from Berlin.'

He shook their hands, Grigat's too. All this glad-handing made him feel as if he were attending an official function. 'Looks like it's going to be one hell of a party,' he said.

District Administrator Wachsmann gazed proudly. 'Few

districts in Masuria commemorate the plebiscite on this type of scale.'

'Might I borrow Herr Wengler a moment?'

'We were discussing the order of ceremony, Inspector.'

'It's all in hand, Gustav!' Wachsmann clapped him on the shoulder. 'You deliver the main speech after I've said a few words of introduction. Musical society to set the tone . . .and then the open-air concert, as always.'

'I'm glad that's all done and dusted,' said Rath. 'It's urgent.' He looked at Wengler's entourage. 'Perhaps, Herr Director, you know somewhere where we might speak in private . . .'

'How about a little stroll in the park?'

Rath agreed and they went on their way. For a moment he was afraid Erich Grigat might feel compelled to join them but, when no invitation was forthcoming, the constable chose to keep the local dignitaries company instead.

'What's so urgent?' Gustav Wengler asked, once they were out of earshot.

'New developments,' Rath said, lighting an Overstolz. 'In our murder inquiry.'

'I've heard you requested a list of employees from the distillery, from 1924.'

'That's right. The trail leads into the past.' He halted and looked at Wengler. 'Does the name Radlewski mean anything to you?'

'Paid a visit to old Naujoks, have you? Grigat mentioned something along those lines.'

'I'm not talking about Martha Radlewski. I'm talking about her son.' Wengler looked astonished. 'It's possible that Artur Radlewski is avenging his mother's death, and that your former employees . . .'

'Revenge? Why? The woman was notorious. She drank herself to death.'

'Perhaps her son sees it differently. Perhaps *he* thinks it was the moonshine that killed her.'

'If he really thinks that ...' Wengler looked Rath in the eye, ' ...then why has he waited this long?'

'Those are questions that still need answering, but he would have a motive, potential knowledge about the poison used, and he has no alibi.'

'A savage who lives alone in the forest wouldn't.'

'I'm being serious, Herr Wengler. Radlewski hasn't been seen for almost nine months. He could be responsible for the killings in the west.' Rath took a deep drag on his Overstolz. 'We need to know if there are other distillery employees who could've been involved in 1924 ...'

'So, that's why you need the list.' Wengler laughed. 'Inspector, you do know that proceedings were discontinued? I mean, you have the file. Nobody knows where this rotgut came from, or who sold it as *Luisenbrand*.'

'That might be true of the courts, perhaps, but that's not what we're talking about here. We're talking about Artur Radlewski. Herr Wengler, my colleagues in Berlin are concerned that Radlewski's vendetta, if that's what this is, might not be over. I share their concern.' He stared back at Wengler. 'I would ask you to take a look at the list. Perhaps something will occur when you see the names.'

Suddenly Gustav Wengler became serious. 'Do you have a cigarette?' Rath opened his case and Wengler helped himself, inhaling greedily as the lighter's flame touched the tobacco. The director thought for a time. 'Inspector,' he said. 'I don't know if this is important, since no charges were ever brought, and there was no mention of it in the paper. But ...my brother.'

'What about your brother?'

'Siegbert was a police officer here. He ...how shall I put this?' Wengler shook his head, as if pained by the memory. 'He was accused of being in cahoots with the moonshiners, or at least of having tipped them off about a raid.'

'Pardon me?'

290

'There was nothing in it.' Wengler threw Rath a hostile glance. 'They found a hideout in the forest by Markowsken, but by the time police arrived there was no one left to arrest.'

'And your brother took the fall?'

'Obviously there was no one there. I'd have been astonished if an operation like that had succeeded. Police uniforms in a forest. That's about as conspicuous as ...'

' ...an Indian in a capital city.'

'Something like that.' Wengler managed a smile. 'At any rate – Siegbert decided to put in for a transfer. With all those rumours swirling around ... Sometimes it's better to make a fresh start.'

'You don't have to tell me,' said Rath. 'So, where did your brother make his fresh start? He could be in danger. We have to warn him.'

'It's a city you're familiar with, Inspector. My brother has been in Berlin for almost eight years, as a traffic officer.'

47

The hollow space under the board between the bedroom and lounge. That is where you have stowed everything you need in case the police call again. Every day you reach inside, fetch the curare pipe, Veronal solution and needles, head to the train station and await your chance. To be alone with him. A single moment will suffice.

You examine the red cloth, which you now fold and place with the other items, and with the red, the memories return.

A red cloth hangs from the railing of the town mill bridge, easily overlooked among all the colours decorating the town. On each entrance to the marketplace they have erected triumphal arches of fir, swathed in black and white and red. *Dieses Land bleibt deutsch*, you read on one; on another, *Das Land ist unser, unser soll es bleiben*. Both proclaim allegiance to the Reich. Polish words are nowhere to be seen. You have emerged from the polling station and are making your way down Deutsche Strasse when you see the red cloth fluttering in the breeze. Your heart pounds; you must fetch your bike from the shed. If you pedal hard, you can make it out to the little lake in half an hour: the place you always meet.

But you don't reach the lake, you don't even reach the shed. As if by magic the trio from the distillery plant themselves in front of you. They are wearing Homeland Service brassards, and even at this hour, appear to be drunk.

'Where's the fire, you dirty Polack?' their leader asks, a man who takes pleasure in tormenting other people.

'Jestem Prußakiem,' you say. They don't like people using this language, especially not to say they are Prussian. You won't tell them how you voted. They will only think their crude propaganda, their threats and their violence have succeeded. They think you are a Polish sympathiser, you don't know why. Perhaps because you come from Warmia and are Catholic. Perhaps because you once protected Marek, the Pole, when the men from the distillery drunkenly abused him in Pritzkus's bar. Perhaps, even, because of your name, though there are many here who don't have German names.

They are drawing closer now, and you realise there was no need to provoke them; they were coming for you anyway.

'That sort of talk'll get you a good thrashing,' the bigmouth says.

'It's long overdue,' the youngest seconds, a giant of a man, a Masurian who ought to know better than to get involved with these thugs, who only spout nationalist rhetoric as a pretext for breaking people's noses. Still, perhaps that is the Masurian tragedy: its people want to be more German than the Germans themselves.

The little one says nothing, but you see the belligerence in his eyes.

You have no choice. You roll up your sleeves, break off a slat from the shore fence and prepare to defend yourself.

Gradually they approach, there is no escaping them now. Behind you there is only the river.

You strike the Masurian giant first, and the strongest of the trio goes to ground. In the meantime the dogged little man has hurled himself at your legs, and you know that if he succeeds in toppling you, all will be lost.

He clings on, no dislodging him, not even a blow from the slat can knock him loose, and though you struggle, eventually you lose your balance and land on the dusty turf. The Masurian is languishing on the grass, forehead bloodied, but now their leader is upon you, gazing down with boundless contempt in his eyes. He kicks you in the solar plexus and suddenly you can't breathe. Still the little man clings to your legs, you can't get up, and now the ringleader is winding up again – when a police whistle pierces the summer air.

48

Up here he issued the commands. He loved the feeling, and it was why he still loved this job, even if it wasn't what it used to be . . .but, wasn't that true of everything? Time was when a whole village had answered to him, then a small town; now it was just an intersection. True, it *was* the busiest in Europe – assuming the information they provided to tourists on Unter den Linden was correct.

Trams approached from every angle, buses droned impatiently; between them, cars and taxicabs flitted through what spaces they could find, the bicycles gleaming in the milling mass like insects blinded by the sun.

He turned the lever, and the traffic filtering through Potsdamer Strasse came to a halt. At the front of the line was a taxicab, behind it the number five bus, and, drawing up alongside the cab, a blonde cyclist inadvertently displaying too much leg as her balance failed her. When they would move again would be his decision alone. Up here in the traffic tower he ruled the world!

There were regulations concerning how long a carriageway could remain closed, but they were subject to interpretation and who the hell was going to check on him? He knew the police commissioner's official car as well as that of his deputy; the murder wagon likewise. If he saw any of them in line, or a fellow officer, he'd switch straight to green, obviously. But not now, with a cute blonde in a summer dress making a show of her legs.

Yes, Siegbert Wengler still loved his job, even if it used to provide more thrills. That said, for a man of his age, a blonde in an airy summer dress afforded exactly the right level of thrill to distract from the tedium of his shift, the greatest challenge of which consisted in climbing the ladder that led inside the traffic tower. He looked at his wristwatch. The relief was late. Scholz, the greenhorn! Had he lost track of time in that toilet cubicle at Potsdamer Bahnhof? Or missed his train? He'd give him what for, and it was hardly the first time! If he had to wait any longer than ten minutes, he'd chalk it up to overtime and leave it to the bloody greenhorn to explain.

In Potsdamer Strasse the first cars began tooting their horns. He took a final glance at the girl's legs before turning the left-hand lever and bringing the traffic on Stresemannstrasse to a standstill. When he switched the lights to green on Potse, the blonde disappeared behind the two gatehouses flanking the carriageway like little temples, pedalling hard into the chaos.

Siegbert Wengler was looking forward to finishing his shift, and stretching his legs. Perhaps he'd take a woman tonight. Only, not at *Jette's* on Potsdamer Strasse; he had to make sure he didn't fall into old habits while the killer was still at large. Thanks to his brother, he could afford one of Jette's girls more or less whenever the fancy took him. Good food, good drink, a woman every now and then, it was more than most fifty-two-year-olds could manage in this city. More than most people his age could hope for from life.

Soon he'd be retiring. Perhaps he'd return home. The hardest thing would be the girls: there wouldn't be too many places like *Jette's* in Treuburg, or in Masuria – period. He'd have to head out to Königsberg, Danzig, even.

At last a man in blue uniform and white sleeves crossed the intersection. He couldn't make out the face under the shako but, by the leather case, it had to be Scholz. Only a greenhorn would transport his sandwiches in a huge thing like that. Still, you needed your sandwiches up here, and a thermos full of coffee went a long way too. It could be draining work in the traffic tower.

The uniform cop had disappeared underneath the tower, his steps already audible on the ladder. Siegbert Wengler noted the change of shift, accurate to the minute, in the notebook that hung by a string from the control panel, packed his lunchbox and thermos, and stood, legs apart, ready to give that slowpoke Scholz the welcome he deserved. To his disappointment, it was a different face that emerged in the hatch door.

'Who are you?' he asked, in the tone he had reserved to read the greenhorn the riot act.

The uniformed officer put down his bag, stood up straight and saluted. 'Beg to report: the relief. Standing in for Constable Scholz!'

'Standing in? First I've heard of it.'

'Constable Scholz sends his apologies. He was taken ill.'

Siegbert Wengler shook his head. So, Scholz was a malingerer too. 'That doesn't excuse *your* tardiness, Constable!'

'Of course not, Sir. My apologies.'

'Do you know your way round the control panel?'

'Yes, Sir.'

Wengler leaned over the notebook to erase the name Scholz and replace it with that of his stand-in. 'Name and rank?' he barked.

Behind him there was no response, and suddenly Wengler realised what it was about this new colleague that had thrown him. The huge leather briefcase on the floor *was* Constable Scholz's, no doubt about it. Still wondering what it could all mean, he felt the man embrace him from behind, and then a stabbing pain in his neck.

He tried to defend himself but the man was too strong, and when, finally, he was released, his legs gave way underneath him. He sank to the floor as if the strength had been drained from his body. He could barely move, his muscles refused to obey.

The uniform cop opened the large case, which really did belong to Scholz, and pulled out a red cloth. 'Recognise me?' he asked, unfolding the cloth and placing it over Wengler's nose and mouth. Wengler tried to shake it off, but couldn't move, he had no choice but to submit, as if paralysed. He couldn't speak, his tongue felt alien in his mouth, like a wet rag. 'You ought to. Because my face is the last thing you'll ever see.'

Wengler gazed into the face, but it was no good, he couldn't place it.

The face disappeared, and when it returned the man held a large bottle of water which he had apparently fetched from the case. Siegbert Wengler started to shake; *those* muscles, it seemed, functioned still.

Then came the water. At first all he felt was the cloth grow damp and clammy, but then the water penetrated the fabric, into his mouth and nose. It spread everywhere, into his jaws, deeper and deeper. He couldn't breathe, it was everywhere. He lay motionless, unable to put up a fight. Only the muscles he had no control over seemed still to function: his heart pounded, reflexes stirred in his throat, he was choking; he tried to throw up, to spew out the water, but couldn't. He thought he was drowning, no, he didn't just think it, he knew, he *was* drowning. Now, at this very moment, as his whole body quivered in the throes of death, he had only seconds to live and didn't know why.

Then the dripping wet towel was removed, and he could

breathe again, despite feeling as if he had just died. Breathe, breathe, breathe, was all he could think of.

'That's how she felt too,' the man said, 'and I couldn't save her. I want you to know how she died.' Wengler stared at the dark, dripping wet cloth. 'Remember now?' his tormentor asked, replacing the dank cloth over his nose and mouth. 'You ought to. You helped lock me up. Back in Marggrabowa.'

Siegbert Wengler felt the damp cold of the fabric on his skin, saw the man lift the bottle, and the thought of the water alone filled him with mortal terror. He'd have screamed in panic if he could, but the screams sounded only in his head, piercing as a siren. The eyes of the man glinted under the shako, as the bottle tilted, and then, just before it reached the cloth and drowned him a second time, he remembered. Siegbert Wengler knew why he must die.

49

Just another half-hour in *Haus Vaterland*. Never before had Charly so looked forward to finishing a shift; she could hardly wait. Any kind of police drudgery would be preferable to this. *Just a few hours overtime* . . .it had ruined her day, her whole weekend in fact. She had been hoping to rummage through Unger's papers undisturbed, but Sundays were the busiest time.

At least she wasn't peeling vegetables. A dishwasher had cancelled at short notice and they had been unable to find a replacement. She wasn't sure why they had asked her, perhaps her onion peeling wasn't up to scratch. She couldn't say if she was any better at washing-up, but had suffered no breakages so far.

She observed Manfred Unger carefully. There was no sign that he'd been intimidated by the two goons from last night, and certainly not that he'd spied his new kitchen maid-cum-office assistant in the same dive. He treated her as he always did, with relative kindness, being less concerned with chiding her than he was the rest of his staff. So far, they hadn't exchanged a word, though she felt his eyes on her the whole time. Whenever she turned around, he was looking at her through the glass window.

Washing dishes might have been kinder on her eyes, but it wasn't a promotion, and she still had her work cut out. The machine had to be fed like a hungry wolf, and, when

300

the dishes emerged, more often than not you had to wash half again by hand. Her apron was soaked through, and in some places the water had penetrated to the skin, where her clothes clung damp to her body.

She'd promised Greta that they'd head out to the Wannsee for a girls' afternoon, a much-needed distraction after her perfunctory exchange with Gereon yesterday. A few hours in the afternoon sun, swimming and browsing a detective novel would be just the ticket. No doubt they'd have to fob off the advances of the odd man, but Greta was a past master, and the more puffed up, the better.

She felt as if she were being watched again, and squinted to the left, only to find that Unger was gone. The office was empty. Suddenly she heard his voice from the other side of the conveyor belt. 'Fräulein Ritter, you've stood there long enough.' She turned round and saw the head chef and a stick-thin boy clad in an apron. Unger pointed at the boy. 'Franzeken here will relieve you.'

She tried not to show her relief. The boy seemed familiar with the machine and got down to work straightaway. Unger was almost smiling, something she had never seen before. He cleared his throat. 'Fräulein Ritter ... They're short of tomatoes in the salad kitchen. Fetch five crates from the store and then you can finish for the day.'

Finish for the day. How good those words sounded, but she was already thinking like a kitchen maid. It didn't matter that she'd made no progress on surveillance, it was time to get the hell out of here!

She threw her dripping apron in the large wash basket next to the time clock, debated whether to put on another apron for the tomatoes, and decided against. Her clothes were due a wash anyway.

She knew the way, but the store was big and disorganised and the tomatoes hard to find. There were several shelves full of fresh vegetables, as well as a few tins. Next to the entrance were four huge crates of potatoes. The tomatoes were in a dark corner towards the back. At least two dozen crates. She wondered how many needed shifting here every day. Finding a handcart, she started loading the crates when an echo sounded from the concrete walls. She had left the heavy door open, but now heard it click shut.

Goddamn it, some idiot had closed the door! Whoever it was, perhaps they'd still be on hand to help.

She loaded the next crate and gave a start. Black-and-white shepherd's check pants. Manfred Unger had arrived as if by magic, watching her go about her work. She put down the crate and stood up straight. 'Crikey!' she said, attempting a smile. 'You gave me quite a fright.'

She didn't say it was the second time already today. Was he checking up on her? Or did he want to speak to her in private about yesterday?

'My apologies,' he said, smiling his strange smile as he drew closer. 'I didn't mean to startle you, Fräulein Ritter. I just wanted to tell you – privately – how glad I am to have you on board. And how much I value your work.'

'Well, thank you very much,' she said, feeling uneasy.

'I hope to have some office work for you soon. Then you won't have to get so dirty. A pretty thing like you.'

'Office work sounds good, thank you, but please don't think I consider this sort of thing beneath me.'

'And you're wet . . .' He looked at her. 'You need to get that dress dry as soon as possible, otherwise you'll catch cold.'

'Lucky I'm about to finish then.' She fetched the last crate from the shelf.

'Yes, lucky.' He stood next to her now, closer than good manners allowed. 'But we still have a good quarter of an hour.' She would have taken a step back, but the shelf was in the way.

At that moment Unger pounced, so suddenly that she

dropped the crate. Seven, eight tomatoes rolled across the floor, but he was unperturbed. He seized her waist and drew her against him. She felt his erection, and then his lips on hers. He tried to thrust his tongue down her throat, but she managed to turn away.

'Herr Unger,' she said in outrage and disgust. 'What are you doing? You're forgetting yourself!'

She heard him panting, and her disgust rose further still. 'Come on,' he said. 'What's the big deal? The door's closed, we won't be disturbed.' She tried to free herself from his vice-like grip. 'I've had my eye on you from the start, and when I saw you in Linkstrasse yesterday, in that dive, I knew. That Ritter, I said to myself, she's a good-time girl.'

'Herr Unger, please.'

So he had seen her yesterday, and drawn the wrong conclusion. The man seemed to think she was some kind of whore.

'You drive me wild,' he panted. 'The way you wiggle your backside when you know I'm watching.'

'Herr Unger, I'm afraid your imagination is running away with you. Now let me go!'

It was no good. He held her firm and began groping her. When he laid his right hand on her breasts, she'd had enough, and gave the bastard a good, hard slap.

He gazed at her blankly, holding his cheek and breathing heavily. Then suddenly those eyes that had been so full of lust moments before showed only contempt. 'So, you're one of those, are you,' he said, shaking his head. 'Drive me wild by the dishwasher. For this!'

'Drive you *wild*? I was working! No one's forcing you to stare at my backside.'

'You mustn't think you're irreplaceable. There are plenty of people who'd do anything to work at *Haus Vaterland*!'

'Well, not me!'

'Oh?' Unger looked as if he were about to spit at her feet. 'But you put out for a black? You goddamn whore.'

'I'm sorry?'

'You heard me!'

There was such contempt in the gaunt head chef's voice that she thought he might actually spit. Instead, he turned around and bolted. She heard the door open again, then click shut.

Her hands were shaking. After taking a deep breath she squatted to pick up the tomatoes. Unger had trodden on one, and she threw its pulpy remains into the bin by the door. The crates were stacked, but it was some time before she felt ready to return to the kitchen. She pushed the handcart in front of her, fists inwardly raised, but there was no sign of Unger, neither in the kitchen nor behind the glass wall of his office. Was he gone already, too embarrassed to confront her? She took the tomatoes through to the salad kitchen and returned the handcart to the store. Then she went to the bathroom and washed her hands thoroughly. It was still early, but she didn't care, she left *Haus Vaterland* as quickly as she could, praying she wouldn't run into Unger again.

In the street she inhaled deeply, as if she'd been holding her breath the whole time she'd been inside. Time for a quick shower at Spenerstrasse to wash away the day's dirt. The U-Bahn steps were on the far side of the building. The Buick was still in Moabit as it didn't fit her cover story. So far she hadn't benefited much from Gereon leaving it, meaning she was looking forward to her Wannsee trip all the more. Perhaps she'd take the Avus and vent her anger on the gas pedal. Fucking men.

There was a build-up of traffic on Stresemannstrasse, apparently stretching all the way back to Anhalter Bahnhof. Less patient drivers turned into side streets or made U-turns; others sought refuge in their horns. The cyclists calmly snaked their way past the cars towards the intersection, until they, too, were obliged to stop. The traffic lights at Potsdamer Platz showed red, and red they stayed.

Was the officer in the tower asleep?

Perhaps he was, for just then she saw a traffic cop emerging from *Josty* and crossing the intersection, where he hastily scaled the ladder leading to the tower. Moments later, the lights on Stresemannstrasse changed to green. An avalanche of metal stirred, and the chorus of horns fell silent.

She was about to make her way to the U-Bahn when she caught sight of a dark-red Horch parked in the shadow of the traffic tower, two of its wheels encroaching on the grass-covered island in the middle of the intersection. A white coat emerged, and as she wondered what Dr Karthaus was doing at Potsdamer Platz, the heavy black murder wagon raced towards her from the direction of Leipziger Strasse, screeching to a halt behind the Horch. Straightaway she knew she wouldn't be going anywhere near the Wannsee that afternoon.

50

Wilhelm Böhm hated being late. It was ironic, therefore, that he had chosen a profession where he was condemned to appear after the horse had bolted. When, that is, someone had died in unnatural or unexplained circumstances, and an investigation had to be launched. Perhaps it explained his notorious ill temper.

At any rate, it explained his ill temper that Sunday afternoon. He had only agreed to standby duty because Inspector Rath was gadding about in East Prussia and A Division were short of men, which, come to think of it, was also the reason he'd taken on Rath's latest case. Someone had to do the work around here. To cap it all, he'd been called out straight after lunch, just when he'd laid his head down for a nap.

He still didn't know exactly what had happened, only that a police officer had died during his shift in the traffic tower. *Probably a heart attack*, he thought, as he hauled his heavy frame up the narrow ladder, *and being no steeplejack here I am running the same risk.*

It was no use. When a policeman died in the line of duty you were obliged to investigate.

A helping hand met him as he gained the hatch. Superintendent Kronberg from ED. Böhm pulled himself up and looked around. The narrow room was busier than its architect would have intended. Aside from Kronberg and Dr Karthaus, a uniform cop, wearing the white gloves and sleeves of the Traffic Police, stared nervously out of the window as he operated the lights. On the floor lay a dead man, likewise a traffic cop, though somewhat older and heavier than his colleague. He looked as though he wouldn't have had long to wait for retirement; just his luck to keel over on duty.

A horn beeped, and the cop at the controls started cursing. 'They're still going crazy on Stresemannstrasse, but I can't keep 'em on green just 'cause they've been stuck on red for the last half-hour.'

He appeared helpless, as if awaiting instructions. Böhm felt he was agitated by the traffic chaos, rather than his dead colleague.

Kronberg handed him an identification. 'Wengler, Siegbert,' he said. 'Sergeant Major. Born 1880 in Danzig.'

Böhm took the identification and nodded. 'Anything else?'

'Still waiting for reinforcements.'

'That'll make things even cosier.' He climbed over Dr Karthaus, who was leaning over the corpse, and approached the traffic officer.

'Was it you who found the corpse?' The man nodded. Operating the lights *and* answering questions was evidently too much. 'Did you know the dead man?' Böhm continued. A shrug. 'Damn it, man, make your report,' the DCI barked without warning. 'Name and rank.'

The cop stood to attention, clicked his heels in fright. 'Eckert. Constable Eckert, Inspector, Sir.'

'Detective Chief Inspector.'

'Detective Chief Inspector. Yes, Sir.'

'There we go!'

'Yes, Sir.'

'Are you Herr Wengler's relief?'

'Beg to report: no, Sir.'

'Do I have to drag it out of you?'

'Yes, Sir. I mean: no, Detective Chief Inspector, Sir!' The cop halted the traffic on Leipziger Strasse and switched the lights on Stresemannstrasse to green. Beads of sweat had formed on his brow. He turned to face Böhm once more. 'Beg to report: I am not the relief, the shift change was over two hours ago. It should be Constable Scholz on duty, but instead I find Sergeant Major Wengler. Dead.'

'So you *did* know the dead man?'

'Not personally, Sir. I knew his name and rank. Bit of a lone wolf.'

'Where is Scholz?'

'I'm afraid I don't know, Sir. Headquarters reported issues at Potsdamer Platz and I was sent to investigate. That's when I found Sergeant Major Wengler.'

'And then?'

'I submitted my report to headquarters, Sir. Then I set things in order.'

'I hope you didn't touch anything!'

'Beg to report, no, Sir. I mean: order on the roads. I didn't touch anything. Apart from the switch for the traffic light signal ...'

'Well, at least you're wearing gloves.'

'Yes, Sir.'

The hatch opened and a prehistoric-looking camera appeared, followed by the head of Andreas Lange. The assistant detective had great difficulty in fitting the camera and tripod stand through the gap.

'Get someone to take over here,' Böhm said to the cop. 'I need to talk to you. Downstairs in the murder wagon.'

'With respect, Sir, you'll have to request relief for me.'

'Can't you call someone yourself?'

'Beg to report: I am not permitted to leave my post to make telephone calls.'

'You don't have to.' Böhm gestured towards the telephone

attached to the control panel. 'What do you think that is, an iron?'

'It's a telephone, Sir!'

'Then why don't you use it, Constable?' Böhm was about to lose his temper.

'I had to telephone from *Café Josty* just now, Sir.' Constable Eckert pointed at the device. 'That thing's as dead as Sergeant Major Wengler.'

It took less than ten minutes for the relief to arrive, and now five officers stood at the intersection regulating traffic the old-fashioned way – by using their arms. Böhm didn't want anyone touching the controls until further notice.

The murder wagon's soft leather bench had been designed for heavyweights like Ernst Gennat. Böhm felt decidedly more at ease than in the cramped confines of the traffic tower. Constable Eckert sat opposite and explained what had happened again for the record. Next to Böhm, Christel Temme eagerly noted each word, including at least twenty '*beg to reports*' and even more '*Yes, Sirs*!'

According to Eckert, it was around half past three when someone noticed that the traffic lights for Stresemannstrasse and Friedrich-Ebert-Strasse had been flashing a continuous red. Traffic Police Headquarters in Magazinstrasse had been informed, and from there they had tried to make contact with the traffic tower. By that stage, however, the line was already dead. Forensics had since confirmed that someone had severed the connection. Headquarters had sent a traffic officer, already on duty in the vicinity, to check that everything was in order – the same Constable Eckert who now sat opposite from Böhm, shako wedged under his arm.

'I climbed back down to call it in, Sir. After that I began dispersing the traffic on Stresemannstrasse.'

Böhm nodded. 'Did you mention that your colleague Scholz had failed to appear for duty.'

'Yes, Sir.'

'Did headquarters offer an explanation? Is Scholz sick?'

Eckert shook his head. 'No, Sir. Constable Scholz's shift began at two. He's usually very reliable.'

Böhm scratched his chin. 'Albeit he failed to show today ...'

'Or came and went.'

'You're saying that Constable Scholz killed his fellow officer?'

'Absolutely not!' Eckert shrugged. 'Perhaps he made a run for it when he saw the body. Lost his nerve.' The constable paused. 'That said ...'

'What do you mean "that said"?'

'The shift change was at two ... but it wasn't until an hour and a half later that anyone noticed the traffic tower was unmanned. That's strange.'

'Strange, indeed.' Böhm scratched his chin. 'What happens if the relief doesn't show? You hold position?'

'Yes, Sir. Of course.'

'So it could be that Wengler continued directing traffic after his shift was over.'

'Beg to report: he'd have contacted headquarters to request relief.'

'Not if the telephone line was down.' Böhm looked at Eckert. 'What would you have done if you were on duty and the relief failed to show? Imagine the line is dead, forget about why.'

The constable hunched his shoulders. 'The same as just now. I'd have gone across to *Josty*, or found a telephone booth and informed headquarters from there. Then held position.'

Böhm nodded. 'Good. That's all for now. You can go, Constable, but please continue to place yourself at our disposal.'

Eckert appeared relieved. He put on his shako, saluted, and withdrew at remarkable speed.

Böhm stepped out to stretch his legs. Any number of people stood outside *Josty* gawping across the intersection at the murder wagon, which enjoyed a certain notoriety in the city. Besides which, it was rare to see cars parked at the foot of the traffic tower. The grass-covered island in the middle of the intersection was the one place you were absolutely forbidden to stop. The rubberneckers were focused on the tails of a white coat flapping in the breeze, Dr Karthaus descending the ladder.

'Well, Doctor?' Böhm said, as the pathologist arrived. 'How's it looking up there?'

'Do you want the good news or the bad?'

'Depends what you mean by "good news".'

Karthaus buttoned his coat. 'There's no doubt what happened up there was murder. More than that, we know the killer's modus operandi.'

'And the bad news?'

'The bad news, Detective Chief Inspector, is that the MO fits with a case that remains unsolved.' He gestured towards the traffic tower. 'The corpse shows signs of drowning.'

Böhm reclaimed his seat on the murder wagon's leather bench. 'And prior to drowning, he was injected . . .'

'Correct,' Karthaus said. 'Which is why I'm going to ask the lab to look for tubocurarine during the blood analysis. That way, we'll have the results sooner.'

51

When Charly arrived at the Castle, Böhm and his men were still not back. She asked what was happening in Homicide, but the duty officer wasn't forthcoming. Michael Steinke was a fellow trainee, a snot-nosed upstart who had come to the Castle from the legal faculty and thought he was a cut above. He seemed to have difficulty passing information to a female colleague. Or perhaps he really *didn't* know anything. Neither reflected well on him.

'Corpse in the traffic tower,' he had said when asked what was going on at Potsdamer Platz. 'I saw to it that Böhm and a few others headed out.'

The idiot just had to go playing the big cheese. As if Böhm would let himself be ordered around by a cadet! Did the man have any idea he was speaking to someone with more than three years' service in Homicide? With a woman, who, while engaged as a stenographer, had contributed to the resolution of no fewer than seven murder investigations?

The telephone rang and Steinke fielded the call with an expression of immense self-importance. He didn't deign to look at her again.

So, there was a dead man in the traffic tower. She had worked that much out when she saw Böhm emerge from the murder wagon. Even so, Steinke wasn't about to reveal anything else. He made a show of turning away, speaking so quietly into the device it was as if he were Secret Service, and Charly a kind of Mata Hari.

She looked for a free typewriter. Might as well use the time to start her report on the *Haus Vaterland* operation. She didn't admit that she wanted it over as soon as possible, nor did she tell the full story of her encounter with Unger in the vegetable store. That was nobody's business but her own, although she could hardly wait to put that bastard behind bars, him and his accomplice! Let the pair rot in jail.

Suddenly she felt horrified at herself, at her thirst for revenge. A policewoman should know better than to let her feelings get in the way. She had almost finished the report when the door opened, and Böhm burst in, grumpy as ever. When he recognised his former stenographer his face brightened momentarily. 'Charly, what are you doing here?'

'Evening, Sir. I thought I'd stop by after seeing the murder wagon underneath the traffic tower.'

She had toyed with the idea of going over when she saw Böhm emerge from the black Maybach, but decided to head to Moabit first, to cancel her trip with Greta and take a shower. She felt dirty everywhere Unger had touched her. After changing into fresh clothes, she drove to Alex and parked Gereon's Buick in the shadow of the railway arches, out of sight of Castle workers entering the building.

Böhm told her what had happened, and Steinke, who was still on the telephone, looked on with envy as the detective chief inspector took *a female cadet* into his confidence.

'You're sure it's our man?' she asked.

'The sequence of events is identical. Paralysis followed by drowning.'

'Has that been confirmed by Pathology?'

'As good as. The perpetrator even left a red cloth at the scene.'

'But a police officer! What does he have to do with the other victims?'

'I don't know, maybe he saw something a week ago. When Lamkau died in *Haus Vaterland*. I've already requested the duty rotas from the Traffic Police. Perhaps we'll get a match.'

She wasn't satisfied with this response – and there was something else that didn't quite fit. 'The rhythm's out,' she said, and Böhm furrowed his brow.

'Pardon me?'

'The rhythm. Until now our killer has struck at intervals of approximately six weeks, but this time only a week has passed.'

'That suggests it could have been a witness.' Böhm rubbed his chin. 'Or a copycat killer. The papers reported everything, even the part about the red cloth.'

She shook her head. Some instinct told her Böhm was mistaken. 'I don't think we're dealing with a typical serial killer here, someone with a psychological disorder.'

'You can say "madman", you know.'

'That's just it. I don't think our killer *is* mad. This is someone who plans his murders carefully. So carefully, in fact, that on one occasion we even ruled murder out.'

'So?'

'The first three victims all lived in different cities, which is why he waited six weeks between each one. But now ...*Haus Vaterland* is just a stone's throw away from Potsdamer Platz and the traffic tower. Lamkau and the dead police officer lived in the same city, meaning he needed less time to prepare.'

'If Sergeant Wengler fits the pattern, then he must have something to do with the other victims. The three of them are linked by this moonshining scandal.' Böhm shook his head. 'Perhaps if Herr Rath would make contact, we'd know more, but it seems he's having quite the time of it in East Prussia.'

'Inspector Rath?' Steinke had thrown the name out there. Charly and Böhm both looked at him. The cadet

314

seemed agitated. 'Excuse me, Sir, but an Inspector Rath did telephone for you this morning . . .'

'And . . .?'

'I took down a memo. It's in your mail tray.'

'A *memo* . . .' Böhm was beside himself.

'Yes, Sir!' Steinke rushed to Böhm's desk and fished a note from one of the filing trays. 'Here it is.'

Charly squinted at the note in Böhm's hands.

DI Rath Telephone call, 11.07 Hotel Salzburger Hof, Treuburg, East Prussia, she read. *Further developments in moonshining scandal. 1924: Siegbert Wengler, Sergeant Major in Berlin! DI Rath suggests surveillance operation; possible next victim should suspicion harden against Radlewksi.*

Signed Cadet Steinke, Homicide

Böhm placed the note to one side. He breathed heavily, fixing the cadet with his gaze, then exploded. 'This is a disgrace!' Steinke ducked as if expecting a beating. 'When did the call come in, goddamn it?'

'I noted it at the top of the page.' Steinke gestured towards the memo. 'Around eleven.'

'You thought I shouldn't see it until tomorrow morning?' Böhm spoke quietly, but sounded no less threatening than before; quite the opposite, in fact.

'I thought . . .' Steinke broke off. He was starting to realise just how badly he had dropped the ball.

'Tomorrow morning,' Böhm continued, 'is when I would have been back on duty. Were it not for the fatality.'

'Which is precisely why I didn't want to disturb you, Sir,' Steinke stammered, falling silent when he saw Böhm's face.

'A fatality that might have been prevented had you relayed the message to me on time.'

'But, Sir, I thought that since you were back on duty tomorrow . . .'

'If that's the case, then perhaps it's best you don't think *at all*!' Böhm was shouting again.

The man cut a pitiful figure, but Charly could understand why Böhm had been so harsh. The DCI took the words out of her mouth: 'If you had managed to relay the message to me, or any one of my team, there is every chance that Sergeant Wengler might still be alive. We might have been able to set a trap for his killer.'

Steinke slumped to his chair and gazed at the floor, as if hoping it would swallow him up. 'I'm sorry, Sir,' he said, almost inaudible.

The situation was becoming unbearable. Despite having treated her as though she didn't exist, Charly felt an urge to comfort the man. *Goddamn maternal instinct*, she thought, *there's no way the bastard would be helping you in the same situation*. She was glad when the door opened and Andreas Lange entered the embarrassed silence, gazing in confusion from one person to the next.

'What are you doing here,' Böhm growled. 'Finished questioning witnesses already?'

'Not yet, Sir. We have around two dozen uniform cops still out searching. We've had most success in *Café Josty*. The ringside seats, if you like.'

'Go on.'

'I think we can more or less reconstruct the sequence of events. It appears that the shift change occurred as normal, at around two o'clock . . .'

'How do you know that?'

Lange held a black notebook aloft. 'The traffic tower duty log,' he said. 'One of Sergeant Major Wengler's final acts was to enter and sign the shift change at seven minutes past two. Constable Scholz's signature is missing, despite his name being given under *relieving officer*. In Sergeant Major Wengler's handwriting.'

'Which means,' Böhm said, 'that Wengler wrote the name when he saw the relief approaching.'

'But Scholz never signed,' Charly said. 'The question is, why?'

316

Lange nodded. 'We have a witness in *Josty* who is certain a uniform cop entered the traffic tower at around two o'clock.'

'At two?' Böhm looked at his wristwatch. 'And the man's still there now, at nearly seven?'

'We questioned him around half past five. He's a writer or something. People like that spend half their lives in cafés. Anyway, the man was clearly watching closely.'

Böhm was sceptical. 'He was, was he? Then tell us what he saw.'

'He saw a traffic cop crossing the intersection shortly after two and climbing the ladder. Everything as normal, he says. Only he didn't see anyone come down. At least not at two, in fact not until . . .' Lange referred to his notebook. '. . .around twenty past three. A few minutes before the chorus of horns began on Stresemannstrasse.'

Böhm was still sceptical. 'Does your witness have nothing better to do than spend the day staring at the traffic tower?'

'He watches, and he writes, is what he told me. It looks like he watches very closely. According to his statement, the man who left the tower at twenty past three was the same man who entered at two.'

'You're saying this man wasn't Constable Scholz?'

'We'll see. My witness is currently waiting on the sketch artist in Interview Room A.'

'Good.' Böhm nodded. 'Let's get a warrant out for this Scholz all the same. Something here doesn't add up.'

'You're right there.' Lange nodded. 'There's something else. Dr Karthaus is now assuming that Sergeant Major Wengler didn't die until at least three . . .'

'So late!' Böhm was disbelieving. 'That can't be right.'

'It could be,' Charly said. The three men looked at her. 'But it would mean that all the while Wengler was dying, his killer was up there directing traffic.'

52

The night shift was the worst. The urinals and toilet bowls looked as if every passenger at Potsdamer Bahnhof had availed of them – with varying degrees of accuracy – before boarding. It was as if the whole world had conspired against him, knowing it was his task to get this disgusting piss-soaked room clean again. He hated it, *hated* it. This was no job for a man, but what could he do? At times like these you were lucky to have work at all.

He wasn't quite finished with the washroom, but wanted to take advantage of the urinals being free. He hated mopping while men peed at the wall, throwing him contemptuous glances if they deigned to look at all. He was about to get started again with his scrubber and bucket when a groan from a cubicle stopped him. No one had entered in the ten minutes or so since he'd begun.

There was another groan. A couple of queers? The thought revolted him. Maybe he should call the police and have Vice lock the dirty bastards up.

Now there was a crash. He crouched; a man was kneeling on the floor. It looked as if he were alone, which was something, at least.

'Hello?' he said tentatively. 'Can I help?' There was another groan. The man in the cubicle tried to stand up, but his legs gave way underneath him. 'Hello? What's the matter? Are you unwell?' He gave the door a shake. Bolted,

318

of course. 'Please open up! Otherwise I can't help you!' The man could be having a heart attack – but how could he help if he couldn't open the door?

The man tried to free the bolt but lacked the strength even for that. There was a helpless jerking sound; the slide must have snagged. Suddenly there was a loud scrape and the door swung open. The man collapsed forward, slamming against the floor tiles. He was clad in underwear and socks.

'What's wrong with you? Should I call the police?'

'Bollisse,' the man slurred. 'I bollisse!'

'What happened? Are you hurt?'

The man managed to prop himself up a little. He seemed pretty dazed, but it wasn't drunkenness. It was almost as if something were paralysing his arm and leg muscles, perhaps even his tongue. He shook his head. 'Not buurtt.' With that, his arms gave way once more.

There was something on the floor of the cubicle, next to the toilet bowl. He went over and picked it up gingerly. A Berlin Police identification with a photo of the unconscious man, though here he smiled and wore a shako. *Erwin Scholz*, it said under the smile, *Police Constable*. Diagonally above was a stamp bearing the Prussian eagle.

53

In bygone times they'd have called it *Kaiserwetter*. The sky was almost indecently blue, the breeze gentle, and the air afizz with the excitement of special days. The town was in festive mood. Flags, pennants and garlands quivered on the fronts around the marketplace, the pavement glistened as after a fresh shower, and the flagpoles fluttered black, white and red, billowing like washing on the line.

Rath had been awakened by the brass band and rose late, having failed to set his alarm. He stood in his dressing gown, gazing out on Germany's largest marketplace. The Treuburgers in their holiday finery lined the square, standing to attention as they listened to the patriotic songs and Prussian marches. A group of youths in brown shirts stood especially straight in their freshly ironed uniforms, resolved to show themselves at their best. Their swastika brassards gleamed as if fresh from the line.

Rath stubbed out his cigarette and went into the bathroom. He felt OK, despite having had far too much to drink last night while attempting to contact Charly. Eschewing the claustrophobic atmosphere of the *Salzburger Hof*, he had taken dinner in the *Kronprinzen*, where his fellow patrons, among them the Berlin tourist family, had watched in bafflement as time and again he interrupted his dinner to make a telephone call.

After dessert, he had asked for a Turkish coffee and called

Carmerstrasse at one or two cigarette intervals, growing more nervous with each failed attempt. Finishing his coffee, he ordered a cognac. Then a second, and a third. At some point he overcame his reservations and telephoned Spenerstrasse, by then drunk enough to contemplate an exchange with Greta. Temporarily setting aside his dislike he inquired politely as to Charly's whereabouts.

Greta's response was curt. 'On duty,' she said. 'No idea when she'll be back.'

He mumbled his thank yous and hung up.

No idea when she'll be back.

Did that mean Charly was still living at Spenerstrasse? To think, he had given her his keys in the hope that she might move in and actually be living with him when he returned from East Prussia. Well, think again.

He ordered another cognac and spent the rest of the evening wallowing in self-pity until, finally, he felt numb enough to head back to his hotel.

There had been no need of an aspirin this morning. A cold shower sufficed. He descended the stairs, placed his key on the shiny counter of the deserted reception and stepped into the sunshine.

The musicians were decidedly better at marching than playing. Reaching Bergstrasse, where Rath now stood with a crowd of onlookers, they wheeled left onto Goldaper Strasse and made their way towards the festival site. The crowd trailed after them like children following the Pied Piper of Hamelin.

He let himself be carried forward, calling on Master Shoemaker Kowalski at the midway point, but to no avail. By the time he reached the park, the musicians had their positions onstage and were playing their final march. Upon finishing they sat down, enjoying the applause of the crowd and turning their attentions to the glasses of beer that had been laid out for them in advance. In the open expanse in front of the war memorial, countless rows of beer tables led

321

to the marquee from which waiters and waitresses emerged carrying fully laden trays.

Spying Kowalski, he fought his way through the masses to join his table. Kowalski made room and introduced the man on his right as 'Uncle Fritz'. Friedrich Kowalski, the cobbler, wasn't nearly as old as Rath had imagined, in his early forties perhaps. Straightaway he stood Rath a beer. Rath offered cigarettes in return.

Moments later, the beer arrived and the band resumed its playing at a volume that precluded normal conversation. Looking around, Rath recognised the blue uniform of Chief Constable Grigat in the front row. Alongside him were two men who were unmistakably parish priests, Catholic and Protestant seated side by side. The sight of the clerical collar and cassock reassured him; anti-Catholic sentiment couldn't be so rife here after all. At the same table were the district administrator and mayor. Evidently the town's dignitaries were gathered, from the grammar school rector to the hospital chief doctor and newspaper editor. Two tables further along was the tourist family from the *Kronprinzen*, the Berliners with the spoiled children. The mother threw Rath a disapproving glance. His fondness for cognac seemed to have left a lasting impression.

At last the band took a break. He was about to turn to Kowalski when he heard a high-pitched voice from behind. 'Inspector?' It was Hella, the waitress from the *Salzburger Hof*. 'Please excuse the interruption,' she said, dropping a curtsey. 'But I didn't see you this morning at the hotel, and there was a telephone call for you. From Berlin.'

'From Berlin? Was it a lady?'

She shook her head. 'A Detective Chief Inspector Blum? He requested that you call back.' The music started up again, obliging her to shout.

'Was it Detective Chief Inspector Böhm? When did he call?'

322

'Pardon me?'

'When?'

She leaned over and spoke loudly in his ear. 'Yesterday evening. I put a note in your pigeonhole ...but then I didn't see you. Anyway, I thought I'd tell you now. Perhaps it's important ...'

'Thank you, Hella,' he said. She stood where she was until he pressed a one-mark coin into her hand. She curtseyed again, flashing him a smile as she returned to her family's table. He gazed after her. The way she lifted her skirt as she sat down ...

So Böhm had called. Well, he'd just have to wait. He focused on his beer; the local brew wasn't so bad. When the band took another break he leaned over to Kowalski. 'How did you get on with that list of names?' he asked.

'I had my hands full with the reading you gave me.'

'And?'

'Zip. Nothing in the paper that might've grabbed Radlewski's attention, and the books you gave me are all about North American Indians. The curare poison comes from South America.'

'Meaning?'

'Meaning there are no recipes for poison.'

'Perhaps the librarian overlooked something.'

'District library's closed today.' Kowalski gestured towards a table in the shadow of the marquee. Maria Cofalka, lady of letters, sat in the company of various men and women, obviously teachers, among whom Rath spotted Karl Rammoser. Rammoser looked over and raised his glass. It seemed the band were taking a longer break; at any rate the musicians' drinks were being replenished.

'What about the list?'

'Give me a few hours.' Kowalski gazed across the site and lowered his voice. 'They're all here, and the tipsier they get, the more likely they are to share.'

323

'Then get going. I need to send the names by lunchtime. Detective Chief Inspector Böhm's requested them already.'

Kowalski nodded and looked towards the front as the district administrator, Wachsmann, buttoned his jacket and climbed the steps to the war memorial to open the official ceremony commemorating the 1920 plebiscite. The whispering at the tables died when the microphone issued its first sound. Wachsmann contented himself with a simple greeting; the majority of his address consisted in listing the names of the local dignitaries present. Rath was pleased that Dr Wachsmann also bid them welcome on behalf of the mayor; there would be no need to submit to this pantomime a second time.

'I would like, in particular,' Wachsmann said, having now worked his way through his list, 'to welcome those here from the west. The Corridor may continue to rupture our Fatherland, but, as your presence demonstrates, we remain very much part of the German Reich, to which we professed our loyalty exactly twelve years ago. Ladies and gentlemen, I welcome those families from Berlin and Pomerania who have holidayed in Masuria for years, unstinting in their solidarity with our beautiful region. I extend an equally warm welcome to all those celebrating the plebiscite anniversary with us today for the first time. May you return, next year, and in ten, in twenty, in fifty years!' His gaze passed among the rows like an itinerant preacher hailing the newly baptised. 'Now, please join me in welcoming to the stage a man who, twelve years ago, fought unswervingly to repel the Polish assault on our hometown! Ladies and gentlemen, please welcome Gustav Wengler!'

From the far reaches of the memorial ground Director Wengler approached at a measured pace, dressed in formal dark suit and top hat. The effect was more dramatic than rising from a table at the front. Rath couldn't help but grin at the thought of him waiting behind a tree, speech

324

tucked under one arm. Despite the obvious artificiality, the people hailed the owner of the Luisenhöhe estate like a tribune. Rath dutifully joined the applause, but felt uneasy. He didn't know what to make of Wachsmann's gushing national pathos, which also featured heavily in Wengler's speech, the opening lines of which were peppered with terms such as *Heimat, Vaterland* and *Treue.* Homeland, Fatherland, Devotion.

The director was the better speaker, which surprised Rath, who had assumed that oratory was the most important weapon in a politician's armoury. Perhaps Wengler was the better politician too. It seemed as if the entrepreneur were the secret ruler of this town – or perhaps there was no secret about it.

'We all know what happened twelve years ago,' Wengler announced. 'To many of you today it will seem only natural that Masuria should have remained German. In fact, it was anything but. We had to fight. In trying to wrest our homeland away, the Poles did everything they could to sow hatred and discord among us ...'

Rath remembered Rammoser's words: that it had been Wengler and his thugs sowing the hatred and discord. How many of their number would be dressed in brown today? The Treuburg SA had commandeered an entire table for itself, and, in point of fact, its members listened more attentively to Wengler than the rest. As far as Rath could see, the estate owner wore no swastika, not even the little lapel badge Hitler's party colleagues were so fond of displaying. Perhaps the man didn't belong to the party, and simply used it for his own ends. Something like Johann Marlow, who presided over the *Berolina* Ringverein without ever having been a member. In Rath's eyes the SA were little more than a gang of criminals, at least in Berlin. Here in Treuburg things were different.

'Their gamble didn't pay off,' Wengler continued.

'We Treuburgers resisted their cunning and trickery and professed our unswerving devotion to the Reich. We did not yield! Even when Polish propaganda and its lies claimed a human life.' He made a brief, but effective pause. 'Most of you know what I am talking about. *Who* I am talking about. A woman from our midst; a woman who gave her life so that she might profess her allegiance to Prussia and Germany. On the day our fate was sealed, the fate of our town and our district, the fate of the whole of Masuria, so too . . .was her fate sealed.' He broke off as if overcome by the memory.

Rath looked around at people gazing in silence towards the front, a few women dabbing their eyes with handkerchiefs. The teachers wore looks of reverence, even Rammoser, though the lines around his mouth suggested he didn't agree with everything Wengler had said. The librarian's expression was easier to interpret. Maria Cofalka regarded Gustav Wengler with distaste, if not outright revulsion. Rath could understand. He, too, was repelled by the theatricality of Wengler's act. He looked at the man's face, unsure if his feelings were genuine, or simply a means of adding emotional authenticity to his yearly address.

'Ladies and gentlemen,' Wengler said now. 'Please be upstanding so that we may commemorate Anna von Mathée's death with a minute's silence.'

Chairs scraped, isolated coughs and whispers died, and an almost religious stillness descended. The only sound was the wind rustling in the trees. Rath gazed into serious faces. Anna von Mathée's death still touched people twelve years after the event.

'I think that most of you know Anna's story,' Wengler continued. 'Most of you are aware of how she was killed; that it happened on the day of the plebiscite, at the hands of one of those alien elements that sought to rob us of our homeland. Most of you know that Anna was my fiancée.

Her death gives me every reason to hate her killer, but today I do not wish to speak of hatred, only love. Nor do I wish to speak of the past, only the future.'

The love Wengler proclaimed was love for the Fatherland, and the future he conjured was music to the ears of the brownshirts alone. Despite his statement to the contrary, the chief of the Homeland Service did not let the past lie. He spoke instead of 'wounds that refused to heal', referring to the Corridor as 'that wedge which has been driven between Prussian body and soul'. Again, the pause was timed to perfection. 'They have separated us from the Fatherland, but they will never tear our German hearts from our breasts! One day we will be bound with the Reich once more, and the humiliation of Versailles erased.'

Rath was familiar with this rhetoric. When a speaker pulled out the stops in this way, he could count on the approval of his public, irrespective of politics or class. Even so, he had never heard anything like the primal jubilation that erupted from the Treuburgers when Wengler finished. Gradually he began to understand why the Nazis, who played on people's feelings in a similar way, had met with such a positive response here, despite the Masurians' Polish roots mitigating against their place in the Nazi world view.

The open-air concert began, so loud it was impossible to hear yourself think. Rath drained his beer and left Kowalski, tapping on his wristwatch as he went. 'I need those names for one o'clock.'

Strolling across the festival site, he realised he wasn't the only one opting to give the musical society's concert a miss. Mothers waited patiently with their offspring by the merry-go-round, while, a few stands along, a group of lads clouted the high striker to impress the lasses. The puck was sent catapulting towards the bell, and the strong man received a kiss from his sweetheart as a reward. Rath made out Hella's blonde pigtails and the brown uniform of the

SA. Her boyfriend wasn't the only brownshirt here. The younger members mostly stood before the high striker or shooting gallery, none of them older than twenty. Those at the gallery were likewise surrounded by village beauties. Uniforms were still important in Germany, Rath mused, if only to impress the fair sex. It was the same at the marksmen's festivals in the Rhineland, youthful sharpshooters prancing in their uniforms to dazzle the girls. Only, the lads here didn't belong to any gun club, but a political goon squad that until recently had been banned.

Rath thought of the Communist posters. Glued under the cover of darkness, here were the boys who'd torn them down.

The scent of roasted almonds and *Lebkuchen* drove him towards more rustic pleasures, and he ordered a *kielbasa* at the stand. Polish sausages were still in demand. He bit inside. Not bad.

'Bon appétit, Inspector.' Behind him stood Karl Rammoser.

'Would you like one too?' Rath asked. 'It's on me.'

'No, thank you. I already have plans.'

'Perhaps I can repay your hospitality another time.'

'Thanks.'

'I'm surprised to see the SA out in uniform.'

'Klaus Fabeck and his boys? I'd rather they celebrated in uniform than brawled with Communists in plain clothes.'

'Wouldn't be much of a fight. There are only two Communists here.'

Rammoser changed topics. 'Maria mentioned you stopped by the district library?'

'That's right. Because of Radlewski.'

'You still suspect poor Artur?'

'Not if he could assure me, in person, that he hasn't set foot outside East Prussia these last few months.'

'Maria's worried about Artur; she thinks you have the wrong man. No one knows him better around here.'

'I can believe that. She was in love with him, wasn't she?'

'I'm too young to know the full story. Apparently, she was smitten at school.'

'Perhaps she still is.'

'Perhaps.' Rammoser glanced at the table of dignitaries where Gustav Wengler now took centre stage; planets orbiting his sun. 'How did you like the speech?'

'Impressive.' Rath couldn't think of a more diplomatic response.

'Many think Wengler should go into politics.'

'If politics is about making yourself popular by telling people what they want to hear, there's no doubt he'd be a success.'

'The way it looks, he sets greater store by his distillery than his political career.'

'At least that way he can't do any damage.'

'Folks here like what he says.'

'So much the worse. Shouldn't you be trying to make peace with Poland? They're your neighbours.'

'You're preaching to the converted but, given Wengler's story, his hatred is understandable.'

'Maybe. I just find it pretty tasteless, the way he . . .'

'Exploits his personal history for effect?'

'Something like that,' Rath agreed. 'He infects the whole town with his hatred. I think it's dangerous. It isn't just the acclaim. It's the people who acclaim him.'

'You have to understand they're afraid of being forgotten, over in the Reich.'

'People rail against the Corridor in the Reich too. Only in Berlin, the Nazis aren't part of the village community.'

'Well, maybe that's because Berlin's no village.'

54

Constable Erwin Scholz lay on his sickbed, wan-faced, skin colour scarcely distinguishable from his bed linen, but he didn't seem to have sustained lasting damage. That was something, at least.

Next step was to discover what had put the poor man out of commission, even if Gräf was certain the blood analysis would point to curare, or some other form of Indian poison. In the meantime he and Lange had become experts in all things South American, though they still hadn't traced the source of the poison that had killed Lamkau and his fellow East Prussians. This despite the industrious Lange borrowing various academic texts to aid them in their inquiry. Perhaps the mysterious killer had cooked up the poison himself, a would-be Indian prowling noiselessly through Berlin murdering its citizens: a gruesome image.

Erwin Scholz knew nothing about that, but then he knew just as little about what had befallen him at Potsdamer Bahnhof, where a member of cleaning staff had found him slouched in the gentlemen's toilets in the middle of the night.

'His body was heavily sedated for hours, and his circulation still hasn't returned to normal,' the doctor had said. 'You need to be patient with him.'

Sadly, patience was the one thing they couldn't afford. The crazy Indian had struck again, and this time the victim was one of their own. As a result, Gennat had chosen to strengthen the *Vaterland* team's reserves. Almost all homicide detectives were now at Böhm's disposal with the exception of the *Phantom* troop, which had been left untouched. For whatever reason, Buddha seemed to dote on Dettmann.

Böhm wanted to recall Rath from East Prussia, but so far his efforts to reach him had proved in vain. Gräf could imagine why. Gereon had never been especially good at keeping Böhm in the loop. In fact, he was a past master at avoiding him, mostly because he couldn't stand the man, but sometimes because he had a lead he didn't want to share.

Well, yesterday he had shared – and, goddamn it, he had been right. Already the Berlin press had wind of it. A dead man in the middle of Potsdamer Platz couldn't be kept secret. Too many people had witnessed the gridlock, and the murder wagon parked at the foot of the traffic tower.

The pale constable looked wretched, but this was no time for sympathy. Gräf took out his notepad, ready to begin. 'How well did you know Sergeant Major Wengler?'

There was a shrug from the bed. 'He was a colleague. Taught me how to use the controls.'

'Is there much teaching involved?'

'Not really. But you know how it is . . .the older generation aren't always so good with technology. Knowing how to operate all the buttons and switches was a source of pride.'

'Were you ever at Wengler's home?'

'No.'

'Do you know where he lives?'

'In Schöneberg, I think.'

'He moved. A few weeks ago.'

'Moved? Where?'

'I was hoping he might have said something to you.'

Yesterday evening, Gräf had called at Wengler's registered home address in Feurigstrasse with a team of forensic technicians. The landlady peered suspiciously through the crack in the door. No wonder. Gone nine, and here were five men whose rumpled suits and tired, sullen faces did not inspire confidence. They looked as if they'd spent most of the afternoon crawling on the floor, which, of course, they had.

'Police? What do you want from me?'

'From you, nothing. We're here for one of your tenants. Siegbert Wengler. We need to take a look at his flat.'

'You have the wrong address. He doesn't live here any more.'

Siegbert Wengler had moved four weeks before, though no one knew where, neither the landlady, with whom he had lived for almost eight years, nor Wengler's Traffic Police colleagues. He had no close friends on the force, at least none that Gräf had spoken to, including Constable Scholz.

'Is it possible he felt threatened?' Gräf asked. 'Did he ever hint at something like that? I mean, was there a reason he lived such a secluded life?'

'I'm sorry, Sir, but Sergeant Major Wengler wasn't much of a talker. Do *you* have any idea who might've killed him?'

'The way it looks, the same man who stole your uniform.' The constable's face grew paler still. Gräf showed him a sketch commissioned by Lange following a witness statement. It had come out pretty generic; the most eye-catching thing was the shako. 'Could it have been this man? Perhaps you noticed him at the station beforehand? Someone behaving suspiciously?'

Constable Scholz gave the sketch a good look before shaking his head. 'I don't recognise the face.'

'Pity. We could've been onto something there.'

Scholz gestured towards the shako. 'The uniform he's wearing is mine, I assume? I'd like to help, but I didn't see the man. I felt him grip me from behind, there was a sting in my neck, and then everything went black.'

'But you're certain it was a man ...'

'Of course ... You think a woman would be capable of overpowering me?' Gräf said nothing. 'In the men's toilets, I'd have noticed a woman straightaway.'

'Do you have any explanation as to why no one realised you'd been attacked?'

'There was no one else around.'

'In the station toilets?'

'It's where I always go before my shift starts. There are no washing facilities in the traffic tower, no toilet either. You have to plan ahead. No way you can work up there with a weak bladder.'

'Plan ahead, understood.' Gräf made a note. 'And you always use the same washroom ...'

Scholz nodded. 'I take the Wannsee line to work. Seems only natural.'

'Just so there are no misunderstandings. You use the same washroom facilities at Potsdamer Bahnhof every day?'

'Yes, for God's sake. Why's it so important?'

'We'll see,' Gräf said. He didn't want to put the man under any more strain, but it looked as if this stranger had spent days, perhaps even weeks, waiting for the opportunity to steal his uniform and gain access to the traffic tower.

55

Goddamn it! Did he have to take care of everything himself? He hung up, ruing the fact that the cabins were equipped with swing doors, but at least now he knew why he hadn't reached Charly yesterday evening, and why Böhm had wanted to speak with him.

Kowalski waited outside the post office. 'What news from Berlin?' he asked, pushing himself up from the wing of the car. 'Are they happy?'

'Get in.' Kowalski obeyed without further comment. Rath sat in the passenger seat. At least *here* he could slam the door.

Kowalski had provided the names at one on the dot, five more distillery workers who, according to the Treuburg gossip mill, were implicated in the moonshining scandal. Two had moved, but three were still employed by the distillery, among them Dietrich Assmann, the operations manager, currently on business in Berlin.

'Good work on your list, Kowalski.' Böhm had noted each name meticulously: Berlin didn't want any more mistakes. No doubt Warrants were already working flat out.

Rath stared out the window as Kowalski rolled the engine. The Communists had been at it again. *Down with Fascism! Join the Communist struggle! Choose List 3!* They must have put them up in broad daylight this time; the slogans were still damp from the paste. Today the marketplace was more or less deserted, save for the pile of wood in its centre. It looked as if the townsfolk were still searching for a heretic to burn.

'If Berlin is happy, why are you in such a bad mood?'

'Kowalski,' Rath said. 'Do you know what a death knock is?'

The assistant detective blanched.

Gustav Wengler, on the other hand, remained composed. More composed, at least, than Rath had dared hope. It was almost as if he had anticipated the news. They had collected him from his employees' table inside the marquee, where celebrations were in full swing. Only once they were at some remove from the hullabaloo did Rath come out with the news. He conveyed the message as per Gennat's training: *Don't blurt it out, but don't wait too long either.*

'Sad news,' he began. 'Your brother in Berlin . . .' Gustav Wengler reached for the cigarette case in his pocket and fumbled out a cigarette. He had understood. 'I'm sorry, Herr Wengler, but your brother is dead. He was killed on duty.'

Wengler placed the cigarette between his lips and checked his pockets for a light or matches, finding neither. Rath gave him a light, lit an Overstolz himself, and explained when and where Sergeant Major Siegbert Wengler had died.

Gennat's next piece of advice was: *Don't quiz them straightaway. Let them talk if they want to. If not, fill in the silence yourself.*

Wengler didn't want to talk.

'We suspect it's the same man who has your former employees on his conscience.'

Wengler took a deep drag. 'Artur Radlewski?' he asked.

'That's how it looks. Only, there's still no trace of him. Seems the man can make himself invisible.'

'Killed on duty, you say?'

Rath wanted to spare Wengler the details for now. 'I'm

335

very sorry to have to break the news at a celebration that already has unhappy associations for you.'

Kowalski kept himself in the background the whole time. Rath could see the situation made him uneasy. No wonder, he had known Siegbert Wengler as a police officer, and even ten years ago his brother Gustav would have been an important town figure.

'We need to ask you a few questions, Herr Wengler,' Rath said.

'I understand. You're only doing your job.'

'We have some names here. Men who were also implicated in the moonshining scandal. I'd like you to help us find them. We need to warn them, and, if possible, protect them. So that no one else dies.'

Wengler took the list Kowalski handed him. 'Assmann is in Berlin,' he said. 'As for the others, let me ask around.'

'Thank you.' Rath waited until Wengler had pocketed the list before posing his next question. 'Your brother – is it possible he suspected he was in danger?'

'We didn't talk much, at least not in the last few years.' Wengler shook his head. 'Damn it. How can someone just cease to exist like that?'

'Did you know your brother had recently moved?'

'He's no longer in Schöneberg?'

'No. I'd hoped you might be able to provide his new address. Your brother doesn't appear to have told anyone where he was moving. If I didn't know better I'd say he was trying to hide – even if he appeared for duty each day as if nothing had happened.'

Wengler drew on his cigarette and gazed thoughtfully into the middle distance, towards the war memorial and the Treuburgers drinking themselves blind on Luisenhöhe Distillery produce. 'You think he moved because he felt threatened?'

'He probably felt safer on duty.'

'Clearly he was wrong.'

'Can you tell us who your brother was friendly with? People with whom he might have shared his new address.'

'Siegbert was never one for friends.' Wengler stubbed out his cigarette. 'Now if you would please excuse me. I'd like to be alone.'

Rath and Kowalski gazed after him as he made his way down to the shore, alone with himself and his thoughts. Suddenly the great man appeared rather lonely.

56

Manfred Unger sat in his office behind the glass pane, watching Charly wide-eyed as she entered the central kitchen four or five hours late in the company of a lone man. After a moment to process what was happening, he rushed to the door and flung it wide open. 'Who the hell do you think you are!' he shouted. 'Swanning in like this. Do you realise what time it is? Collect your papers, and get out!'

'We'll be on our way soon enough, Herr Unger.' Lange showed his identification, and suddenly the head chef appeared to twig. 'Only, you'll be coming with us.'

'On what grounds?'

'How about multiple extortion? I would ask you to come quietly. It's not in your interests to make a scene.'

'But ...' Unger gestured towards the central kitchen, his realm. 'The work here ...'

'You needn't worry on that score, Herr Unger,' Charly said. 'There are plenty of people who'd do anything to work at *Haus Vaterland*.'

He gawped at her, still apparently unaware of her role. He looked at Lange. 'Did that little bitch report me? Don't believe a word she says. Fucking Sarotti-sweetheart.'

'I'd advise you to choose your words more carefully,' Lange said. '*Little bitch* is an inappropriate way to describe a CID officer.'

'Pardon me?' Unger stood open-mouthed, looking unusually stupid.

'Fräulein Ritter here is a CID cadet,' Lange explained.

'What's the world coming to?' Unger said, shaking his head. 'Women police officers!'

'You'd do well to get used to it. You'll be seeing rather a lot of Fräulein Ritter in the coming days.'

'It won't be long before we have a woman *minister*. Chancellor, even, knowing these Social Democrats.'

'Keep this up, Herr Unger, and I'll have a squad of uniform officers cuff you and turn your office upside down.' Lange took a couple of official-looking documents from his pocket. 'These search and arrest warrants give me every right.' He smiled at the chef. 'So, how about we tone things down a notch, and wrap this up as discreetly as possible.'

Unger said nothing more. They closed the door and showed him to a chair. Lange took up position while Charly filled two cardboard boxes with files, and the contents of Unger's desk. The man threw her a venomous glance. Through the glass pane, she could see that just about every kitchen employee had realised that something was up. They carried on as before, but continued to look furtively in Unger's direction.

Lange took one of the heavy boxes, and gestured for Unger to take the other.

'Why would I do that?'

'Very well,' Lange said. 'Fräulein Ritter? Put a call through to the 16th precinct and request assistance with a defiant suspect, and with carrying boxes.'

She reached for the receiver and was on the verge of dialling when Unger had second thoughts. He lifted the box sulkily from the desk. She held the door open and they left the office, encountering a fat man at the time clock who was putting on his chef's hat. Unger stared at him.

'Fritzsche? What are you doing here?'

The fat man smiled in embarrassment. 'Director Fleischer called to say I'd be standing in for the day.'

'I think it'll be longer than that,' Lange said.

Carrying his cardboard box in front of him as they left the central kitchen, Manfred Unger looked like an employee who had just been given the sack.

57

By now the atmosphere was far removed from the solemn patriotism of the morning speeches. People were laughing and having a good time, while the first inebriates stared into space or began weaving their way home. Soon a fight would break out, and new couples would form. Devoid of all the nationalist bombast, this was just another run-of-the-mill public festival. Behind the war memorial, on the bridge leading over the light railway platform, the celebrations were no louder than a distant murmur.

Rath tapped an Overstolz against the lid of his cigarette case and gazed over the sports ground towards the lake and public baths. He had sent Kowalski to remind old Adamek of their agreement, and was glad to have a minute to himself. Informing a person that a relative, or friend, had died, sometimes in violent circumstances, was a part of the job he despised – even if that person was as slippery as Gustav Wengler. He threw the match onto the railway tracks.

A voice called out behind him, and he gave a start. 'Inspector, do you have a moment?' Maria Cofalka, the librarian, stood looking at him, appearing altogether less shy – and sober – than before. 'If it suits you, of course...'

'Absolutely.' He tried to sound friendly. 'Is it to do with Artur Radlewski?'

'You could say that.' Maria Cofalka smiled and suddenly

appeared ten years younger. Probably the same ten years added by her bun. 'Karl tells me you can be trusted. Herr Rammoser, I mean.'

'I'm honoured. Is there something you'd like to tell me in confidence?'

'Perhaps,' she said. 'What do you make of Herr Wengler?'

'In my line of work it doesn't matter what I *make* of someone. What matters is what they've done, and what you can tell me.'

'You're probably right. What did Wengler want to speak with you about just now?'

'You were watching?'

'I just happened to see the pair of you strolling through the park. Was it something important?'

'You'll understand that I can't go into detail. Only, it wasn't Wengler who wanted to speak with me. I had bad news for him.'

'I'm sorry to hear that.' She seemed surprised. 'His brother?'

'How did you know?'

'You suspect Artur of killing these moonshiners, don't you? The ones responsible for his mother's death.' Rath nodded. 'That's not his style, believe me. Artur has always let Wengler's moonshiners go about their business in peace. Even though they brew and smuggle their rotgut in his forest.'

'They're not *Wengler*'s moonshiners, though, are they? Gustav Wengler has nothing to do with all that.'

'That's certainly the impression he likes to convey but, Inspector, you shouldn't believe everything Gustav Wengler tells you.'

'You don't like him very much, do you?'

'I have my reasons.'

'Perhaps you should enlighten me.'

'That's why I'm here.' She looked around to check no one

was listening. Whatever she had to say, it was costing her a lot of effort. 'Don't believe Wengler's stories, Inspector. About his fiancée and her death. It's lies, all of it.'

'Let's head down to the lake. We can talk in private there.'

'Apologies, Inspector. I'm not in the habit of speaking ill of people.' The noise grew ever quieter the nearer they approached the lake. 'It's just ...I have the feeling no one here can separate good from evil any more.'

'And Gustav Wengler is evil?'

She agreed without a moment's hesitation. 'Gustav Wengler is a hypocrite. He sent an innocent man to jail. The Polack didn't kill Anna von Mathée.'

'Who?'

'The Polack. The great Polish agitator Wengler never tires of mentioning in his speeches.'

'Polack, eh? Sounds like he might be onto something.'

'That's just the name he was given by Wengler and his men. His real name was Polakowski.'

'Was?'

'He died trying to escape from Wartenburg Jail. He's buried in the cemetery over by the lake.'

'The Catholic cemetery ...'

'Being Catholic was his first mistake – alongside his Polish name. At least in the eyes of the Homeland Service. His second was to want no part in the anti-Polish frenzy of twelve years ago.'

'He *didn't* belong to the Agitation Bureau?'

'He was a doctor. A young registrar who worked at the hospital over on Graudenzer Strasse.'

'A doctor who spoke up for the Polish cause ...'

'I'm afraid you've let yourself be taken in, Inspector, just like everyone else. Jakub Polakowski didn't speak up for the Polish cause; he spoke up for Polish people.'

'I'm sorry. Go on.'

'Back in those days brawls were a common occurrence.

343

On one occasion alongside a member of the Agitation Bureau, one of Wengler's goons was hurt. Lamkau.' Rath nodded. 'Both men needed treatment, but Polakowski's mistake was to tend to the Bureau member, Roeska, first, who was unconscious and the more seriously hurt. Suffice it to say, the decision didn't go down well with Lamkau and Wengler and the others. After that Dr Polakowski became the Polack.'

'How do you know all this?'

'The man often came by the library, and I can tell you one thing. He never took out any Polish books, although we had any number back then. Still do, in fact, even today, when Polish is only spoken behind closed doors.'

'Why are you telling me this?'

'You're a police officer. Perhaps you'll see that justice is served. Jakub Polakowski didn't kill Anna von Mathée, he was just a convenient scapegoat. Wengler serves up the same old lie each year, and people here are only too happy to believe it. It soothes their conscience about the bad old days. The Poles were much worse, they'll say, they actually *killed* someone, when all we did was fight, or smash windows, or set fire to barns.'

She had talked herself into a rage.

'I'm not sure there's much I can do for you,' Rath said. 'Who benefits if I go digging up these old stories? Not Polakowski. He's already dead.'

'It was Siegbert Wengler who arrested him . . .'

'So?'

'He knew that Polakowski was innocent, and Gustav Wengler knew it too. Yet they took him to court, and both made statements against him.'

'You realise these are pretty enormous accusations you're making?'

'I appreciate that, Inspector, but you're the first person I've told.'

344

'Karl Rammoser doesn't know?'

She shook her head. 'No one here does. No one would believe me. Like I say, you're the first I've told.'

'Why do you suppose I'll believe you?'

She took a folder full of papers from her bag, some of which were so curled and yellowed that they must have got very wet once upon a time. 'Read these, then decide whether you should take another look at the Polakowski file.' She pressed the folder into his hand. He felt a little ambushed. He had underestimated her. 'Inspector, you have to promise me something,' she said. 'Don't show this folder to anyone. Don't tell anyone where you got it. No one, do you hear, not even Karl Rammoser . . .'

'I don't know if . . .'

'Look after it.' She gave him a pleading look. 'This is . . .something very private. It isn't easy for me to part with, but you have to make sacrifices for the truth. Take the time and read it, I beg you.'

He looked at the closely written papers. 'What is this?'

'That,' Maria Cofalka said, 'is the truth about Anna von Mathée's death.'

58

The truth about Anna von Mathée's death wasn't easy to read, scrawled as it was in tiny letters, and with the ink smudged in various places or grown faded.

Rath began leafing through the papers immediately, taking up position on a bench by the shore and doing his best to decipher a few lines, but it was mostly guesswork. The only thing he could discern with any conviction was the signature that concluded each text, even if the word itself made little sense. *Tokala*, he read, and, after comparing a few times, he felt certain he was right, since the word appeared over and over again in the documents. Someone was writing about themselves in the third person . . .

Tokala will never live among humans again, ran one of the opening lines. The letters, if indeed that's what they were, had no date, no salutation, no sender, just a signature that was always the same.

There was no point carrying on; he'd need a magnifying glass to get anywhere with these. He snapped the folder shut and strolled along the shore towards town, passing the district office and reaching the Catholic cemetery. Noticeably smaller than its Protestant counterpart, it was nevertheless better situated, behind the modest Catholic church by the lake. He didn't take long to find Jakub Polakowski's grave. Plain, with a wrought-iron cross, there were no flowers, nor anything to suggest it was looked after.

For love is strong as death;
jealousy is cruel as the grave:
The coals thereof are coals of fire,
which hath a most vehement flame.

Jakub Polakowski

*18th May 1895
† 5th August 1930

Why had the man been buried in Treuburg, when he had no relatives or friends here to tend to his grave? Why hadn't they laid him to rest in the prison cemetery at Wartenburg? Jakub Polakowski was only thirty-five when he died, scarcely older than Rath now. A generation betrayed. He'd probably fought in the war, and, barely two years later, they'd thrown him in jail for a murder he hadn't committed. If, that is, what Maria Cofalka had said was right.

Jakub Polakowski didn't kill Anna von Mathée, he was just a convenient scapegoat.

Rath returned to the marketplace, but the stationer was closed, the bookstore likewise. Almost all shops had ceased trading; only the *Treuburger Zeitung* remained open.

'A magnifying glass?' a secretary said from behind the counter. 'There should be one in the editorial office. I don't know if I can lend it out, though. Herr Ziegler will be here any moment. His article on the plebiscite anniversary is due in tomorrow's edition.'

Rath showed his identification. 'Would it be possible for me to use the magnifying glass here?'

'I'll see what I can do.'

She smiled and disappeared towards the back. Rath looked around. On a table by the wall was a pile of old newspapers from 1920. Evidently the editor, Ziegler, would be making use of the archive for his latest report. He leafed curiously through the pages, tickled by the Polish Agitation Bureau, which was having difficulty *recruiting a female copyist*; even the *500 Mk. monthly salary* had failed to find any takers.

The hateful atmosphere so prevalent in those days could be inferred from an editorial. *We must sow hatred*, Rath read, *in the same way that we have learned to hate Germany's external enemies, so must we now punish its internal enemies with our hatred and scorn. Mediation is impossible; it is only through extremes that Germany can recapture what it was before the war.*

This chauvinistic crowing had its roots in the Empire, and was still fashionable in the Republic, at least in German National and Nazi circles. He had heard it again during the speeches this morning; the same crowing that had cost one brother his life and driven the other from his homeland.

The secretary returned holding an enormous magnifying glass.

'That should do it. Many thanks,' Rath said, sitting at the visitor's table with Cofalka's folder. Even now the task was no easier. First he had to get used to the handwriting. Soon, however, he was on his way.

No, Tokala will never live among humans again. Living among humans would signal death, just as it signalled death for his mother. The truth must speak without him. And it will, for Winchinchala will reveal it as she sees fit. She knows the world of humans and how to move within it, Tokala does not.

Winchinchala must understand him. He cannot go back, never again. They will imprison him, no matter what he says, and being imprisoned is worse, even, than death. Tokala has no other choice but to carry on with his life, alone in his solitude and in his guilt.

348

What happened at the little lake cannot be undone. Niyaha Luta, the woman with the red feathers in her dress, is dead, and nothing can bring her back to life. Tokala fled and returned too late; he will never forgive himself for that. If he knew how he could put things right, he would.

He will never forget how she lay in the shallow water. The wicked man is gone, she is alone again, only her body remains, rocking gently with the waves, eyes looking up at the blue sky, seeing nothing now. Her dress is torn to shreds, between her legs streaks of blood ripple in the water.

Tokala hears the clatter of a bicycle up in the forest, and crawls back inside his hiding place; he sees a man approach the shore, the same man Niyaha Luta had been expecting – when the wicked man came. He looks as if he has been fighting.

And then he spies her in the water. He kneels as he reaches her; her corpse. It is as if someone has sapped the life from his knees. He lifts her head out of the water, gently, as if afraid he might hurt her.

Tokala stays hidden, he doesn't dare breathe.

The man takes her head in his lap and strokes it, kneeling in the water as he silently mourns her death. His face has turned to stone.

A bell rang as the door opened behind him. Rath looked up. Gustav Wengler entered with one of the men from the dignitaries' table, a fat, moustachioed type suffering from shortness of breath. Wengler spoke animatedly, apparently no longer grieving for his dead brother. When he saw Rath, he blinked in surprise.

'Inspector,' he said, before the fat man could get a word out. 'What are you doing here?'

Rath shoved the papers back inside the folder. 'I lent the inspector here a magnifying glass,' the secretary said.

'Then I'll need it back,' the editor growled.

'Of course, I'm finished anyway. Many thanks.' Rath handed the man his magnifying glass and turned towards Wengler. 'Are you assisting with the article on the plebiscite anniversary?'

'I don't need any assistance,' the editor protested. 'But tomorrow's edition will naturally include an interview with the chief of the Homeland Service.'

'In that case, gentlemen,' Rath moved towards the door, 'keep up the good work.'

'What have you got there?' Wengler asked, gesturing towards the folder.

'Just a few papers. Hard to read, very small handwriting.' He opened the door and the bell rang once more.

'Did Maria Cofalka give you those?' Wengler asked.

Goddamn it! The man had seen them together, or it had been one of his many informers. Best to brush it aside.

'I don't wish to take up any more of your time. Goodbye, gentlemen, madam.' Rath tipped his hat and left the offices of the *Treuburger Zeitung*, folder wedged under his arm. In the street he turned around. Through the glass door Gustav Wengler eyed him with undisguised suspicion.

59

At last they had something to go on. Like all duty officers, Siegbert Wengler had left an emergency contact number with Traffic Police Headquarters. It had been updated four weeks ago, the only indication that his circumstances had changed. It wasn't a Schöneberg number, but belonged, instead, to a butcher's near Anhalter Bahnhof, in Kreuzberg.

Gräf stowed whatever photos of Wengler he could find, commandeered a couple of forensic technicians and made his way over. After yesterday's disaster, when it became clear that not even Wengler's brother knew the dead man's address, he had put in another call to Traffic Police. Whether the strike would gain Böhm's approval was moot, but at least he could feel better about himself.

Approval or not, the DCI had failed to provide any additional officers, leaving him to deal with Forensics alone again. For once Lange or Charly would have sufficed, but they were still occupied with the blackmail case from *Haus Vaterland*. Today they would pass it, along with the two suspects, onto Arthur Nebe and his colleagues in Robbery, who were responsible for extortion under threat of force. It seemed less and less likely that the case was connected with the dead men, but it was good that someone like Nebe, who had solved several homicides in the past, was involved. If there *was* a link, he'd be the one to find it.

The butcher's was in Kleinbeerenstrasse. Despite being close to the Philharmonic, as well as Wilhelmstrasse and the government buildings, the houses became more run-down the further one ventured from Möckernstrasse. Gräf left the ED men in the car and entered to find a red-cheeked woman gazing at him expectantly. The selection in the glass cabinet didn't inspire much confidence, everything fatty and stringy, bone shards for boiling. Meat for people who couldn't afford it.

The woman looked disappointed when she realised he wasn't intending to buy anything.

'Herr Siegbert Wengler,' he said, showing her a photo of the deceased without his shako, 'left your telephone line as his contact number. Can you tell me where he lives?'

'I'd have to ask my husband,' she said, suspiciously. 'Who wants to know?' He placed his identification next to the photo. 'I'm a colleague of Herr Wengler's.'

She studied his identification closely. 'Are you really a police officer?'

He took out his disc. 'Any reason to be suspicious?'

'Herr Wengler said at some point someone might come looking for him. In which case we should say nothing.'

'He was afraid of someone,' Gräf said, 'and rightly so. He was murdered.'

'Good God!'

'You can rest assured, my colleagues and I are trying to find out who was responsible. Now, will you please tell me where he lived.'

More than that, the butcher's wife had a key.

Wengler's apartment was located in the same block, albeit in the rear building. She led them across the yard and up two flights of stairs until they stood outside a wooden door. The nameplate was blank, and inside was messy. Judging by the newspapers on the floor, Siegbert Wengler had followed the horses. A pair of trousers and a shirt rested casually over the back of a chair. Without further ado the ED officers set about securing fingerprints.

Gräf pulled on a pair of gloves to avoid the technicians' wrath, before examining the desk by the window. The most interesting items were to be found in the enclosed drawer. Three death notices, one from Dortmund, one from Wittenberge, one from Berlin, confirmed Siegbert Wengler's links to Lamkau, Wawerka and Simoneit.

He handed the death notices to the ED officers and turned back to the drawer. Something had caught his eye. The plain, black notebook seemed familiar somehow. It wasn't like those used by CID, but bigger and thicker, a real doorstopper. Soon he was staring at columns of figures.

At that moment he knew where he had seen it before. They had confiscated it from Herbert Lamkau's office about a week ago. He leafed through and found a pencil mark he'd made himself.

'Over here,' he said to one of the forensic technicians, who reluctantly obeyed. He handed him the notebook. 'See if you can get any fingerprints. The more, the merrier.'

60

Rath realised he'd had too much to drink after all. Before returning to the celebrations, he'd tried to continue reading the letters in his hotel room but, without the aid of a magnifying glass, it proved impossible. No matter how hard he strained, he could decipher no more than two or three words per sentence.

He wanted to speak with Maria Cofalka again, but found her neither at the festival site nor during the evening's final act: a torchlit procession that included a farewell performance from the musical society and climaxed at the marketplace with the lighting of the great fire.

If what he'd managed to read was true, then the librarian was right: Gustav Wengler's tale of the wicked Pole who'd murdered an upstanding German girl was built on a lie.

Outside the *Kronprinzen* he ran into Karl Rammoser, who was celebrating the evening's final throes with his teaching colleagues. 'Maria will be sleeping it off somewhere,' he said. 'She can't take her drink.' In contrast with the group of teachers, with whom Rath sat quaffing into the long, summer night. The rest of the town, on the other hand, seemed to be asleep as he finally started for home.

Reaching the *Salzburger Hof* well past midnight he caught the owner's daughter off guard with her SA man. The pair stood in an entranceway next to the hotel; Fabeck was talking insistently. Hella spotted the returning guest and smiled. Rath smiled back just as Fabeck turned around. Seeing Rath, Fabeck pulled Hella towards him and gave her a lingering kiss. Rath couldn't help but grin: all the while Fabeck's tongue was working in her mouth she gazed unashamedly in his direction. This Hella was no country cousin.

As he stood in the bathroom brushing his teeth, he thought again of Artur Radlewski, the man who called himself Tokala. The man who had scalped his own father and fled into the woods; who had witnessed a murder and felt guilty for not having prevented it; and who was clearly far removed from the feeble-minded wood sprite everyone took him for.

For a moment he was tempted to retrieve the letters from the drawer, but without the magnifying glass it was hopeless. Besides, he was far too tired, and too drunk. He undressed, lay down and fell asleep as soon as he hit the mattress, where the Masurian Indian haunted his dreams as a noble savage, appearing almost exactly as he'd pictured Winnetou as a child, an honourable Apache who roamed the Masurian forests until he reached a lake, in whose shallows a dead girl lay.

Suddenly it was Rath who stood leaning over the lifeless beauty, recognising her face framed by the black hair floating on the surface, and scaring himself half to death. Charly, it was Charly!

Startled out of sleep, he opened his eyes wide and stared into darkness, heart pounding wildly, breathing heavily as if he, himself, were about to drown. His hand searched for her. He needed a moment to work out where he was. There had been too many grisly stories in the last few days, but...what was that? It was pitch black in the room save for a strip of moonlight that had found its way through the crack between the heavy curtains, and nestled on the wall next to his bed.

He felt for his Walther on the bedside table. Still unable to see anything in the darkness, he was no longer sure the noise was real. But he had sensed it. There was someone in his room. Locating the pistol, he fumbled it out of its holster and released the safety catch. 'Is anyone there?' he asked. No response. 'Who's there? Show yourself! I'm armed!'

A white shadow flitted to his bed.

'Sshh.' A hissing noise, surprisingly loud, and a warm, slender finger on his lips. The strip of moonlight confirmed who it was. Her blonde hair was down, but still wavy from her untied braids. Hella let her finger linger on his lips and drew her face closer. Her big eyes sparkled, gazing at him inscrutably. He could make out her nightshirt and her breasts silhouetted inside.

She pressed her mouth on his and her tongue blazed a trail through his lips. She smelled of toothpaste and raspberry juice. He realised he had kissed her back without meaning to, and pulled away. 'Hella, this is . . .'

Her finger returned to his lips. 'Sshh,' she whispered, and before he knew what was happening, she lay next to him in bed, snuggling closer as she slipped under the covers. She knew what to touch, and how to touch it.

61

When Rath awakened the next morning, Hella was gone. He had fallen asleep beside her, his night devoid of nightmares, but now her side was empty. It wasn't even warm. At least she had taken her nightshirt.

It was years since anything like this had happened. Even during those long months when Charly had been in Paris, he had lived like a monk, in spite of the numerous temptations a city like Berlin afforded a man in his early thirties. On one occasion a lustful grass widow had picked him up in *Kakadu* and they had kissed wildly in the taxi as they tentatively explored each other's bodies. In her bedroom, with champagne standing ready in its cooler, he remembered Charly and essayed a last-minute about-turn, leaving the woman to bombard him with abuse as she contemplated another night of solitude.

It ought to have been a lesson, but now, no sooner than he was engaged to marry, *this*!

Idiot. She couldn't have been older than eighteen or nineteen at most.

But by God, she was exciting.

Is that all you can think of?

He padded into the bathroom and took a shower. The water was so cold he cried out, but he didn't care about the other residents. Afterwards he felt better, lucid enough to put her out of mind; this girl about whom he knew only that he wasn't her first man. At least, he thought, he had one over the idiot brownshirt.

He looked at his watch; time to go. Emerging from the bathroom he felt ravenous, but remembered who would be on waitress duty, and resolved to give the ample *Salzburger Hof* breakfast a miss.

Stealing downstairs he found Hermann Rickert, hotel owner and father of Hella, at reception. He issued a brief greeting, wrestling with the image of the man reaching behind for his shotgun – but Rickert was polite as ever, and he emerged onto the street unscathed. Outside, it smelled as if half the town had burned down with the remains of yesterday's fire still smouldering.

He strolled to a café next to the newspaper offices, where that morning's edition hung in a wooden holder by the hall stand. He drank a coffee and ate a ham roll as he skimmed its contents. A special feature was devoted to the celebrations, with a second page recalling the events of twelve years ago. The results of the plebiscite, he read, had been projected onto the wall outside the offices of the *Oletzkoer Zeitung*, as it was then.

> *Each new result that went Germany's way was greeted with cheers and rejoicing, the tide of enthusiasm reaching its peak when, shortly before midnight, the overall outcome was announced. Only two votes for Poland, the rest for Germany. Minutes later a torchlit procession was underway, and a fire ignited in the marketplace.*

The birth of the Treuburg legend. Now he knew the significance of last night: it was a commemorative burning.

Gustav Wengler would be delighted. Not only was his speech praised, it was captured in three separate photographs, with advertisements for *Mathée Luisenbrand* and *Treuburger Bärenfang* appearing on either side of the double spread. There was no sign of an interview, however. Wengler's quotes were carried almost verbatim from the speech. No doubt he had placed his manuscript at the editor's disposal.

Rath left his money on the table and set off. He bought a foldable pocket magnifying glass from Dytfeld's bookshop, and headed back across the marketplace. He still had an hour.

His hotel room was just as he'd left it. He took a deep breath, relieved not to find Hella Rickert making up his bed. After hanging out the *Do Not Disturb* sign, he locked the door, sat at the desk and flipped open the magnifying glass. Opening the drawer to retrieve the folder he realised it was gone. He looked in the second drawer. Nothing.

Perhaps he had taken it out yesterday after all? He tried to recall, but his memory was blank. Why, oh why, had he drunk so much? Imagine being constantly led astray by a village school teacher.

Led astray . . .

That bitch!

When he came downstairs Hermann Rickert was still at reception, though there was no sign of his daughter. The sight of Rickert dampened his ardour. Had he seen Hella there alone, he'd have put her across his knee!

'Is there something I can do for you, Inspector?' the hotelier asked politely.

He cleared his throat and leaned over the counter. 'Listen . . . a black folder hasn't been handed in since yesterday evening, has it?'

'Sorry.' Rickert gave an apologetic shrug.

'It should be in my room somewhere.'

'We have a safe for valuable items . . .'

'It isn't valuable, just a plain black folder with papers inside.'

'If the papers are of value . . . you should have entrusted them to me.'

'No, there's nothing of value, at least *material* value, but it could be evidence!'

'Like I said, we have a safe. You ought to have ...'

'Where's your daughter?'

'What are you trying to say? My daughter's no thief!' Hermann Rickert was indignant. 'Besides she hasn't been in your room today.'

Rath resolved to keep his counsel. 'Tell her to keep her eyes peeled for a black folder when she does her rounds. Perhaps it slipped behind a cupboard. Please inform me immediately if you find it.'

'Certainly, Inspector.' The hotelier gave him that look of obsequiousness he so hated.

'Just to be clear, Herr Rickert. These are important documents. I hope they turn up, otherwise I might find myself obliged to have your premises searched, and your guests submitted to questioning.'

The hotelier blanched. 'But, Inspector! This is a house of impeccable repute! I've no doubt this will soon be resolved.'

'Then see that it is.'

'Certainly, Inspector.'

He returned to his room. Knowing it was futile, he searched high and low, behind every cupboard, in each drawer and under the bed. There was no sign. Hella must have taken it. He wondered why, but there wasn't time to pursue the thought. Today was the day they entered the forest.

At the bottom of the stairs, he saw that both reception and dining room were deserted, the only sound the clattering of pans from the kitchen. He peered through the swing door, but didn't recognise any of the staff.

He hoped the threat of a police search would be enough to retrieve the folder. Perhaps Hella Rickert was simply a kleptomaniac, and her father was already taking her to task.

He crossed over to Goldaper Strasse and rang the

shoemaker's bell. The Wanderer gleamed outside; Kowalski must have washed it after collecting it from the site.

Uncle Friedrich opened and bade him enter, looking him up and down. 'You're not going into the forest dressed like that?'

He shrugged. 'How else?'

The answer came in the form of Anton Kowalski, who looked as if he were planning an Alpine crossing with full rucksack, knee breeches, checked shirt and coarse knee-length socks. Sturdy hiking boots completed the ensemble. In brogues and grey suit, Rath was his antithesis.

'You need good shoes,' the shoemaker said firmly. 'The forest is swampy; moorland everywhere.'

'Our guide will take us round any bogholes.'

'Even so, you need good shoes.'

'This isn't the Sauerland Mountaineering Society.' Both Kowalskis stared blankly. 'Don't worry about it.'

'My uncle's right, Sir. If we're heading into the forest you need something sturdier. We're not talking about some park. The hut's out on the moors.'

Rath pointed towards his brogues. 'That's the sturdiest pair I own.'

Friedrich Kowalski looked down. 'Wait a moment,' he said. 'I'll be right back.'

'What's going on?' Rath asked.

Moments later Kowalski's uncle returned carrying hiking boots that looked brand new. 'Try these on. Finished working on them two weeks ago. They're from Studienrat Damerau, the teacher next door.' Amazingly, they were a fit. 'Of course, I'll have to pledge Herr Damerau a small loan fee ...'

'How much?'

'One mark.'

Rath rummaged for a coin. 'Give Herr Damerau my thanks.'

With that they set off. Kowalski drove as Rath tied his shoelaces a second time. He hoped they really were all right; the last thing he needed was blisters. They were certainly sturdy enough, and handmade to perfection.

He bade Kowalski stop outside the *Salzburger Hof*, and took his brogues up to his room. The bed was still unmade. Hella would be in for it tonight, if the folder still hadn't turned up.

He made no mention of last night's incident to Kowalski, who had his mind firmly set on the Kaubuk. Rath had never seen him so excited. No doubt it was the thrill of the chase.

On the Lega bridge, halfway towards Adamek's house, they ran into Erich Grigat. The police constable tipped his shako in greeting, and the two officers saluted in return.

'Let's make a little detour to Luisenhöhe,' Rath said when they were on Lindenallee, on the road out of town. Kowalski furrowed his brow, but did as bidden.

Outside the estate house, Wengler's servant was loading a suitcase into a maroon-coloured Mercedes. Rath motioned for Kowalski to park behind the gleaming sedan and got out. The servant pretended not to have seen him, and stalked back inside.

Rath debated what he might say to the man, when Wengler appeared, buttoning his coat. 'Inspector! Good morning.'

'You're going somewhere?' Rath asked.

'Berlin.' Wengler cleared his throat. 'To settle my brother's estate, and take care of the funeral arrangements.'

'Of course. My apologies for disturbing you again. You were going to tell me how to reach your former employees. Assmann, and the others on the list.'

'I've had the addresses collated for you. I'll send for it now.'

'Not necessary.' Rath took out a card and wrote a name on the reverse. 'Since you're going to be in Berlin, why

362

not report to Detective Chief Inspector Böhm at Police Headquarters, Alexanderplatz.'

Wengler took the card. 'I'll do that, Inspector. Many thanks.'

'One more thing...' said Rath. Wengler's eyes were devoid of grief or rage, or indeed of any expression at all. 'Your brother...how long did he serve as a police officer in Treuburg?'

'He started during the war. Why?'

'I'm looking for possible motives. Police officers often make enemies in their job.'

'You can say that again.'

Rath ignored the allusion. 'The question is, is it possible there are other cases besides the moonshining scandal that your brother could have been involved in?'

'How do you mean?'

'Anything that could have created bad blood.'

'I thought you were looking for this Radlewski?'

'We are. We're about to head into the Markowsken forest. They say his hideout's there somewhere.'

'Then go and find him – and stop harassing me.'

'Herr Wengler, I'm sorry if my questions are bothering you, but I'm only doing my job. We want to find your brother's killer and whoever murdered your former employees.'

'I realise that. I'm sorry.'

'They'll ask you the same thing in Berlin. Perhaps you should use the journey to think about your response.'

Wengler nodded. 'I'll do that, Inspector. I promise.'

Rath tipped his hat. 'Safe trip, anyhow.'

He climbed into the Wanderer and looked back through the rear mirror as Kowalski turned towards the driveway. Wengler stared after them until they'd disappeared around the bend behind the avenue trees.

62

Old Adamek waited on the bench outside his shanty, cheroot dangling from his mouth. In contrast to Kowalski, his outfit was unlikely to meet with Sauerland Mountaineering Society Statutes. It looked as if it hadn't been washed since Christmas, if, indeed, it had been washed at all. His trousers were more patch than original, his jacket bloodstained, and his shoes were tied with wire. He greeted Rath's suit with a raised eyebrow and snarl; the coarse hiking boots alone appeared to satisfy him.

He was astonished when asked to get into the car. 'We're heading into the forest,' he said. 'Crate like that's no good to us.'

'It'll take us as far as Markowsken,' Kowalski said. 'We'll manage the rest on foot.'

Reluctantly, Adamek agreed, and Rath guessed the man had never set foot inside a car. A horse and carriage was probably the only means of transportation he'd ever used; perhaps the railways during the war, out of necessity. Either way he was used to travelling on foot. Huddled on the rear seat, he clung to the shotgun wedged between his thighs. Did he mean to go hunting, or did he never leave the house unarmed?

They reached Markowsken via a pretty mountain road, noticeably higher above sea level than Treuburg and its lake. Shortly before the entrance they passed a little grove, with stone crosses between its young trees. 'Military cemetery,' Kowalski explained, without being asked. 'Russians and Germans at peace together.'

On the rear seat Adamek mumbled something. Rath recalled that the old man had fought the Russians in the war. Perhaps some of his comrades were buried here, along with one or two enemies – or former enemies. Rath was reminded, not for the first time, how much the Masurians had suffered during the war. People had died in the Rhineland of hunger and deprivation, but the actual war had largely played out beyond the border. Here in East Prussia, battles had raged, and whole towns and villages were destroyed before Hindenburg finally drove the Russians out at Tannenberg. No wonder the Masurians worshipped the man.

Kowalski parked at the end of the village. 'This is where you're from, isn't it?' Rath said. 'Don't you want to call in on your parents?'

'They don't live here any more. My father is with his fellow soldiers, where we came in.'

'I'm sorry. I didn't know.'

'You don't have to be sorry, I don't know any different. I was just a boy when it happened. Five years old when my mother told me Papa was dead. You accept these things as a child, you think it's normal. First you turn five, then your father dies, then you go to school.'

'What about your mother?'

'She remarried a few years after the war and moved to America.' Kowalski looked at him. 'I didn't want to go, so Uncle Fritz looked after me.'

Rath fell silent. He didn't want to probe any further.

In the meantime Adamek had exited the vehicle and started walking, following the village road until he turned onto a path. 'We'd best make sure we don't lose our guide,' Rath said. The old man set a quick pace, but it wasn't just his head start that made it hard to keep up. With his long legs he covered the ground quickly, and soon Rath was out of breath. 'Wait a moment,' he cried, and, surprisingly, Adamek came to a halt. 'I need a break. Please.'

Kowalski opened his rucksack and took out a canteen along with several smoked sausages. He offered one to Rath. 'No, thank you. I'd rather have water.'

Kowalski passed him the canteen, and he took a few sips. Adamek declined. 'Best keep moving,' the old man said. 'It's a long way.'

'Fine,' Rath said. 'But a little slower, please. You'd almost think you were trying to run off.'

Adamek nodded and started out again, slower than before, but still at a brisk enough clip. At least they were still following a path. Upon reaching a clearing, however, it came to an end, and soon they were moving through the middle of the forest, over sandy, grassy terrain, which shifted underfoot, but was held together here and there by moss. Rath was glad of his new shoes. Suddenly they were moving downhill; behind the tree trunks something glistened brightly. 'What's that?' he asked.

Adamek turned around. 'The little lake. It doesn't have a name, but beyond is the Kaubuk's domain.'

The little lake. He couldn't help thinking of Radlewski's lines. 'Is that where Anna von Mathée was found?'

Adamek nodded, apparently astonished.

They continued downhill for a time, soon reaching the shore. The bank was relatively steep, but the water so shallow the sandy bottom could be seen twinkling in the sun.

This was where Anna von Mathée met her death, he thought. This was where she was found. If only he could have seen what Artur Radlewski saw twelve years ago ...

'We need to keep going, Sir!' Kowalski said, following Adamek along the shore.

'Just a moment,' Rath said. 'I have to take a look at something.'

366

He'd spotted a tree trunk or, rather, a thick branch, jutting almost horizontally across the lake, illuminated by sunlight. Something was carved in the bark. He took off his shoes, rolled up his trouser legs and waded the few metres across. The water only reached up to his ankles, but was still decidedly cold.

There was a heart carved in the bark, pitted now and bulging, as if it had been carved a hundred years ago – or maybe twelve. Just a run-of-the-mill heart with initials. He tried to decipher the letters. *A.M.* and *J.P.*, he read, initials artfully entwined. He tried to mirror the effect in his notebook. Anna had eschewed the *von* in her name.

J.P.

He snapped his notebook shut. Jakub Polakowski and Anna von Mathée were lovers. Did Maria Cofalka know? He'd have a lot of questions for the librarian when they returned later tonight.

'Sir? What are you doing? We need to keep moving.'

'Coming.'

He waded back to the shore, put on his socks and shoes and rejoined the others.

'What were you doing?'

'I thought I'd seen something, but it was nothing.'

Kowalski raised an eyebrow, but there was no time for discussion, Adamek had already set off. Reaching the other end of the lake they emerged back into the forest, moving through thick undergrowth where the soil was sandy at first, before it became stony and covered in moss. They had been on the move for an hour by the time they reached a clearing at the end of a pinewood.

'One of us has to stay here,' Adamek said. 'Keep watch for Polish border guards.'

'*Polish* border guards?' Rath asked.

Adamek nodded and gestured back the way they came. 'The pinewood's still Prussia.'

'You realise that beyond this border the Prussian Police have no authority?'

'Not my problem,' said Adamek. 'You wanted to see the Kaubuk's hut. Well, it's over there. The Kaubuk doesn't care whether it's in Poland or Prussia, and neither do I.'

'So where is it? Poland or Prussia?'

'Prussia, if I remember rightly, but no one keeps tabs here on the moors.'

'Then why don't we stay in *Prussia*?'

'If you want to get as close as possible we need to go through Polish woodland. Going by the moors is longer, and more dangerous.'

'Very well,' Rath said. 'Kowalski, you stand guard, but make sure you stay on Prussian territory. We don't want an international incident. If you see a Polish border officer, discharge your weapon.'

'Pardon me?' Kowalski went pale.

'In the air! To warn us.'

'Shooting at the border isn't a good idea,' Adamek said. 'Better to call. Like an owl.' He demonstrated.

'Can you do that, Kowalski?' Rath asked.

Kowalski's attempt sounded halfway authentic. At the very least it was loud.

Adamek put a finger to his lips. 'We need to be quiet,' he said, before disappearing with his shotgun. Into Polish woodland. Rath followed, and after no more than ten minutes the old Masurian came to a halt. Having reached the edge, they gazed out over marshland overgrown with weeds, shrubbery and brush. Dead tree trunks jutted out of the ground.

'Stop,' Adamek said, raising a hand. 'This is where the moor begins. Every step is dangerous.' Rath nodded respectfully. Adamek pointed into the wilderness. 'His hut's over there.'

'Good,' Rath said. 'Let's go.' The old man looked at him

as if he'd made an indecent proposal. 'You said you'd take me to the Kaubuk's hut.'

'I said I'd *show* you his hut.' Adamek pointed towards the marshland, behind which, somewhere, the forest began again. 'Use the tall pine to take your bearings. Keep going in that direction and it's another five hundred metres or so, not far. Be careful. You'll need to watch every step.'

'Then take me. You know your way around.'

'Not on the moors.'

'Do you want money? We should have discussed this before. How much do you want? Perhaps we can come to some arrangement.'

The old man shook his head. 'It's too dangerous.'

'If you're not brave enough, then get me Kowalski. Get me Prussian CID!'

Adamek was unmoved. He nodded and disappeared back into the woods.

Rath sat on a warm stone and gazed over the moor. Looking in the direction Adamek had shown, he tried to imagine how a hut might appear in the middle of this inhospitable scrub. There was no doubt it was an ideal location for someone wanting to be left in peace. He listened for Kowalski's warning cry, but none came. The last thing he needed was to be picked up by a Polish border patrol.

It wasn't just Kowalski's warning cry that failed to materialise, however. Neither he nor Adamek were anywhere to be seen. Where the hell had they got to? He took the cigarette case from his pocket and lit an Overstolz. Immediately he felt calmer. Not even the thought of Polish border officers could daunt him. Let them come, he'd make his excuses. He was a tourist who'd got lost while taking a stroll. They were sure to believe him, so long as they didn't find his service pistol and identification.

By the time he stubbed out his cigarette on a stone, there

was still no sign. Maybe they were talking and Adamek would take them to the hut after all? Maybe the old man just needed a little persuading in Masurian.

The sun was already low in the west. He headed back into the woods. It wasn't so far to the clearing where Kowalski was keeping watch. Adamek hadn't deviated much from the straight and narrow. He trudged on, but needed more than a quarter of an hour to reach a clearing. He wasn't sure if it was where they'd left Kowalski or not. Either way, neither man was here.

He looked around, recognising the forked trunk where they'd emerged from the pinewood. No doubt about it, it was the same clearing. And those pines were in Prussia, so to hell with the secrecy.

'Kowalski?' he cried, as loud as he could. 'Adamek?' No response. 'Kowalski! Adamek? Where are you?'

Nothing. No reaction. No sound. Just a few birds fluttering somewhere nearby.

'Kowalski! Goddamn it!'

His voice echoed, but the woods issued no response.

The only possible explanation was that Adamek and the assistant detective had taken another route to Radlewski's hut and they had missed each other. He went back towards the hut, calling their names at regular intervals. No response. By the time he reached the moor, the sun had disappeared behind the trees.

Something wasn't right. Had they been picked up by Polish guards? Time and again the newspapers were full of border incidents, mostly in Silesia, but why shouldn't it happen in East Prussia too?

But then he'd have been picked up too, wouldn't he? The way he'd cried out just now?

There was another possibility, of course: the bastards had stitched him up. Why? Because Kowalski was too much of a coward, and wanted to forestall his command?

It was pointless thinking about it. All that mattered was that they were gone.

He gazed over the moor. Five hundred metres to Radlewski's hideout, Adamek had said, but that was madness, he was alone here in the wilds. There was no way he was setting foot on that moor, even if the hut was only a stone's throw distant. Assuming, of course, Adamek was telling the truth. Or was this revenge for their exchange in Pritzkus's dive?

He returned to the clearing, retracing his steps without difficulty. Arriving at the border he lit an Overstolz, his second-last, and tried to take his bearings. The sun was setting in the west: wasn't that where he needed to go? If he held slightly north, he'd be fine. North was to the right of west. No problem.

He entered the Prussian pinewood in good spirits, now assuming he was on the right track. At least he was no longer in Poland, and, if he didn't reach the forest edge or the little lake, so long as he continued in a straight line he was bound to hit upon a path or perhaps even a road at some point.

That was the plan, but after an hour's strenuous walking he still hadn't made it out. In the meantime it had grown darker. Soon it would be dusk.

Damn it! He had no torch, nothing – but at least he had good shoes.

He couldn't help remembering when he and Charly had got lost by the Müggelsee, and gradually his faith in his sense of direction started to evaporate. On that occasion it was actually Kirie who'd led them astray. Without *her*, his chances were probably greater. A compass would have been good; soon he'd no longer be able to take his bearings by the sun. Even now the diffuse light filtering through the treetops gave little indication of where it was setting, or, indeed, had already set.

He fought his growing sense of panic and yomped on. In the meantime his eyes had grown accustomed to the darkness, and he could still discern the tree trunks that stood behind and alongside each other in unrelenting uniformity. There was nothing to suggest the forest was about to end.

'Kowalski!' he shouted again, knowing it was futile. 'Adamek!'

The wood responded with brutal silence.

At last he made out a glimmer of light. The forest edge. Soon he'd be back by the lake, no need to panic, but when he emerged he stood at another clearing. Not, thankfully, his starting point: at least he hadn't been going round in circles.

Apart from that, he had no idea where he was. Overhead the sky was full of stars, and a crescent moon beamed over the tips of the trees. Grounds for optimism at last. In spite of his disappointment he felt something akin to relief. On this clear evening he'd have enough light. Now, where did the moon rise? Was it in the east like the sun? Or west? Or somewhere else entirely?

He'd given up on finding his way back to Markowsken. By now it'd be enough to hit upon any path leading to civilisation. If, indeed, that's what Masuria was. *Where culture ends, there Masuria begins*. In his present state even a peasant's cottage without electricity or running water would look like paradise, and the prospect of being picked up by a Polish border patrol had lost its edge. At least they'd get him out of here.

The moonlight was so bright that he could see little beasts leaping in all directions to avoid his tread. Grasshoppers, he thought at first, but he wasn't moving over grass, rather, soft moss, and, bending down, he saw that they were in fact tiny frogs. There was something reassuring about the sight, the place couldn't be entirely unsuited to life. He yomped gamely on, wondering whether the moon really did rise in

372

the east, when the moss under his feet gave way and he stepped into something damp and soggy. A mudhole!

Again, he recalled his Müggelsee adventure. On that occasion they had also found themselves in marshland, costing him a shoe. Well, not this time. The thought of struggling through this interminable forest in his stockings spurred him on. He just had to make sure he didn't pull up his foot too fast. He tried, cautiously, but felt it sink deeper. He had to shift his weight somehow, and took a small step with his free right leg, straight into another mudhole. Everything below the layer of moss, on which the frogs had just now been hopping, seemed, suddenly, to swim.

He leaned forward and tried to reach his left foot with his hand. In vain: he felt himself sink deeper.

This wasn't just some mudhole. How much moorland was there here, goddamn it? For there was no doubting the landscape was more idyllic than the spot Adamek had shown him; with its shrubs and moss carpet it reminded him of the Wahner Heath. There were no dead trees, no indication that the environment was unsuited to life. It couldn't be Radlewski's patch.

Don't panic, he told himself, laying his forearms and hands on the undulating moss as he tried to get a hold, but there was nothing to hold *him*. The carpet of grass and moss pitched on the water and gave way under his weight. All he had achieved was to make the hole in which he stood larger still, as if he were digging a pond. The more he struggled, the firmer and colder the moor's grip.

He was afraid of being swallowed entirely when he remembered his natural history. Buoyancy would prevent him from becoming submerged. The only mortal danger lay in not being discovered, as exposure could take hold in a matter of hours.

Already he felt the cold penetrating deeper in his body, even with the heat of the day still in the air. He'd lost feeling in his legs and had difficulty moving them. The midges were out in force and he shooed them away by waving his arms, until realising that this, too, only made him sink deeper. He was completely dependent on outside help, and had the creeping sense that he'd never been so far removed from a human dwelling in all his life.

'Help!' he cried, as loud as he could. 'Help!'

His cry echoed in the moonlit night. He listened, heard the treetops rustling in the wind, heard an owl screech, otherwise nothing. The owl wasn't Kowalski. 'Help,' he cried again, and there was a swishing sound at the edge of the forest. He turned his head so that he could see better. A massive shadow lumbered towards him.

Were there still wolves here? he wondered. Don't go attracting any beasts of prey! Before he could make out its contours, however, the shadow disappeared.

His face itched everywhere, but by now he'd given up trying to bat away the midges. He felt himself being stung on the upper lip, and realised he was shivering, could even hear his teeth chatter. By God, it was cold!

He closed his eyes and tried to think clearly, but it was growing more and more difficult. Again, he heard a rustling noise, and opened his eyes wide to see a massive form leaning over him, gazing curiously. A head with a huge set of antlers. He couldn't believe his eyes. An elk. An elk gawped at him, watching him die.

He couldn't help thinking of Charly's words at the airport. *Perhaps you'll see an elk*.

Charly. Would that botched goodbye at Tempelhof be their final evening together? Would he really die like this, at the very start of their journey? When he'd been unfaithful to her for the first time. He thought of last night with Hella. Suddenly all this felt like a punishment.

No, there was no *meaning* to any of it. Death was just as meaningless as life. He remembered the military cemetery at Markowsken. Anyone who spoke of death being meaningful, of laying down one's life for the Fatherland, of dying a hero's death, was a goddamn liar. It was all nonsense. Meaningless as it was, he wanted to live, damn it, *live*.

'Come on,' he said to the elk, cautiously, so as not to scare it. 'Just one more step.'

The large head did indeed draw closer; the beast seemed to trust this man jutting out of the ground. Rath had read somewhere that, unlike roe deer or stags, elks were rarely frightened of people. Not this one, anyway. It was now or never.

Quick as a flash he grabbed for the antlers, thought for a moment he could feel soft skin, when the beast jumped back and jerked its head up. He clutched at thin air as it took another step towards the brush before trotting majestically away, illuminated by the moonlight.

He gazed after it until it'd gone.

Idiot! he thought, driving away your only friend out here.

'Help,' he cried again, astonished by the frailty of his voice. Could this mercilessly cold moor really have sapped so much strength out of him? Had he lost his mind?

He thought of his pistol, and fumbled the Walther out of its holster. His hands could barely grip the cold steel, but somehow he managed to release the safety catch and fire. The recoil almost threw the pistol out of his frozen hand but at the last moment he caught it and stowed it back in the holster. Perhaps he would need it again if there really were wolves.

Despair crept inside him, worse than the cold. Hopelessness drowned him like heavy, black, rotten ink, a viscous sludge spreading everywhere. At the same time somewhere deep inside was an irrepressible will to live that fought to get near the surface.

In the meantime the midges no longer concerned him; let

them devour him, he wouldn't resist. And then he thought he must be delirious.

Again a beast emerged from the brush, a huge black dog which reminded him of an illustration from his copy of *The Hound of the Baskervilles*, a huge, great hellhound. Now was the moment to reach for his pistol, but he couldn't, his muscles no longer obeyed, only shivered.

He closed his eyes, ready to die. If this hellhound wasn't the product of his imagination, then it would surely eat him. And, if he *had* imagined it, it would be gone as soon as he opened his eyes.

He kept his eyes closed, sensing his eyelids were the only muscles still capable of obeying, and when, after a time, he opened them again, he saw that he had not been eaten, and that the dog had, indeed, disappeared. In its place was a figure reminiscent of another illustration from his childhood books. Or, rather, two: Robinson Crusoe, and Leatherstocking.

A man stood there with an unbelievably wild full beard and long, shaggy hair, dressed in leather and hides, bow and quiver across his shoulders; on his head a beaver-fur cap.

Rath stared at the vision and then closed his eyes with his mouth relaxing into a peaceful smile. Even his shivering had ceased. He felt a deep sense of peace, and, all of a sudden, a great warmth in spite of the cold. With that he was plunged, once and for all, into darkness. A darkness no longer reached by the crescent moon.

PART III

Prussia

18th July to 6th August 1932

It is seldom, that liberty of any kind is lost all at once.

David Hume

63

Black-and-white flags were everywhere, even on the coffin, which, amidst all the rest, seemed strangely incidental. Never had there been so many flags at a police funeral, colleagues said, although, since it was her first time, Charly was no judge. She just knew she hated it. The pomp, the ironed uniforms, the bombastic speeches – if this was what it meant to pay your last respects she wanted no part.

The church was nigh-on empty, with rows of pews unoccupied. These days in Berlin a dead policeman was nothing out of the ordinary; more and more officers were being caught in the fire between Communists and Nazis. Others were killed in cold blood, like Officers Anlauf and Lenk the previous year.

There were few mourners, but the coffin positively drowned in wreaths. Custom dictated that both Police Commissioner Grzesinski and Uniform Commander Heimannsberg should lay one, though neither had appeared in person. Grzesinski's deputy, Bernhard Weiss, gave the eulogy, an honour usually bestowed upon police officers killed by Communists or Nazis, but the dead man had, like them, died in the line of duty.

Given the treasury's long-standing money problems, it was no surprise that the floral tributes had nothing to do with the Free State of Prussia. The dead policeman's brother had ensured events could proceed with the kind of ceremony normally reserved for dead ministers or members of the Hohenzollern dynasty. Most of the wreaths could be ascribed to his financial clout and influence. The *Marggrabowa Homeland Service* had gifted one, as had the *Treuburg Citizenry*, but the most impressive came from Gustav Wengler himself: a sumptuous arrangement of white and dark-violet, almost black, asters. *In Everlasting Memory*, the ribbon read, *Your Brother, Gustav*.

Charly tried to listen to Weiss's speech but couldn't. No matter, she was here to keep an eye on Wengler, who sat diagonally in front of her in the first row with his head bowed. She had encountered him once already, when he'd presented himself at headquarters and answered the questions the *Vaterland* team had in connection with his brother's death, and the events of 1924. Afterwards it became clear that Charly wasn't alone in thinking he might be holding something back.

It would have been useful to consult Gereon, but no one had heard from him in days.

Though still registered at his Treuburg hotel, he had failed to return calls from headquarters. 'Gereon Rath missing in action' was by now an all too familiar trope, and Böhm was beside himself.

Even more vexing was his failure to contact her. If he *had* done so, she might have covered for him. She'd have given him a piece of her mind, of course, but never in a million years would she have shopped him to Böhm. Didn't he trust her, or was he simply trying to avoid the inevitable quarrel?

In the meantime she had relieved Erika Voss of her canine duties and moved into Carmerstrasse with Kirie, in the hope that he might call there, but the line was so dead she wondered if it was even connected.

One evening she decided she'd had enough and telephoned his hotel. Inspector Rath was currently unavailable, said a voice on the line, and it wasn't certain when he would be back. The porter noted her request, but Gereon's call never came. She hardly dared try again, to suffer the staff skating politely around his absence. Having called at all times of day and night, she asked herself if he was sleeping there at all. But then ...where *was* he sleeping ...? The bastard!

Nor could she reach him through the Treuburg Police, since he hadn't shared the details of his investigation with his Masurian colleagues. The local chief constable was decidedly miffed. She could just imagine Gereon treating him with the arrogance of a big-city cop investigating a small-town crime – seasoned with a good dose of Rathian pig-headedness. Gereon Rath, one-man investigation machine. God, she hated it. If he would just give them *something*, or was he planning to arrest Artur Radlewski on his own?

The Treuburg Police seemed not to trust him, and the same was true in Berlin, with the exception of Gräf, perhaps, and a few others.

She focused on the job in hand. She couldn't work this Gustav Wengler out. How he listened to Weiss in a spirit of reverence, when she knew that he harboured Nazi sympathies, and would not be pleased that a Jew was delivering his brother's final address. Slippery: the word could have been coined for the man.

Maybe they'd crack him without Gereon's help. They had cited him to appear at Alex again before leaving town, and this time they had a surprise in store.

64

The clock tower on the administration building showed twenty past nine. Bright neon lit the grounds and was reflected in the water of the harbour basin.

Reinhold Gräf looked down from high above the quay, in the cabin of a loading crane belonging to the Berlin Harbour and Warehouse Company, through a set of field glasses taken from police stocks. A lone ship was being discharged, otherwise all was quiet. Most harbour workers were gone, with only a couple of dozen still on their feet – as well as a platoon of anti-riot officers currently hidden from view.

Until last year Warehouse 2 had been where the Ford company assembled its cars for the German market, before shifting production to a factory in Cologne, contributing at once to Berlin's growing unemployment and the vacancy rate of its warehouses. It was the ideal hideout for a hundred or more waiting officers. The Chief Customs Office had suggested it, and Berlin CID had put in its men as discreetly as possible, with civilian coats thrown over their uniforms, their weapons and shakos stowed in crates. They looked like a company of workers charged with restoring the warehouse to life. Detective Chief Inspector Böhm and a senior customs official were last to enter. Böhm issued the men with their instructions, and distributed their shakos and carbines.

Gräf gazed at the telephone beside the levers and buttons, fearing the slightest touch might set the crane in motion.

The phones were used by crane drivers to co-ordinate with the foremen at ground level, but Gräf's was connected directly with Warehouse 2. He knew this, but still gave a start when it rang.

'Yes?'

'Anything doing?'

'Nothing.'

Nine o'clock, Lamkau's notebook had said. Nine o'clock, Tuesday night. Five hundred crates, each containing twenty-four bottles. Stacks of paper – and even more schnapps. Enough to bring serious charges, but they didn't know which boat, only which harbour, and here in the northern basin as many as five vessels were moored.

He was wondering whether someone had smelled a rat when there was movement on Westhafenstrasse. They were coming. One vehicle after another rolled onto the site via the eastern gate, five lily-white delivery vans bearing slogans for *Mathée Luisenbrand* and *Treuburger Bärenfang*. Gräf hadn't expected the Lamkau firm to transport such a delicate load so openly. Perhaps they were wrong, and the contents was the legitimate, taxed product of the Luisenhöhe distillery? But then why would Lamkau have entered the delivery date in a notebook otherwise recording illegal income that had no place in official company documents?

The vans pulled up at the loading bay next to the warehouse and Gräf used his field glasses to check the name of the ship they had stopped beside. *MS Erika*.

A few men appeared on deck and opened the loading hatches. Others emerged from the vans. Each vehicle held two men, clad in the uniform of the Lamkau firm. He was surprised at first, but anything else would have been more conspicuous. The men weren't doing anything illegal, just loading a cargo ship with crates of schnapps, identical to those Gräf had seen in the lift at *Haus Vaterland*, next to Lamkau's dead body.

The difference was that these crates held illegally distilled rotgut rather than brand product. No doubt it was for the American market, where it would be shipped with the aid of the *Concordia* Ringverein.

At least, that's what he hoped. If not, they could be made to look very foolish.

A gangway slid out from the ship, and the men formed a chain from the first truck. It wasn't long before they were loading at breakneck pace, like a bucket brigade – only with crates. He reached for the telephone and waited for Böhm to pick up. 'Now,' he said. 'Warehouse 2, westside, the *MS Erika*. Five trucks, all told about a dozen men. None armed so far as I can see, but possible some are carrying – above all, those on board.'

A few seconds later a large sliding door opened and the customs inspector stepped onto the loading ramp, behind him Wilhelm Böhm, megaphone in hand. Lamkau's men didn't notice until the uniform cops took up position on the ramp, carbines at the ready. 'Your attention, please,' Böhm's voice echoed. 'This is the police!'

A lone crate crashed to the floor.

'That's right,' Böhm continued. 'Drop the crates, and place your hands in the air. You're surrounded and under arrest. As of this moment these goods are the property of the Berlin Chief Customs Office.'

A driver climbed into his van and stepped on the gas. The engine roared as the vehicle raced across the quay, perilously close to the harbour edge. Two men jumped aside to avoid being knocked down. The driver was headed for Westhafen-strasse, but the eastern gate was locked, guarded by armed uniform cops. The van screeched into a turn, but no one gave chase. Heedless flight only confirmed that an illegal operation had been blown. Encountering more armed offic-ers, the driver gave up and exited the truck with hands in the air. Gräf stowed his field glasses and began the descent.

Arriving below, he heard diesel engines and saw the police vehicles stationed behind the admin building move in. The smugglers had their hands in the air, and made no move to resist arrest.

The cops who weren't busy with handcuffs began loading the crates, not just from the Lamkau vans, but also from the quay and cargo ship. Böhm already had a crate open, and fished out a bottle. He took a sniff, made a disgusted face, and passed the bottle to Gräf.

It looked like the *Luisenbrand* served all over Berlin, but smelled more like methylated spirit than high-end Korn. They'd need to undertake a chemical analysis for the courts, but there was no doubt about it. This was rotgut of the cheapest order. Could they really be palming it off as a German speciality to the Yanks? Gräf wondered how much money was to be made smuggling alcohol into the US given the current dollar exchange rate. Evidently enough to justify doing so on a large scale.

He looked at the men. On board were a few villains whose mugs no doubt already graced the rogues' gallery, but the men from the delivery vans were just normal Lamkau firm employees. He thought he recognised one or two from the company offices at Tempelhof.

The men took their places on the vehicle platform next to their smuggled goods, and suddenly there was a loud crash of metal. Gräf looked round to see a Lamkau van door fly open and a cop hitting the ground. A white overall flitted through the night like a ghost. Goddamn it!

They must have overlooked someone hidden in the front van, and he had slammed the heavy rear door against the unsuspecting cop's head. Now he fled across the quay, overalls flapping.

'Halt!' Böhm cried into the megaphone. 'Stay where you are! Or we'll be forced to shoot!'

The man turned and, in the pale neon light, Gräf thought

he recognised Dietrich Assmann, the East Prussian heading up the Lamkau operation to support the grieving widow. But the man kept running, and Gräf could no longer be sure.

'Stay where you are,' the megaphone sounded again. 'Or we'll shoot.'

A warning shot was fired in line with police protocol. When most crooks would have given up, this one just ran faster.

A second shot ripped through the night, and Gräf was afraid the operation would claim its first fatality when the white overalls appeared to take off, and seemed, for a moment, to be flying, before dropping like a lead weight and disappearing behind the wall of the landing stage. He chased after a couple of cops as they ran towards the harbour edge, and shone his torch on the water below, still foaming from the body's impact.

'There!' The torch beam caught something white rising slowly to the surface, the overalls borne upwards by air bubbles. The fugitive had disappeared.

65

It was late, the office dark and deserted. Gräf had gone out to the Westhafen with Böhm, and Erika Voss had finished for the day. Charly switched on the light and hung her coat on the stand. Surveillance work wasn't popular, which was why it was usually left to the cadets. She had been shadowing Gustav Wengler since early morning. For most of the time he had been with relations from Danzig, who had stayed on after the funeral. Now they were back in their hotel. It didn't look as if he would make for the harbour anytime soon, but they would stay on him all the same.

Lange had relieved her about an hour ago, and while he sat in the green Opel outside the Eden Hotel, awaiting their target's next move, she headed back to police headquarters. She didn't know where else she could go.

Despite taking mental leave of the flat in Spenerstrasse, she hadn't found the courage to tell Greta about the changes in her life and, even after spending the last few nights, she still felt like a stranger in Charlottenburg. The flat was too big, especially when she was alone. Perhaps if she'd been able to keep Kirie . . . but the surveillance operation had meant handing canine duties back to Erika Voss. She fetched the *Vaterland* case from the shelf.

Herbert Lamkau. Three crimes converged in the person of the deceased spirits merchant: murder, blackmail and bootlegging. How were they linked?

387

By now, blackmail was beyond doubt. Riedel and Unger sat in custody awaiting trial, each blaming the other, which only made things easier. Skimming Nebe's interrogation transcripts, she couldn't help but smile. The way he had duped the pair was a thing of beauty. A throwaway remark had led Unger to believe Riedel had dropped him in it, which resulted in the head chef doing the dirty on his partner. The back-and-forth had continued between interview rooms, culminating in two written confessions waiting to be signed.

By accusing Lamkau of selling cheap rotgut, Unger and Riedel had unwittingly touched a nerve. The Lamkau firm was indeed pedalling moonshine, the proceeds of which were painstakingly recorded in the notebook Gräf had recovered from Siegbert Wengler's flat. It had taken some time for police to decipher the columns of numbers, but it had been worth it. Though still unsure how and when Wengler might have stolen the notebook, they were no longer in any doubt that he *had*.

Even so, Wengler hadn't been able to protect Lamkau from his blackmailers. That task had fallen to others. Charly had recognised one of the men she'd seen in Linkstrasse in the rogues' gallery: Rudolf Haas, aka *Lovely Rudi*, the right hand man of *Concordia* chief Paul Marczewski, also known as Polish-Paule. Though still unidentified, there was every reason to assume Haas's accomplice was, likewise, a fully paid-up member of the *Concordia* Ringverein. Charly wondered if the pair hadn't been involved in Lamkau's death, or whether it was a vendetta, as Gereon suspected, pursued by a man whose mother had fallen foul of the company's rotgut. What Gereon didn't know, because no one could possibly have told him, was that Lamkau was still at it eight years on. Which meant there could be countless additional victims, and therefore, countless additional people with grounds for revenge.

Gereon. Goddamn it! She was thinking about him again.

She looked out of the window, but dusk had already turned to darkness, and all she could see was her yawning reflection. She was tired. If only she knew where he was, the swine!

She was starting to worry. Had something happened to him? No, the Treuburg authorities would have been in touch – or that colleague from Königsberg he'd mentioned on the telephone.

She decided to try his hotel again, no matter how ridiculous it might feel. At least in Carmerstrasse she could use the telephone without colleagues listening. To say nothing of Greta. Her friend would have killed herself laughing if she'd known Charly was worried about a man. The truth was she wasn't sure if it *was* worry; it could just be anger at the bastard's stubborn refusal to get in touch.

66

Strange smells. Animal sweat and herbs. Camomile and vinegar. Light behind the darkness. A gleam behind the eyes.

Dream scraps. Memories.

The moon.

Charly's smile.

Slipping out of reach.

Eyes open. Stinging light.

A wooden spoon. Steaming fluid. Disgusting smell. Animal sweat. Herbs. Camomile and vinegar.

Drink, drink!

A gnarled voice.

Turn away. Close eyes.

Charly's smile.

A jolt towards the light.

Infernal grin, black beast, teeth bared; red, panting tongue. Above, a blonde beard.

No strength, no fight.

Drink!

Gnarled voice. Behind the beard.

The spoon again. Disgusting taste, bitter and oily and hot. Involuntary swallow. Camomile and vinegar and honey and herbs.

A sudden shiver. Enveloping warmth. Great fatigue.

Fatigue that excludes all else.

Falling back.
Eyelids.
Heavy.
Closed.
Darkness, sleep, death.
Peace, at last.
Peace, leave me in peace.
Dark, deadly sleep.
Charly's smile.
Peace.
At last.

67

Dietrich Assmann sat at the table in Interview Room B and shrugged his shoulders. Just as he had done umpteen times already. Böhm might have kept score.

The Lamkau firm meant to offload a large shipment last night at the Westhafen.

Shrug.

The *MS Erika*, port of destination Hamburg.

Shrug.

The consignment wasn't accounted for in the freight documents.

Shrug.

The crates contained illegally distilled schnapps, in original *Luisenbrand* bottles.

Shrug.

Some twelve thousand bottles, the majority already on board, the rest stowed in five delivery vans, property of the Lamkau firm, Berlin-Tempelhof, parked at the Westhafen northern quay. Seized in their entirety by the Chief Customs Office, Berlin.

Shrug.

According to the freight documents, the consignment contained three hundred tons of rapeseed oil, to be offloaded onto the high-sea freighter *MS Tsingtao* at Hamburg. Its destination: Hoboken, New Jersey.

Shrug.

Böhm stood, arms folded, listening, as Chief Customs Inspector Bruno Kressin continued his fruitless questioning. With every shrug of Assmann's shoulders, he felt his blood pressure rise. Staying patient during a lengthy interrogation had never been one of his strengths, which was why he had given Kressin, under whose jurisdiction the Lamkau firm's illegal activities fell, the floor.

For a full quarter of an hour he gritted his teeth and listened. For a full quarter of an hour he displayed the patience of a saint – but no more. 'Don't just sit there playing the innocent!' he yelled without warning, and Dietrich Assmann instinctively recoiled. Böhm beat his fist against the table. 'They were Lamkau trucks, Herr Assmann.'

For once Assmann offered more than a shrug. 'Could be,' he said. 'But I didn't send 'em.'

'No?'

'No. How many times? Do you think asking the same questions as your colleague will get you a different answer? Change the goddamn record. I can't tell you a thing.'

'Can't, or don't want to?' Böhm fixed Assmann with his bulldog-gaze. 'We'll question you for as long as it takes to get a sensible answer. Why would almost the entire fleet of Lamkau firm vehicles head out to the Westhafen if the managing director hadn't given the instruction?'

'Acting managing director.'

'And why should your employees, Lamkau firm drivers and warehousers, meet with men who are part of the *Concordia* Ringverein to load moonshine onto a cargo boat?'

'What do I know? Perhaps they did so on the instruction of their *former* managing director. Or, it was someone acting under their own steam who roped the others in.'

'You had nothing to do with it, then?'

'That's what I've been saying this whole time.'

'Then why were you there?'

'Pardon me?'

'You were at the Westhafen last night.'

'Rubbish!'

'So tell me where you were around half past nine ...'

'I was eating my dinner.'

'Cut the crap. You were at the Westhafen! A CID officer recognised you.'

'This officer of yours, got issues with his eyes, has he?'

'Word is you're quite the swimmer. Where did you dispose of your wet things? When my colleagues met you at half past twelve in your hotel, you were in evening dress.'

'I don't know what you're driving at.'

'I just hope you didn't catch cold in the harbour basin.'

'What are you talking about? That your officer too? I think you'd better send him to an optician.'

'In the *eyes* of the court, police testimony carries serious weight, Herr Assmann.'

'I wasn't at the Westhafen, goddamn it, I was in the *Rheingold*!'

'And I've no doubt you can prove it. So what did you eat, in the *Rheingold*?'

'Venison loin.'

Böhm made a note. 'We'll check the menu.'

'Please do.'

'But that won't be enough to prove you were there.'

'How about the bill? Would that suffice?'

'Better than nothing. Do you have it there?'

'I didn't pay.'

'Then who was kind enough to pick up the tab?'

'My boss.' Assmann grinned. 'Gustav Wengler. Director of the Luisenhöhe distillery.'

Böhm rose to his feet. 'Kressin, carry on without me for now.'

Charly could tell the man didn't take her seriously. He seemed to think she was a secretary or second stenographer, even though Hilda Steffens was the only one with a pad in her hand. She had clearly introduced herself and stated her function, but Gustav Wengler was stumped by the very idea of a female CID officer. Or perhaps he had a problem with women in general.

Apparently he thought the uniform cop by the door of Interview Room A was more important than the woman sitting across from him. 'How long do you propose to keep me here?' Wengler asked the man. 'I have appointments to attend.'

The cop gazed sternly, impassive as a castle guard.

'Appointments can be postponed, Herr Wengler,' Charly replied. 'You received our summons four days ago, leaving you more than enough time to rearrange your diary.'

Wengler looked at her in indignation and confusion. 'I was summoned to an interview. And what happens? I'm here in good time, and the Herr Inspector is nowhere to be seen.'

'That's because there is no *Herr* Inspector. I'll be the one asking the questions.' She smiled politely, savouring the look on Wengler's face. 'I'm sure it's in your interests to have the matter of your brother's death resolved.'

'I'm just surprised your colleagues didn't ask these questions when I was here last Friday.'

'An investigation like this yields new information all the time.'

'New information? How exciting.'

Hilda Steffens sat at the ready, and Charly began. 'Dietrich Assmann is the operations manager of the Luisenhöhe distillery in Treuburg?'

'You call that new information?'

'Why did you send your operations manager to Berlin? Herr Assmann has been here more than a week.'

'Edith Lamkau requested my help.'

'So you send your most vital employee?'

'My *best* employee. The Lamkau firm plays a decisive role in distributing our product through Central Germany. It's in my own interests for business in Berlin to get back on its feet.'

'How well do you know Herr Assmann?'

'What kind of question is that?'

'One I'd like you to answer. Is it a purely business relationship, or are you also personally acquainted?'

'The former.'

'How well did you know your brother?'

'You do ask strange questions.'

'Just concentrate on answering them.'

'Eight hundred kilometres makes it hard to stay in touch. I wasn't aware of his last address, if that's what you're alluding to, nor the danger he was in.'

'And Herbert Lamkau?'

'What the hell do you want from me? Tell me what you're driving at.'

'Let me see. Tainted schnapps containing dangerously high levels of methanol, marketed in *Luisenbrand* bottles ...'

'Isn't it about time you stopped digging up these old stories?'

'The question is: what you know about them? Now, as well as back then.'

'I've explained all this to your esteemed colleague in Treuburg. Doesn't he pass information like this on?'

Sadly, not always, Charly thought. 'Herr Wengler,' she said. 'I'm afraid these stories aren't quite as old as you think. Yesterday evening, working with the Chief Customs Office, the Berlin Police seized a large consignment of lethal rotgut stowed in *Mathée Luisenbrand* original bottles.'

'Pardon me?' Wengler's surprise appeared genuine, but what did genuine mean with a man like this?

'The goods were to be loaded onto a cargo boat at the Westhafen by Lamkau employees, whose vans were stationed alongside the quay.'

'You seriously think I'm involved? Who do you think a scheme like this hurts most? The *Luisenbrand* name! The good reputation of our company, and the *Mathée* brand!'

'I don't think anything, Herr Wengler. I'm just trying to establish the facts. Do you know how the Berlin Police were aware of the operation? It was thanks to a black book found in your dead brother's apartment. A book from Herbert Lamkau's private desk that was seized with other company papers, that your brother must have stolen from headquarters.'

She didn't mention the *Nordpiraten* informant who had revealed important information about the *Concordia* Ringverein's illegal dealings with Lamkau and the Americans.

Wengler shook his head. 'To think, back then I believed Siegbert when he told me he wasn't involved.'

'He doesn't appear to have been the driving force.'

'Lamkau?' Wengler asked. 'The rat. He swore to me never again. Dragging my company's good name through the mire!'

'I'd be surprised if Herbert Lamkau was behind it. Given that the deal passed off yesterday, almost three weeks after his death.'

'What surprises *me* is that such large quantities were contained in original *Luisenbrand* bottles. Someone from the distillery must have been helping him. One of his old accomplices, perhaps . . .'

Charly tried to read Wengler's thoughts, in vain.

The door opened and Detective Chief Inspector Böhm burst into the room. 'Excuse the interruption, Charly,' he said. 'Can I speak with you a moment?'

Wenger gazed at her curiously as she re-entered the room. She took her time, sat down, and opened her notepad. She had no need to take down what Böhm had told her outside

– nor did she want to mitigate the effect an open notebook could have on a potential suspect. After a moment she lit a Juno, before striking like a snake. 'Herr Wengler, where were you yesterday evening between nine and ten o'clock?'

'I was having dinner. In the *Rheingold*. Why do you ask?'

'The *Rheingold*. The food's good there. What did you have?'

'Venison loin.'

Charly nodded and made a note. The response had come without hesitation. As if the answer had been agreed in advance. 'Can anyone confirm that? You must surely have kept the receipt.'

'I'm not sure what I'm being accused of here. I thought this was about my brother's death?'

'I want to know who you had dinner with yesterday.'

'Relatives. Uncle Leopold and his family. They were here for the funeral, and returned to Danzig this morning.'

Now Charly was surprised. She had been expecting a different answer. Perhaps Wengler was keeping Assmann's name back for the end, so that it sounded more credible when he finally remembered him? He said nothing more.

'No one else?'

'No.'

Charly looked at her notebook. 'Your operations manager Dietrich Assmann claims you had dinner with him yesterday in the *Rheingold*.'

'He must have the date wrong. We met for dinner on Sunday evening, but at Kempinski's, not in the *Rheingold*.'

Gustav Wengler smiled, but Charly could hardly imagine he was unaware of what he was doing. Did he really think he could save his own neck so easily? That his old comrade Assmann would give it up just like that?

68

They were obliged to let Gustav Wengler go, but Lange continued to dog his heels. Dietrich Assmann, on the other hand, was afforded the privilege of lunch in his private cell. Charly wondered if inmates were served the same muck as staff in the canteen. The mashed potatoes could have served as paste in another life, while the pork was stringy and lukewarm. She took a serviette and stowed the meat carefully inside, for Kirie. The rest she could just about stomach. The sauerkraut even bordered on edible.

Wilhelm Böhm's plate was clean. The man had a horse's appetite, with taste buds to shame a garbage truck. 'When should we bring Assmann back in?' she asked, lighting a cigarette.

'We'll let him stew another hour or so.'

'I wonder what he'll do when he realises his alibi's fallen through?'

'Let's hope he implicates Gustav Wengler.'

'We shouldn't forget this is a murder inquiry. Bootlegging is a matter for Customs.'

'Of course. Only, it looks like there's a link between our murders and the illegal distilling of *Luisenbrand*. Remember that four of those involved are dead, making anyone else who's mixed up a potential victim, Assmann and Wengler included.'

'I can't shake the feeling this investigation's jinxed.'

Charly shook her head. 'We keep finding more and more crimes, yet we're still no closer to catching the killer.'

Böhm agreed. 'It'd be good to know what Inspector Rath has turned up in East Prussia. I'd be a lot happier if we could bring this Indian in. Apparently Rath's sent his colleague back to Königsberg. To me that sounds like he's concluded his investigation. So, why hasn't he come back?' He leaned across the table and lowered his voice. 'You're on good terms with the man. Can you explain why he hasn't made contact in over a week? Just between ourselves, Charly.'

She almost choked on her Sinalco. She had any number of explanations, the majority of which she had no desire to share with Wilhelm Böhm. She had already cursed Gereon a thousand times inside. With a more reliable person you could feel your anxiety was justified, but with Gereon you never knew whether to feel anxious or simply annoyed.

She shrugged her shoulders and stubbed out her cigarette. 'Time for work. Inspector Rath will be in touch. If not, we'll soon find him back at his desk as if nothing's happened.'

'Now *that* I can believe,' Böhm said, and stood up. 'But you're right: to work!'

A strange commotion disturbed police corridors, distinct from the usual midday ruckus. Officers stood in small groups speaking quietly, watching the passage leading to the police commissioner's office.

Charly and Böhm pushed to the front to see the unfamiliar grey of the Reichswehr. A captain escorted a police colonel and a civilian to the police commissioner's office.

'The uniform cop is Colonel Poten,' Böhm said. 'He used to be in charge of the police academy at Eiche.'

'So what's he doing turning up here with a Reichswehr captain?'

'Rumour has it that Poten's to replace Heimannsberg,'

another officer whispered. 'They say the man in plain clothes is the new commissioner.'

'Pardon me?'

'Apparently the entire police executive is to be replaced.' The officer handed her the morning paper. *Dangerous Plans*, ran the headline in the *Berliner Tageblatt*. *Papen as Reich Commissioner?*

She glanced at the headline. What was now happening had been in the air since Sunday, when bloody exchanges between Communists and Nazis claimed sixteen lives. Gunfire had erupted on the streets of Altona, a provincial town in far away Holstein, after an SA troop in full regalia had marched through a Communist district. The Prussian Police had called for assistance from neighbouring Hamburg, and the national press had questioned whether the Prussian state government and police force still had the ball at their feet. There were calls for a Reich commissioner to be appointed so that the Social Democrat minority government led by that stubborn East Prussian Otto Braun might be deposed. In short: Prussia was to be co-governed by the Reich.

It was nothing less than a call to arms.

Reich Chancellor Franz von Papen, whose major political contribution to date had been the lifting of the SA ban, without which the exchanges in Altona would never have occurred, had travelled to Hindenburg's East Prussian estate at Neudeck to persuade the aged president of the necessity of such a measure. Papen, who had no Reichstag majority and had been appointed chancellor by the grace of Hindenburg himself, had his heart set on becoming Reich commissioner for Prussia.

The move would signal the end of Prussian democracy, one of the few remaining bastions of democracy in Germany, which was precisely what this reactionary Franz von Papen, dreaming of the Kaiser's return or a military dictatorship – no one was quite sure which – had in mind.

Böhm and Charly watched in silence as the captain and his men halted outside Grzesinski's door and knocked, to be admitted by the commissioner's secretary as if they were expected.

They made their way back to A Division in silence. At length, Böhm spoke. 'So, Papen and his barons have been so bold.'

Charly was surprised. It was rare for the Bulldog to express his political views in police circles, but a line had been crossed. Suddenly politics were an indelible part of Castle life, and Böhm was deeply unhappy. 'Do you think Prime Minister Braun's already been deposed?' she asked.

'Otto Braun won't go without a fight.' Böhm opened the glass door to Homicide like a gentleman of the old school. 'I can't imagine that Grzesinski's about to clear his desk either. As for Dr Weiss ...' Seeing a few colleagues standing in the corridor, he started whispering again. 'With any luck, this farce will go the same way as the Kapp Putsch.'

Charly had run into Albert Grzesinski in the stairwell only this morning. Dressed in cutaway coat and top hat, he was scheduled to attend Superintendent Mercier's funeral at three. Now, in his mourning dress, he was obliged to receive a Reichswehr captain. She'd have given anything to know what was playing out behind those doors.

There was still no news half an hour later when they took Dietrich Assmann back to the interview room. It looked as if Grzesinski was still in office. No doubt Böhm was right, and the whole thing would just fizzle out. There was no way the police commissioner and his deputy would relinquish their roles without a fight. She looked at the man sitting opposite.

'This is Officer Ritter,' Böhm said, and Assmann gazed curiously. 'It was she who spoke with Director Wengler this morning. Your boss – and alibi.'

Assmann furrowed his brow. 'And?'

'To cut a long story short,' Charly said, 'Herr Wengler denies being with you yesterday evening. He claims to have last seen you on Sunday night.'

Dietrich Assmann was temporarily lost for words. 'It's a trick,' he said finally. 'You're trying to pull the wool over my eyes.'

'I'd be happy to provide a copy of his written statement.' Böhm didn't move as he spoke. It was as if a marble statue were moving its lips. 'If you like, I can arrange a sit-down with Herr Wengler.'

'I want a lawyer,' Assmann said at length.

'Should I have someone call Dr Schröder?' Böhm asked. 'I understand you're one of his clients?'

'Not any more.'

No wonder the man wanted to switch lawyers, Charly thought. Helmut Schröder was the Berlin solicitor representing Gustav Wengler.

69

Rath opened his eyes and stared into a set of fanged jaws. An animal skull. His mind whirred, but he couldn't remember where he was. The skull, which might have been from a fox, lay on a rack beside his bed. He looked around the inside of a wooden hut, crudely assembled. Its walls were tree trunks grouted with loam and mostly covered in animal hides, which also served as bedside rugs.

He felt cold sweat on his skin but, now that his initial confusion was past, he realised he felt as rested as he had in a long time. It was as if, after months of wakefulness, he had finally been granted a decent night's sleep.

Where the hell are you, Gereon Rath? And how did you get here?

He searched his memory but found only fragments of dark dreams.

The man with the beard; the hellhound; the elk.

What had happened to him?

Daylight filtered in through two small windows. Sunshine. He heard birds chirping outside, saw green branches. The hut contained a small table and lone chair. In a corner of the room was a hearth, its joists capped with a thick, sooty layer of loam. An opening had been left in the roof, through which the sun now shone. On a kind of grating metal pots and pans stood covered in soot.

Already he could guess who the cabin's architect was, and

looking at the wall opposite he felt his hunch confirmed. Though likewise crudely assembled, there was something here that didn't quite match its surroundings. Rath was gazing at a bookshelf.

He had gained the Kaubuk's hut.

His hand reached to the side where his holster normally lay. Gone. His Walther PP was gone too, along with his jacket, trousers, shoes and socks. He lay in his underwear, covered in a heavy, red-brown pelt that hadn't lost its animal smell. The bed was lower than most. He pulled back the pelt and tried to stand, but his legs wouldn't obey and he collapsed in a heap.

His circulation seemed back to normal, but his legs felt like rubber hoses when he tried to stand. He summoned his strength and tried again, gripping a beam. All of a sudden he felt hunger, and an insatiable thirst. Would there be anything to eat or drink here?

Like a cripple he moved through the room hand over hand, finding water in a wooden pitcher, which he smelled and found to be good. He savoured the feeling of it running down his throat. His muscles grew accustomed to carrying him once more, but movement took more out of him than anticipated. He sat on a stool next to the window and looked at the shelf.

Many of the spines were familiar: novels by Karl May and a few volumes of *Leatherstocking*, perhaps the same editions he'd read as a child. But here they lined the shelves of a grown man, worn and thumbed. Alongside were a few new editions: Fritz Steuben's *Der fliegende Pfeil*, Gabriel Ferry's *Waldläufer*, a German translation of Mayne Reid's *The Scalp Hunters*, as well as a range of non-fiction books with titles such as *The Indians of North America* and *Life on the Prairie*.

He stood and tried holding his weight without the support of his hands and, to some extent, it worked. There was no immediate danger of falling over. On a tin plate near the hearth was a small, bandy leg. Meat of some kind, but it was fried to a crisp, and he was hungry.

He reached for the haunch, or whatever it might be, and bit into it, tearing away as much as he could, and nibbling at it, teeth bared, until it was gone. His craving for meat made him feel like a predator. The taste was familiar, rabbit perhaps. Although, it hadn't looked like rabbit – nor did the gnawed bone. He replaced it on the tin plate, which reminded him of the plates they had used during the war. Carefully, he moved to the door, taking a stick as a precaution.

The sun was high in the sky. How long had he been asleep? There were midges everywhere, but he batted them away. Next to the entrance was an almost full rain barrel. He drank with both hands, shovelling water on his face to waken himself. The hut was perfectly camouflaged by trees and bushes but, a few steps to either side, and the scrub was so thick as to make it invisible.

The landscape wasn't nearly as bleak as that which Adamek had shown him. He groped his way forward with the stick, but soon found himself in a deepish water hole. He circled the hut and realised it was situated on a kind of island, surrounded by moorland on all sides. It was a mystery how Radlewski came and went here. He'd have to know the moors like the back of his hand, or at least better than old Adamek.

The chances of escape were slim. He knew now why he hadn't been tied, but Radlewski hadn't killed him either. Perhaps that was still to come?

Inside again, he scoured every receptacle until he located his suit in a large chest. It was a little damp, and unbelievably dirty, especially the trousers, but it was better than traipsing around in his underwear. He dressed, donning socks and Herr Damerau's sturdy boots, which seemed to have survived the episode intact.

He felt his inside jacket pocket. His cigarette case was still there, though it was empty, of course. He snapped it shut. The little magnifying glass was there too. He'd have preferred the cigarettes.

He returned to the stool and examined the books. At length he removed one from the shelf, opened it, and a sheaf of papers sailed to the ground. He crouched to retrieve it. Not bookmarks, as he'd thought initially, but letters, written in an elegant, curved hand.

Dear Artur,

I know I won't be able to entice you from the wilderness, and sometimes I understand you only too well. But I cannot choose the same path as you; I couldn't live like that, I'm not strong enough. That's why I choose this path, because I know how much you cherish the world of language and the written word. Perhaps in this way we can even establish something akin to a friendship. You don't have to reply, but if you don't want me to write, just leave my letter here on your next visit. I'll place it inside the pages of a book you want to borrow.

He didn't have to read to the end to know that Maria Cofalka had written these lines, and that they marked the start of their correspondence. Rath had already guessed it was the librarian who'd initiated the exchange. Using the books she laid out for Radlewski as a kind of mailbox seemed like a natural solution.

She'd written to her childhood crush again and again and, at some point, Artur Radlewski, who was sensible to the written word, had responded. He had christened her Winchinchala, whatever that meant. With the exception of Nscho-tschi Rath didn't know any Indian names.

He gathered up the letters and placed them back inside the book before returning it to the shelf.

His curiosity was further roused by an item of furniture that stood next to the window. A table with a slanting top, a kind of desk or bureau, adorned, incredibly, by an inkwell and ink. Where in the hell ... The paraffin lamp that stood on the table was most likely stolen too, along with a few other implements Rath now recognised: tools, metal pots and pans, a washboard.

So this was where Artur Radlewski sat to write his strange, indecipherable letters to Treuburg's librarian. The letters that Hella Rickert had stolen from his drawer!

More and more memories surfaced. The day in Treuburg. The missing letters. The expedition to the Markowsken forest. The little lake. Old Adamek, who set a ferocious pace before suddenly vanishing with Kowalski. The moonlit night. The moor. How he'd given up the ghost. When Radlewski had appeared, the Kaubuk ...

He couldn't remember anything after that. He felt his head for a bump, his neck for a puncture site, but there was nothing.

What would the Kaubuk do when he realised his unwanted guest was awake? He must know by now that Rath was a police officer: badge and identification were gone, along with his service pistol.

At least he wouldn't kill him; if he wanted him dead he'd have killed him long ago.

Rath opened a drawer in the desk and was astonished to find piles of virgin white paper. Standing side by side were various leather-bound notebooks, some good as new, others well worn.

He snapped open his pocket magnifying glass and

attempted to decipher a few lines of Radlewski's tiny handwriting. Diaries, no doubt about it. In order to preserve his sanity out here in the wilds, Artur Radlewski had kept a diary.

The notebooks were from a stationer. The inkwell and letter paper too, no doubt. Rath sat down and opened the book that looked the oldest and most worn. Radlewski had filled the pages with the same tiny script he had used to write his letters to Maria Cofalka.

On the move again, stealing through the forest, he leaves his shelter and advances through the trees. No one will hear him, no one will see him. There is a heaviness in the air, deep in the thicket he feels the warmth; summer has arrived with a vengeance. Tokala pauses and takes a deep breath. The scent of lime-tree blossom and winter barley fills the air in the fields over by Markowsken, and already he can smell the lake ...

70

Dietrich Assmann didn't trust them. His alibi had collapsed, but still he was cautious. Playing the blackmailers Unger and Riedel off against each other had been a doddle in comparison, but Assmann smelled a trap and, for the time being, refused to say anything against his alleged accomplice. It didn't matter whether it was the customs man, Kressin, asking the questions, or CID Officers Ritter and Böhm. Even Charly made him wary; he wouldn't fall for her kindness.

After three and a half hours of more or less fruitless questioning, Böhm had Assmann escorted back to his cell. They had already requested an arrest warrant from the magistrate. Time was on their side. Sooner or later, Dietrich Assmann would be in absolutely no doubt that his boss had left him in the lurch and would make his statement, whereupon they could, likewise, issue a warrant for Wengler's arrest – or so they hoped. They just had to make sure he didn't give them the slip in the meantime. Fortunately Gräf, who had taken the day shift, was a dab hand at surveillance. They had chosen to deploy a new officer with each shift, alternating between CID and Customs so that Wengler didn't smell a rat.

'What do you think? Will Assmann make a statement today?' Bruno Kressin asked. The man was dry as a bone.

Böhm shook his head. 'Let him sleep on it, I say, and speak to his lawyer. Tomorrow he'll be ripe.'

'Why would Assmann choose an alibi like that if he

couldn't be sure Wengler would cover him?' Charly asked.

'Maybe,' Böhm said, 'he *was* sure.'

The customs man nodded, and it seemed plausible to Charly too.

Suddenly there was a commotion outside, loud voices, cries. The officers looked at one another. Charly exited the interview room and stepped into the corridor, crossing to the stairwell where various colleagues had gathered. She heard Böhm and Kressin follow, but didn't turn around, the action before her was too compelling.

She didn't know what had happened in the hours they had spent interrogating Dietrich Assmann, or what had taken place in the police commissioner's office. She only knew that Albert Grzesinski hadn't found the time to change his clothes. Flanked by two soldiers, he still wore his mourning suit. The Reichswehr had arrested the Berlin police commissioner and were relieving him of office.

Behind Grzesinski followed Deputy Police Commissioner Bernhard Weiss, uniform immaculate as always, and Uniform Commander Magnus Heimannsberg, each man escorted, in turn, by two Reichswehr officers. Though the eyes under the steel helmets stared straight ahead, the young men were clearly afraid that the members of the Berlin police force, hundreds of whom were employed here at Alex alone, might foil the arrest. Yet not a hand stirred; officers whispered and murmured, grew indignant, but none intervened.

The customs officer mumbled an apology along the lines of 'best not to interfere in police matters', and took his leave.

Charly couldn't believe it. They had *actually* been so bold. Papen and his reactionary ministers didn't just want to take the Free State of Prussia, the only province that had been continuously governed by the Social Democrats since the war, they wanted its police force too. It wasn't enough

411

to exile the interior minister, they had to replace the entire Berlin Police executive: the Social Democrat Grzesinski, the Liberal Weiss and the Catholic Centrist Heimannsberg.

'They can't get away with this,' Charly said to Böhm. 'We have to do something!'

'The commissioner need only say the word, and thousands of men will stand behind him.'

'Then let him, goddamn it. He's going without a fight, like a lamb to the slaughter.'

'He knows what he's doing. Armed resistance could provoke a civil war between the police and Reichswehr. The bloodshed would be worse than 1919.'

'Papen can't want civil war. No one can. Isn't there enough violence on our streets as it is?'

'What Papen wants certainly isn't democracy.'

The black cutaway and top hat was a fitting outfit, even if Grzesinski had been prevented from attending Superintendent Mercier's funeral. A fitting outfit with which to mourn the death of Prussian democracy.

More and more office doors opened, and more and more officers stepped into the corridor to look, pushing towards the stairwell to watch the soldiers in field grey leading away their superiors. A few colleagues, above all those in uniform, showed their respect to the police chiefs by performing a military salute.

'Long live the Republic!' someone cried suddenly, and the faces under the steel helmets looked about nervously.

'Long live the Republic!' More and more officers joined the cry, and now Charly, too, cried at the top of her voice, and even Böhm, whom she'd not have thought capable of such a thing, stood by her side and chanted. 'Long live the Republic. Long live our chiefs!'

The cry echoed through the corridors and stairwell, growing ever louder. 'Long live the Republic. Long live our chiefs!'

With increasing nervousness, the youthful soldiers gazed left and right, hands on their weapons, ready to fire. At any moment a CID officer could draw his service pistol and shoot. The Prussian Police could put an end to this nonsense.

No one did, of course. The officers assembled were far too Prussian. In the absence of an explicit command, no one would reach for a weapon, but the disregard in which these insurrectionists were held was plain to see.

Amidst the chants of her colleagues, every so often an isolated cry of 'Freedom!' rang out, and Charly felt a hitherto unknown sense of pride in the Berlin Police and her Prussian homeland. Notwithstanding men like Dettmann, she felt inordinately proud to be a part of this police body which, despite the Reich government's display of force, stood in democratic solidarity with its executive officers.

The officers followed the cortège through the stairwell down to the ground floor, and Charly stood with them. Right now she didn't care about Gustav Wengler, Dietrich Assmann and the rest, she was simply glad to be a part of the Prussian police force, protesting against its most senior officers being led away like criminals.

Below on Alexanderstrasse was a Mercedes with a Reichswehr number plate, into which Grzesinski now climbed with the Reichswehr captain. Heimannsberg and Weiss followed in a second and third car. Where they were headed, no one could say, only that it was somewhere out west.

Once the cars had disappeared around a corner, Charly looked up at the brick façade of police headquarters. Almost all Castle windows were open, everywhere officers stood following the unworthy spectacle, and the cries that moments before had filled the stairwell resounded still from open windows and the mouths of colleagues: 'Long live the Republic! Long live our chiefs!'

But Charly no longer felt any desire to join them. Suddenly she recognised the futility of their actions. Her pride and euphoria evaporated, and she felt only impotence. She sensed, no, she *knew*, that, in the face of the Reich government's staggering effrontery, words could never be enough. She looked across for Wilhelm Böhm but couldn't find him among her fellow officers, and with only unfamiliar faces for company she felt utterly alone.

It was Wednesday evening, shortly after half past five, and the death knell for Prussian democracy had just sounded.

71

Rath didn't know how many pages he'd read. They were confused and not necessarily in chronological order, but made for fascinating reading all the same. The style was similar to the letters, only here Radlewski seemed to reveal more of himself. Sometimes relating details from his everyday life, sometimes dim memories from childhood, they were filled even now with hatred for his father and love for his mother. But there was one event he kept coming back to, the same event he'd described to Maria Cofalka: the murder of Anna von Mathée in the shallows of the little lake.

Radlewski had seen a man rape Anna, and failed to intervene. Returning to the same spot, full of remorse, he had found her dead.

How many times had he recounted the scene? The young woman's corpse floating on the water as, still stunned, he registered the fact of her death. A young man discovering her body. The killer returning to the scene of the crime in the company of a uniformed police officer. The same officer striking the grieving young man with the butt of his revolver as he knelt by the corpse. Even the perpetrators' exchange was recorded.

'Should we drown the dirty Polack, here and now?' the cop asks.

The wicked one shakes his head. 'Let him pay for it,' he says. 'Let him spend the rest of his miserable life paying for it.'

And then he looks at the cop, as if he can issue him with instructions.

'Arrest him,' he says. 'Arrest him, and we'll have him tried. Let everyone know what he has done.'

There was no mention of the name Polakowski, but perhaps Radlewski hadn't known the young registrar. Who else could it be?

Should we drown the dirty Polack?

Rath thought back to the furniture dealer on the aeroplane. He, too, had spoken of *dirty Polacks*. In jest, perhaps, but the sentiment was real. In the meantime, far too many Germans spoke of their Polish neighbours in a hate-filled and contemptuous manner. Not that the Poles were any less guilty, the feelings cut both ways.

He spun around as, suddenly, the door flew open. He felt as if he had been caught out. Whatever form these notebooks might take, they were still a man's private diaries. The book was snatched from him, and he was pushed from the chair with no more than a twist of the hand.

Landing on the floor he gazed at the force of nature that stood above him. Artur Radlewski was bareheaded, his hair plaited in two braids and complemented by an Indian-style headband. With his full beard and leather garb the man only partially resembled the vision of his dreams.

Seeing the Kaubuk in person, fever now dissipated, Rath knew that, with his long hair and beard, there was no way this man could have wandered the streets of Dortmund, Wittenberge and Berlin avenging his mother's death. He'd have been spotted immediately. Even in Berlin, where events that might elsewhere trigger a popular uprising were greeted with a shrug, *someone* would have seen him. As

416

for the enormous black dog that stood guarding the door, tongue hanging out of its mouth . . .

'Herr Radlewski!' Rath chose to be friendly, knowing the man understood High German. He smiled. 'Good to meet you after all this time.' Radlewski silently removed the notebooks from the table, and stowed them back inside whatever this strange item of furniture might be. 'You rescued me from the moor. Many thanks.'

Radlewski threw him a suspicious glance as he placed the diaries alongside the letter paper, muttering sullenly.

'I came to, not knowing where I was. When I saw your books, I thought I might find some clue there.'

Radlewski's gaze flitted between Rath and the desk. Though no less suspicious, his expression was at least a little friendlier. Or rather, a little less unfriendly.

'My apologies. I had just opened the book when you came in,' Rath lied.

Radlewski mumbled something and went to the hearth, finding the tin plate with the gnawed-off bone. On top of everything else, it looked as if Rath had bolted his lunch. He took the plate and looked at his guest.

'That was me. Apologies.' Rath wondered if the apologies would ever stop. 'But . . .I was ravenous. I'll pay for it if you like. As well as any other inconvenience you've suffered on my behalf. If you just tell me where my wallet is.'

'You'll pay for nothing. You're my guest.' The blonde beard could speak, and the voice wasn't nearly as dry as Rath had imagined. No doubt he spoke regularly with his dog. The beast, at any rate, wasn't surprised to hear its master, but remained in the door, watching Rath. 'I've made another catch.'

'Catch?'

'Just needs to be skinned and gutted, then we can roast it.'

With that he disappeared outside. The dog remained in the door. Rath didn't move.

Soon Radlewski returned, holding a metal skewer on which three scrawny, suspiciously small-looking rodents with long tails were impaled one on top of the other.

'Are those . . .rats?' Rath asked.

'Rats?' Radlewski laughed. 'Yes, rats.' Giggling, he reached into a small bag and rubbed the bloody, skinned animals with salt. Rath's stomach briefly threatened to rebel, but soon settled. 'Special rats,' Radlewski continued, stoking a small fire. His cackling was starting to grate. 'Tree rats!'

'Tree rats?'

'Squirrels,' Radlewski said, hanging the skewer with the three animals over the hearth. He was still shaking his head and grinning in amusement.

Rath breathed a sigh of relief, though he didn't especially feel like eating another squirrel.

Radlewski set the meat on the tin plate and handed it to him. 'Eat,' he said, taking a second animal from the skewer and biting. 'You need to eat. You were sick.'

Rath examined the skinned, roasted *thing* on his plate, so stringy it really was more reminiscent of rat than squirrel, closed his eyes and bit inside. His stomach didn't protest.

The two men ate in silence for a time until, when Radlewski offered some of the third squirrel, Rath gratefully declined. Radlewski shared it with the dog. 'What are you doing here?' he asked suddenly. 'What are you doing in my forest?'

Your forest, Rath almost asked, thinking the possessive pronoun incongruous. 'I'm a police officer,' he said. 'I catch killers.'

'I'm aware you're a police officer, but you're not from here.'

'No.' Rath debated whether he should tell Radlewski the truth, but it was so clear the man had nothing to do with the curare murders that he preferred to keep it to himself.

'Why are you here?'

'I wanted to meet you.' At least it wasn't a lie; it sounded almost friendly.

'You won't bring me in. I'm no killer. I just wanted justice.'

'What do you mean?'

'My father. I assume that's why you're here?' The fourteen-year-old boy who had scalped his father.

'No,' Rath said. 'You witnessed the murder of Anna von Mathée,' he said at length. Radlewski looked at him. Surprised, perhaps even a little upset. 'You need to testify in court. You saw the man who killed Anna. An innocent man went to jail.'

He had said too much, he could see straightaway from Radlewski's reaction. The man was thinking. 'You read them,' the Kaubuk said at last, the old suspicion returning to his voice. 'You read my notebooks.'

'No more than a glance, but Maria Cofalka . . .'

'I'm not leaving the forest,' Radlewski said. 'I'll never return to the world of men! Did Maria send you?'

'Yes and no, it's . . .'

'I'm not leaving my forest,' Radlewski interrupted. 'Neither you nor anyone else can persuade me.'

'I just want . . .'

Radlewski stood up. Seeing his size Rath started. No wonder everyone here spoke of the Kaubuk. He was really not the kind of man you'd want to run into alone in the forest. 'You're fit and healthy again,' Radlewski said. 'You don't need nursing any more. Time for you to leave.'

'You nursed me?'

'You had a bad fever, but now you need to return to your people, and never enter my forest again!' As he spoke, Radlewski fetched a canteen from a windowsill next to the hearth. Seizing Rath so suddenly that there was no chance for him to react, he forced his jaw open and held the bottle to his mouth. 'Drink,' he said over and over. 'Drink!'

Rath had no choice, so firmly were the Kaubuk's thumb and index finger wedged between his jaw, as if he were a horse being bridled.

The broth tasted better than the Kaubuk's dirty fingers, and soon Rath realised he was dozing off.

What the hell had the bastard given him? Was he trying to poison him? Why ...? Wh ...y?

The only response came in the form of darkness, enveloping him once more.

72

At eight the lights went out, and it grew colder. Dietrich Assmann wrapped himself in his blanket and shivered on the plank bed.

So, he'd have to spend a night here, but the lawyer would get him out soon after. Hopefully the man was good. He'd have preferred Dr Schröder, but Schröder ate out of Gustav Wengler's hand and, as matters stood, wouldn't be much use – if, that is, Gustav really *was* trying to do the dirty on him.

He still couldn't believe it. Why would Gustav Wengler collapse his alibi? Everything had been agreed. True, the shipment at the Westhafen had gone belly up, but that was hardly his fault! He'd bust a gut to ensure they kept to the delivery date, despite the problems created by Lamkau's death. It wasn't his fault they'd been grassed up. Some arsehole from *Concordia*, no doubt. Unlike Gustav Wengler, he'd never entirely trusted its members.

The truth was, he was proud of how he'd dodged the cops, how he'd obtained a set of dry clothes and returned to the hotel. He'd have thought Gustav might reward such commitment. After all, he could have died.

He still wasn't sure the cops hadn't simply laid a trap. Every fibre of his being resisted believing that Gustav Wengler had dropped him just like that. Gustav must understand that a man like Dietrich Assmann wouldn't go down without a

421

fight. Or perhaps it was all part of the plan? Just like in '24 when Lamkau and his gang were sacrificed to save the firm. Even Siegbert Wengler had left Masuria back then, though not before ensuring it was worth his while.

Wengler might have something similar in mind now. Perhaps Schröder would pay him a visit tomorrow with an offer. Time would tell, but the figure would need to be substantial. Assmann knew the locations of all the moonshine stills, knew the men who worked in them, the transport routes and more. More than Lamkau had ever known, and information like that had to be worth something.

Requesting his own lawyer couldn't hurt. He might even get more out of it. Since '24 business had grown exponentially. He wouldn't let himself be fobbed off like those two stiffs. He'd ask for more than Lamkau, and could do so with a clear conscience.

He couldn't help remembering the last thing the brawny inspector had said before returning him to his stinking cell. 'You should be mindful, Herr Assmann, that the murders of your former colleagues are linked to moonshining. If you're in any way involved, it's best you let us know. That way we can protect you. You could be next.'

The man had no idea. He'd washed his hands of old lady Radlewski's death back in '24, just like Gustav Wengler, which was how he'd been able to take on the role of manager. He was in about as much danger as Wengler himself.

Despite the darkness sleep refused to come. Perhaps that was part of prison life. You had all the time in the world, you just couldn't use it, not even for sleeping.

In the pitch black everything seemed impossibly loud; every door that slammed, every squeak, cough, slurp, sob, whine and snore. The jerky melody of church bells penetrated the gloom of his cell.

Üb immer Treue und Redlichkeit. Always practise Truth and Honesty.

Despite his infinite fatigue, sleep continued to elude him, and darkness deadened his sense of time. Suddenly, there was movement and a light came on in the corridor outside.

He heard steps, then saw two men halt outside his cell, a uniformed guard and a plain-clothes officer in a rumpled suit. The guard jangled a set of keys. 'Here's your man,' he said, pointing to the cell.

A loud echo came back from the bare walls as the key rattled in the lock. 'You've got company,' the guard said.

Assmann sat up. 'I thought it was lights out.'

'Take it up with reception in the morning. If CID want to see you, it's lights on.'

'CID?'

'I'm sorry to disturb your sleep, Herr Assmann, but there are a few things I'd like to get straight,' the plain-clothes man said, stepping inside. Assmann sat up when he showed his badge, suddenly wide awake, and nervous. What did they want from him *now*?

The guard locked the cell door from the outside. 'Inspector, Sir!'

'I'll call when I'm done.' The inspector sat next to Assmann on the plank bed.

'What do you want from me? Don't you think your colleagues upstairs have done enough?'

'That was the day shift,' the man said. 'I'm nights.'

So they were working him over in shifts now? Fucking cops. 'Can I smoke?'

'Feel free.' The cop made an inviting gesture with his hand. Assmann fingered the last cigarette out of his case, the one he had been saving for the morning. The inspector said nothing.

Night shift! They could question him until they were blue in the face. Dietrich Assmann wouldn't say a thing until he knew where he stood. Once he'd spoken with his lawyer, and Gustav Wengler.

All of a sudden it was pitch black as before. The embers of the cigarette shone like a glow-worm and threw reddish light on this strange inspector who still hadn't asked a question. Was he trying to intimidate him with silence? Assmann shook his head and took a long drag, knowing it was his one cigarette for the night. Looking to the side, he was surprised to see that the face of the man, who moments before had sat beside him on the plank bed, was gone.

73

It smelled of damp grass. A chill on the skin.

Letters carved in stone.

In the wan light a snail that appeared almost black.

Rath looked up at a gravestone.

For a moment he thought he was in a nightmare, but the ache in his neck told him it was real.

The gravestone bore a different name than his own.

Gefr. Szudarsky, Res. Inf. R 49.

He was familiar with such abbreviations. The 49th Reserve Infantry Regiment. A dead private who had fought for Kaiser and Fatherland in '14.

He looked around. More graves, arranged in file. Even in death the Prussians kept to march formation. Moonlight shone on the stones.

Suddenly, he knew where he was: the military cemetery near Markowsken.

He read more names. All had died in the same year, 1914. Many sounded Polish, but it wasn't just Prussian war graves, Russian soldiers were buried here too – some of whom also had Polish-sounding names.

The Masurians had given their lives for Prussia and the Kaiser; the Masovians for Russian-Poland and the Tsar.

What a difference a simple border made, but then again perhaps not. Everyone here was dead, irrespective of which side they had fought on.

Standing up he was obliged to support himself on Prussian Private Szudarsky's grave. Radlewski must have doped him. He could vaguely remember stumbling through the forest, more or less out of his mind, urged on by the Kaubuk and his dog. After a while he felt the strength in his legs begin to return.

He looked down at himself. His grey suit was for the garbage. He felt his left side, detecting his shoulder holster and service pistol. Even his wallet was there. He looked inside: not a penny missing, identification present and correct. Artur Radlewski and his accursed moor had spat him out just as they had found him. The only thing he didn't have was cigarettes.

He made for the road. It was seven or eight kilometres to Treuburg if he went right via Krupinnen, but he had a different destination in mind, and bore left instead. The moon lit the way. Gazing above him he knew he must have been gone longer than a night or two, much longer in fact. The crescent moon that had looked on as he lay dying was already on the wane.

The spire of the village church rose dark and forbidding in the night sky. He walked the final metres to the main road, hoping not to meet anyone, his suit utterly soiled, his hair matted and, feeling his chin and cheeks, he knew that a shave was long overdue. A light was on in the schoolhouse. He knocked and, at length, Karl Rammoser opened the door.

The teacher's eyes opened wide at the sight of him. Perhaps he took him for the Kaubuk. 'Inspector,' he said. 'What are you doing here so late? I thought you'd returned to Berlin long ago.'

'Can I come in? I'll tell you everything.'

'Of course.'

On the dining table in the teacher's apartment stood a bottle of homebrew and a glass, alongside an open book.

426

Rammoser fetched a second glass from the cupboard. 'Drink? You look as if you could use one.'

'Do you think I could have a cigarette too? I need the nicotine more.' Rath looked around. 'Where's your housekeeper?'

'Erna? Finished for the night.'

The wall clock showed just before midnight.

'What day is it today?'

'Wednesday.'

'I mean, what's the date?'

'20th July. Do you need the year too?' Rath shook his head. He had been missing for over a week. Why hadn't anyone come looking for him? Rammoser gave him a cigarette and a light. 'Don't take this the wrong way, Inspector, but you look appalling.'

'Thank you very much.' Rath took a deep drag and felt the nicotine course through his veins. At last. 'How about you? Where have you been?' He gestured towards the teacher's black suit. Rammoser had loosened his tie.

'You really don't know?' Rammoser furrowed his brow.

'These past few days I've been a world away, quite literally.'

'Maria Cofalka is dead.'

Rath had to sit down. 'I'm sorry to hear that,' he said. 'You were good friends, weren't you?'

'Very good.' Rammoser poured schnapps into the two glasses and sat beside him. 'Maria was probably the best friend you could have in this town.' The teacher raised his glass, and the men toasted and drank.

'How did she die?' Rath asked.

'Drowned, in the Treuburg Lake. They found her body near the public baths. People are talking of suicide, but I think it was an accident. Maria would never have killed herself. She must have slipped on the landing stage, banged her head against something and lost consciousness.'

427

Rath couldn't bring himself to mention the letters Maria Cofalka had entrusted to him before her death. The letters that had been stolen from his hotel room.

'But we were talking about you,' said Rammoser. 'Everyone thought you'd gone back to Berlin.'

'Who's been saying that?'

'That's the word in *Pritzkus's*. I don't know who started the rumour.'

'Old Adamek perhaps?' Rath asked. 'It's him I've to thank for all this. I almost died because of it.'

'Go on.' Rath told the schoolmaster the tale of his moorland odyssey, and his rescue by the Kaubuk. 'Artur Radlewski? So he's still alive.'

'He saved my life,' said Rath.

'Is that why you didn't arrest him? Or did he convince you of his innocence?'

'Most of the time I lay unconscious, running a fever. When we finally had the chance to talk he wasn't exactly friendly. I fear I may have outstayed my welcome.' He lit another cigarette. 'He doped me. It was like I blacked out. I have a dim memory of walking with him through the night, before I came to in the military cemetery by Markowsken.'

'So now you're summoning all police reserves in the Oletzko district to fetch him from his murky lair?'

Rath shook his head. 'No need to worry about that. Firstly, I don't bear grudges. Secondly, far as I'm concerned Radlewski still has a little credit in the bank. And thirdly, I'm certain he isn't behind the series of murders I came here to solve.'

Rammoser gave a satisfied nod, as if his favourite student had just given the correct answer. 'You think old Adamek purposefully lured you onto the moor?'

'Yes, otherwise he'd have come looking for me. Instead of spinning some yarn about my having gone back to Berlin.'

'We don't know if the rumours stem from him.'

'We know he's done nothing to dispel them.'

'Adamek doesn't say much when he drinks at *Pritzkus's*. You should know that,' said Rammoser. 'Why would he do it?'

'If only I knew ...' Rath said. 'Perhaps he has a score to settle with me.'

'I think you're misjudging the old boy.'

'We'll see. Either way, I'd like to hear what he has to say.'

74

A Division briefing felt more like a memorial service. Rumour had it that all division and squad team leaders had reported to the new command earlier that morning. Everywhere Charly looked were embarrassed faces. Ernst Gennat appeared later than usual, as usual giving nothing away. He stepped onto the platform and all conversation ceased.

'We are all aware that decisive changes were made to our institution yesterday,' he began. 'Nevertheless, in the coming days I expect you to fulfil your duties just as scrupulously as you would otherwise. Obey the commands of your superiors as ever, and go about your work.'

'With respect, Sir,' Wilhelm Böhm cut in, 'that's just it. We don't know who our superiors are.'

'Until further notice, Dr Melcher will be in charge.'

'What do you mean, "until further notice"?'

'Until the matter has been subjected to a judicial inquiry. In the meantime these issues mustn't prevent us from carrying on with our work. God knows, we have enough cases awaiting resolution.' The officers weren't happy. 'Now don't be looking like that. Kurt Melcher is by no means the worst commissioner, if his reputation in Essen is anything to go by.'

'That might be true, Sir.' Wilhelm Böhm wouldn't let go. 'But for myself and many colleagues, it's the manner of his appointment that jars.'

Gennat nodded. 'We don't know if the change in personnel was right, or rather, rightful, but we live in a constitutional state, and these are matters for the courts to decide. Meanwhile, all we can do is carry on.'

'I'm not so sure about that,' Charly said, surprised she'd found the courage to speak in a room full of men, but she couldn't hold back any longer. 'What I mean is that I'm no longer sure we *do* live in a constitutional state.' She lifted a copy of *Berliner Tageblatt*. 'If what the paper says is true, then what we witnessed yesterday was a cold-blooded putsch, and Papen has thwarted Prussian democracy in one fell swoop. And whatever our new commissioner's reputation, he's hardly known as a democrat.' She looked around. Not all colleagues were nodding.

'Surely it's more important that he's a good chief.' The calm voice belonged to Arthur Nebe. He gave Charly a friendly smile. 'Sadly, this institution has had its share of democrats who've turned out to be poor criminal investigators.'

Böhm beat Charly to it. 'I hope that number doesn't include Grzesinski and Dr Weiss,' he said.

'I'm just saying that professional competence is more important than political persuasion.'

'I'd have expected a little more loyalty to our old chiefs, especially from you,' Böhm argued. 'The support you've received from Dr Weiss, you ought to be grateful to him for the rest of your life.'

'That kind of patronage, Detective Chief Inspector, goes hand in hand with performance!'

'Gentlemen, please,' Gennat intervened. 'Let's put these squabbles to one side. Everyone is entitled to their own political views, but they should not be a point of discussion here. Dr Melcher's professional competence is undisputed. He has led Essen Police Headquarters with distinction since the war.' He looked sternly at Böhm and Charly.

431

'And the democratic credentials of a man who belonged to Stresemann's party are beyond question.'

Charly wasn't so sure. Kurt Melcher's move was self-seeking, the very fact that he'd been present at the putsch spoke against him, but she said nothing more and Böhm, too, fell silent. Gennat was right; they shouldn't discuss these matters here. It sowed discord, and wouldn't solve any of the issues raised by yesterday's events.

'I expect . . .' Buddha continued, but then the door flew open, and those assembled remained none the wiser as to his expectations.

Cadet Steinke stood in the door looking agitated. 'Please excuse the interruption, Sir,' he said. The man was out of breath, as if he had sprinted the distance from Homicide to the small meeting room. 'But something terrible has happened.'

'Come on then, man. Out with it,' Gennat said, as Steinke paused for breath.

'It's . . .Prisoner Assmann . . .here in police custody . . .'

'Assmann? He's my prisoner,' Böhm said. 'Don't tell me the man has escaped, or that some shyster has got him off?'

'Worse. I'm afraid Prisoner Assmann is dead.'

75

In the *Salzburger Hof* the breakfast tables were already being cleared. Hella Rickert gazed at Rath wide-eyed, but said nothing, simply turned towards the kitchen door with her tray of dirty crockery, offering him a perfect view of her rear.

Forbearance is not acquittance, he thought, and crossed to reception. No one there. He slammed the bell so hard it might have been a high striker.

He felt ready to take on the entire Rickert family if necessary. Rammoser had let him sleep, waking him around nine. After a bath, a decent shave, and a proper breakfast with coffee – *sans* leg of squirrel – he felt almost human again. Rammoser had offered a replacement suit from his wardrobe. The trousers were a little short and the jacket had patches on its elbows, but otherwise it was a perfect fit, even if it made him look like a village teacher. A village teacher returning from a school trip, for Rath still wore Herr Damerau's mud-encrusted hiking boots.

He had caught the ten o'clock from Wielitzken. Rammoser had recommended that he find a doctor, but upon reaching Treuburg station the first thing he did was buy three ten-packs of Overstolz. After that he made for the telephone booths and requested a long-distance call to Berlin, lighting the first cigarette as he waited to be connected. He asked for Charly's extension, but got Böhm instead, and hung up without a word. He had no desire to be recalled while there was still business to attend to here. In the *Salzburger Hof*, for example.

He slammed the bell again and Hermann Rickert appeared straightaway, looking him up and down, as if to make sure it really was his sometime guest. 'Inspector, what a surprise!'

'Isn't it just?'

'You left without notifying us. We were somewhat taken aback.'

'Old Adamek could have told you where I was.'

The hotelier looked at him blankly. 'I asked Chief Constable Grigat, but apparently you kept him in the dark.'

'He said that?'

'I had to have your room cleared, as we had a number of guests over the weekend. You're welcome to have it back.'

'How kind.' Rath wasn't sure Hermann Rickert noted his sarcasm.

'You ought to have told us you were staying out of town. We'd have kept your case here for you.'

'I'm afraid that wasn't possible.'

'Well, I don't mean to be awkward. How about we just charge you for the case? A week in left luggage.' Rickert smiled his politest hotelier's smile.

'Most obliging. Then I'd like to have my old room back.'

'Of course.' Rickert fetched the key from the board. 'I'll have your case brought up immediately.'

'Thank you.' Rath nodded. 'And ...you'll remember I'd lost something before my ...departure? Did you manage to ...?'

'But of course! My apologies, how could I forget?' Rickert stooped to retrieve a black folder from behind the counter.

'Where did you find it?'

'It was my daughter, actually. She found it while clearing

your room for our weekend guests, on Sonnabend. It must have slipped behind the bed.'

'I see.' Rath took the folder and key, and headed up to his room.

On entering, the first thing he did was check that the letters were all there. At least one was missing, the lines he'd been reading prior to the theft. As for the rest, he couldn't be sure – and the only person who knew for certain was dead. The news about Maria Cofalka had shaken him. Her death was neither accident nor suicide, nor was it a coincidence.

There was a knock: not Hella, but Reimund, the Rickert's factotum. In one hand he held a suitcase, in the other a pair of brogues. Rath put on the shoes, but hung his brown suit in the wardrobe, the only one left for the journey back to Berlin. He locked the folder in the desk, pocketed the key and exited the hotel. First stop was Goldaper Strasse, where he called at the shoemaker's workshop. Friedrich Kowalski wore a leather apron and held a small hammer in his hand. He looked surprised.

'I wanted to return these,' Rath said, dropping the muddy boots on the floor so that the crusts flaked off. 'Please send my regards to Herr Damerau and tell him many thanks. They were a great help.'

'Inspector!' The shoemaker looked at the shoes, then at Rath. 'I thought you weren't coming back.'

'I nearly didn't.' Rath peered inside the hall. 'Where's your esteemed nephew?'

'In Königsberg.'

'In Königsberg. I see. What's he doing there?'

'Working, what else? He was recalled, about a week ago now.'

'And the fact that he abandoned me in the forest? That didn't bother anyone here?'

'I'm sorry?'

'That's right, your nephew abandoned me. He and old Adamek. I almost died out there on the moors.'

'Come inside, Inspector.' A short time later Rath sat with a cup of tea at Kowalski's kitchen table. 'I'm afraid I don't quite understand,' the cobbler said. 'You sent him back yourself, didn't you? With a message for Grigat.'

'The last thing I told your nephew was to keep watch by some clearing on the border. By the time I returned he and Adamek were both gone.'

Kowalski shook his head. 'That's not like Anton. He never lets anyone down.'

'What's this about a message for Grigat?'

'He didn't tell me. He had to set off pretty much right away after returning from the district office. Königsberg needed him urgently, him and the car.'

'No one thought to ask about me?'

'Anton was rather vague, but somehow we all assumed you no longer needed his help.'

Rath nodded pensively. Someone here was playing him false, and there were no prizes for guessing who.

Wilhelm Adamek sat outside his shanty whittling an enormous stick. He registered Rath's appearance with a twitch of his eyebrows and returned to his work. If he was surprised at seeing the missing inspector he gave no sign. He examined his stick, stuck out his lower lip and continued carving. Rath wondered if he should be wary of the knife. His Walther might not be loaded, but it should serve for intimidation purposes.

'Hello to you, too,' he said. 'Safely returned from the forest, I see?'

Adamek threw him a brief glance and carried on with his whittling. Rath tried to assess the old-timer's strength. Even under normal circumstances a man like Wilhelm Adamek might have the better of him. After a week in bed with fever, and still wobbly on his legs, there was no question. Diplomacy, then. He couldn't just yank the man up by the collar.

'I was looking for you, recently. Why didn't you come back for me?'

'I'd brought you to your destination.' Adamek didn't even look up.

'You left me in the lurch.'

'I had to escort your colleague back.'

'Don't talk nonsense. What did you say to Kowalski to make him go with you? That I was sending him back with a message for Chief Constable Grigat? What kind of message? That I'd manage just fine on my own in the wilds, and didn't need his help?' Rath was shouting, but didn't care. The composure with which this *outlaw* sat whittling made him incandescent. 'I would have died on the moors, if someone hadn't pulled me out!'

Adamek looked up and raised his eyebrows. 'I'm sorry,' he said. 'I didn't want that.'

It sounded genuine. Rath was surprised. 'Then you shouldn't have abandoned me in the forest.'

'Like I said, I'm sorry.'

The old-timer's face was hard to read. 'It wasn't your idea, then?' Adamek said nothing. 'Who put you up to it?' More and more splints rained down in front of the bench. 'Who?'

'I can't say!'

'So, someone *did* put you up to it!' Adamek looked at Rath with a mixture of anger and contempt. 'Tell me who it was. Did they blackmail you?' Adamek's knife carved ever larger splints, this was wood-chopping now. 'Your poaching, was it? Did someone threaten to turn you in?'

All of a sudden the old man sprang to his feet and hurled the knife into the bench where it quivered for some time. 'Listen to me,' he said. 'There's only one thing I want from life, and that is to be left in peace!'

437

'I don't like being abandoned.'

'I never abandoned anyone!'

'There's someone else who won't leave you in peace, isn't there? Someone who urged you to teach that puffed-up inspector a lesson. *See that he's had his fill of Masuria, and on the first train back to that hotbed of vice he calls home*! So that life here can carry on as normal. Is that it?' Adamek was silent. 'Well, let me tell you and your fellow Treuburgers something. You won't get rid of me so easily! There are far too many secrets in this town, and it's time someone lifted the lid. Now, kindly tell your mystery employer that's precisely what I intend to do!'

Was that a grin on his face? Adamek seemed to have enjoyed Rath's outburst. 'Why don't you tell him yourself?' he said.

76

For as long as she had worked at the Castle, Charly had given the holding cells a wide berth. Now the smell and crude remarks that greeted her arrival appeared to justify her decision. At least the man in here would be keeping his comments to himself. Dietrich Assmann lay on the plank bed, covered by a thin woollen blanket. His eyes were closed, at first glance he looked as if he were sleeping.

'We didn't realise until reveille,' the guard told Ernst Gennat. 'When we saw he wasn't moving, we went in. The rest you know.'

'The rest we know,' Gennat gave the guard a hostile look. 'This man was an important witness and he was was killed on your watch! For God's sake, are people no longer safe in jail?'

'I wasn't on duty last night,' the guard said.

'You're in charge here, man!'

'Yes, Sir.'

'I demand to know how it could have happened.'

'In theory, Sir, no one can get in or out of here without our say-so.'

'In theory,' Gennat repeated. 'Yet somehow a killer got in *and* out. You can't tell me this was suicide.' He shook his head. 'It's a disgrace! Murder in a police cell! If the press gets wind of this ... I want this resolved. I need whatever

439

logs are kept here on my desk. *Now*. And round up everyone who was on duty last night.'

'This moment?' the guard asked, kneading his cap in his hands.

'Yesterday.'

'Yes, Sir!'

For some years Gennat had preferred to pull the strings from the comfort of his office, but now the bodies were coming to him. He didn't even have to leave headquarters to reach Dietrich Assmann's corpse, just cross to the holding cells in the southern wing and head upstairs to Solitary on the second floor.

Böhm was there too, alongside Lange, and Cadet Steinke, who had called it in. All stood outside the narrow cell watching the forensic technicians go about their business.

Gennat approached the corpse, whose neck Dr Karthaus was examining.

Meanwhile all we can do is carry on. Well, here was Buddha showing the way. Charly didn't know if it was right, but perhaps there really was no other choice. Did it really matter if their commissioner's name was Grzesinski or Melcher, if he was a Social Democrat or National Liberal?

Whatever, it looked as if their killer had struck again. Dietrich Assmann lay dead on his plank bed. The mattress and upper portion of the woollen blanket were wet, and on the bedpost hung a red cloth still damp with water. She went over and examined it, sniffing at the red fabric. 'It smells like camphor,' she said.

Lange finished photographing the corpse and steered the camera towards the cloth. 'She's right. Pitralon, I'd say.'

'Pitralon?' Gennat said curiously, joining them. 'Aftershave?'

'Seems our man applied it before his death,' Dr Karthaus said. 'The corpse smells as if it's been freshly shaved. Although the chin is quite stubbly.'

440

'Am I right in thinking these cloths are placed over the victim's nose and mouth, and then drenched in water?' Gennat asked.

'You're saying the smell transferred onto the cloth from Assmann's face?'

'Precisely.'

'Isn't it too intense for that?' Charly asked. 'Seems more likely the cloth was dipped in aftershave.'

'Take a photo of the cloth, Lange, then Kronberg can bag it for examination.'

'Yes, Sir.'

Gennat turned towards Kronberg, who was speaking with Böhm. 'Well?'

The ED man shrugged. 'We don't know how the perpetrator got in and out. There are no signs of forced entry. Nothing to indicate the use of a picklock.'

'He must have got in somehow.'

'Perhaps he had a key.'

'You're saying it was one of the guards?'

'We shouldn't rule anything out, but actually what I meant is perhaps someone had a key *cut*. Or got hold of one somehow. Wouldn't be the first time a key had fallen into the wrong hands.'

'We'll ask around the relevant people.'

Gennat was famous for his contacts in the Ringvereine, as well as for his network of informants. If anyone could discover who had keys to the holding cells at Alex, it was him. 'When you examine that cloth,' he said to Kronberg, 'I'd like to know why it smells like that, and if it's a match for the others.'

While Gennat was speaking, Charly looked round the cell and found a cigarette stub under the plank bed. She knelt beside Dr Karthaus and lifted it with a pair of tweezers. It had only been half-smoked. 'Take a look at this,' she said. Gennat and Böhm turned towards her. 'Strange, don't you think?'

'Why?' Böhm asked. 'You're permitted to smoke in police custody.'

'That's true,' Gennat said, 'but in here you smoke each cigarette as if it's your last. What you don't do is smoke half and stub the rest out. I think that's what you're getting at, am I right, Fräulein Ritter?'

Charly nodded, but she was embarrassed. She felt like an insufferable know-it-all. Luckily Böhm didn't hold it against her.

Dr Karthaus joined them. 'Did I hear you right? You're permitted to smoke in here?' He fetched his cigarette case from his overalls and lit up.

'So long as you don't stub it out on the floor.'

'No problem.' Karthaus removed a tin case from his overalls. A pocket ashtray. 'I know my place where Forensics are concerned.'

'Have you anything for us?' Böhm asked. 'Death by drowning? The usual?'

'Depends on how you look at it. If by *usual* you mean that the man is dead, then yes.' The pathologist inhaled deeply. 'If, on the other hand, you are asking whether we are dealing with the same sequence of events as in previous cases, then I'm afraid I must disappoint.' Böhm looked surprised, and the doctor seemed to enjoy it. He gestured towards the corpse with the cigarette. 'I've searched his neck for a puncture site. There's nothing.'

'Perhaps the killer injected a different part of his body?'

'We'll have to wait for the autopsy. However, while examining his neck I made another discovery.' Karthaus took another long drag and pointed at the corpse a second time. 'Unless I'm very much mistaken, the man has a broken neck.'

77

Erich Grigat was adjusting his shako before the wall mirror when Rath barged through the door. 'How the hell did you get in here?' he asked.

'My apologies, Sir,' his secretary replied. 'This gentleman completely ignored me. He didn't even knock, just came …'

'It's fine, Fräulein Bikowski. Let me see to the inspector. Why not go for your lunch? If you need anything, I'll be in the *Salzburger Hof.*'

The secretary nodded and left, but not before throwing Rath a hostile glance. 'I think it's in your interests that this conversation remain confidential,' he said, closing the door.

'I can't see what there is to discuss, Inspector. You've told me nothing of your movements so far, and your Berlin colleagues clearly likewise. Your superior was in touch on several occasions. Unfortunately there was nothing I could say to him.'

'No?' Rath looked at Grigat's twitching moustache. 'You couldn't have let Berlin know where I've spent the last few days?'

'I'm sorry?'

'What did you say to old Adamek? Did you threaten him? Say you'd no longer turn a blind eye to his poaching? What about your beloved venison loin?'

'I don't know what you're talking about.'

443

'We ran into you on our way to Adamek's. You'd just come from there, hadn't you?'

'Stop speaking in riddles.'

'Granted, you didn't mean to kill me. You probably just wanted to run me out of your pretty little town. Well, too bad!'

'What are you talking about?'

'Or were you acting on someone else's behalf, instructing old Adamek to abandon me in the forest like that?'

'Are you implying the Treuburg Police can be bought?'

'Depends what you mean by "bought"? Perhaps you were just doing someone a favour. In Cologne we call it *Klüngel*. Cabal.'

'And here we call it calumny. I'm warning you, stop making baseless accusations!' It felt as if Grigat might challenge him to a duel.

'Need I remind you . . .' Rath placed the letter from Bernhard Weiss on the desk. 'That the deputy commissioner of the Berlin Police has expressly requested that you provide me with support. Therefore, I advise you to lay your cards on the table. Tell me who wanted rid of me and I won't lodge a complaint. Otherwise, your conduct could be interpreted as insubordination. No doubt you're aware of Dr Weiss's connections in the Interior Ministry?'

Grigat lifted the official letter. 'As far as I'm concerned the only thing that paper's good for is wiping your arse.'

'Pardon me?'

'You heard me!'

'Do you realise what you're saying? This is a letter from Berlin Deputy Police Commissioner Bernhard Weiss . . .'

'Your *Isidore* has no authority here! The Berlin Police commissioner's name is Kurt Melcher, and your Dr Weiss can count himself lucky he hasn't had his Jewish arse spanked.' For a moment Rath thought Grigat had gone mad. He fetched a communication from on top of his filing tray.

'Came over the ticker this morning. Grzesinski, Weiss and Heimannsberg have all been removed from office. About time someone cleaned up this Social Democrat pigsty.'

'No, Severing would never allow it!'

'The Interior Minister has also been removed, the entire Prussian government in fact, bunch of red bastards. Hindenburg has appointed the Reich chancellor as Reich commissioner for Prussia.'

'Show me!'

Grigat handed Rath the teleprinter message informing all Prussian police and gendarmerie stations that the Prussian minority government had been removed from office, along with the Berlin Police executive. Until further notice Prussia would be governed by a Reich commissioner.

'This ...can't be. It's a ...putsch,' Rath stammered.

'I'd choose your words carefully if I were you,' Grigat said, now holding the upper hand. 'Otherwise I might find *myself* compelled to make a complaint against *you*! My patience with you and your bizarre code of ethics is at an end!' He grasped the document and waved towards the door. 'Now, be so kind as to leave my office, otherwise I'll have you removed by force.'

Rath thought better of answering back. Silently he folded Bernhard Weiss's letter and stowed it in his pocket, before leaving Grigat and the district administrative office behind. *Damn it*, he thought, *a hell of a lot has happened in the days you've been gone*.

There was a telephone booth outside the district court. He took out his wallet and counted his change, knowing it was only a matter of time before Treuburg's chief of police declared him *persona non grata*.

Robert Naujoks was reliable. The Lyck train got in at half past two. Rath met him on the platform. Naujoks opened his leather bag and removed a thick lever arch file: the

445

Mathée case. 'Pretty old hat, this,' he said. 'You think you can find something in here that implicates Gustav Wengler? The victim was his fiancée.'

'We'll see. All I'll say is things are about to get seriously hot for our distillery-owning friend.'

Naujoks took the file from his bag. 'The Mathée case was closed when I took up office here, the killer long since in jail. It was still talked about though.'

'It's still talked about today. Only thing is, they got the wrong man – and I think lots of people knew it, too. Gustav Wengler included.'

Naujoks looked around as if someone might be listening. 'We shouldn't speak so openly.'

Rath gestured towards the station restaurant. 'Can I buy you a coffee?'

'That's kind, but no. Too many people here still know me. It's better we're not seen together.'

'Perhaps you're right.'

'Look after yourself. If there's one thing Treuburgers don't like it's nosy police officers.'

'You can say that again.'

'I'll be on the next train back out to Lyck.' Naujoks looked at his watch. 'Leaves in half an hour. I'll take my coffee alone. You should find yourself someplace quiet, too.'

Rath took his leave of the retired constable, thanking him once more. Naujoks waved and vanished inside the restaurant.

Exiting the station building, file tucked under his arm, he wondered where he could go. Nowhere sprang to mind. Even prior to Naujoks's warning, he felt as if his every move were being monitored, as if the whole town was conspiring against him.

Then, all at once, the solution presented itself. The light railway that ran from Mierunsken to Schwentainen was

446

only a stone's throw distant. Perfect: the next train departed in ten minutes. Rath purchased his ticket.

The line didn't just have a narrower gauge than the Reichsbahn, its cars were smaller too. The train to Schwentainen, which called to mind a toy locomotive, stood at the platform, engine steaming away. He found an empty compartment, and bagged a window seat.

According to the timetable the train stopped at every milk churn, but that was just fine. The first station, shortly after Treuburg, was Luisenhöhe, where he could see the brick chimneys of the distillery. A few people got off, no one got on, and the train continued. Now certain that no subsequent passenger would recognise him, he opened the file and began to read.

The train needed a good half-hour to reach Schwentainen. After almost a dozen additional stops, he had acquired a basic working knowledge of the Mathée homicide from July 1920.

He was surprised by how many names he recognised. Sergeant Siegbert Wengler had found Anna von Mathée dead on Sunday, 11th July 1920, at around three thirty, in the shallows of a small, unnamed lake in the forest behind Markowsken. Wengler had apparently discovered a man crouched over the corpse, whom, upon violently resisting arrest, he had neutralised with the butt of his rifle and led away from the forest in handcuffs as a *prime suspect in the murder of Anna von Mathée*. The man's name: Jakub Polakowski.

The dead girl's horse was tied to a tree by a nearby clearing; Polakowski's bicycle stood next to the shore.

Sergeant Wengler had then pronounced Anna von Mathée dead before taking leave of the crime scene and requesting a doctor. Prior to that, he had pulled her body towards the shore and closed her eyes, exactly the sort of thing Gennat had been trying to prevent simple-minded uniform cops

447

doing for years. Ordering things, *then* calling for CID, was a habit those first on the scene couldn't seem to kick.

In Anna von Mathée's case, no one had been especially worried. CID officers from Lyck reconstructed the chain of events using Wengler's witness statement, alongside clues found at the site, and the autopsy report. The reconstruction had the suspect follow Anna von Mathée to the lake on his bicycle, perhaps to watch her bathe, only for desire to get the better of him. When she tried to defend herself he drowned her.

There were all sorts of suppositions in the text. According to Wengler, the plebiscite's bleak prognosis for Poland could have filled Polakowski with hatred against all things German, speculation aided by the fact that the suspect had instigated a quarrel against three members of the Marggrabowa Homeland Service on the morning of the same day. An appendix provided the details. Again, the names of those involved were familiar: Herbert Lamkau, August Simoneit and Hans Wawerka. Wengler had actually placed Polakowski under arrest for a short time.

Around an hour after Polakowski's release, Anna von Mathée's fiancé had arrived at the police station to report her missing, Anna having failed to appear for lunch at the Luisenhöhe estate. Witnesses had seen her riding out to the Markowsken forest in the late morning. So, the search began.

It was striking that Sergeant Wengler had only mentioned the name of this fiancé on one occasion, at a point that could be easily overlooked, as if he were somehow embarrassed to have set out in search of the missing girl with a family member. For the man with whom he scoured the forest, before eventually arriving at the little lake, was none other than Anna's fiancé himself, was none other than his own brother, the superintendent at Luisenhöhe: Gustav Wengler.

The wicked man, as the Kaubuk called him. The man who had returned to the scene of his crime.

78

Dr Karthaus had moved quickly. Dietrich Assmann's corpse still lay covered by a white cotton sheet as the pathologist met the *Vaterland* team down in the hallowed halls of the morgue.

Charly felt uneasy entering the autopsy room, which would be one reason why Wilhelm Böhm had brought her along. It was something any CID cadet assigned to Homicide, however temporarily, must experience. In the days she'd worked as a stenographer for A Division, Böhm and Gennat had valued her theories and deductions, but they had never brought her here. The smell, a mix of human blood and disinfectant, took some getting used to, but her curiosity outweighed any sense of disgust.

Most officers had remained in the Castle to assist Gennat in interrogating the squad of guards. It was still unclear how on earth the killer had gained access to the cells.

'That was quick, Doctor,' Böhm said, and Karthaus arched an eyebrow in surprise. Praise from the chief inspector was as rare as a snowflake in August.

'Superintendent Gennat asked me to prioritise this autopsy, and there were several details that struck me as odd during my initial examination.'

'The broken neck.'

'Right! At first I thought it could be a result of the water torture. If you tie your victims up and put the fear of death in them, some react so violently that they break their bones.'

'But our man doesn't secure his victims, he paralyses them,' Charly said.

'Not this time.' Karthaus had their undivided attention. 'The blood analysis is still pending, but I'd be willing to bet it shows negative. I couldn't find a single puncture site.'

'So, he did tie Assmann up?' Böhm asked.

'That's what I thought, but there are no signs of a struggle, nothing to indicate the man was tied.'

'What about the water on the plank bed, the wet cloth? That points to water torture.'

'That's what it's *supposed* to point to, certainly. However, we only found water in the trachea, and it got in post-mortem.'

'Nothing in the lungs.'

Karthaus shook his head.

'A copycat,' Charly suggested.

'That's what I suspect too,' said Karthaus. 'Nothing points to the victim having been exposed to the *tormenta de toca*, let alone having died as a result. Which was his great good fortune, if you can speak of fortune when a man has died. Most likely he barely noticed a thing, except, perhaps, for the lights going out. Metaphorically speaking.' He threw Charly an apologetic glance. 'To come back to the water: I've examined samples from both the plank bed and the victim's hair, as well as the residue from the red cloth. The strange smell – it is indeed Pitralon. I found traces of camphor in the water, camphor and alcohol. It was mixed with aftershave, albeit heavily diluted.'

'Could it be from the victim?' Böhm asked.

'Unlikely, but I have another explanation.' Karthaus pointed to the covered corpse. 'The man's neck was broken by someone who knew what he was doing, someone trained in close combat, or similar. Everything else is for the purposes of misdirection.' The pathologist looked at the two CID officers. 'He didn't have a lot of time to prepare. He had to improvise. As for the water used to simulate the *tormenta de toca*...my guess is that the perpetrator brought it into the cell using an empty or almost empty bottle of Pitralon, because he had nothing else to hand.'

79

Rath went for a stroll. He'd have liked to go straight back to Treuburg, but the next train wasn't for another hour and a half. So he strolled, file under his arm, through the town. Schwentainen was a ribbon settlement on the shore of a lake bearing the same name, with a small church, on whose spire red roof tiles gleamed in the sun. Perhaps being forced to walk like this was good. He needed to think.

Now wasn't the time to confront Gustav Wengler, whatever his instincts told him. He tried to place what he'd read into some kind of order, comparing it with the lines from Radlewski's diary.

It was a fix-up, all of it. From Anna's death right up to Jakub Polakowski's murder trial.

The Homeland Service boys had deliberately embroiled Polakowski in a fight, so that Gustav Wengler could calmly go about cornering Anna at the lake where she met her paramour in secret. Near the tree in whose bark the young couple had immortalised their love.

Was her murder planned? Her rape? Or was it just meant to be a talk, which had spiralled out of control? A brutal murder for which the Wengler brothers had found the perfect scapegoat in Jakub Polakowski?

Rath left Schwentainen, passing over a narrow headland separating two lakes from one another, and reaching the village on the other shore where a sign read: *Suleyken*,

452

Oletzko District, Administrative Region of Gumbinnen.

He sat on a jetty and gazed at the roofs of Schwentainen lining the opposite shore, a breathtakingly beautiful scene. Nothing could disturb the idyll here in the Oletzko District, Gumbinnen, and certainly not the truth that Maria Cofalka had closed in on.

They had buried her only yesterday, but already Rath was determined to exhume her body. The librarian might be dead, but her case was far from closed.

80

When Charly returned to the Castle with Böhm, they found Vosskamp, the head guard, sitting in Gennat's office. Trudchen Steiner, Gennat's secretary, waved them through. 'The superintendent has requested your presence,' she said.

Before Charly could confirm they were both needed, Böhm pushed her through the door. 'So?' Gennat said, his coffee poured. 'What's the word from Pathology?'

'It's a copycat,' Böhm said. 'He broke Assmann's neck, doused him with water and left a red handkerchief to throw us off the scent. Well, we've caught it now.'

'There were traces of aftershave in the water,' Charly said.

'Interesting.' Gennat shovelled three spoonfuls of sugar into his coffee, stirring slowly and deliberately. 'A copycat, then. That tallies with Forensics's findings. We still don't know anything about the others, but the handkerchief from this morning came from the textile section in Tietz, right here on Alexanderplatz.'

'That was quick.'

'One of Kronberg's men recognised it. He bought one himself a few days ago.'

'Then the man's a suspect,' Charly joked.

'You're closer to the truth than you might like.' Buddha

looked at the guard on his sofa. 'In the meantime Herr Vosskamp and I have solved one or two riddles.'

Vosskamp interpreted this as an invitation to make his report. He cleared his throat. 'Yes,' he said, placing his cup to one side. 'We've questioned the duty guards on both late and night shifts and pieced together Herr Assmann's final hours. The prisoner received a visit at twelve minutes past nine, from a detective inspector.'

Charly's ears pricked up.

'What inspector?' Böhm asked. 'I didn't send anyone up to him in the middle of the night. Or did Customs . . .?'

'No, it was a detective inspector,' Vosskamp said. 'At least according to our log.'

'Based on what we know so far,' Gennat said, 'this is the man who has Dietrich Assmann on his conscience.'

'What do you mean? Did an interrogation spiral out of control?'

'We don't know yet.' Gennat shrugged. 'The guard swears that everything was as normal when he fetched the officer from the cell. He claims the prisoner was already asleep.'

'Or dead,' Charly said, immediately irritated by her lapse in control.

'Yes, Fräulein Ritter,' Gennat said. 'That's what I think too.' He glanced at a sheet of paper. 'It was nine thirty-seven when the officer called for the guard, which was also when he left the cell wing.'

'After which point there were no other incidents of note,' Vosskamp said. He clearly thought it significant.

'If he's in the log then he must have left a name,' Böhm said. 'So why aren't we grilling him as we speak?'

Gennat opened the log and passed it to Böhm. 'The entry's there, at the bottom.'

Böhm took the book and looked inside. Charly squinted at the page. Prisoner name, cell number, visitor name and length of visit were all neatly recorded. The last entry bore yesterday's date and pertained to Dietrich Assmann. She could see the name and signature. No doubt about it, it looked the same as on all those letters he had sent to Paris: the book was signed: *Gereon Rath*.

81

There was only one fresh grave at the Catholic cemetery in Treuburg. Already the wreaths and flowers were starting to wilt; it smelled of herbs, topsoil and holy water. Maria Cofalka didn't have a headstone yet, but Rath knew he was in the right place. He'd purchased flowers en route after depositing the homicide file at the train station, in the same locker he'd left his suitcase prior to meeting Naujoks.

He laid the bouquet beside the wreaths and, before he knew what he was doing, sank to his knees. He wasn't especially devout, didn't even know if he still believed – but he felt responsible for the death of this woman whom Wengler had ordered killed. For the distillery owner wasn't only interested in preserving the legend of Anna von Mathée's death, but also in concealing a murder he himself had committed, and, with the help of his brother, falsely attributed to another man.

If Rath hadn't let the papers Maria Cofalka entrusted to him be stolen, then perhaps she would still be alive. He felt an urgent need to ask for her forgiveness, but this was ridiculous, kneeling before a mound of earth, communing with a dead woman.

She can't hear you, goddamn it, it's too late!

Still, he spoke with her, apologised that he would soon be disrupting her peace so that the circumstances of her death might come to light, in this town where all else, it seemed, was swept under the carpet at the bidding of just one man.

Wanting to confront this man, Rath had alighted from the train the station before Treuburg and walked up to the estate house, finding only Fischer, the private secretary, according to whom, Wengler was still in Berlin. Having settled his brother's estate he would now depart on business, and wouldn't return for at least a week.

Was the nimble-minded Fischer aware what kind of man he worked for, that Gustav Wengler had his own fiancée on his conscience, and more people besides? Perhaps the secretary was in cahoots with him?

Rath stood up and wiped the dirt from his knees. Jakub Polakowski's grave was close by, and, passing it, he read its inscription once more.

For love is strong as death; jealousy is cruel as the grave. The coals thereof are coals of fire, which hath a most vehement flame.

Love. Rath wondered who was responsible for Polakowski being buried here, and for these verses. Perhaps the same person who was responsible for the murders. Someone who knew who first deprived Jakub Polakowski of the love of his life, then sent him to jail for her murder.

If he hadn't known better, he'd have suspected Maria Cofalka, who had worked in a hospital during the war and would be familiar with needles. As a woman, she'd have been able to get close to her victims without arousing suspicion, right until the needle entered the jugular. But Maria had been in Treuburg when Siegbert Wengler was killed in Berlin. Rath had questioned her in the library the day before.

Perhaps she'd had an accomplice who would finish the job now that she was dead? He needed to find out who else had been close to Jakub Polakowski.

Or he could keep his findings to himself, and let things

slide. He could cross his fingers that this mysterious avenger would catch up with Gustav Wengler and subject him to as torturous a death as Wengler had Anna von Mathée.

He shook his head. He couldn't. He'd have liked to, but he couldn't. There was a madman on the loose who had killed four people; not innocents, perhaps, but four people all the same. People who hadn't deserved to die, just as Gustav Wengler didn't deserve to die.

No, the only right course of action was bringing Gustav Wengler to trial.

On Bergstrasse, just before the marketplace, he was met by around a dozen SA officers, led by Klaus Fabeck, Hella's boyfriend. Fabeck glowered at him with the typical SA gaze, a strange mix of hatred and contempt. You could be forgiven for thinking the brownshirts practised it. As if it were a forward march, or a kick to the solar plexus.

He stood in the troop's way, and Fabeck raised his hand and bade his men halt. At least the idiots were well-trained.

'Well,' Rath said. 'What feats of heroism await?' Fabeck stared in silence. 'What's on today's agenda? Theft, murder, the usual?'

At last Fabeck found his voice. 'How about decking the local gobshite?'

'Bet you feel strong with all these men behind you, but that doesn't mean you can incite your girlfriend to steal.'

'What are you talking about?'

'You know very well.'

'Get out of my way!'

'Order your lads about all you like, but I'm a Prussian CID officer.' Rath pulled out his badge, just in case there was anyone who didn't know. 'Didn't your girl tell you? She had to con her way to the letters.'

'Con her way to the letters?' The youth was stupider than

459

he looked. The SA needed people like him. The problem was they were ten a penny.

'Using her feminine wiles.'

Fabeck turned red. 'What are you trying to say?

'Let's not worry about that now. Ask her yourself. Maybe it wasn't the letters she was after. Maybe she just wanted . . .'

'Shut your mouth!' Fabeck barked.

'All right, all right,' Rath said. 'Like I say, these letters, they're evidence. I hope you haven't destroyed them, otherwise you're looking at a pretty serious offence. Return them, and I'll forget the whole thing.'

The SA man spat at his feet. 'You're addressing an SA Rottenführer!'

'I'm addressing a boy. That brownshirt doesn't make you a man.'

'Don't get fresh with me.'

'Don't get fresh with me, *Inspector*. The police might look kindly upon you here, but in Berlin we know you're little more than a gang of thugs.'

'Is that so? Then perhaps we should show you just how *thuggish* we can be.'

'You'd attack a Prussian officer?'

'Why? You going to report us? How many witnesses d'you think will testify in your favour? No one can stand you here.'

'I wasn't thinking so much of reporting you,' Rath drew his Walther, 'as defending myself. So, who's first?' The brownshirts took a step back. 'If I were you, I'd be setting my sights a little lower. Now, let's talk about Maria Cofalka.'

'That Papist tramp?' one of the SA youths said, catching a hostile glance from his Rottenführer.

'That's not how I'd describe her. I'm Catholic too, and, as luck would have it, you boys are my number one suspects.'

'There's nothing for you here,' Fabeck said. 'You're not

460

authorised, and no one gives a damn what your Isidore in Berlin says. The Prussian Police has been cured of its Jews.'

'You've a real problem with other religions, huh? You boys ought to be more tolerant, especially as Prussians.' He held them in check with his Walther. 'Jews or no, a Prussian Police homicide unit will be questioning you soon enough.'

He left the brownshirts where they were and proceeded to the train station. It was a good feeling, knowing he'd made an enemy of Wengler's thugs at last, and an even better feeling, knowing his bags were already packed.

82

Charly didn't know what to think any more. Where was Gereon? What was going on? Why hadn't the bastard been in touch? It looked like his signature, but she couldn't seriously believe he'd paid a visit to police custody yesterday to kill a prisoner. As for leaving his name behind ... Someone must be playing a nasty trick.

Gennat seemed to think so, too. Even so, he had asked to speak to her once he'd dismissed Böhm and Vosskamp.

Buddha knew about their engagement, and hoped, therefore, that she could shed some light on where Gereon was, and what he was doing. But she couldn't. Gereon Rath was the same unreliable shitbag he'd always been. He went his own way whenever the mood took him, and the rest of the world could go hang. An engagement ring wasn't about to change that.

She fetched the ring from her purse, where she'd kept it ever since that memorable day two weeks ago. She wasn't sure whether to put it back on her finger or hurl it at his feet – if, that is, he ever showed his face again.

Where in the hell was he, goddamn it? She slammed her fist against the table. He had left her his car, his dog, the key to his flat and an engagement ring. Only, there had been no word from him in over a week. Should she be worried? Too late, she already was, but admitting it only made her angrier.

She wondered whether to call the hotel and make a fool of herself. Again.

It was time to go home. She was the only one still here wondering about who'd passed themselves off as Gereon. The guard hadn't asked for an identification, a simple badge had sufficed. Well, any idiot could get hold of a badge, even if it was a punishable offence, and you could always forge a signature. Though in this case the forgery came close to the original, meaning it must be someone who had access to the genuine article. Perhaps she would suggest to Gennat that they looked into it again tomorrow, instead of badgering her with questions she couldn't answer.

The telephone rang, and she started. Erika Voss's direct line when she had gone home hours ago, taking Kirie with her.

Charly hesitated a moment, but picked up. 'Ritter, Inspector Rath's office.'

'Apparatebau Rath, Rath am Apparat.'

She was so taken aback that for an instant she said nothing. Several instants, in fact. She felt tears in her eyes, so relieved was she to hear his voice. The bastard! She held the receiver in her hand and let the tears flow. At least he couldn't see her.

'Hello, Charly? Are you still there?'

'You bastard!' She couldn't think of anything else to say.

'Charly, don't get worked up. I don't have much change. I'm calling from a telephone booth at the train station . . .'

'Which train station?'

'There aren't too many in Treuburg.'

'You're still in Treuburg?'

'Where else?' He ceased playing the comedian. 'Charly, I'm sorry,' she heard him say. 'I know this is late in coming. But . . . I was out of the picture for a while there.'

'A while!' She couldn't help it, it just came out. 'I haven't heard a single fucking word from you in over a week!'

'I was unconscious with fever most of the time.'

'My God, Gereon, what happened?'

'It's a long story, much too long for a trunk call. I'll tell you when I'm home. The main thing is I'm OK.'

'If you're coming back make sure they don't arrest you. There's been a warrant out for the last three hours.' She told him what had happened.

'Someone's played a dirty trick.'

'That's what I think, and perhaps if you'd submitted your report from Treuburg more often, Böhm and Gennat would think so too.'

'They don't seriously believe I'd kill one of Wengler's people?'

'Up until five minutes ago even *I* wasn't sure.'

'A hell of a lot has happened here. That Indian business was a red herring; he isn't our man.'

'How do you know?'

'I was with him. He saved my life.'

'Pardon me?'

'I'll tell you later. Believe me, it couldn't have been him. Long hair, straggly beard. He'd have been spotted right away.'

'That won't please Böhm.'

'Perhaps he'll come round once he hears what I have to say about motive. It *is* a vendetta, we were right, but it isn't about the moonshining scandal, it's about murder. A murder Gustav Wengler committed twelve years ago.'

'Can you prove it?'

'Not yet, but I know. He even made sure someone else was convicted.'

'The man who's out for revenge.'

'No. He died trying to escape, but someone's avenging *him*. Avenging everyone involved. Don't let Wengler out of your sight; I'm pretty sure he's next in line.'

'We're watching him.'

464

'Good.'

'So, who's this mysterious avenger?'

'Some relative, a friend, no idea. I'll know soon enough.'

'What do you have in mind?'

'I need to take care of something here, then I'll be on my way.'

'Aren't you at the train station already?'

'I have a ticket for the overnighter tomorrow evening. I'll be at Bahnhof Zoo the day after tomorrow, just after six. It'd mean a lot if you ...'

'The day *after* tomorrow? What ...?'

The line beeped and the connection was interrupted. She rattled the cradle impatiently. Nothing doing.

'Operator? Why was this call ended?'

'Sorry,' came the reply. 'The caller ran out of money.'

Charly hung up. How was she supposed to get hold of him now? She hesitated before reaching again for the telephone and asking for the *Salzburger Hof*. 'Ritter here, good evening. I'm sorry to disturb you again. I heard that Inspector Rath, your guest from Berlin, is back in Treuburg, and wondered if you could pass on a messa ...'

'I'm sorry, Fräulein Ritter,' the hotelier interrupted. 'Bad timing. The inspector checked out at lunchtime today.'

'Oh ...I see.'

'I do apologise.'

She hung up and stared at the black Bakelite. What in the hell was Gereon up to? The telephone gave nothing away, and at length she took her coat and switched off the light.

As she closed the office door a voice behind her asked, 'All alone?'

It was Harald Dettmann. 'We meet again,' he said, grinning his nasty grin. 'Working late?'

'Leave me alone, Dettmann!' She tried to evade him, but he moved with her, and her evasion became a kind of retreat. He pressed her back into the corridor, towards the glass wall and into the corner. 'Let me go! What is this?'

'I'd never have thought you were such a snitch.'

'What do you want?'

Dettmann shook his head. 'You just *had* to go to your fancy pants hero, didn't you, give him a good suck, then bawl your eyes out on his shoulder.'

'Cut it out! Let me go!'

Dettmann pressed his arms against the wall, trapping her so that she couldn't move left or right. She smelled the sweat of his armpits, his aftershave, and turned her face away. 'Listen to me, lady, then I'll let you go. There's no one here you can go crying to. They've sent your Gereon packing, and everyone else has finished for the night.'

'I'll be reporting this to Superintendent Gennat!'

'What have I ever done to you except voice my opinion? Believe me, there are plenty who think women have no place in Homicide.' He looked down at her with a mix of disdain, hatred and disgust.

Charly felt impotent, and helpless. She had no desire to sit on the toilet crying her eyes out again. She thought of Gereon, how he had fought her corner. OK, so he had played a little dirty, but at least he had done something.

You have to do something too, she thought, *you can't spend your whole life running from men like this.*

Dettmann pushed himself off the wall and stood, wide-legged, observing his victim with a certain satisfaction as he lit a cigarette.

It really was no more than a stupid power game. He had wanted to intimidate her, but was too cowardly to actually do anything. All he was interested in was humiliation.

She looked into his dull eyes, held her ground when he blew cigarette smoke in her face and, without so much as batting an eyelash, aimed a short, sharp kick between his legs.

83

This time Rath dragged Karl Rammoser out of bed. The teacher had thrown on a dressing gown and looked at him bleary-eyed. It wasn't even that late.

'My apologies,' Rath said, 'but I thought as long as the trains are still running to Wielitzken, it's OK to knock on people's doors.'

Rammoser glanced at the time, then at the suitcase by Rath's feet. 'That was the last train.'

'Correct.' Rath cleared his throat. 'Seeing as the sofa in your staffroom is so comfortable, and school hasn't started yet...I wondered if I might ask for your hospitality again.'

Rammoser gestured towards the suitcase. 'Are you planning on moving in?'

'One night only. Tomorrow morning I catch the train to Allenstein, and from there it's on to Berlin. It's just...I don't feel safe in the *Salzburger Hof* any longer. I picked a fight with the SA and it's better they don't know where I am.'

'You did what?' Rammoser gazed to the left and right, but the streets of Wielitzken were deserted. He pulled Rath into the schoolhouse and closed the door. 'Did anyone see you?'

'No one else got off the train.'

'Let's hope the SA haven't got wind of where you're staying.'

'They think I'm in Allenstein, at least that's what I told the hotel. The Rickert family are on good terms with the SA.'

'The daughter, above all,' Rammoser said. He led Rath into the lounge and set two glasses on the table. 'I have to get a fresh bottle from the classroom.'

Rath lit a cigarette. He couldn't help thinking back to his telephone conversation with Charly. Should he tell Rammoser there was a warrant out for his arrest, and that he was suspected of murder? Best not: this SA business had spooked him enough.

'I've brought your clothes,' he said when Rammoser returned. 'Thanks again.'

'No trouble.' Rammoser filled their glasses. 'Now, why would you pick a fight with the SA, in Treuburg of all places? You do know what they're about here, don't you?'

'They're Wengler's thugs, you told me yourself. The same thugs who have Maria Cofalka on their conscience.'

'I'm sorry?' Rammoser set down his glass without drinking from it. 'Why would the SA kill Maria? They beat up Communists, sure, but a harmless librarian?'

'Rottenführer Fabeck didn't deny it.'

'Fabeck? Even in school the boy was a horror. King of the playground, maybe, but hardly the sharpest tool.'

'You know him?'

'I taught him, and he's a sorry example of the human species. But a murderer?'

'Better men than Klaus Fabeck have resorted to murder, believe me. Especially when they can hide behind an organisation.'

'Why? Maria would never have picked a fight with that lot. She wouldn't have gone within ten metres of them. She acted like any person in their right mind, whose head wasn't turned by this Hitler's recent performance in Lötzen. That is to say, she took no notice of the brownshirts. She treated the little shits as if they were still the same schoolboys borrowing books by Karl May and Mark Twain.'

'They aren't schoolboys any more.'

'No.' Rammoser drained the contents of his glass and wiped his mouth.

Rath drank a small sip. This bottle seemed even stronger than the last. 'Maria Cofalka didn't pick a fight with the SA,' he said. 'She became a danger for Gustav Wengler. That's why she had to die.'

Rammoser suddenly appeared very pensive. He topped up their glasses while Rath told him the story of the letters and their contents, and how they had been stolen from his hotel room (though he no more than sketched Hella Rickert's role). He told him how the decisive pages were missing when the letters were returned, the pages that suggested Jakub Polakowski was innocent.

'Damn it,' Rammoser said, when he finished. 'I should have known. I should have protected Maria.'

'How could you have known? I was the first person she told about her correspondence with Radlewski. It's me who failed. It's me who should have protected her.'

'You don't know the full story. At the plebiscite anniversary two years ago, Maria had a little too much to drink. It didn't happen often. She almost never drank, but sometimes I had the feeling that alcohol was the only way she could stomach Wengler acting like the Fatherland's saviour. Anyway – at some point late in the day, when everyone had forgotten Wengler's speech and just wanted to have a good time, she publicly accused him of murder.'

'But she was so shy, so delicate.'

'Maria was stronger than you realise.'

'How did Wengler react?'

'He said she was a drunk who didn't know what she was talking about. Truth be told it was an easy sell. Besides, most people, myself included, thought she was alluding to Martha Radlewski's death.'

'Which was old news.'

'The rumours didn't stick, even in '24. Remember, this was just some alcoholic who'd drunk herself to death. No one blamed Wengler.'

'Which means no one took Maria Cofalka seriously . . .'

'No. Myself and a few friends brought her home. We were afraid she might make a fool of herself, perhaps even put her job on the line. She slept it off, and the next day no more was said on the matter. Maybe she didn't remember, she was pretty drunk.'

'Maybe she needed some Dutch courage to confront the great Wengler.'

'Maybe.'

'It must have taken a little Dutch courage to entrust those letters to me too.'

'Our courageous girl,' Rammoser said, and drank. He turned his face away, and Rath said nothing more.

84

You pack what you need, the rest you will throw on the stove. You take the small case, no deadweight, you can buy the tubocurarine over there. Discovered in transit, drugs will only spell trouble.

Sobotka's wanted poster falls into your hands, and you don't know if you should pack it, or throw it in the oven. Already it has begun to yellow.

Escaped Prisoner.

Wanted: Franz Sobotka, *thirty-two years old, of Altschöneberg, near Allenstein, sentenced to twenty years for the armed robbery of at least fifteen rural savings and Raifeissen banks in the administrative regions of Allenstein and Königsberg. Sobotka, who escaped while engaged in road construction work east of Wartenburg, has been at large since 5th August 1930.*

The description that followed was perfectly adequate, but would have no chance of success.

You remember the day you met Sobotka. A man who never lost his vital energy, he managed to awaken new hope even in you.

Though perhaps hope is the wrong word.

Still, with Sobotka you laughed again for the first time in years; laughed, despite thinking you had forgotten how. In him you found something akin to friendship. After all those years spent thinking mankind was doomed to solitude; that anything else was just an illusion.

Perhaps Sobotka's friendship was an illusion, but still you laughed at his jokes. You were never angry when he teased you, and afterwards flashed his pearly white smile – because you knew he never meant offence. You felt that warmth again, which only friendship can provide, and so what did it matter if it was based on illusion?

Yes, he made your life bearable again, but you never approved of his escape plans, which he harboured and shared with you from the start. You had no desire to escape from these walls, which afforded you a strange security; you wouldn't have known what to do on the outside, if there was anything you could do at all.

Then came the day in early summer when everything changed. *Everything*.

It was the first visitor you'd ever received in Wartenburg, notwithstanding your public defender, who didn't so much defend you during your trial at Lyck District Court as work on you to take a reduced sentence, for the purposes of which he extracted a confession. You let him extract it, of course, through your silence. It was clear the public prosecutor stood in thrall to the Wengler brothers and their corrupt witnesses. They wanted to send you away for murder, make an example of an alleged Polish sympathiser. Even the police officer had given a false statement; said you'd started the fight with the distillery trio, that he'd locked you up for it and released you an hour later.

It wasn't true; you were in that miserable cell more than two hours before you could head out to the lake, and find her.

You no longer recall what happened next. It was as if

472

your soul had already left your body as it sat breathing and staring blankly at the lake, and made its way in search of her, whose earthly form lay dead and pale in the water.

Only in court did you learn you must have been crouched by the water more than an hour holding vigil at her corpse, when the policeman emerged from the forest and felled you with the butt of his rifle. The same man who prevented you from saving her life.

There was only one question in that courtroom left unresolved: the true identity of Anna's killer.

You had to wait ten years for an answer.

You couldn't place her at first, sitting on the visitor's chair, shy, hands on her lap, gaze lowered. Wartenburg was no place for a woman like her. Only when she lifted her head and looked at you, did you recognise her.

Maria. The librarian.

You could have almost cried, so greatly did it move you, so little had you expected it. Here was someone from your former life.

She lowered her voice and told you an incredible tale, mentioned there was a witness to Anna's death.

That she knew who Anna's killer was.

By the time visiting was over, your views on jailbreak had gone full circle.

To Sobotka's great delight. For you were part of his plan. They always chained you together during the construction work prisoners carried out in the summer of 1930. The steel ankle shackles kept your hands free so that you could work.

Guards with carbines looked on. They relied more on the shackles than their rifles. The chains could only be cut by a blacksmith prepared to involve himself with escaped convicts.

Sobotka knew which guard was the most careless, having spent months planning and observing the routines, waiting for the decisive moment when the midday heat was at its peak, and the man responsible for your sector sat in the shade and dozed, and almost fell asleep.

It worked out better than you could have hoped.

You made it to the forest before he raised the alarm. There you could let go of the chains, the jangling no longer mattered; you just had to reach the lake before the wardens arrived with the dogs. It would take time for the canine unit to be deployed.

There were many lakes in the woods near Wartenburg, and you chose the first you came upon. It had no landing stage, no boat, nothing. You managed to swim across, just, already you could hear the yapping of hounds as you emerged from the water on the other side. Sobotka grinned, because he knew the dogs would lose your scent at the shore.

Even the shackles didn't concern him; the railway line to Insterburg ran through the middle of the forest.

'Not dangerous,' he had explained with a characteristic grin when mentioning it for the first time. 'Not dangerous.'

You nodded back then, because you didn't take his crazy ideas seriously. Because for you they were just theories that could never be implemented in practice.

And yet . . .

The railway line was the only sign of civilisation far and wide.

It was quiet, a few birds chirruping, wind rustling in the treetops. No dogs. They had lost your scent.

Sobotka lay on the track bed and instructed you to follow suit. On the outside. 'It isn't so dangerous there,' he said.

'I don't think it's dangerous at all.'

'Not for the person on the outside.'

'But for you.'

'So long as there's nothing hanging from the train, it'll be fine. The cars are high enough. I just have to duck.' His grin. 'This is the Prussian Ostbahn. There won't be

474

anything under their trains. No metal parts, no loose screws. Nothing.'

You remember that you believed him. What else could you do? You lay beside him, likewise on your stomach, just the track between you now, and above the track the chain that held your shackles together.

As you lay down you heard the track vibrating.

Sobotka said nothing, simply covered the back of his head with his hands. You were about to follow suit when you shielded your ears to try and block out the vibrations, which were accompanied now by a rattling sound.

The train was approaching.

85

The longer the conversation went on, the worse Charly felt. As if yesterday's grilling wasn't bad enough, there was now the matter of Gereon's telephone call. She had told Gennat about it straightaway, and there had been no let-up since. 'You know this means you're shielding a wanted man.'

'I'm not shielding anyone. I don't know where he is. You think he's any more open with me?'

'Unless something has changed, you're engaged so, yes, I'd expect a degree of openness between you. Besides, it was *you* he called, no one else.'

'He called headquarters!' Charly lit a cigarette angrily. 'I just happened to be there.'

'But you didn't tell anyone.'

'It was around eight, half past. I told you straightaway this morning. It didn't seem necessary last night.'

She didn't mention how Dettmann had got in the way. She'd been happy just to leave the station without further indignity.

'We could have tipped Warrants off,' Gennat said. 'You know how important time is in our work.'

'Tipped them off...how? He didn't actually tell me where he was.'

'Is that really true?'

'As soon as the connection was interrupted, I telephoned

476

his Treuburg hotel. He checked out yesterday at midday. He was calling from a train station.'

'Then he's still in East Prussia.'

'Or in the Corridor. He was planning on coming back, that much he did tell me.' She didn't say that Gereon wouldn't be arriving until early tomorrow morning. Perhaps all this would have blown over by then. 'At least we know he's alive,' she said, stubbing out the cigarette with enough force to burn a hole in the ashtray. Her anger didn't stem from Gennat's persistence, more that she felt obliged to lie. To *Buddha*, whom she worshipped more than any man she'd ever worked for.

He adopted a more conciliatory tone. 'Wengler's operations manager is killed, Inspector Rath falls under suspicion, and a day later he gets in touch claiming Gustav Wengler's a murderer. It can't be a coincidence, can it?' Charly was tired, weary of these questions. 'Do you believe him? That Wengler, is a murderer?'

'He can't prove it yet. He said so himself.' She looked at Gennat. 'But, yes, I believe him.'

She wondered whether Buddha would buy it. Her tone gave him reason to doubt.

'So who's after Wengler, then? Who is this sinister avenging angel?'

'If Gereon says he'll find out, then you can be sure he will. He'll do everything in his power.'

'That's precisely what I'm afraid of,' Gennat said.

His secretary knocked and opened the door. 'Excuse me, Sir, but Andreas Lange is here to see you. He says it's urgent.'

'Send him in,' Buddha grunted. Moments later, Lange stood in Gennat's office, hat in hand and a little out of breath.

'It's Gustav Wengler,' he said, without taking a seat. 'He's gone.'

'Gone where?' Gennat asked.

'Boarded the train to Danzig at Friedrichstrasse. I could scarcely get on with him.'

'No problem,' Gennat said. 'I'll inform Officer Muhl in Danzig. They can intercept him at the train station, and assume surveillance duties.'

'It's the Free City of Danzig,' Lange said. 'The German Police has no authority there.'

'Perhaps that is why Wengler is headed there, but John Muhl is a Prussian and an old friend. He'll be glad to help.'

86

The night train through the Corridor didn't leave for another four and a half hours, so Rath used the time to visit the jail where Jakub Polakowski had been wrongly interned until his fatal escape attempt two years before. The prison director was happy to receive him, so, shortly after arriving at Allenstein train station, he made his way over by taxi.

The smell of prisons was unmistakable, whether you were in Klingelpütz, Plötzensee or Tegel: urine and sweat, mixed with dust and steel and fear. As soon as he passed through the security gates he knew he was in a place of confinement. Wartenburg Jail had originally been conceived as a monastery and, certainly, he knew of no other detention facility with a church steeple as the dominant feature. It was almost idyllically situated on a peninsula, separated from Wartenburg town centre with its brick church by the mill pond.

Rath doubted whether the prisoners would appreciate the view, but...

Imagine Polakowski languishing here, his lover murdered by the man who helped send him to jail.

A guard entered the waiting room. 'The director will see you now.' He had been ushered into the estate house at Luisenhöhe to meet Gustav Wengler with similar words. The prison director's office was on the small side, but looked across the water onto the town. Clearly, East Prussian officials understood the value of a good view.

Prison Director Karl Henning was a thin man with even thinner hair, who greeted Rath kindly and offered him a rickety chair.

'Beautiful location,' Rath said, cautiously taking his seat. The chair felt as if it might snap at any moment. 'May I smoke?'

'Feel free.' Henning gestured towards an ashtray on the desk, and Rath took out his case. 'Are you interested in someone in particular?'

'Yes, Director. Jakub Polakowski. Sentenced to life imprisonment for murder. Committed on 7th November 1920.'

'You're aware the man is dead? He perished during an escape attempt.'

'Yes, but I'd like to know whether he had any relatives or close friends. Who visited him during his time here?'

'I can tell you exactly. We keep a book.' Henning reached for the telephone on his desk. 'Grundmann? Bring me the Polakowski file, Jakub, prisoner four-six-six-slash-twenty.'

Rath still hadn't finished his cigarette when a young, overzealous type appeared with a thin file, which he placed on the director's desk. Henning didn't need long. 'Here we are . . .' He leafed back and forth, as if the odd page were missing, then continued. 'If this is correct, then in the ten plus years Jakub Polakowski was here, he received only one visitor.' He shook his head. 'I remember thinking the man was very isolated, but I didn't realise the full extent.'

'Who visited him, and when? It's very important. The man could have been a killer, someone taking revenge on Polakowski's account.'

'It wasn't a man,' Henning said. He passed the file across the desk and pointed to the name entered there, alongside a full address.

Cofalka, Maria, Librarian, Treuburg, Administrative Region of Gumbinnen, Seestrasse 3.

It wasn't the name he'd been expecting. He'd reckoned with another Polakowski, some distant relative or other, but in spite, or indeed *because*, of this, he felt the same tingling sensation he always did when potentially decisive developments began to emerge.

'This was just a matter of days before his escape attempt,' Henning said, shaking his head. 'Tragic. When he finally receives a visit, he chooses to break out and forfeit his life.'

'Perhaps he broke out because he suddenly had a reason to live?'

'You mean, he fell in love with his visitor?' Henning shrugged. 'Perhaps you're right. It wouldn't be the first time.'

'What actually happened? Was he shot?'

'No.' Henning didn't have to consult the file to tell the story. 'Polakowski was engaged in road construction work with a number of other prisoners. A guard lost concentration and he escaped, together with the prisoner he was chained to. A crafty bank robber named Sobotka.'

'They were chained together? Wouldn't that render any escape attempt hopeless?'

'That's what we thought,' Henning said. 'That only a madman would try it. Or, rather *madmen*. Whatever, Sobotka managed it – we're still looking for him today.' Henning adopted a serious expression. He didn't enjoy discussing the subject. 'And Polakowski, the poor fellow, whom Sobotka had incited to flee in the first place, was the one who died.'

'Go on.'

The director explained how they had found Polakowski's corpse on the railway line between Allenstein and Insterburg. Of Sobotka there was no trace.

'Could I take another look at the file?' Rath asked.

Moments later Rath sat with the Polakowski file in an empty office, whose windows looked onto a prison

481

courtyard. In the watchtower two men stood with loaded carbines. He lit a cigarette and leafed through the file. A serious man gazed out of the photo, a man who had abandoned hope.

He checked the date in the visitor log. *Maria Cofalka, Treuburg librarian, residence ibidem, Seestrasse 3* had visited Prisoner Jakub Polakowski on 27th July 1930 at 17h, a Sunday. Exactly a week after the plebiscite anniversary during which she'd accused Gustav Wengler of murder.

Maria Cofalka had let Polakowski in on her secret! Following her visit, prisoner 466/20 had a reason to live again, but not because he had fallen in love with the librarian. Not love, but hatred, had been the driving force behind his escape, which took place one and half weeks later, at one thirty on a Tuesday afternoon. Shortly after five they had recovered his corpse.

The prison file came to a close on that date, 5th August 1930, with the stamped remark: *Deceased*.

Rath leafed back to the photograph. The sight set something inside him in motion, a vague feeling which he tried, once more, to grasp until, all of a sudden, he realised what it was. He knew this man. His appearance might have changed, but the eyes left him in no doubt. It was a man he had met a short while ago, but not in Treuburg. In Berlin.

87

Charly felt a little queasy inside. It was her first armed operation, and she was still a relative novice with the gun. Gennat had insisted she take it.

Buddha himself held position in the Castle. By his own account, Hartmut Janke lived on the fourth floor, and for the overweight superintendent that was a step too far. He had enough difficulty negotiating the single flight of stairs up to A Division. Perhaps – and it wasn't just Charly who thought this – it was why he was wont to sleep in his office, where he'd had a small bedroom made up years ago for those nights he was obliged to work late. Such nights were commonplace for Gennat, as they were for any CID officer who took the job seriously. Nights such as tonight.

It was already gone eight when the uniform cops took up position in the stairwell. By now all escape routes were blocked, with additional officers posted in the courtyard and on the street below. The squad leader nodded to Böhm, and he knocked on the wooden door. No response. Böhm knocked a second time.

'Herr Janke? Are you there? Please excuse the late interruption, but I need to speak with you urgently. CID. We have some questions regarding the *Haus Vaterland* murder three weeks ago. It won't take long.'

There was nothing from behind the door.

Charly was wondering if she should volunteer her lock-picking skills, when Böhm wound back and aimed a mighty kick at the door frame, lifting it off its hinges. Wood splintered, and there was a loud crack.

Uniform stormed the apartment.

Charly followed at a respectful distance, weapon drawn for form's sake. She held it primed, barrel in the air, but only because it looked better, and she didn't want to embarrass herself in front of colleagues.

She had told Gennat and Böhm about Gereon's call right away. The first thing Buddha said was: 'I hope you know where he is this time.'

'Not right this moment, but I do know he telephoned from a jail.'

'Pardon me?'

'From Wartenburg, a jail in East Prussia. He recognised Janke, aka Polakowski, from the files.'

Gennat had acted immediately, enlisting a squad of a hundred officers in case Polakowski should attempt to resist arrest or flee. In the rear courtyard uniform cops stood at every entrance and exit point, stretching all the way to Müllerstrasse. Even in Wedding, such a large police presence didn't go unnoticed.

No one was home. They swept the flat in less than thirty seconds. The windows were all closed from the inside, meaning Janke hadn't fled via the fire escape. Böhm made a beeline for the bedroom and wardrobe. The hangers were all empty except for one, which held the uniform of the Berlin Security Corps.

Otherwise the cupboards had been cleared. Even the bed had been stripped. There were no pictures, though the tiny holes in the wallpaper revealed that any number of items must have hung above the desk. Charly found a scrap of newspaper on the floor. It was scarcely yellowed. A black

484

line that might have been part of a border was the only sign of printer's ink.

It looked like it was the only trace the man had left behind. The squad officers handed over to Forensics, but they found nothing either: no red handkerchiefs, no envelopes, no tubocurarine, not even any fingerprints.

'It's as if he wiped everything down before leaving,' said Charly.

'What about the uniform?' Böhm asked.

'No prints, if that's what you mean. Looks as if it's been dry-cleaned.'

'Take a look at this.' A second technician had lifted a plank from the wooden floorboard between the hallway and parlour. Right under the door frame. 'It's hollow under here.'

'So?'

Charly and Böhm drew closer. The ED man shrugged in disappointment. 'Empty.'

Even so, Charly felt sure this was where Janke kept the items that a routine police check would have no business uncovering. 'See if you can't find something. After all ...' she said.

'What do you mean? It's empty.'

'I mean, little things. Things you might need a magnifying glass for, and better light. Glass shards, perhaps, or dried liquid residue, anything like that. Then check if the glass might be part of a hypodermic syringe, or if the liquid's curare.'

In the corner where three rooms abutted one another was a small, pot-bellied stove. Charly took a handkerchief and opened the hatch. 'There's ash inside,' she said, and one of Kronberg's men rushed over. 'It's still warm.'

The technician took the poker and carefully probed the ashes. It was mostly paper. Then he fished something from the black-grey mass which disintegrated upon touch, the only thing to have survived the gorging flames. Just a little edge of paper, but it was clear it was from a death notice. A few of the letters were even legible:

> *thy victory*
> *omable wisdom*
> *suddenly and unex*
> *sy life.*

Now Charly was certain. They had found his hideout; it was really him.

Hartmut Janke, the guard who had provided information so willingly in *Haus Vaterland*, had previously been known as Jakub Polakowski, and he had killed four men.

88

Rath saw them as the train pulled in: a dog and its mistress. Was he imagining things or did Charly look ever so slightly peeved? She certainly wasn't carrying a bouquet of flowers. Quite the role reversal, he thought. Three weeks ago he and Kirie had waited here, perhaps even on the same platform, although on that occasion her train had arrived from the west.

He waved, but they still hadn't seen him. Of course, she had every right to be peeved. Even so, he hoped she was a little glad to see him, just as he was glad to see her standing there with Kirie.

He was among the first to alight from the train and, as he did so, a smile appeared on her face after all. There you are, see!

He pushed past the other travellers streaming onto the platform, until, finally, he reached them. Kirie wagged her tail wildly, dancing excitedly back and forth, and Charly gazed at him sternly, smiling all the while. He took her in his arms and held her fast, buried his nose in her hair and breathed in her scent like an addict. 'I'm sorry,' he whispered in her ear.

'About what?'

'Everything. About being away so long, about your not knowing where I was.' He looked at her. 'I was missing in action.'

487

'You're telling me.'

'Seriously. I got lost in the forest. I would have died on the moors, but for ...' He broke off. 'I'd rather tell you at home over a cup of coffee.'

'Coffee's waiting.'

'Great – what about Polakowski?' They descended the steps to the car.

'Gave notice to his employer and cleared his flat.'

'Hopefully he didn't smell a rat. Or perhaps he's en route to his next vic ... Where's Wengler?'

'Danzig.'

'Danzig? His home city.'

'We suspect he's visiting family there. Local CID are informed. They met him at the train station, and won't let him out of their sight.'

'We should send on a description of Polakowski, ideally with a photo.'

'What photo?'

'From his prison file.'

'You said Gustav Wengler was a killer?'

'I'd stake my next promotion on it.'

'Whenever that might be.' Charly laughed, then grew serious again. 'You know he's wriggled his way out of this bootlegging business. He shopped his operations manager, Dietrich Assmann.'

'The dead man from the cells?'

'Precisely.'

'Then Wengler's behind his murder, too. Perhaps he told this police impersonator to use my name, as a little payback for making his life hell in Treuburg.' He looked at Charly. 'Let's hope he can't wriggle his way out of a murder rap. He's already eliminated one potential witness.'

'What do you mean?'

'Maria Cofalka, the librarian from Treuburg. The trouble is, we can't prove anything. The only person who saw Gustav Wengler killing his fiancée twelve years ago wouldn't make much of an impression in court. That's assuming we can lure him out of his forest in the first place.'

'Radlewski?'

'An oddball, for sure, but no killer. If he has any role in this case, it's as a witness. At least, in theory.'

They reached the Buick, which Charly had parked beneath the railway bridge on Hardenbergstrasse. Rath was so busy stowing his case on the dickey that he failed to notice the three men until it was too late. All carried pistols.

'I hope you're not going to make any trouble, Rath,' said one.

He turned around. Wilhelm Böhm's service revolver was trained on him.

'What the hell is this? You're arresting me? When I'd have come in straight after breakfast!'

'Better safe than sorry.' Böhm gestured towards the road where a green Opel had pulled over. Rath started towards it. Kirie didn't understand what was happening, and ran back and forth between master and Buick. Charly was inconsolable.

'I'm sorry, Gereon. I had no idea. They must have followed me.' She threw Böhm a hostile glance, and suddenly Rath knew things weren't half as bad as they seemed. For the first time they shared a common enemy: Wilhelm Böhm. It was almost enough to draw a smile. Maybe she was starting to realise what a bastard he was.

He sat on the rear seat of the green Opel, and greeted the driver. 'Mertens. I'm sorry you were awakened so early on my account.'

'Don't worry about it, Sir.'

A plain-clothes officer whom Rath didn't recognise threw his case into the boot, and Böhm heaved his heavy frame onto the rear seat. 'Looks like you'll be taking your breakfast at headquarters,' he said, and signalled for Mertens to start.

In the rear mirror Rath saw Charly and Kirie standing next to the Buick, growing ever smaller until a bus crossed Hardenbergstrasse and they disappeared from view.

89

At least Böhm hadn't put cuffs on him.

'Are you actually arresting me?' Rath asked as the car passed the roundabout by the Gedächtniskirche.

'I have a warrant, but I'm appealing to your common sense.'

'Sir, this is ridiculous! Arresting me like a criminal. Somewhere out there, someone is dying with laughter.'

'The magistrate saw grounds for a murder charge. That isn't to say I share his opinion.'

'Then why are you arresting me?'

'Because I can,' Böhm growled. The rest of the journey passed in silence, but when Rath saw the cake tray in Gennat's office he knew everything would be all right, in spite of Buddha's frosty greeting.

'Inspector Rath,' he said. 'Do we really have to *arrest* you to make you submit your report?'

'It's a simple misunderstanding. I . . .'

Gennat interrupted him. 'It is anything but a misunderstanding. We had no other way of ending your game of hide-and-seek. Now, will you please tell us what is going on? What have you been doing in East Prussia? Then we might understand why Dietrich Assmann had to die, and the charges against you can be dropped.'

'With respect, Sir, and as I've already said to Böhm here, I'd have come in straight after breakf . . .'

'Well,' Buddha said. 'What's wrong with having your breakfast *here*?' He poured coffee. 'I hope you had a good trip.'

Rath sat. 'Yes, Sir, thank you. At least there was no flying involved.' He lit an Overstolz and took a sip of coffee. For the moment he ignored the cake Gennat had shovelled on his plate, and focused on telling his story from beginning to end. The only details he omitted were the exact circumstances of Hella Rickert's theft.

By the time he'd finished, Gennat had demolished three slices of cake. 'You're certain about this Anna von Mathée's death?'

'Quite certain. Radlewski would have no cause to implicate an innocent man. In fact he blames himself for failing to prevent Anna's murder. I think these diaries were a way of alleviating his guilty conscience. There's no reason to doubt them.'

Gennat agreed, and for once even Böhm seemed convinced.

'So this Radlewski saved your life,' Gennat said. 'And you're certain that Polakowski is the man with four people on his conscience?'

'Working as a guard in *Haus Vaterland* he'd have opportunity. There was no need for him to leave the crime scene afterwards, because no one suspected him.'

'Do you have a photo?' Böhm asked.

'In the prison file – in my suitcase.'

Böhm snapped it open and took the photograph from the file. 'We should show this to Constable Scholz, from the traffic tower. Perhaps he'll recognise his attacker.'

Gennat nodded, and Böhm disappeared with the photo.

'Now that we're alone,' Buddha said. 'I'm aware of your issues with Böhm, but the fact that you didn't even contact your fiancée ...I'm afraid *that* I simply can't let slide. You need to apologise to Charly, and make sure you never treat her like that again, otherwise you'll have me to deal with and, believe me, that's a road you take at your peril.'

Rath felt almost moved that Buddha was so concerned for Charly's well-being. 'Beg to report: I have already apologised, and it won't happen again.'

'Good. Now eat your nutcake.' With Gennat, that, too, was an order it paid to obey. 'What I'm wondering is,' Buddha continued, 'if you're right, and everything up to this point has been a prelude to the killing of Gustav Wengler, then why hasn't Polakowski done the deed by now? The man was in Berlin for more than a week.'

Rath had his mouth full. He swallowed before answering. 'Wengler was under surveillance the whole time, wasn't he?'

'He still is. Danzig CID Chief Muhl called me last night. Wengler's staying at the Hotel Eden. Two of Muhl's men are stationed in a car outside.'

'They should stay on him. Polakowski might fall into their hands.'

'Our priority is to warn Wengler about Polakowski.'

'So that he smells a rat, and discovers we've been digging up these old stories? Wengler knows that Polakowski is after him, because that's how Polakowski wanted it. Think of the death notices, the whole rigmarole. With respect, Sir, if we warn Wengler – about something he's probably already aware of – then all we'll be doing is giving him the chance to get rid of incriminating evidence. It's hard enough to pin Anna von Mathée's murder on him as it is.'

'In my view it's more important to prevent a murder than solve one that's already occurred,' Gennat said seriously. 'Wengler is the victim here, or at least potential victim. It's *Polakowski* who's the suspect.'

'My fear is that Wengler will stop at nothing to conceal his own guilt. He had the Treuburg librarian killed when he learned she was in contact with Radlewski.'

493

'What?' Gennat raised his eyebrows. 'You're certain about that?'

'More or less. I think he roped in the local SA to do his dirty work. Its members are in thrall to him somehow.'

'Wengler's a Nazi?'

'He doesn't hawk it about,' said Rath, 'but I suspect if he ever officially entered politics, you'd find one of those swastika pins on his lapel.' He replaced his cake fork on the table, and lit an Overstolz in the hope that Gennat wouldn't offer him seconds. It seemed to work. 'I think Wengler has Assmann on his conscience too, and is trying to frame me.'

'While we're on the subject.' Gennat cleared his throat. 'For my part I don't believe you're guilty, but that doesn't mean we can spare you the routine. Fingerprints, identification parade with the guard personnel. That much at least.'

'If it's the only way.'

'I'm afraid it is,' Gennat said. 'We've already requested a comparison of signatures. Whoever broke into Dietrich Assmann's cell made a pretty decent fist of yours.'

Rath wondered who might have provided Wengler with his signature. Hella Rickert? Her father, perhaps? The corrupt small-town policeman, Grigat? There were various possibilities.

The door opened and a black dog entered. A woman stood in the door looking angry.

'Fräulein Ritter. What are you doing here?' Gennat asked.

'I thought I might stop by and see what was happening, after Detective Chief Inspector Böhm snatched my fiancé away without so much as a word. You're not seriously arresting him as a suspect in the Assmann case? If you even *think* about putting him in a cell, I tell you this now. I'll be baking a file in his cake.'

Rath could scarcely conceal his pride.

'As for you,' she shouted. 'Wipe that grin off your face.

494

If you just played things by the book for once, we'd have been spared all this fuss.'

'I've already explained that much, Fräulein Ritter.' Gennat was amused. 'I think he's seen the error of his ways.'

'I should think so too!'

'Why don't you join us?' Gennat clapped the surface of the green armchair next to his. 'Coffee?'

'Thank you.' She sat down, still hopping mad. Rath would have liked to embrace her, but had to make do with ruffling Kirie's fur.

Gennat poured coffee, while Charly lit a Juno. She was beginning to calm down. 'Has Kronberg been in touch?' she asked.

Buddha looked at his watch. 'Right now Superintendent Kronberg will be eating his breakfast, if he's up at all.'

'I mean ED in general. They were planning to work through the night.'

Rath must have had a big question mark on his face.

'We found a few items in Janke, aka Polakowski's, flat yesterday,' Gennat explained. 'Kronberg promised us the results today.'

Charly stood up to leave with Gereon, but Gennat held her back. 'Fräulein Ritter, could you stay a moment, please? I need to speak with you, in private.'

'Certainly, Sir.'

She shrugged at Gereon as he exited the office, wondering what Gennat wanted that couldn't have been discussed before. Buddha poured more coffee and she lit another cigarette. 'Would you like some more cake?'

'No, thank you, Sir.'

'I wanted to thank you, Fräulein Ritter, for your contribution here. You've provided sterling service.' It sounded like goodbye. She said nothing. 'It is not least thanks to your efforts that our investigation here will soon be concluded, give or take the odd warrant.' He looked her in the eye, and she could see he wasn't finding this easy. 'Superintendent Wieking wants you back, and I'm afraid I'm running out of reasons to keep you, Charly. From Monday you'll report to G Division.' Buddha proffered a hand. 'It was a pleasure working with you. Think fondly of us.'

She shook his hand. 'Perhaps there'll be other opportunities to collaborate.'

'Perhaps.' Gennat didn't sound as if it were likely.

Charly smiled bravely but, in the corridor outside she could have cried. So, it was back to G Division, back to Karin van Almsick and Wedding youth gangs, to neglected children and fallen girls. She had always known her stint in Homicide could be no more than an interlude; that, for women CID officers, day-to-day policing occupied a different plane.

And now, of all times, here came Dettmann! The inspector eyed her suspiciously, but kept a respectful distance. It didn't stop her from smelling his aftershave as he passed. Pitralon? Whatever it was, it was overpowering. He must have applied it liberally, as if he had just bought himself a new bottle.

She stopped and turned around. Dettmann had disappeared inside his office. An idea flashed through her mind, something so fantastic she could hardly take it seriously. Yet it wouldn't let go.

90

Rath had difficulty keeping his eyes open. He was lacking in sleep, and motivation, having too little to do with ongoing investigations in the Castle. Somehow he felt he no longer belonged, and Böhm made little effort to disabuse him of the notion. He was more or less a spare part while others went about their work. At his desk he decided to put a call through to Königsberg. 'Assistant Detective Kowalski, please,' he said to the switchboard girl.

Kowalski was delighted to hear from him, but inconsolable nonetheless. 'My uncle told me what happened, Sir. I'm sorry. I thought I had to report to Grigat, and he sent me back to Königsberg. You know how it is: orders are orders.'

'What did Adamek tell you to say?'

'That you'd requested backup, more men to arrest the Kaubuk. I thought Adamek would stay with you. He did go back into the forest. How was I to know Grigat had put him up to it?'

'Well, anyway, I survived.'

'And now you're back in Berlin.'

'Indeed I am, and I have news.' He told Kowalski the whole story and, though disappointed the Kaubuk wasn't their man, Kowalski was flattered that Rath had kept him in the loop. Indeed, that he had telephoned at all. 'Wengler, a killer? Are you sure?'

'More or less. Only, I don't have proof.'

'There must be something out there.'

'I wouldn't bet on it after twelve years. Besides, if you listen to my superiors, Wengler's a victim who needs protection. For now we have to concentrate on Polakowski. After that, we'll see.'

Kowalski hesitated. 'I wanted to tell you, Sir, how much I enjoyed working with you.' Rath didn't know how to respond. No one had ever told him that before. He mumbled a hasty goodbye and hung up.

Just as he was contemplating taking Kirie for a stroll, Kronberg appeared in Homicide. Rath joined the others in Böhm's office so that he could listen to the forensics man. Charly was nowhere to be seen; what on earth could she and Gennat still be discussing?

'The newspaper scraps from Janke's,' Kronberg said, 'are identical to two death notices found in the Wengler flat. The Lamkau notice, and the Simoneit notice. The Lamkau notice from the *Kreuz-Zeitung* is a 100 per cent match. Regarding Simoneit, we can, at the very least, confirm that the paper is the same as that used to print the *Volkszeitung für die Ost- und Westprignitz*. There are more details here.' He laid the file on the table.

'Many thanks for your efficiency, Herr Kronberg,' Böhm said. The forensics man nodded modestly.

Typical, Rath thought: has his people work through the night, then takes all the glory himself. Böhm was already hunched over the report when Kronberg produced a second file from his leather bag.

'I have something else,' he said. 'It looks as though we've been able to trace the source of the tubocurarine.' That, too, was typical of Kronberg. He always saved the most important news for last.

Strangely enough, they had got there by way of the red handkerchiefs. These didn't, as previously suspected, hail from Berlin, but rather, Königsberg, from a large quantity of fabric and off-the-peg clothing that had been stolen two years before from the Junkerstrasse-based *Moser* firm. The guilty party was a notorious burglary ring that had somehow managed to evade justice, despite its methods being well known to Königsberg Police.

Which was how colleagues there *also* knew that the same ring had broken into the University Clinic two nights later and, besides various drugs and narcotic agents, made off with large quantities of an anaesthetic that was the focus of current institute research. A muscle relaxant based on the curare poison of the South American Indians, obtained from the pareira root. Its name: tubocurarine.

Polakowski, it seemed, had obtained the handkerchiefs and narcotics from one and the same source.

Rath took Kirie by the lead and went out. At Alexanderplatz he found a telephone booth and put in another call to Königsberg.

Not even the dog was there. Without Kirie and Gereon, Charly felt that much lonelier at her desk. She was still in the outer office with Erika Voss, but got along decidedly better with her than during her first days in Homicide. No doubt due to the absence of a certain Gereon Rath.

'The inspector's taken the dog for a walk,' the secretary said, and for a moment, Charly was tempted to head to Alexanderplatz in search of them, but just then Böhm bustled through the door to ask that she have copies of Polakowski's photo made and distributed to all major police stations in Prussia. 'Plus a dozen to Warrants here at Alex.'

She went upstairs to Photographics, which was housed on the same floor as ED. The lab workers were not known for their efficiency, which was why it was best to wait in person and make a nuisance of yourself, otherwise it could take an age to get your prints.

This, then, would be her final act in A Division: having copies made and sent to all and sundry. Nice. Still, it would be a damn sight more interesting than sharing an office with Karin van Almsick again on Monday.

Then there was this business with Dettmann, the scent of his aftershave, and the thought it had triggered. Perhaps she was going mad, but the idea, or, rather, the images, that had flashed through her mind were so realistic it was as if she had lived through them herself. A police officer breaking a prisoner's neck.

She had seen these images often enough in the last few days; it was how her mind worked when speculating on the particulars of a crime. Poor Dietrich Assmann had been murdered over and over again in her imagination, always with the same jerking motion, but now, for the first time, the killer had a face.

91

By the time Rath returned, most colleagues had already finished for the weekend, but Charly sat alone at her desk bagging photos. He recognised Jakub Polakowski's mugshot. 'Can you send one to police headquarters in Königsberg?'

'Done!' She showed him an envelope, addressed to the commissioner.

'Then send another, care of Assistant Detective Kowalski.'

'No problem. We have more than enough prints.' She passed him a photo and an envelope. 'You can take the address from the previous.'

He added a few lines of thanks on lettered paper to go with the photograph. By the time he was finished Charly had bagged at least another five prints and cover notes, but she seemed strangely brusque.

'I'm sorry,' he said. 'I didn't mean to treat you like my secretary ...' He showed her the letter to Kowalski. 'See. I'm not so useless after all.'

'It's fine,' she said, but her face told a different story.

'Has Dettmann been bothering you again?'

'No, no. Don't worry. He's been avoiding me actually.'

'It's better that way.' He felt a certain pride. Perhaps his performance in Dettmann's office had achieved something after all.

Charly forced a smile. 'Soon there'll be no chance of

Dettmann running into me, apart from in the canteen, perhaps.' She hesitated a moment. 'I ... On Monday, I'll be returning to G Division.'

'Your guest appearance is over?' he said, trying to sound sympathetic.

In truth he was relieved. He had been unhappy working so closely with her. It felt restrictive somehow, as if his every move were being monitored, when in fact they'd only spent three days together on the *Vaterland* team. The rest of the time he'd been gadding about in East Prussia. Thinking of her curiosity, and his fondness for secrecy ...well, perhaps it was no bad thing she was being reassigned. But seeing her face, he knew he had to comfort her. He took her in his arms, and in the same instant she began sobbing.

This was the second time in a matter of weeks when, normally, she'd have fought back tears at all costs. For a moment he wondered if she might be pregnant ...

He held her, and she had a good cry on his shoulder. 'Sorry, Gereon,' she said after a while, smiling again amidst the tears. 'I'm just a silly goose.'

He dabbed at her damp cheeks with his handkerchief. 'No,' he said. 'You're not a goose.'

It took a moment for the penny to drop, then she started banging her fists against his chest. 'You cad,' she said, but she was still smiling. 'I did know it was only temporary, but somehow it got me when Gennat said I'd be back with Superintendent Wieking from Monday.' She shrugged. 'He's right, though. The investigation's as good as closed. Finding Jakub Polakowski is a job for Warrants now.'

'I'm not so sure. We still don't have anything on Gustav Wengler.'

'You've really got it in for him, haven't you? Don't forget, he's the one in danger.'

'I won't, but it doesn't change the fact that he killed a young girl – and ordered the death of an innocent librarian to cover it up. Then there's his old mucker, Assmann.'

All of a sudden Charly's smile evaporated.

She wanted to tell him, but couldn't. What could she say? Describe the images playing over and over again in her mind, of Harald Dettmann wringing Dietrich Assmann's neck? How she heard the crack of bones breaking, saw Assmann's cigarette fall to floor and Dettmann stamp it out?

No, it would only lead to more strife.

She leaned on his shoulder as he steered the Buick west via Tiergartenstrasse. He threw her a quick sideways glance and put his arm around her. She was surprised at herself, at her need for affection, her reluctance to make trouble. For once, all she wanted was a peaceful weekend.

She gazed at the windscreen wipers struggling against the rain, which had set in just as they were leaving the Castle, and savoured his presence beside her. In the drizzle she could just make out the spire of the Gedächtniskirche. She decided she couldn't hold it in any longer. She had to say something, if only to see how he reacted. 'This business with Assmann. Do you really think it was a colleague?'

'More likely the badge was a fake.'

'Still, I wouldn't put it past ... Dettmann, say.'

'The man's an arsehole, but that doesn't make him a killer. Don't take things so personally.'

'I just mean I wouldn't put it past him.'

'Anyone's capable of murder. That's one of the first things Gennat teaches you.'

'Anyone? Does that include you?'

He hesitated before continuing. 'That isn't funny.'

'Sorry.' She sat up and looked at him. 'I know. That signature business was a dirty trick, but someone like Dettmann is just waiting for a chance like that.'

She could see he was thinking. Even so, she knew what he was about to say. 'It was Gustav Wengler trying to make trouble for me, just like in East Prussia. I'm starting to become a nuisance and I'm telling you, it feels good. It means I'm on the right track.'

'You seem to want to pin something on Wengler at all costs.'

'*Pin* something?' Gereon looked at her, outraged. 'The bastard killed his fiancée! Then cashed in on her death.'

'You can't prove it.'

'Oh, I'll prove it, don't you worry. If not that he killed his fiancée, then Maria Cofalka, or Dietrich Assmann.'

'But he didn't kill *them*, you said so yourself.'

'No.' Gereon gave a bitter laugh. 'Gustav Wengler no longer kills for himself. He has people kill for him. What's the point in being director otherwise?'

'Gereon, I think you're getting too wound up. Talk about taking things personally.'

'Oh, I am, am I? The way I see it, I'm the only one who's actually *interested* in this. Everyone else just wants Polakowski.'

'I hardly think Gennat's taking a murder in police custody lightly.'

'No, but he hasn't questioned Wengler either, has he?'

'Because it wouldn't help matters.'

'Wengler's behind Assmann's murder, it's obvious, so that there's no one left to testify against him.'

'You realise if he'd given him an alibi, we'd have had to let *both* of them go.'

'Perhaps he wanted rid of him. Perhaps Assmann had become a nuisance.'

'Perhaps,' Charly said. 'Just like the others. I didn't get the impression he mourned any of them, not even his brother. You could be right: he wanted rid of Assmann.'

They reached Carmerstrasse, parking outside the gate. 'There's no way he hired Harald Dettmann to do it. The pair don't even know each other.'

504

'No,' Charly said. Gereon was right. Dettmann was so busy with his Phantom, he'd barely checked in with the *Vaterland* team these past weeks. Yet she couldn't shake the image of him breaking Dietrich Assmann's neck; dousing a red handkerchief with water from a Pitralon bottle, tying the hanky to the bedpost as he poured the remaining water over Assmann's face – before covering the dead man's corpse to make it look as if he were asleep.

92

It is quiet now, everyone is asleep. You, too, could use some rest, but you know you will find no peace until you step off the train at Königsberg. The rattling of steel wheels; once upon a time it soothed you, rocking you gently to sleep, but not now, and never again.

Königsberg. It is two years since you were last here, but still you remember where you must go.

The dive bar in Vogelgasse is so narrow you can scarcely believe it has a back room. A back room where, in exchange for money, anything can be yours: information and weapons, narcotics of all kinds, and a new life.

You remember your first visit.

'I need a passport.'

'No problem, but it'll cost you.'

'I have money.'

Sobotka's stash was still hidden in the forest by Allenstein, near a village called Altschönberg, his birthplace. Fifteen thousand marks. Money for Sobotka to start over once he was out; money for you to start over now, yourself.

'There's more.'

'We can get hold of anything.'

'Even tubocurarine?'

'What's that?'

'An anaesthetic adjuvant. They're using it for research

purposes at the University Clinic, Department of Anaesthetics. Lange Reihe.'

'We don't need the address.' You recall the suspicion in his eyes as he looked you up and down. 'It won't come cheap.'

'I told you: I have money.' He looked down wide-eyed as you laid a thousand-mark note on the desk. 'Four more, if you can get hold of everything, and grant me a small favour.'

'We don't kill people.'

'No.' You showed him the iron shackle under the right trouser leg of your elegant new suit. 'I need to get rid of this. Today.' You knew then that you had won his respect. 'I need some addresses. Four East Prussians, who moved west from Marggrabowa.'

'It's called Treuburg now.'

You nodded. You were aware that the world had changed. You passed a note across the desk containing the names, along with your additional requests.

You are rid of the shackles the same day, and, two weeks later, you have everything you need. A new identity, four addresses, and enough tubocurarine to kill an elephant.

The rattle of the train keeps you awake, eating away at your thoughts and rekindling unhappy memories.

The vibration of the tracks.

The railway line in the pine forest near Wartenburg.

Sobotka on the crossties, hands on the back of his neck, the ankle chain that binds you straddling the shiny metal.

You pull your legs outwards so that the chain sits tight as possible on the tracks.

By now the vibrations come paired with other noises. You choose not to protect your neck, covering your ears as the train rushes towards you, growing ever louder. You cover your ears and pull the chain tight, awaiting the inevitable.

Even covering your ears, the train is so loud that you start to shake; beads of sweat run down your skin, making you grow cold, as the wind rages all around.

You close your eyes and wait for it to be over – but it takes an age.

A cacophony sweeps over you, a violent screech, thunder and rumble, and you are shaken by a painful blow to your leg.

You wait for the ear-splitting roar to die, not daring to move. You hear more screeching, further and further away until, at last, it subsides.

You open your eyes. Pain in your right leg. Instinctively you reach for it, but feel no wound. The chain has loosened, it must have struck against your shin, a bruise, nothing more.

You'll limp, perhaps, but you'll carry on. Both of you must now make yourselves scarce. The driver has halted the train and will soon sound the alarm. It will take time for them to get out here and pick up your trail, but it won't take forever.

You sit up. Your triumphant grin fades when you gaze towards the track bed.

Sobotka's powerful frame looks almost unscathed, but he is now lying on his back. A hand is missing, so too his face.

Something struck his head, or perhaps his head met with the onrushing train. All you know is that his grin, which could banish all dread from this world, has been replaced by a bloody pulp.

You feel sick, but the fear makes you act, the fear of being locked up again.

Someone is thinking in your place as you remove your prison garb and switch it with Sobotka's. Swap your number 466/20 with his 573/26.

Then you strike out into the forest, moving as fast as you can. Before the driver arrives, before the search party arrives, before the dogs arrive. Before they find the dead man with the prison number 466/20.

You run through the forest and scream; despite everything that has happened, you are overcome by a hitherto unknown sense of exhilaration. It is freedom you feel: a freedom that only death can provide.

93

Rath had no choice but to lie. It was true that he couldn't meet her for lunch in the police canteen, he just hadn't been entirely honest as to why.

'I'm out in the field,' he had said, and he had indeed canvassed several of the witnesses who claimed to have seen Jakub Polakowski in Berlin over the weekend. Still, he was finished with that long before the lunch break. As predicted, all three visits were in vain. An old lady suspected her neighbour, whose radio was constantly blaring; an unemployed bookkeeper's report had clearly been driven by boredom; which left only the third witness, a kiosk owner, who claimed to have seen Polakowski at Schlesischer Bahnhof on Friday. When Rath showed him the photo, which was considerably sharper than the copy in the newspapers, he nodded. 'That's him, I'd wager. Saw him Friday morning carrying a small case.'

The man couldn't say where Polakowski was headed, couldn't even remember the exact time. Rath made a few notes, but held little hope of picking up his trail. You could go almost anywhere from Schlesischer Bahnhof, which had its own S-Bahn platform.

He'd finished his list around twenty past eleven, but chose not to return to Alex. Instead he'd lied to Charly, on the day they'd made their engagement public in the Castle. Gennat had announced it that morning in briefing, and Harald Dettmann gazed stonily in Rath's direction as others joined the applause.

They could have been in the canteen toasting the fact that everyone knew. Instead, he was moving through Friedrichshain towards the banks of the Spree. Walking down Mühlenstrasse, cigarette dangling and hands in his coat pockets, he proceeded towards the Oberbaum Bridge and the Osthafen where, this time last year, Red Hugo, head of the *Berolina* Ringverein, had vanished without trace.

The black Adler sedan that rolled past and stopped on the street corner looked out of place in a neighbourhood like this, characterised as it was by industry, poverty and petty crime. Even so, its paintwork didn't have so much as a scratch. Everyone here knew who the vehicle belonged to, as, of course, did Rath.

The driver's door opened, and a well-dressed Chinese emerged. The man wore a long, black ponytail under his hat, and nodded briefly at Rath as he opened the rear door.

'Thank you, Liang,' Rath said, taking his place on the back seat, next to a powerfully built man who put the papers he'd been reading to one side.

'Long time, no see, Inspector,' said Johann Marlow.

'I've been out of town.'

'Might I invite you for lunch? There's a Chinese restaurant close by.'

'Thank you, I already have plans.'

'Let's take a little drive.' Marlow gave Liang a signal and the sedan started rolling. They turned onto Warschauer Strasse.

'Thank you for meeting me like this,' Rath said, though it went against the grain to express gratitude to such a man. He needed his help though, so had grasped the nettle once more. As time passed he grew increasingly inured to its sting.

Marlow had always behaved honourably towards

511

him, which was more than could be said for some of his so-called colleagues. Arseholes like Harald Dettmann and Frank Brenner, or traitors like Bruno Wolter and Sebastian Tornow. Even a man like Andreas Lange didn't always play with an open hand; the same went for Böhm and Gennat, of course, to say nothing of the various police commissioners he had served under.

'What can I do for you?'

Rath lit a fresh cigarette. 'Where would I go if I was looking for a contract killer, here in Berlin?'

Marlow laughed. 'You mean to dispose of your superiors? You won't get any help from me or *Berolina* for that kind of service.'

'What about *Concordia*?'

'Same code. Murder is off limits.'

The Ringvereine controlled organised crime in the city, but nearly all of them shied away from murder, at least those who could afford the luxury of a code of honour.

Marlow looked at him sceptically. 'What would you like to know, Inspector?'

'A witness was killed in police custody last week. By a professional.' He didn't want to reveal any more. Neither that the killer had posed as a police officer, nor, this went without saying, whose name he had used.

'Do you think *Concordia* are behind it?'

'I think a man named Gustav Wengler is behind it. A suspected bootlegger, who does business with *Concordia*. I believe that, with the help of *Concordia*, Wengler has neutralised a troublesome witness.'

'I'm afraid you're barking up the wrong tree, Inspector!' Marlow tapped a cigarette against the lid of his case.

'What do you mean?'

'*Concordia* no longer have any dealings with Wengler.'

'Only last week *Concordia* men were involved in loading Wengler's moonshine onto a boat at the Westhafen.'

'Also the moment that their long-standing arrangement came to an end.'

'Wait a minute. You're saying *Concordia* deal directly with the Luisenhöhe distillery?'

'*Dealt*. Like I said. How else do you think they get their hands on so many original bottles? And they're important; the Yanks pay top dollar for market products, take it from someone who knows.' Rath thought of the two thousand dollars in his mailbox. 'What's actually inside isn't important. You have to assume our associates over there dilute the product even further. With water and medicinal alcohol, or worse. Poor Yanks.' Marlow shook his head and laughed.

'But this arrangement is now over?'

'The *Pirates* drove *Concordia* out of business, if you ask me with the express approval of Gustav Wengler.' Marlow took a drag on his cigarette. 'If a witness needed eliminating, it'd be Hermann Lapke who ordered it, the head of the *Nordpiraten*.' The gangster grinned. 'If I were you, Inspector, I'd be asking around at police headquarters. Who knows, perhaps you'll find your killer there.'

Rath was astonished. He was certain he hadn't mentioned the police impersonator and his fake badge. Charly's words flashed through his mind – but surely Dettmann had even less to do with a Ringverein than Gustav Wengler?

'What do the *Pirates* have against *Concordia*? I thought it was *Berolina* they had it in for?'

'Lapke's decided to leave us in peace for the time being.' Marlow inhaled appreciatively. 'Though he's leaning on *Concordia* pretty hard. Five of their members have now been killed and, according to the papers, you were the investigating officer.'

'The Phantom.' Rath nodded thoughtfully. 'The victims were all linked to *Concordia* ...'

'No doubt some of them wouldn't want it inscribed on

513

their gravestones, Riemann, the Charlottenburg lawyer, for instance ...but, yes, the Phantom's victims have all been necessary in some way for Marczewski's business deals.'

'Polish-Paule?'

'I wouldn't call him that, unless you want to get yourself shot. Though he's a perfectly charming fellow otherwise.'

'He's Masurian?'

'Prussian, at any rate. Came to Berlin a few years ago from Königsberg.'

'Then Wengler knows him from the old days.'

'Possibly, though they're no longer friends. Marczewski's afraid he's next on the Phantom's list, and went to ground several days ago.'

'So the *Pirates* are behind all the Phantom murders?'

'Lapke's behind them. Ever since he was released from Tegel a year ago, he seems to be on astonishingly good terms with the police.'

'What are you saying?'

'That it's no coincidence he was spared by the *Weisse Hand*, unlike his friend Höller.'

'You're saying Lapke was in cahoots with the *Weisse Hand*?'

'Perhaps he still is.'

'The *Weisse Hand* no longer exists. We broke it last year.'

'The man who kills on Lapke's behalf is one of your colleagues, Inspector, believe me. Whatever name you give him.'

'The Phantom's a sniper; the victim from police custody had his neck broken.'

'I'd be surprised if Lapke gave the job to someone new.'

'So who is it?'

'If I knew that, he'd have been exposed by now. Or killed.'

'You're well informed.'

'In my line, information is the alpha and omega,' Marlow

514

said, and Rath remembered his father's saying. *Knowledge is power*.

He fell silent and stubbed out his cigarette in the ashtray. It was about the same size as the Buick's glove compartment. 'Do you think that Paul Marczewski would be willing to testify against Gustav Wengler?'

'You really want to get this Wengler, don't you?' Marlow said. 'If it hurts the *Pirates*, you have my support. That said, I can't imagine Marczewski will make the greatest impression in court, and he'll hardly be crazy on the idea either. But ...' – he threw his cigarette out the window. – '...I'll see what I can do.'

94

Charly hadn't been at her desk half a day and already felt she was in a rut. At the weekend she had laboured under the illusion that she still worked for Homicide, discussing the dead man in the cells with Gereon and mentioning Dettmann by name on several more occasions. In the meantime her colleagues in G had picked up the girl gang from Wedding. Questioning had taken place while she'd been seconded to the *Vaterland* team, and now she had to sift through the transcripts with Karin van Almsick, looking for contradictions or inconsistencies.

Somehow she couldn't help sympathising with these girls who threatened their fellow U-Bahn passengers with switchblades, which they took great pleasure in opening in front of their victims' faces.

The youngest was fourteen, the oldest seventeen. All were homeless, orphaned girls trying to make ends meet. Charly couldn't help thinking of Alex, whom she'd met a year ago. Where might she be now? Initially she'd feared she might stumble on the name Alexandra Reinhold in the transcripts, and was glad to be proved wrong. Alex, too, had stolen, and used a knife from time to time, but Charly liked her all the same. Hopefully, one way or another, she'd soon have her life back on track, along with her friend Vicky.

'Penny for your thoughts.' Karin van Almsick was a very

nosy colleague. 'Let me guess, you're thinking about him?'

News of their engagement had been made public that morning in G as well as A Division. She'd received the congratulations of her colleagues, and promised to bring a cake the next day. 'Actually, no,' she said. 'If I'm honest, I don't think of Gereon much at all.'

She tried to focus on the transcripts, but her colleague wouldn't allow it. 'How long have you known one another? Pfeiffer from Juvenile Crime says you worked in Homicide three years ago as a stenographer.'

'That is indeed where I met Gereon Rath. It's plain you're a CID officer.'

Her colleague smiled blissfully, not realising that Charly was being sarcastic. 'How long have you been together?'

'We were together and then we weren't – but we got there in the end.'

Karin van Almsick gazed sympathetically. 'How awful!'

'There are other men out there.'

The throwaway remark was astonishing to her colleague. 'You're not serious?'

'Pardon me?'

'About there being other men. You haven't actually...' She seemed fit to burst.

'Yes, there have been other men in my life. Some serious, some not so. You've got to be able to compare. You do it while shopping, so why not when it actually matters?'

Karin van Almsick needed a few moments to close her mouth. She was a country girl, from Wriezen or somewhere, shocked by Berlin morals, or Berlin moral depravity, as she'd no doubt have it. 'Why don't I make us a tea,' she said, and smiled, obviously glad to be escaping temporarily. Charly gazed after her. Better to come out with it now than spend the next God knows how long beating about the bush.

Karin van Almsick returned from the tea-kitchen sooner

than expected. The door flew open and she stood in the office, minus the teapot but short of breath and white as a sheet. 'There's someone outside,' she said.

'So?'

She took a deep breath, looking as though she'd just encountered the Devil himself. 'A Negro,' she said at length. 'Charly . . .there's a Negro outside who wants to speak with you.'

95

Rath couldn't bear the waiting, but what choice did he have? What a crackpot idea, going to Gennat *now*! Did he really think he'd be waved straight through? But that was just it, he wasn't thinking, or at least, he wasn't thinking straight. He had knocked, and Trudchen Steiner had motioned for him to take a seat, and so now here he was, and there was nothing he could do.

The mood he was in, it was torture. There were a thousand things he'd rather be doing than waiting for an audience with Gennat, but perhaps it was better he couldn't do them now. Better he couldn't storm into her office and ask who the hell she ate lunch with whenever he turned her down.

Finishing with Marlow, he had wanted a quick snack before returning to the Castle. He'd never have gone near *Aschinger* if he thought she'd be there. Instinctively he sought cover behind a fat woman in the queue, his guilty conscience at work, as ever, following his latest rendezvous with the gangster.

That was when he saw she wasn't alone. In *Aschinger* of all places, where half the station went for their lunch, she sat in full view: Fräulein Charlotte Ritter, newly engaged to Herr Gereon Rath, as most colleagues knew since this morning, eating her lunch without her fiancé. Only, she wasn't alone.

Alongside at her window table was a black man. A black man who displayed his dazzling white teeth just as Rath looked over. Charly was laughing about whatever it was he'd said, so fixed on her companion that she failed to notice her fiancé in the queue. Rath resisted the temptation to give the man a good smack, choosing, instead, to beat a retreat.

If he hadn't just come from meeting Johann Marlow he'd have taken her to task, and hounded the black out of the restaurant, but if there was one thing Charly must not know it was Marlow's excellent relationship with the Berlin Police, viz. Gereon Rath. So, perhaps it was wise that he hadn't. Even if it'd have made him feel better. Perhaps.

What kind of man was this? Why was she meeting him, and why had she never mentioned a black acquaintance? One thing was for certain: this was no lawyer.

He stared at the Hindenburg portrait in Gennat's outer office and tried to think of something else, but the same images kept flitting through his mind. Charly, sitting with a black man, laughing. Trudchen Steiner finally stopped the merry-go-round in his head. 'The superintendent will see you now.'

Ernst Gennat sat at his desk. 'What is it that's so important?' he asked.

My fiancée is having secret meetings with a Negro.

'How is Officer Dettmann getting on with the Phantom case?'

It wasn't the most poised opening. Gennat eyed him suspiciously. 'Do you want your old case back, Inspector?'

Of course he did, and if he could take Gustav Wengler down at the same time, so much the better. 'Of course not, Sir, it's . . .' He lit a cigarette. Rarely had he felt so nervous in this office. Perhaps it was because his thoughts kept turning to Charly. 'I might have some fresh insight regarding the case . . .'

520

'I thought the *Vaterland* team was focusing on the search for Jakub Polakowski?'

'Precisely how I came upon the information, Sir, or rather, in connection with our investigation into Gustav Wengler.'

'Your primary concern should be Polakowski,' Gennat said. 'He's our suspect. Wengler is the victim, or *potential* victim. We are keeping him under surveillance to protect him.'

'With respect, Sir, Gustav Wengler is a killer, and bootlegger, who had his long-time operations manager murdered to conceal his shady deals.'

'That's little more than a theory at this stage.'

'I have evidence to substantiate it. Wengler has played two Ringvereine against each other, by switching allegiance from *Concordia* to the *Nordpiraten*.'

'What are you driving at?'

'The murder in police custody could be the work of the Phantom. The man kills on Hermann Lapke's behalf – who was doing his new business associate Wengler a good turn.'

Gennat's expression grew serious, even startled, as he reached for the telephone. 'Fräulein Steiner, under no circumstances am I to be disturbed in the next ten minutes. Not even by you.' He hung up. 'Who have you already spoken to about this?'

Charly's meeting a Negro.

'Spoken to?'

'About your suspicion.'

'No one, Sir. You're the first.'

'Then let it stay that way.' Gennat furrowed his brow. 'Tell me how your suspicion came about. The Phantom is a sniper, and Assmann had his neck broken.'

'It had to be done quickly, and police custody is the worst possible place for a sniper.'

'Where do you have your information?'

'An informant from the *Berolina* Ringverein told me the Phantom is Lapke's personal hit man.'

'*Berolina* ...'

'Yes. A Ringverein on good terms with *Concordia*, in whose orbit most, if not all, of the Phantom's victims moved.'

'You think the *Pirates* are stirring things up again?'

'Perhaps even Lapke himself.' Rath lowered his voice. 'There are whispers that Lapke was in league with the *Weisse Hand* last year, and that this Phantom is a remnant, so to speak, of that time. Which would mean ...'

' ...the Phantom's a police officer,' Gennat said.

'Which also explains how he gained access to the cells. All we have to do now is show the guard from Wednesday evening pictures of all CID offic ...'

'I fear that could be tricky. Herr Studer has been missing for three days.' Gennat adopted a conspiratorial expression. 'What I'm about to tell you, Inspector, must stay in this room. Can I rely on you?'

'Of course, Sir.'

Gennat threw him another searching glance before continuing. 'The Phantom killings actually began in autumn '31, shortly after the *Weisse Hand* was broken. We suspect someone slipped through our fingers at the time, who has since made a career of his hobby. A lucrative one, at that.'

'Murdering criminals or their accomplices, and earning money on the side.' Rath stubbed out his cigarette. 'So it really is a police officer?'

'Not a word to anyone, do you hear.' Gennat gave him a piercing look, and Rath nodded as if hypnotised. 'We are not only certain it's a police colleague. We know which one.'

522

96

A further four days passed, and still Jakub Polakowski hadn't been found. By now all major police stations in Prussia had a photo, and Warrants had scoured the whole of Berlin, along with every town Polakowski had visited during his vendetta.

The Danzig Criminal Police had also been issued with photos, but Polakowski hadn't appeared outside Wengler's hotel, the Eden, where the distillery owner occasionally met with lawyers or family members. Clearly he wanted to put his dead brother's affairs in order, and perhaps do a little bootlegging on the side.

The man had been in his home city for a week now, and Rath wondered when he would return to business in Treuburg, especially since his manager was dead and the distillery was operating without a leader. Perhaps he had already anointed a successor? Whatever, he'd have to return tomorrow at the latest, since there was no way someone as politically-minded as Gustav Wengler would miss the Reichstag elections.

The previous four days had been hard on Rath. Buddha's secret weighed heavily. He'd have liked to tell Charly, but it was Gennat's express wish that not even she be admitted. The secrecy was worse than last year, when they had disbanded the *Weisse Hand*, a clandestine troop of frustrated police officers who had taken it upon themselves to eliminate career criminals using vigilante justice.

Apparently the troop's last remaining member was still out there killing, only now he did so against a fee. Rath wasn't entirely surprised when Gennat gave him the name. 'Detective Inspector Dettmann.'

'Dettmann, but you gave him his own case? Why, so he can eliminate all evidence?'

'There is no evidence. I wanted to lull him into a false sense of security.'

'You'd have been better making an arrest.'

'Without proof, that's not possible.'

Gennat was right. They had no proof, only clues that would never stick in court, and would have to be patient.

As luck would have it Rath wasn't alone in guarding a secret. Charly hadn't said a word about this black she'd eaten lunch with on Monday. Rath thought he'd heard colleagues gossiping about it in the canteen, but the whispering died as soon as he entered the room. Even so, he was certain he'd caught the word *black*, and the scorn and pity in the eyes of colleagues. He'd tried not to think about it, remembering Hella Rickert in Masuria. There was no way he'd be telling Charly about Hella, it was none of her business. He wondered if that was why she'd failed to mention ...

His jealousy grew by the day. Rarely had he slept with Charly so often as in recent times, and it was starting to feel as if he were doing it to possess her, that she might belong to *him* and no one else.

Who was this black, and why hadn't she said anything about him? He'd briefly considered hiring a private detective, only to abandon the idea, since it would mean yielding to his jealousy. Besides, Berlin sleuths were a notoriously shady bunch.

Meanwhile, normal service had resumed in A Division.

Charly had been recalled at exactly the right time and didn't complain, simply got on with it. Clearly she was on good terms with her office colleague, and no one in G seemed to envy her having spent three weeks in Homicide.

Three times this week he had eaten lunch with her in the canteen, introducing her as *my fiancée, Fräulein Ritter*, and enjoyed being seen together at last.

Perhaps it was jealousy that bound him to her, but he didn't care. Already they were living a kind of trial marriage, sitting together in the evenings, listening to the radio or records, and talking about work. As well as keeping their own secrets. Perhaps that, too, was part of married life. He tried to make peace with the idea, however difficult he found it.

On Sunday they would cast their vote together, as he'd promised they would. He still didn't know where to put his cross. The whole thing seemed pretty pointless. At the end of the day, it'd be Hindenburg who had the final say on the identity of his chancellor, and perhaps it was better that way. The Nazis were beneath the old man; there was no way he'd let one of them run the country.

Rath's sole wish was that Nazi and Communist votes might tumble, reducing the frequency of street battles. Perhaps the new government would ban the SA and SS again, so that life in Berlin and elsewhere in Prussia might return halfway to normal. That way the police wouldn't have to keep hearing about how they had lost control.

With all these questions running through his mind, one refused to let go: who *in the hell* was this black man?

Perhaps on polling Sunday he'd casually steer conversation onto the Nazis and their asinine racism. Were there even black Germans? It was a legitimate question, surely?

He put the thought to one side and concentrated on the file in front of him. He'd spent much of the week trying to write down everything that had happened in Masuria. He hated drudge work like this, but at last the report was ready for Böhm. Hopefully it wouldn't be thrown back in his face.

Perhaps Böhm was no longer here. Most colleagues had finished for the weekend. Charly had said her goodbyes about an hour ago, after arranging to go shopping with Greta. Or was she meeting ... Again his thoughts turned to the black man, sitting with her at the window table in Aschinger.

The telephone rang, the call he'd been waiting for all week. 'Kowalski. I see you're racking up overtime, just like me.'

'I've been spending a lot of time with my colleagues in Robbery Division.'

'And?'

'This university break-in from October '30 ...' He paused, as if to make sure no one was listening. 'Nothing was ever proved, but my colleagues are certain it was Marczewski's gang. Their prints are all over it.'

'Marczewski?'

'It's how the gang's still known, though the boss has been in Berlin a few years now.'

'Polish-Paule.'

'Pardon me?'

'That's what we call him here. He took over a Ringverein. Clearly a major player where bootlegging's concerned.'

'There's an informant. I showed him the photo you sent, and he recognised the man.'

'And?' Rath felt his hunting instinct awaken.

'He says not only did this man buy the stuff from the clinic, he ordered the theft himself; knew exactly where the drugs could be found.'

'Interesting.'

'It wasn't the only job he gave Marczewski's men either. He wanted a new passport, as well as the addresses of four Treuburgers who'd moved away.'

'Let me guess: these four men are no longer with us?'

'You got it.'

'Did these gang members know they were handing a killer his victims on a plate?'

'The informant denies it, but that lot would sell their grandmothers. Polakowski must have laid down thousands of marks – just like that, enough to make any hood go weak at the knees. Only thing I'm wondering is how a fugitive could have so much cash.'

'His jail-friend was a bank robber, wasn't he? It's probably from his stash. Thank you, Kowalski. Excellent work.'

'Thank you, Sir, anytime, but there's one more thing. Our informant saved the best until last ...'

'Go on.'

'He was there again.'

'Who?'

'Polakowski paid another visit to Marczewski's gang last Sunday. He needed more tubocurarine, and he got it.'

Wilhelm Böhm was still at his desk, but dressed in his hat and coat and speaking on the telephone. 'Keep your eyes open. He'll be back soon enough.'

'What's the matter?' Rath asked.

'Our colleagues from Danzig. They've lost Gustav Wengler, somewhere in the covered market.'

Rath placed a thick file on Böhm's desk. 'Apropos Wengler,' he said. 'My Masurian operation. Here's the report.'

'Finally.' Böhm reached across and opened it. 'About time.' There was no such thing as a friendly thank you from Wilhelm Böhm.

'I think you'll find it's pretty comprehensive.' Rath was unsure whether or not he should report Kowalski's call.

Böhm looked up from skimming the file. 'Was there something else, Inspector?'

527

'Yes and no.'

Böhm furrowed his brow.

'Polakowski,' Rath said. 'I think he's in Treuburg, waiting for Gustav Wengler.'

'What makes you say that?'

'Just a feeling.'

'Why not check if this *feeling* has any substance, and get in touch with the local police? A man like Polakowski should stick out like a sore thumb.'

'With respect, Sir, I don't trust the police in Treuburg.' Rath gestured towards his report. 'As far as I'm concerned, Chief Constable Grigat's perfectly capable of killing Polakowski himself.'

'A police officer who kills?'

'No doubt he'd dress it up as self-defence, or say Polakowski was trying to escape. Grigat and Wengler are in cahoots, and it's not in Wengler's interests that Polakowski should fall into police hands, the sole witness in an age-old homicide case.'

'A mass murderer, besides.'

'That doesn't mean vigilante justice should prevail.'

'Hmm.' Böhm rubbed his chin.

'What sort of impression does it make if Berlin asks for assistance on the basis of a *feeling*?

'Yet you expect me to green-light an expensive operation on precisely the same grounds?'

'It's the weekend,' Rath said. 'It could always be an unofficial trip.'

'Don't you want to cast your vote tomorrow?'

'There are more important things.' Rath started downstairs. On this occasion 'hmm' would have to suffice. If he let Böhm say anything else, he'd only end up back in his office.

The Buick had a full tank, and he had over a hundred marks in his wallet. More than enough. He steered onto

Kaiserstrasse, then Frankfurter Allee. There was a build-up as far as Lichtenberg, but once he was past the S-Bahn bridge he could step on the gas.

He'd have liked to take Charly with him, but she was with her friend on Tauentzienstrasse, spending her hard-earned cash. Screw it, there was no way of reaching her, but perhaps it was better if she didn't come, thinking of Hella Rickert, and the prospect of their crossing paths.

He knew what he had to do, and he had to be quick about it. If he made good time, the journey would take around fifteen hours. Gustav Wengler would be back in Treuburg tomorrow at the latest to cast his vote, and he wanted to be there too. He drove as fast as he could, but still took almost five hours to reach the border. In Schneidemühl, the last German town before the Corridor, he found a gas station with a coin telephone. He made his way over while the attendant looked after the Buick. It was almost eight, she'd be long home by now.

The connection wasn't good; Charly's voice scratched in the receiver. 'Gereon, where are you? Overtime again?'

'No.' He decided to make it short and sweet, to tell the truth for once, instead of talking all around it. 'I'm at a gas station,' he said. 'In Schneidemühl.'

'Sorry?'

'In Schneidemühl, on the Polish border.'

Charly stressed each individual word. 'What. Are. You. Doing. In. Schneidemühl?' By the time she finished, she was shouting.

'Settle down. It's Polakowski. I know where he is.'

'Going it alone again. Gereon, didn't you want to . . .?'

'I'm not going it alone. Böhm knows.' She was speechless. Great. 'Don't worry, Charly. I have to say goodbye, I'm out of coins. I love you.' He hung up.

It wasn't far to the border, but he wasn't the only one

heading to East Prussia for the weekend. A long queue had formed in front of the checkpoint. Gennat hadn't been exaggerating. First of all he required a transit visa, which cost him sixty marks and no little patience, before it was finally stamped and signed. It took just as long for the serious-minded Polish border officials to search his car, in the process of which they discovered one of Kirie's rubber balls, which Rath had misplaced long ago.

Next, his Walther was confiscated. In its place he was issued with a receipt, which entitled him to reclaim the pistol on his return journey. On top of everything else, he then had to pay a toll of five Zloty. The officials refused to take Reichsmark, meaning he had to use the bureau de change, where the commission bordered on daylight robbery. He was beginning to regret taking the car. The train ride had been more pleasant; even the plane had been preferable, despite his fear of flying, but there was no going back now that the paperwork was complete. His transit visa granted him twenty-four hours to clear the Corridor; he did so in two and a half. Bromberg and Thorn were both pretty towns but, fearing the hostility of Polish border officials might be matched inland, he carried on, refusing to stop until he'd reached German Eylau, and with it Prussian territory once more.

Entering East Prussia proved far easier than entering Poland; the border officials requested his visa, his passport and his driving licence. No more than half an hour, and he was back on German soil.

In the meantime it was just after midnight.

97

A pleasant day greeted Charly as she stepped outside with Kirie. She felt the sun on her skin, and a gentle breeze made her forget her fatigue. She was so angry she had barely slept. Gereon bloody Rath, but she wasn't so much angry at him, as at her own stupidity, at having to stay put while he was gallivanting round the country. This time he hadn't even left her the car. Couldn't he have flown again? It seemed highly unlikely that he was hot-footing it back to Masuria with Böhm's blessing.

To think, she had been looking forward to getting out of town together, and to casting their vote. She couldn't help thinking back to the last week, during which she had rehearsed eagerly for married life. Was this part of it too? Spending her weekends alone? Not if Charlotte Ritter had anything to do with it! She'd catch up on that Wannsee trip she still owed Greta. Her polling station was in Moabit anyway; she could call by Spenerstrasse at the same time, perhaps even spend the night. Her role in life wasn't restricted to keeping Gereon's bed warm!

She pulled hard on the lead as she crossed the street. Kirie, who had been slow to react, looked at her in astonishment, and she immediately regretted venting her anger on the poor beast. Kirie was least of all to blame for her master's antics.

At Steinplatz she came to a halt in front of an advertising pillar bearing election posters. *Down with the system*, demanded the Communists. *The Workers have awakened*, the Nazis proclaimed. Here in Charlottenburg, these slogans would most likely fall on deaf ears, though the German National People's Party might gain traction with their *Power to the Reich President*, with Hindenburg at its core. None of the three parties were interested in democracy. As far as these elections went, they were interested in power, and power alone.

She was about to cross to the park when a man emerged from a bright, imposing-looking house on the corner. Donning his hat he looked through thick spectacles as he made his way towards her.

Charly couldn't contain her surprise. 'Deputy Commissioner, Sir,' she cried. ' Good morning.'

Bernhard Weiss lifted his hat. 'Good morning, Fräulein Ritter.' He hadn't needed a moment to remember her name, which flattered her more than she cared to admit. 'I fear you're one of the few who still recognise that title.'

'You're still in charge as far as I'm concerned, Sir.'

'Strictly speaking, I'm only on leave of absence. I signed a declaration in custody which prevents me from exercising any official powers.'

'Your removal from office wasn't legal. As for our government – that was a putsch.'

'These are matters for the State Court to decide.'

Charly's next question had been on her mind ever since she had seen Reichswehr soldiers leading away her superiors like criminals. 'Why didn't we defend ourselves?' she asked. 'Twenty thousand police officers. We could have prevented this putsch.'

'No doubt Prime Minister Braun and Commissioner Grzesinski didn't want to risk civil war. Enough blood has been spilled already.' Weiss gestured towards the advertising pillar. 'Who knows, perhaps these elections will result in a new government.'

'You think an election can really change anything?' Charly asked, smiling as she saw his face. 'Don't worry, I haven't given up hope. Of course I'll be voting. I'm just sorry I couldn't do more.'

'I wouldn't give our Republic up yet.' Weiss stroked Kirie, who was sniffing at his shoe. 'Is this your dog?'

'I . . .she belongs to Inspector Rath. I'm looking after her while he's in East Prussia.'

'Rath still isn't back?'

'He's gone again. I think he's on the trail of a murder suspect, but, honestly, I'm not sure any more. I was reassigned from Homicide last week.'

Weiss seemed surprised that she was still looking after Rath's dog. For a moment she considered mentioning their engagement, but it hardly seemed appropriate.

'You live here?' she asked, pointing towards the house from which Weiss had just emerged.

'Not yet, but this is where my family and I will be moving to. We need to vacate our official apartment in Charlottenburg within the next few weeks.'

Charly felt a great sadness. 'So it's permanent, your withdrawal from police office?'

'I hope to be reclaiming my desk at Alex very soon. Once the State Court has delivered its verdict, or the new Reich government.'

'If there *is* a new government, and it isn't worse than the one we already have.'

98

Rath pulled over just before Allenstein, parking on a forest path, struggling to keep his eyes open. When he awakened it was already dawn. He washed using water from a nearby stream, and drove on, encountering more and more people the closer he came to Treuburg. Again and again he had to brake as a horse and cart straggled along. Occasionally he met a group of pedestrians, who stood gawping at the Buick and took an age to clear the road. It was almost midday when he arrived in Treuburg, suit rumpled and stomach rumbling.

The Masurians were on their way to church and the polls. Almost all the towns and villages he had driven through were decked out for election day, with people hanging flags out of windows to denote their political persuasion. Far too many swastikas, he thought, far too much black-white-and-red, and not nearly enough black-red-and-gold.

Approaching from Lyck he could already make out the Treuburg water tower, but instead of holding course, he bore left and drove up to Luisenhöhe. The staff in the estate house were surprised to see him again. Yes, Herr Wengler had returned, yesterday evening in fact, but unfortunately he wasn't home. After church he had gone to vote, and he still had business to attend to in town.

When was he expected?

A shrug.

'I need to find Herr Wengler. It's a matter of life and death.'

The servant looked at Rath as if he had never heard such nonsense. 'I see,' he said. 'I'll pass that on.'

'It might be too late by then. Just tell me where I can find him.'

'Try the marketplace, that's where Herr Wengler's polling station is.'

In Treuburg, too, flags hung from windows. Lots of black-white-and-red, interspersed with swastikas. There was even a little black-red-and-gold on show. Only Communist colours were absent; perhaps the Nazis had burned their flags.

The girls' school on the marketplace had been transformed into a polling station. Outside the entrance stood a few of Fabeck's SA boys, brown shirts freshly ironed, hair parted straight as a die. They threw Rath dirty glances but, in the absence of their Rottenführer, seemed unsure whether to take matters further. 'Berliners aren't permitted to vote here,' said one, as Rath pushed past.

'Who wants to vote with people like your Führer standing?'

Before the youth could respond, he disappeared inside. Dressed in their Sunday best, the Treuburgers were fulfilling their patriotic duty. Gustav Wengler was nowhere to be seen. 'The Herr Director has voted already,' one of the polling officers said. No more information was forthcoming.

Outside, he found Klaus Fabeck and troops blocking his path. 'If it isn't our busybody friend from Berlin,' Fabeck said. 'SA-officer Brandt tells me you've been insulting the Führer ...'

'Have I?' Rath lit a cigarette. 'Well, he isn't *my* Führer. I'm sorry if I hurt your tender feelings for the man. I forgot you lot are all gay.'

'You're lucky it's polling day, Inspector. Once these

535

elections are over, you'd better watch out. People like you will be first for the chop.'

'People like me?'

'Those who mock the Führer. Once Adolf Hitler assumes his rightful position as leader of the German Volk, only true Germans ...'

'He didn't even make it to Reich President,' Rath interrupted. 'Perhaps it's time Herr Hitler headed back to Austria. Half a year ago he didn't have citizenship, now he's telling us what it means to be German?'

Fabeck stood poised to attack, but his two companions held him back.

'Leave it, Klaus,' said one. 'He's a cop. He's trying to provoke you, so he can lock you up.'

Rath lifted his hat. 'I bid you good day.'

Without hurrying he made sure to put a little distance between himself and the group. Fists inwardly raised, he readied himself to strike, but the attack never came.

Outside the *Kronprinzen* he ran into Karl Rammoser, who sat on the terrace in the shade. 'Inspector, what are you doing back in Masuria?'

'Try keeping me away.'

'Isn't it polling day in Berlin?'

'I have more important things to do. I'm looking for Gustav Wengler.'

'I saw him about an hour ago, coming out of the polling station. Exchanged a few words with the SA lads, then got in his car.'

'Well, he isn't home. I was up there just now.'

'Then I assume he's gone for a drive. He does that sometimes, just hops in his car and drives around, out to some lake, or forest.'

'It is pretty around here.'

'You're telling me. Only, not everyone has a Mercedes to enjoy it.'

'A Buick will do just fine.' He gestured towards his car, which was parked down by the roadside. 'Can I drive you home?'

'Too early for me, I'm afraid. I'm meeting someone for lunch.'

'Well, then ...' Rath tipped his hat by way of goodbye.

He wondered how long he could leave the Buick by the marketplace before the SA slashed his tyres. It hardly faded into the background, besides being the only vehicle here with IA plates. It seemed even the Berlin tourist family had returned in time to vote. All other cars bore the East Prussian registration IC.

He got in his car and considered where Polakowski might be hiding. He had no idea. This trip to Treuburg might be a crackpot idea, yet he knew Polakowski was here somewhere, waiting to complete his revenge.

He settled down. If Wengler was in his Mercedes then he was safe, for the time being. Whether that was true at Luisenhöhe was another matter.

At least he had managed to pick up the trail again after Danzig. That ought to pacify Böhm somewhat. He started the engine and set off. Perhaps he should take a leaf out of Wengler's book and enjoy the scenery, and maybe he'd meet the maroon-coloured Mercedes along the way.

Something on the Lega bridge was flapping in the breeze. He reversed a few metres and looked out the side window. A red handkerchief was tied to the railing. He pulled over and got out of the car. No doubt about it, it was the same as the one they'd recovered from the lift at *Haus Vaterland*. In the traffic tower at Potsdamer Platz; in Wittenberge and in Dortmund. Fearing the worst he gazed over the railing, scouring the Lega's shallow waters for a corpse.

He took a deep breath before climbing down to the river to check underneath the bridge. Only when he was certain there was no body did he return to the handkerchief. It was dry.

Suddenly it dawned on him that the red handkerchiefs were a signal to Polakowski's victims, rather than a simple means of torture. The same signal had lured Anna von Mathée to her death – and Jakub Polakowski to ruin.

Rath got into the Buick and drove to Markowsken without filling up. He'd only have enough for another few kilometres but couldn't afford to be late. Wengler had almost certainly seen the sign.

Apart from two horse carriages, the road was clear. His instincts hadn't betrayed him: the red Mercedes was parked by the edge of the forest.

Gustav Wengler wanted rid of this man who threatened his legend, this man who knew his status was founded on lies and hypocrisy. Did he think he had the edge on Polakowski? That was what Herbert Lamkau and Siegbert Wengler had thought, until Polakowski administered his needle and resistance was crushed. Did Wengler realise exactly how his brother had died?

Rath drove into the forest until the road became track, parked and started walking. He didn't know how far it was, couldn't be sure he wouldn't get lost again without Adamek and his local knowledge; but still he continued, until suddenly he saw the water sparkle through the trees.

He considered calling out loud, so that he could bring home the folly of Polakowski's endeavour, but then the man would be warned, and he would never catch him. And Rath wanted to catch him. Not just because he was a mass murderer, but because he might be a viable witness in the case against Gustav Wengler. He worked his way through the forest until he could see the little lake – but it was too late.

Standing in the shallows over Gustav Wengler's inert body was Hartmut Janke, aka Jakub Polakowski, the man whose life Wengler had so utterly destroyed. Wengler's head was submerged, but Polakowski pulled it out. Wengler gasped for air, but not as frantically as someone who fears he will drown. The tubocurarine must be at work. Polakowski apparently spoke with Wengler, who sat listlessly in the water.

Rath imagined Polakowski speaking with his other victims, reminding them of their sins, of the harm they had visited on himself and Anna, even asking about Gustav Wengler, as, slowly, he ended their lives.

Then he realised he wasn't alone in the forest. A man was crouched behind a thick pine trunk, brown suit scarcely visible against its surroundings. It was Erich Grigat in plain clothes, his weapon drawn and trained on Polakowski. He meant to shoot Polakowski dead first time, and not hit Gustav Wengler by mistake.

Rath could have made short work of things with his service pistol, but it was locked in a Polish border office.

Down by the water Polakowski was still speaking, and Grigat had eyes only for the killer and his next victim. Rath grabbed a stick from the forest floor, and approached the chief constable slowly from behind, making sure he didn't step on any withered branches that might give him away. It was a trick he had from reading Karl May, although perhaps fortune looked kindly on him. As Gustav Wengler's head was thrust underwater a second time, he struck, and Grigat slumped to his knees before collapsing sideways on the soft forest floor. His service pistol, a Luger, fell out of his hand. Rath claimed it, walked the final few metres to the shore, and emerged from the shadow of the trees.

Polakowski didn't see him, hadn't heard him above the splash. Wengler lay on his back, face submerged in the water. A few bubbles rose to the surface, otherwise all was still. Wengler didn't so much as twitch.

Rath caught himself taking pleasure in the scene: the great Gustav Wengler drowned by his own wretched victim. Wasn't that just, and didn't he deserve to die? Should he, Rath, not simply wait until Polakowski had completed his task before making his arrest? He just needed to stay quiet, to avoid startling Polakowski and preventing him from carrying out the execution, but the other part of Rath's conscience was already working. His right hand released the safety catch on Grigat's Luger and held it at the ready, as his feet continued towards the shore. It was time to end this.

'CID, Berlin,' he said. 'I'm armed. Please do as I say.' Polakowski's body grew rigid. Though the man's back was to him, Rath felt certain it was devoid of expression. 'Remove the man from the water. Slowly and carefully.'

Polakowski lifted Wengler by the shoulders. No sooner did his head surface than he took a deep, heavy breath. The escaped convict, who had spent long years wrongfully languishing in jail, held his victim and tormentor above the water.

'Bring him ashore.'

Rath didn't know if that would save Wengler. He had no idea if and when the curare would exert its deadly effect, or if Wengler already had too much water in his lungs. Polakowski seized Wengler's body under the armpits and dragged him slowly towards the shore.

'Now lay him down, place your hands in the air and turn around.'

Polakowski obeyed, but turned so quickly that Rath scarcely knew what was happening, knocking the Luger out of his hand in a single motion. The pistol landed in the undergrowth, and Polakowski was on him.

The man was strong and deadly serious. Polakowski took his neck in a chokehold. He couldn't prise his hands free. He wriggled and thrashed his legs, reared up, but it was no use. Polakowski stayed on top, hands squeezing mercilessly until, suddenly, his grip loosened and he toppled to the side like a felled tree.

Rath gripped his neck and looked up. Gustav Wengler stood over him, holding Grigat's Luger in his hand, which glistened with Jakub Polakowski's blood. Rath was confused. It was strange to see a firearm used as a primitive cudgel, but it had worked, Polakowski had been immobilised. Wengler had saved his life.

Rath would never have thought he'd have to feel grateful towards the man, yet here he was. 'You need a doctor,' he said. 'He's injected you with tubocurarine. Probably in a fatal dose. It's a miracle you can even stand.'

'You disappoint me, Inspector!' said Wengler. 'I thought you were more intelligent than that, and less scrupulous.' He grew more serious. 'I'd hoped you'd shoot the swine. The man was trying to kill me.'

'He didn't inject you with paralytic poison?'

'He injected me with something, and I'm sure he believed it was the Devil's work.' Wengler laughed. 'When really it was saline solution.' He gestured towards a large tree by the shore. 'The needle lay hidden there for days. I had a hunch he'd want to finish things here, and asked Erich to keep an eye on the lake. It was no problem to switch the needles.'

'Then you were playacting? Why?'

Wengler looked at the weapon. 'Did you get this off Erich? That isn't nice, you know. It's his service pistol. Where is he, by the way?'

'Sleeping the sleep of the just. Now explain: why the dying swan?'

'Why, indeed? To manufacture a situation where the bastard could be gunned down without Erich being brought to trial.'

'It was all planned?'

'Inspector, for more than two years I have known that Polakowski was outside, planning his revenge. He made the mistake of obtaining false papers from Paul Marczewski of all people. In Königsberg. Without realising I do business with the man.'

'*Did* business with the man.'

'I see you're well informed. Yes, sadly I had to end our business partnership but, back then, it proved very useful. When the Polack started making inquiries about my people, Marczewski naturally informed me right away.'

'You knew the whole time? Why didn't you protect your men?'

'Why should I? They'd become a nuisance. The sins of one's youth.' He shook his head. 'Inspector, I'm trying to legitimise my business operation and these tales of moonshining are damaging.'

'But ...your own brother ...'

'If you must know, Siegbert was a corrupt bastard. Sooner or later he'd have blackmailed me if I'd interrupted my payments. He'd cost me far too much already, and he was a lazy swine.'

'Then Polakowski acted in your interests.'

'You know, he thought he was scaring me with those death notices. I was *pleased* with his work. How much do you think it'd have cost to pay someone for all that?'

'Well, you ought to know. You paid for Assmann, didn't you? Or did Lapke go halves with you?'

'Inspector, if you're so clever, why is it I have to do your work for you?'

Wengler raised Grigat's pistol and aimed at the unconscious Polakowski. Rath closed his eyes.

'Wengler, you can't! I'll have you for this.'

'You think you're going to survive?' He aimed the pistol at Rath. 'First I'm going to shoot the Polack, then I'm going to shoot you. Afterwards we'll cook up a nice story about how you tried to save me, but died a hero's death. Poor Grigat sustained a blow to the head during the struggle, of course, but will testify to my version of events. A police witness always looks good.'

'I'm warning you, Wengler. My colleagues will be here any moment.'

Wengler laughed. 'Even you don't believe that. The way Grigat tells it, you'd rather run from your colleagues than keep them informed.' Suddenly his laughter died, and he gazed over the barrel with an ice-cold expression. 'Any more and you'll be first to go.'

'Wengler, you wretched ...'

Creature, Rath was about to say, but he ran out of time. He heard a whirring sound, then a noise that sounded like a fence post being driven into a quagmire. A shot struck his shoulder and threw him backwards looking up. Gustav Wengler stood as before, Luger smoking in his hand. In his neck was a long, thin arrow.

Wengler dropped the pistol and reached with both hands for his throat, gasping for air as he tried to remove the shaft. The next arrow struck him in the left eye and it was as if he had been snap-frozen. He stared rigidly towards the lake, at a thick shrub on the other side of the little bay, before tilting like a tree slowly torn from its roots, falling sideways into the water and landing on his back.

Rath sat up, only now aware of the pain in his shoulder. Wengler's lifeless body lay in the shallows. Two arrows, one in his throat, one in his left eye, protruded like solitary reeds.

99

Again Rath sat on Ernst Gennat's green armchair, only this time things were more serious. This was no dirty trick. A man had died during a police operation, and not just any man but a Treuburg luminary, whose obituary served as a moving tribute to national pathos everywhere.

> On the day that ought to have been his greatest triumph; the day on which nationalist forces saw an unparalleled upsurge in his beloved Treuburg, Gustav Wengler, philanthropist sans pareil, died in a hail of Berlin Police bullets.

Rath was familiar with this kind of tone. He had endured similar in Cologne, and eventually been forced to leave. He didn't care what they wrote about him in Treuburg, but Erich Grigat was more than making up for it, despite the counter statement issued to the *Treuburger Zeitung* by Berlin Police Headquarters, refuting the paper's more outrageous claims. The police constable was still on sick leave, recovering from a serious head injury with relatives in Elbing, and had already put in for a transfer.

It was probably for the best, even if Editor Ziegler wouldn't be able to preserve Gustav Wengler's reputation forever. Maria Cofalka's death was being investigated. Königsberg CID had a Homicide unit on site, which included Anton

Kowalski, and, by their last telephone conversation, it was only a matter of time before the deceased Wengler was implicated by one of Fabeck's troop. At least here, it seemed time was working in justice's favour. Each SA man that sat in custody was a victory for public security. Since the vote the brownshirts had stepped up their brutal and often fatal assaults. The surge in Nazi votes promised anything but stability.

Gennat glanced at Rath's report and shook his head. 'Well I never.' The superintendent gestured towards his sling. 'How's the shoulder?'

'Fine, thank you. Bandage comes off next week.'

The blood-soaked bandage and sling that held his arm steady made a wretched impression, but had been a great help in mollifying Charly. Confined to his bed by doctor's orders, he had been moved by her concern. So much so that he'd almost forgotten about the pain.

'I still don't understand why you took Chief Constable Grigat's service pistol.'

'To arm myself. Mine was with Polish border officers in Wirsitz. I knew Polakowski couldn't be far away.'

Gennat raised his eyebrows. 'Yet it was Gustav Wengler who was shot!'

'That was self-defence, as I've already explained to police in Lyck and Gumbinnen. As well as your good self.'

'You know how we like to hear things again and again. What I'm interested in, is how this situation came about.' Gennat leafed through Rath's report. 'You went down to the lake alone, leaving the police constable up in the forest, unarmed ...'

'That's correct, Sir.'

'There you came upon Jakub Polakowski ...'

' ...who was lying in wait for Gustav Wengler. There was a blackmail letter in Wengler's car.'

That much was true. Perhaps Polakowski had drawn

545

inspiration from Riedel and Unger, of whose endeavours in *Haus Vaterland* he must surely have been aware. At any rate, he had threatened to expose Gustav Wengler not only as a moonshiner, but a killer to boot. Having tortured every one of Wengler's trusted allies to death, there was no doubting what he knew. Even so, he didn't want simply to destroy Wengler's reputation, built as it was on lies. He wanted to destroy the man entirely.

'Then,' Gennat continued. 'You were about to arrest Polakowski ...'

'Correct. There was a warrant out. An alleged mass murderer ...'

'A warrant that is still current, since apparently you let this *alleged* mass murderer escape.'

'I'm sorry, Sir.' A little contrition couldn't hurt.

'Back to the lake: you were keeping Polakowski in check with Grigat's Luger ...'

'Everything was under control until Gustav Wengler appeared.'

'It was he who felled Grigat from behind, up in the forest ...'

'That's what we assume, Sir.'

'Why? If Wengler had the police in his pocket, as you've always maintained?'

'That was an error. Chief Constable Grigat is a loyal representative of the Prussian police force, a man of integrity.'

'Wengler threatened you with a pistol?'

'Yes, Sir. He meant to kill Polakowski. I'd interfered with his trap. I instructed him to lay down his weapon.'

'An instruction he refused to carry out.'

Rath took a drag on his cigarette. 'As you can see from the report, he then demanded that I lay aside *my* weapon. That's when I informed him that he, too, was under arrest: that he had knowingly sanctioned the death of his former associates, including that of his brother, and was responsible for the deaths of Maria Cofalka and Dietrich Assmann.'

'Which was enough to make him shoot.'

Rath's left shoulder hurt. 'Clearly.' He stubbed out his cigarette with his right hand. 'I didn't think that was in any doubt.'

Gennat again glanced at the file. 'I can understand your first shot,' he said. 'A classic case of self-defence, but why did you shoot Wengler in the eye after you'd immobilised him with a shot to the neck?'

'I don't know, Sir. I pulled down on the trigger twice. I realise it was an error, but it happened. Perhaps it was a reflex after Wengler hit me, mortal terror, whatever . . . in situations like that you don't always think clearly. You react . . .'

'But you should. Think. It's what police officers are trained to do. Especially before using their weapons; before having recourse to *fire*!'

'Yes, Sir.'

'The weapon used to shoot you . . . could it have been a Luger too? Our colleagues were unable to trace the bullet.'

'I don't know, Sir. It's possible.'

'Your wound would suggest as much.' Gennat sighed. 'Shame we don't have it.'

'Yes, Sir.' Rath appeared contrite again. 'I'm sorry I let Polakowski give me the slip, but he threatened me with Wengler's gun, which he had claimed for himself.'

'You were armed too. Why didn't you take up the chase?'

'I had to see to Gustav Wengler first. He was still alive at that point.'

'And, of course, Chief Constable Grigat was no longer armed.' Gennat struck the file with the flat of his hand. 'Rath, my good man. I'm having trouble believing even half of this outlandish tale.'

'I can't help it if the truth is outlandish, Sir.'

Gennat fixed him in the eyes, so deep that Rath grew uneasy. 'I guess we'll never know what really happened at this lake in Masuria.'

Let's hope so, Rath thought. *Otherwise they'll make Artur Radlewski's life hell, and he deserves it least of all.*

'I've told you everything I know, Sir.'

'Let's put it this way: you haven't once contradicted yourself and, as your statement tallies with that of Chief Constable Grigat, there's an end to it.'

Dealing with Grigat had been easier than Rath anticipated. The fact that Gustav Wengler was dead, and the bullets in his corpse came from the constable's service Luger, made it a damn sight easier to win the man over, and cook up a halfway credible explanation for the whole shemozzle.

Gennat tapped Rath's report with the flat of his hand. 'This won't be the last time you're questioned on this. Investigation proceedings aren't over, not by a long shot.'

'I'm aware of that, Sir.' Rath tried not to show discomfort at Buddha's stern gaze.

'I hope that killing a man and allowing a mass murderer to escape can be squared with your conscience.'

'Forgive me, Sir.'

Gennat shook his head. 'Sometimes, Herr Rath, you're a little too Catholic for your own good.'

'What do you mean, Sir?'

'The fact that you're constantly seeking forgiveness. How many times is it you've sat here now? I'm neither your confessor, nor the dear Lord himself. Go to confession to have your sins absolved, not my office!'

'I haven't been to confession in a long time, Sir.'

'Perhaps you should.' Buddha snapped the file shut. 'You're lucky, Herr Rath, that alongside Chief Constable Grigat and Assistant Detective Kowalski, both Fräulein Ritter and Wilhelm Böhm have put in a good word for you.

And that, right now, I need people like you. People who aren't interested in politics, but in solving crimes.'

Rath stubbed out his cigarette, safe in the knowledge that, whatever investigation proceedings were still to come, he'd survive. As for his conscience and visiting confession, Buddha need have no worries there. He was at peace with himself – for the most part.

He looked at his watch and stood up. 'Might I remind you, Sir? We have an appointment.'

100

Though it was mid-August, an uncomfortable chill rose from the harbour basin, a biting wind. Rath parked the Buick outside the warehouse and opened the passenger door. Having squeezed himself into the vehicle, Gennat only barely made it out.

Rath turned up his collar and looked around. At the opposite end of the basin a ship was being loaded, otherwise all was quiet. With his arm still in the sling he felt vulnerable. Driving had been a challenge in itself but, having now arrived, he was certain they had nothing to fear. The Westhafen was *Concordia* territory; no one from the *Pirates* would show his face here. Even if there was a traitor in *Concordia* ranks, as Rath suspected, their chief was the only one who knew of this arrangement. That much had been guaranteed by Marlow.

Rath had met Marczewski on one previous occasion, in Marlow's office at Ostbahnhof, shortly after returning from East Prussia. 'So, you're from Königsberg?' he'd asked, and Paul Marczewski had shaken his head.

'Rastenburg. Like many Masurians, I moved west for work.'

'You're Masurian? Then why is your nickname Polish-Paule?'

'Your guess is as good as mine. We Masurians are caught between two stools: too German for the Polish, too Polish for the Germans. Believe me, though. The majority of people decried as Polacks here in Berlin or the Westphalian mines have Prussian passports.'

Gustav Wengler had indeed known about Polakowski's vendetta, and done nothing about it. It seemed that, meaning to go legitimate and make his position unassailable, the time was right to get rid of his former partners in crime. Lamkau, Simoneit, Wawerka, and his own brother, Siegbert.

'It was the strangest thing,' Marczewski said. 'The man appearing like that, and asking about the very people we do business with. Did business with.' Needless to say the former Königsberg gangster had informed his business associate Gustav Wengler. 'Had I known the bastard would leave me in the lurch, I'd never have warned him. It's a good thing you dealt with him.'

Rath didn't know how to take this compliment, but he did know that he didn't mourn Gustav Wengler.

Buddha wheezed as he climbed the small staircase to the concrete loading ramp. Rath followed behind. No sooner had they reached it than a door opened and a man stepped out. 'May I introduce Paul Marczewski, Sir.'

'Pleased to meet you.'

Rath was surprised at Buddha's easy manner. The pair shook hands, the chief of the *Concordia* Ringverein and the head of Berlin Homicide.

'Come in,' Marczewski said. 'It's warmer inside.'

The warehouse really was just a warehouse, bearing no comparison with Marlow's office at Ostbahnhof, which called to mind the fireplace room of an English country house. Marczewski was less assuming, contenting himself with a table and a few chairs. They sat down. On the table stood three glasses and a bottle of *Mathée Luisenbrand*. Marczewski poured. 'Don't worry,' he said, 'it's the real thing.'

The *Luisenbrand* tasted as Rath knew it from Treuburg.

This was no rotgut, though nor was it as tasty as Rammoser's homebrew.

'It seems,' Marczewski began, lighting a cigarette, 'that the Berlin Police and *Concordia* have a mutual problem ...'

'Indeed,' Gennat said. 'Inspector Rath tells me you'd be willing to help bring it to a resolution.'

'The Phantom, as the papers have dubbed him, has been responsible for the deaths of five of my men. With each killing he has sought to weaken my organisation. From what I understand ...' he drew on his cigarette, ' ...I'm next.'

'How do you know?'

'Since the operation at the Westhafen, seven of my men have been detained in custody. If they take me now, *Concordia* will be finished. Why do you think I've gone into hiding?'

Gennat looked at him pensively. 'You're saying the Phantom will strike as soon as you show yourself in public?'

'You can bet on it.' Marczewski sipped on his *Luisenbrand* and recharged their glasses. 'Am I right in thinking the Phantom always takes aim at his victims' chests?'

'You are indeed.'

'What about these bulletproof vests I've been reading about in the papers? Do you have something like that?' Buddha nodded. 'Our founder's day celebration is in two weeks, at the *Habsburger Hof* ballroom on Stresemannstrasse. We'd be delighted to have the pleasure of your company, Superintendent.'

Gennat looked at Marczewski out of narrow eyes. 'The *Habsburger Hof*? That's right opposite Europahaus, isn't it?'

'The perfect location for a sniper, but perhaps preparations can be made.'

Gennat nodded pensively. 'I'm quite certain they can be, Herr Marczewski. And thank you for the invitation.'

'Then you accept?'

'I accept.'

Paul Marczewski shook Gennat's hand and took his leave. Rath noted his laughter lines. Marlow was right, he was a charming fellow, even if Rath was loath to consider how many men's lives he might have on his conscience, and precisely what Marlow understood by 'charming fellow'.

Still, that didn't matter. Marczewski was helping them lay a trap for a dangerous contract killer, the last remaining member of the *Weisse Hand*.

'What do you say, Rath,' Gennat said, when they were back among themselves. 'Care to join me at *Concordia*'s celebrations?'

'Perhaps from across the street. Europahaus is, in fact, the ideal location for a sniper.' He lit a cigarette. 'It would be my pleasure, Sir, to arrest Harald Dettmann in person.'

Gennat smiled, and they went silently into the clear night. The stars twinkled bright in the dark water of the harbour basin, above the sickle of a crescent moon. Perhaps everything would turn out just fine.

Epilogue

Monday, 30th April 1945

The four men pay him no heed. Instead of guarding him, they drink and smoke and laugh and play cards.

Tokala doesn't stir, doesn't move a muscle. His face is devoid of emotion. He sits with fixed gaze, dignified in his captivity, like his heroes.

Captured at last. He had always expected it, ever since the day he killed the wicked man at the little lake. How many years have passed since? In all that time they haven't once come looking for him, have kept away from his forest. Despite his violating the agreement and meddling in their world.

He expected the men from the surrounding villages and town to come and fetch him, but in fact it was these soldiers, who have suddenly sprouted everywhere in their strange uniforms. They treat him like a murderer, even though they cannot know he has killed.

All these years Tokala has hated himself for not having prevented Niyaha Luta's death. Even today he can still hear the splash of her arms and legs as they writhe against the shallow water; still see the wicked man shift on top of her as he submerges her again and again ...

Tokala never thought he'd see him again, but then, many summers later, the wicked man stood at the lake once more. Tokala sat tight in his hiding place, in the same bush where he had witnessed Niyaha Luta's murder all those years before. The wicked man had grown fatter, but Tokala recognised him and stayed where he was, watching everything.

He saw another burst forth from the forest and jam something in the wicked man's neck, not a knife, but a glass arrow; saw how the wicked man collapsed, sank to his knees, and was dragged into the water; how the policeman now appeared, the one who had almost perished on the moor.

Tokala didn't understood why the two men were suddenly fighting, rolling about as they wrestled on the floor.

Then the wicked man got up, knocked his assailant out and threatened the policeman with a pistol.

And Tokala felt the same old impotence return.

The wicked man meant to escape. Again.

This time Tokala wouldn't allow it, and reached inside his quiver. He couldn't help it, even though he knew the arrows would betray him, that the police would come for him, the people from the town.

There was no other way, it had to be done.

He didn't understand what happened after. The police officer pulled the arrows from the dead man's neck and left eye and threw them far into the lake, where they sank. Then he took the pistol and fired twice, one bullet for each hollow.

Tokala didn't understand, and eventually withdrew to his forest. Sat with Odakota and waited, but neither the police nor anyone else came looking for him. After a time, he began to venture out again.

Soon after, flags had fluttered from the houses of the town, red and white, with black swastikas; and Tokala saw men in uniform, so many uniforms, more than there had ever been under the Kaiser. Some change had occurred. Even a man who dwelt on the moors couldn't fail to perceive it.

Winchinchala no longer wrote, or laid books out for him, and Tokala looked for her and found her grave down by the lake. One last time he ventured into town with flowers from the moor, but since then he has never returned among men, not even to fetch his books.

Then, the uniforms hadn't lied, war broke out. Tokala thought it didn't concern him, like the first war, during which he'd avoided the soldiers in his forest as he did all others. They didn't find his hut, since no one was familiar with the moorland on which it stood, no one apart from himself and Odakota, his black dog friend.

It needed a second war and new soldiers to catch him. He was careless. He had thought the fighting was over because the shooting had stopped. And perhaps it had – but the soldiers were still there.

They picked him up.

They must be Russian. He can just about understand them. They don't know what to make of him, of that much he is certain. They almost shot him, just like that, but at the last minute an officer had pushed the soldier's machine gun to one side, and the wild face and slit eyes had stood and followed the salvo as it was swallowed by the moor.

Tokala had already closed his eyes in anticipation of death, but this is no deliverance. The worst possible thing has happened. They have locked him up.

These are evil men. They shot Odakota in front of his eyes, he had to watch his beloved pet die while tied to a chair. He pulled hard on his shackles, but all it achieved was to tip the chair, to the raucous amusement of the soldiers.

They say he is a spy, a lone fighter, a werewolf; they have offered him any number of possibilities to which he might say 'yes'. Have spoken to him in Russian, Polish and German, and he has met them with silence in all three. He bore his suffering like a man. Not a single cry of pain came from his lips.

Now they have put him in this crate, which roared skywards no sooner had they thrown him onto the worn leather of his seat. They are taking him to specialists in Moscow, the officer says, who also speaks German, very good German in fact, they would get it out of him, see what kind of man he was.

Clearly they have never seen his like before.

He sits by the window as the aeroplane gently shakes, listens to the hum and roar, and looks out, sees the country spread out beneath him, the forests and lakes, the land of his forefathers. He sees how beautiful it is. And suddenly he is overcome by an immense love for his homeland. He has always loved this country, but never before has he appreciated it so clearly as now.

All of a sudden, he knows what he must do, knows how he can recapture his freedom.

He looks around. Four soldiers sit with him in the cabin, smoking and playing cards. They are not watching him, thinking him safe, up here in the air.

He is still bound, but only by the arms, which they have tied in front of his chest so that he may sit.

The door latch: he has seen how it works, how they closed it before. He is still Tokala, the fox. He is sly, he is deft, and he is quick.

It is only two or three steps, then he is by the door, slides the bolt back with both hands; the door flies open almost of its own accord.

Suddenly there is a loud roar, more violent than the dull rumble to which they have so far been exposed; the wind reaches inside their metal shell and pulls on his clothes.

Waziyata.

The north wind itself has come to claim its son.

A cry issues from behind and Tokala turns around. The

wind has blown the playing cards from the table, and they whirl through the cabin, as the men jump to their feet. Tokala sees the fear in the soldiers' eyes. Four machine guns are pointed at him. Four men cry out. *Step back from the door and get down* – but he refuses to obey. One of them draws a bead and repeats his threat to shoot. Panic speaks from his voice.

Tokala knows the man won't fire, knows they cannot prevent his escape. He doesn't have to do anything, simply tips forward, and feels Waziyata seize him and press against his chest.

For a moment it takes his breath away. The raging, blustering wind is so loud that no other sound reaches his ears, not even the rumble of the plane.

Abandoning himself to the wind he had closed his eyes, but now he opens them, and sees the lakes and forests that were his life draw ever nearer.

He understands how he is one of the chosen few, those who shortly before death are granted witness to the beauty and immensity of creation, not simply to see it, but *feel* it in their body and soul, and, amidst such beauty and immensity, acknowledge how small and insignificant human life is. This comforts him, as nothing ever has before, not even his mother's breathing when he was still an infant. The acknowledgement of how miniscule, how ugly, he really is, and that it doesn't matter because, in spite of everything, he is a part of this all-encompassing beauty and immensity.

This is what he thinks; feels; knows, and with a smile on his face and the wind in his hair, he crashes onto the hard surface of a secluded forest lake.

And that is the moment he receives his new name.

Mitakuye Oyasin.

We are all one.

Author's Note

This is a work of fiction, which means the vast majority of it is simply invented. There was not, for instance, a Luisenhöhe estate near Marggrabowa/Treuburg, just as there was no Mathée schnapps distillery or products. Nor did any of the events related in this novel occur on the Elisenhöhe estate (which served as the model for its fictional counterpart) or, indeed, in the city of Treuburg. Any similarities with living or dead people are, therefore, entirely coincidental. Of all the Treuburg citizens appearing in the story, only the district administrator and mayor do so under their historically documented names.

There was never a Masurian Indian called Artur Radlewski, and, though Masuria is rich in lakes and moorland, the little lake, and the Kaubuk's impregnable patch of moor in the forest near Markowsken (which is today called Markowskie) exist in my imagination alone. The same is not true of the military cemetery, however, which is still to be found today, next to the road leading into Markowskie.

Likewise, it's a fact that as early as 1928, that is to say before the onset of the Nazis' wave of Germanisation, Marggrabowa changed its name to Treuburg. Anti-Polish and anti-German resentments on both sides of the East Prussian border were all too real. Sadly, it is also true that the Masurians, who ever since 1920 had been connected with the German Reich by a transit route that passed through Poland, the so-called Polish Corridor, felt abandoned by the Reich and its governments and, in the spring of 1932, acclaimed Adolf Hitler as though he were the saviour. The man, who in time, would become the death of their culture.

Also historically documented are the events which took place at Berlin Police Headquarters on 20th July 1932, the arrest of the Social Democrat Police Commissioner Grzesinski and the entire police executive. If not for the reactionary Reich government's suppression of Prussian democracy and the Berlin police force, it is doubtful whether the Nazis would have seized power with quite such ease six months later.

Large parts of this novel are set in a world which has ceased to exist. The old Masuria, in which Polish and German cultures coincided with others, and achieved a happy symbiosis, was crushed between the millstones of Nationalism; between Germanisation and Polonisation. Masuria's multi-ethnic culture, which could have served as a bridge between the cultures of Germany and of Poland, sadly had no place in a world enslaved by nationalist mania.

V.K., April 2012

The inspiration for the hit TV series

1929: When a car is hauled out of the canal with a mutilated corpse inside, Detective Inspector Gereon Rath claims the case. Soon his inquiries drag him ever-deeper into Weimar Berlin's underworld of cocaine, prostitution, gunrunning and shady politics.

'The first in a series that's been wildly popular cleverly captures the dark and dangerous period of the Weimer Republic before it slides into the ultimate evil of Nazism.'

Kirkus Reviews

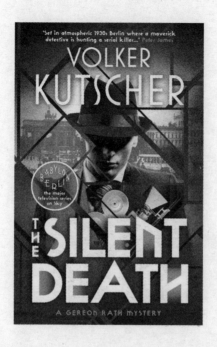

1930: Silent movie actress Betty Winter is killed on set after a lighting system falls on her. Inspector Gereon Rath suspects sabotage. Talkies are destroying careers in a world already bubbling with studio wars and sexual politics. Then another actress is found dead, this time with her vocal cords removed.

'Set in atmospheric 1930s Berlin where a maverick detective is hunting a serial killer *The Silent Death*, like its predecessor, *Babylon Berlin*, owes much to its author's commitment to historical accuracy and the cynical feel of the times.'

Peter James

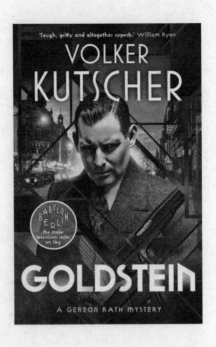

'Tough, gritty and altogether superb.' William Ryan

VOLKER
KUTSCHER

BABYLON
BERLIN
the major
television series
on Sky

GOLDSTEIN

A GEREON RATH MYSTERY

1931: Abraham Goldstein, professional hit man, arrives in
Berlin from New York. Gereon Rath is assigned to keep him
out of action – a boring job when the city's stores are being
robbed, an underworld power struggle is playing out, and
Nazi brownshirts are patrolling the streets. But Goldstein
will surprise them all.

'*Goldstein* is maybe the best of the series so far ... like the
bastard love child of Christopher Isherwood and Raymond
Chandler.' ***CrimeReads***

www.sandstonepress.com

facebook.com/SandstonePress/

@SandstonePress